About the Authors

Katie Meyer is a Florida native with a firm belief in happy endings. She studied English and Religion before getting a degree in Veterinary Technology. A former Veterinary Technician and dog trainer, she now spends her days homeschooling her children, writing and snuggling with her many pets. Her guilty pleasures include chocolate, *Downton Abbey*, and cheap champagne. Credit for her romance writing goes to her parents and her husband, who taught her what true love really is.

Sharon Archer has always been a bit of a dreamer. Her school reports regularly said, 'Sharon would do much better in (fill in the subject) if she would stop daydreaming'. Yet all of that daydreaming paid off! After years of trial and error, Sharon won herself a finalist position two years running for the Emma Darcy Award and hasn't looked back (or stopped writing) since. Sharon lives in Australia with her husband, Glenn.

Author **Helen R. Myers** is a Texan by choice, and when not writing, she's spoiling her four rescued dogs. An avid follower of the news and student of astrology, she enjoys comparing planetary aspects with daily world events. To decompress, she experiments with all forms of gardening and cooking with the produce she raises. You can contact her through her website at helenr.myers.com

Animal Magnetism

Animal Magnetism: A Forever Home

KATIE MEYER

SHARON ARCHER

HELEN R. MYERS

MILLS & BOON

First Published in Great Britain 2021
By Mills & Boon, an imprint of HarperCollins*Publishers*
1 London Bridge Street, London, SE1 9GF

ANIMAL MAGNETISM: A FOREVER HOME
© 2021 Harlequin Books S.A.

A Valentine for the Veterinarian © 2016 Katie Meyer
Single Father: Wife and Mother Wanted © 2009 Sharon Archer
Groomed for Love © 2014 Helen R. Myers

ISBN: 978-0-263-28163-7

MIX
Paper from
responsible sources

FSC
www.fsc.org

FSC® C007454

This book is produced from independently certified FSC™ paper to ensure responsible forest management.

For more information visit: www.harpercollins.co.uk/green

Printed and bound in Spain
by CPI, Barcelona

A VALENTINE FOR THE VETERINARIAN

KATIE MEYER

Ean, for picking up the slack
and never complaining about it.

My mom and my son, Michael,
for babysitting the littles when I had
a deadline and needed some quiet.

My agent Jill,
for guiding me through the process.

And my editorial team, especially Carly and
Jennifer, for finding my (numerous) mistakes
and making me look good.

Chapter One

"Grace, you just saved my life. How can I ever repay you?"

The woman behind the counter rolled her eyes. "It's just coffee, Dr. Marshall, not the fountain of youth. If you leave a few coins in the tip jar, we'll call it even."

Cassie clutched the cardboard cup like a lifeline, inhaling the rich aroma. "I had an emergency call last night, ended up performing a C-section on a schnauzer at three a.m., and then was double-booked all day. So right now your caffeinated nectar is my only hope of making it through the meeting I'm going to." She paid for her coffee and took a cautious sip of the scalding brew. "You're my hero."

"That kind of flattery will get you the last cinnamon scone, if you want it."

"Have I ever turned down a free baked good?" Cassie

accepted the small white bag with the proffered pastry. "Thanks. This ought to keep me out of trouble until I can get some dinner."

"Speaking of trouble, here comes that new sheriff's deputy. I'd be willing to break a few rules if it would get him to notice me." Grace craned her neck to see more clearly out the curtained front window. "Don't you think he looks like a man who could handle my rebellious side?"

Cassie nearly spit out her coffee. If Grace Keville, sole proprietor of Sandcastle Bakery, had a rebellious side, she'd kept it well hidden. Even after a full day of baking and serving customers, she looked prim and proper in a crisp pastel blouse and tailored pants. From her lacy apron to her dainty bun, she was the epitome of order and discipline. Not to mention she was happily married and the mother of three. "You've never rebelled a day in your life."

Grace sniffed. "Maybe not, but that man makes me consider it. Hard."

Rebellion wasn't all it was cracked up to be. She'd been there, done that, and had considerably more than a T-shirt to show for it. She started to say as much, but stopped at the jingle of the door chimes behind her. Turning at the sound, she caught her breath at the sight of the intense man heading toward her with long, ground-eating strides.

No wonder Grace was infatuated. The man looked like he'd just stepped out of a Hollywood action movie rather than the quiet streets of Paradise, Florida. Thick, dark hair framed a chiseled face with just a hint of five-o'clock shadow. His eyes were the exact color of the espresso that scented the air, and reflected a focus that only men in law enforcement seemed to have. Even without the uniform she'd have known him for a cop. Sexy? Sure. But still a cop. And she'd had her fill of those.

"I'm here to pick up an order. Should be under Santiago."

Grace grabbed a large box from the top of a display case. "I've got it right here—an assortment of cookies, right?"

"That's right."

"What, no doughnuts?" Uh-oh, did she say that out loud?

He gave Cassie a long look before quirking up one side of his mouth. "Sorry to ruin the stereotype."

Grace glared at Cassie before attempting to smooth things over. "Deputy Santiago, I'm Grace. I'm the one you spoke to earlier on the phone. And this is Dr. Cassie Marshall, our resident veterinarian."

"Nice to meet you Grace, Dr. Marshall." He nodded at each in turn. "And off duty it's Alex, please." He smiled then, a real smile, and suddenly the room was too warm, too charged, for comfort. The man's smile was as lethal as the gun strapped to his hip—more potent than any Taser. Unsettled by her instant response, Cassie headed for the door. It wasn't like her to speak without thinking; she needed to get out of there before she embarrassed herself more than she already had.

"Let me get that." He reached the door before her, balancing the large cookie box in one hand and pulling open the door with the other. After her own snide comment, his politeness poked at her conscience.

"Sorry about the doughnut remark." There, her conscience was clear.

"I've heard worse." His expression hardened for a minute. "Don't worry about it."

She wouldn't; she had way too many other concerns to keep her occupied. Including the meeting she was going to be late to, if she didn't hurry. She nodded politely, then made a beeline for her hatchback. Setting the coffee in a cup holder, she cranked the engine and popped in a CD of popular love songs. She had less than ten minutes to put aside all the worries tumbling through her mind and get herself in a Valentine's Day kind of mood.

Alex watched the silver hatchback drive away, noting she kept the small vehicle well under the speed limit. Few people were gutsy enough to speed in front of a sheriff's deputy—but then again, the average person didn't spout off jokes about cops to his face, either. There had been resentment in those blue eyes. She'd disliked him—or at the least the uniform—on sight. He was used to gang members and drug dealers treating him that way, but a cute veterinarian? His gut said there was a story there, but he didn't need to make enemies in his new hometown. He had plenty of those back in Miami.

A loud bark snapped him out of his thoughts.

"I'm coming, boy."

At this point, he and his canine partner, Rex, were in the honeymoon period of their relationship, and the dog still got excited whenever he saw Alex return. Unlocking the car, he couldn't help but smile at the goofy expression on the German Shepherd's face. As a trained K-9, Rex was a criminal's worst nightmare, but to Alex he was the best part of his new job.

He'd never expected to live in a small-time town like Paradise, had never wanted to leave Miami. But when he testified against his partner, the department had turned against him. It didn't matter that Rick was guilty. Alex was the one they turned on.

He'd known that refusing to lie during his deposition meant saying goodbye to any chance of promotion. He could live with that. But when his name and address were leaked to a local gang he'd investigated, things changed.

Putting his own life at risk, that was just part of the job. Messing with his family, that was a different story. When his mom had come home one day to find threats spray-painted on her walls and her house trashed, he'd known they couldn't stay.

He could still see her standing in her ruined kitchen, white with fear. She'd aged ten years that humid night.

Guilt clawed at him. What kind of son was he to lead danger straight to her doorstep? He'd resigned the next day and spent his two-week notice hunting down the scum responsible.

Then he'd packed up and looked for a job, any job, where he could start fresh without a target on his back. When a position in the Palmetto County Sheriff's office became open, he'd jumped on it. Working with a K-9 unit was a dream come true; he'd often volunteered time with the unit back home. That experience, plus a stellar record, had landed him the position.

Having the dog around eased the loneliness of being in a new city and made the long night shifts required of newbies seem a little shorter.

Thankfully, his mom had been willing to move, too. She'd lived in Miami ever since she and his father emigrated from Puerto Rico. He'd worried she would fight against leaving, but she'd agreed almost immediately. Her lack of argument told him she was more rattled than she'd admitted.

And of course there was Jessica, his younger sister, to think about, too. She was away at college, but still lived at home on school holidays. His mom wouldn't want her in the line of fire, even if she wasn't afraid for herself.

Now Paradise was their home and all that was behind them.

As he drove down what passed for Main Street, he scanned the tidy storefronts, more out of habit than caution. The tiny island community couldn't be more different from fast-paced south Florida. Instead of high rises and strip malls, there were bungalows and family-owned shops. Miami had a vibrant, intoxicating culture, but working in law enforcement, he'd spent his hours in the less picturesque parts of town. Here, even the poorest neighborhoods were tidy and well kept.

Of course, nowhere was perfect, not even Paradise. Which was why he was missing valuable sleep in order to attend the Share the Love volunteer meeting. The sheriff's department was pairing with the county's department of children's services in a fundraiser, a Valentine's Day dance. The money raised would be used to start up a mentor program for at-risk kids. Some were in foster care and many had parents serving time or were in trouble themselves. When the department had posted a flier about the program, he'd been the first to volunteer. He'd been on the other side of that story; it was time to give back.

It took only a few minutes to cross the island and

reach the Sandpiper Inn, the venue for tonight's orga-
nizational meeting. The largest building on the island,
it often was the site of community events.

Pulling into the gravel lot, he was surprised to see
most of the parking spaces were full. Either the Sandpiper had a lot of midweek guests or the meeting was
going to be larger than he'd expected.

He grabbed the box on the passenger seat and left the
engine running, thankful for the special environmental
controls that kept things safe for his furry partner. Late
January in Florida tended to be mild, but could sometimes still hit dangerous temperatures. "Sorry, buddy,
but I think this is a human-only kind of thing."

Rex grumbled but settled down, his big head resting
on his paws when Alex locked the car.

"Are you following me?" The voice came from behind him and sounded hauntingly familiar.

The prickly veterinarian from the bakery.

She was standing where the parking area opened onto
the shaded path to the inn's entrance. Her strawberry-
blond hair caught the rays of the setting sun, strands
blowing in her face with the breeze. Eyes snapping, she
waited for him to respond.

"I'm not stalking you, if that's what you mean." His
jaw clenched at the insinuation. "I'm a law enforcement
officer, not a criminal."

Her face softened slightly, and he caught a glimpse
of sadness in her eyes. "Sorry, it's just that in this town,
there isn't always a difference."

Chapter Two

Well, that was embarrassing. Cassie truly did try to think before speaking, but some days she was more successful than others. What had she been thinking, accusing him of following her? It had been months since the accident; she needed to stop jumping at shadows.

"Mommy, look what Miss Jillian helped me make!" Cassie's daughter, Emma, came bounding down the stairs of the picturesque inn with the energy and volume befitting a marching band, not a four-year-old. "I made Valentine's cards!"

Behind, at a more sedate pace, came Cassie's best friend and employee, Jillian Caruso. With her mass of black curls and pale skin, she looked like a princess out of a fairy tale, despite her casual jeans and sweater. Right now she also looked a tad guilty. "Before you say anything, this wasn't my fault. I told her I would help her make some, but all the ideas were hers."

Cassie arched an eyebrow, but let it go. She was just grateful Jillian had been willing to entertain Emma. Normally her mom watched Emma after her preschool let out, but today there had been a schedule conflict. Emma was much happier playing at the inn than being stuck with Cassie at the clinic yet again. "Hi, sunshine. I missed you." She swept her up in a hug, letting go of the tension that had dogged her all day. This was why she worked so hard. This little girl was the most important thing in her world and worth all the long hours and missed sleep of the past few months. "Are you having fun?"

"She should be," Jillian broke in. "She's been here less than an hour and we've already played on the playground, looked for seashells on the beach and made brownies."

"Are you a policeman? Did my mommy do something bad?"

Cassie had almost forgotten the deputy behind her. Blushing, she set Emma back down and turned to find him a few feet away, smiling as if she hadn't just bitten his head off.

"Hello, sweetie. I'm Alex. What's your name?"

"I'm Emma. Are you going to take someone to jail?"

"Not today. Unless there are any bad guys here?" His dimples showed when he smiled. Cops should not have dimples.

"Nope, just me and Miss Jillian and Mr. Nic. And Murphy. He's their dog. And a bunch of people for the meeting. But they're going to help kids, so they can't be bad, right?" Her little brows furrowed as she thought.

"Probably not. Helping kids is a good thing. Are you going to help?"

Emma's curls bounced as she nodded. "Yup, I get to help with the decorations. Mommy said so. And I get to come to the big Valentine's Day dance. I'm going to wear a red dress."

"A red dress? Sounds like a great party." He raised his gaze to the third member of the group.

"Hi, I'm Jillian. Welcome to the Sandpiper Inn." She offered her hand to the handsome deputy.

"Nice to meet you. Alex Santiago. Thanks for offering to host the meeting here."

Jillian smiled, her face lighting up. "We're happy to do it. I grew up in foster care myself—I know how hard it can be. Even the best foster families often can't always give the kids as much attention as they need. It will be great if we can get a real mentor program started."

If Alex was surprised by Jillian's casual mention of her childhood, he didn't show it. He just nodded and held out the box he'd picked up at the bakery. "I brought cookies, if you have somewhere I can put them. I figured at least a few people might not have had a chance to grab dinner yet."

Oh, boy. Shame heated Cassie's cheeks. She'd been stereotyping him with the old cops-and-doughnuts line when he'd actually been buying refreshments to share with others—at a charity event, no less.

The sight of the uniform might set her teeth on edge, but that was no reason to be openly rude to him. The car accident that had injured her father so badly had been caused by a single out-of-control deputy, but she couldn't blame the man in front of her just because they both wore the same badge.

"Ooh, can I have a cookie?" Emma looked up at

Alex, practically batting her eyelashes. "I've been very good."

He laughed, and the lines around his eyes softened. "That's up to your mom, princess."

Emma turned pleading eyes to Cassie, whose heart melted. "Since you've been good, yes, one. But just one. Jillian said you've already had a brownie, and I don't want you bouncing off the walls on a sugar high." She nodded a thank you to Alex for letting her make the decision. "Now, let's see those valentines you were telling me about." She brushed off the niggling bit of envy that she hadn't been the one making valentines with her daughter. Maybe that was why Jillian looked concerned about them?

"Cassie, maybe you should wait and read those later?" Jillian cautioned, nodding toward Alex.

Cassie darted a glance at the cop still standing on the stairs with them. He shrugged, then moved past them. "I'll just go find a place to set these down. See you inside."

Why was Jillian acting so tense over this? They were just paper hearts and glitter, not a manifesto. Taking them from Emma's slightly grubby fist, she continued up to the massive front door of the Sandpiper.

The first card boasted a crudely drawn bouquet of flowers, and the words MOM and LOVE circled by pink and purple hearts. "Thank you, sweetie, I love it." She shuffled that one to the back and opened the next one. This time there were happy faces covering the pink paper, and Jillian's name, misspelled, at the center. "Beautiful!" Smiling, she opened the last heart-shaped card and then froze, almost stumbling as her daughter pushed past her into the warmth of the lobby.

The words on the page had instantly imprinted on her brain, but she read them again anyway.

To Daddy. Painstakingly spelled out in red and gold sequins.

She felt a hand on her shoulder. Jillian's eyes were wide with sympathy. "I'm sorry. I didn't know what to do. I told her I'd help her make valentines, but I had no idea…"

Cassie straightened her spine. She'd talk to Emma about it. Make her understand, somehow, that this particular valentine was going to remain unsent. Her head began to throb.

"Don't worry. It's not your fault," Cassie told Jillian.

It's mine.

Alex kept an eye on the door as he mingled and shook hands in the spacious lobby. Observation was second nature at this point, and he wanted to see how that little scene out front played out. What was the big deal about a couple of valentines? Maybe it was nothing, but an overactive sense of curiosity came with the job.

He was munching on a tiny crustless sandwich when Cassie entered the room. Her daughter and friend followed, but she was the one that drew him, made him want to know more. There was something about the fiery redhead that made her impossible to ignore. Yes, she was pretty in a girl-next-door way, with a petite build and freckled complexion. But it was more than that. Her quick temper should have been off-putting. Instead, her transparency put him at ease. Every emotion showed on her face—there was no hidden agenda. In his line of work, he spent most of his time trying to figure out what someone wasn't saying, but this woman was an open book.

And right now, she looked like she needed a friend. Her pale skin was flushed, and she had a tight look around her eyes, as if she was fighting off a headache. Moving toward her, drawn by instinct more than conscious thought, he offered her a drink. "Water?"

"Hmm?" She looked down at the unopened bottle he held in his hand. "Yes, thank you." Taking a tentative sip, she screwed the cap back on. "Listen, about the coffee shop. I'm sorry I was rude. It was a dumb joke. I just...well, it wasn't about you, specifically."

"Not a fan of cops, are you?"

She winced. "That obvious?"

"Let's see. You made a cop joke in front of a cop. Then you equated law enforcement with criminal behavior. It wasn't a hard case to crack."

Her eyes widened, and then she smiled. A heart-stopping smile that reached her eyes and made him wish he could do more for her than hand her a bottle of water. This must have been how Helen caused all that trouble in Troy. His heart thudded in his chest, warning him to look away.

His eyes landed on her daughter, who had snuck to the far side of the table to liberate another cookie. "She's beautiful."

The smile got even brighter. "Thanks."

"Just like her mother."

Instantly her smile vanished, and her gaze grew guarded. "I should go find a seat, before they're all taken."

He hadn't meant the compliment as a pick-up line, but she obviously thought he was hitting on her and was putting as much space between them as possible. She wasn't wearing a ring, but he'd heard medical people didn't always wear them because of the constant hand-washing. Great. She was probably married. Now she had a reason to dislike him personally, rather than just cops in general.

Unable to come up with a reason to follow her, he hung back to watch the proceedings from the rear of the room, a small crowd filling the seats in front of him. These were his neighbors now, his community. Getting to know them had to be top priority if he wanted to be effective at his job. Hopefully volunteering like this would be a step in that direction. He had other, more personal reasons for wanting to volunteer, but no one needed to know that. He didn't need his past coloring his chances at a future here.

At the front of the room, the woman he'd spoken to earlier, Jillian, stood and called for everyone's attention. "Welcome to the Sandpiper, and thank you for taking the time to help with such a worthwhile project. As most of you know, I was a foster child myself, so I know firsthand how hard that life can be. And what a difference a caring person can make. I'm really thankful we have so many people interested in volunteering, and that, in addition to working with children's services, we will also be partnering with the Palmetto County Sheriff's Department. They will be sponsoring a group of kids for the program as well, kids who are in a difficult spot and might need some extra help. Deputy Santiago is here representing the department tonight and will be volunteering his own time to this important project." She smiled at him, and he raised a hand in acknowledgment. Several of the townspeople turned and sized him up. Many offered warm smiles; a few nodded in acceptance.

Jillian finished, then introduced the chairwoman of the event, Mrs. Rosenberg, a diminutive senior citizen decked out in a leopard-print track suit. As she listed off the various jobs, he made a mental note to sign up for the setup crew. A strong back would be welcome when it came time to move tables and hang decorations, and it sounded a heck of a lot better than messing with tissue paper and glitter for the decorating committee.

Finally, the talking was over. Everyone milled around, catching up on gossip as they waited to sign up on the clipboards on the front table. He started that way, easing through the crowd as best as he could, given that everyone there seemed to want to greet him personally. He'd exchanged small talk with half a dozen people and was less than halfway across the room when he felt a tug on his sleeve.

"Deputy?"

It was the chairwoman, now sporting rhinestone spectacles and wielding a clipboard.

"Yes, ma'am?"

"You're new in town, aren't you?" The question was just shy of an accusation, and the shrewd eyes behind the glasses were every bit as sharp as a seasoned detective's.

"I am." He extended a hand. "Alex Santiago. Nice to meet you."

She gripped him with a wiry strength, then spoke over his shoulder. "Hold on, Tom, I'll be right there." Turning her attention back to him, she smiled. "I have to go handle that. But don't worry. I'll get you signed up myself."

Grateful that he wouldn't have to fight the crowd, he backtracked to the front door. He was almost there when it hit him. "Mrs. Rosenberg?"

From across the room she turned. "Yes?"

"Which committee are you signing me up for?"

"Oh, all of them, of course."

Of course.

Cassie spent most of the drive home trying to figure out what to say to Emma about her valentines. She still wasn't sure how to explain things in a way a four-year-old could understand, but she'd come up with something. She always did.

She set her purse down on the counter and put the old-fashioned kettle on the stove. "Emma, go put your backpack in your room, and get ready for your bath, please. I'll be right there." It was so late she was tempted to skip the bath part of bedtime, but changing the schedule would undoubtedly backfire and keep the tyke up later in the long run. Besides, after an afternoon romping on the beach and exploring the Sandpiper's sprawling grounds, her daughter was in dire need of a scrub-down.

Enjoying the brief quiet, she kicked off her sensible shoes and opened the sliding door to the patio. The screened room was her favorite part of the house, especially at this time of year. The air was chilly by Florida standards, but still comfortable. Right now she would have loved to curl up on the old chaise with her tea and a cozy mystery, but tonight, like most nights, there just wasn't time.

"Mommy, I'm ready for my bath."

"Okay, I'm coming." Duty called. Taking a last breath of the crisp night air, she caught the scent of the Lady of the Night orchid she'd been babying. It would bloom for only a few nights; hopefully she'd get a chance to enjoy it. But for now, she closed the door and went to find her daughter, stopping to fill her mug with boiling water and an herbal tea bag.

Emma was waiting in the bathroom, stripped down to her birthday suit and clutching her favorite rubber ducky. "Bubbles?" she asked hopefully.

"Bubbles. But only a quick bath tonight. It's late."

The little girl nodded solemnly. "Okay, Mommy."

Cassie's heart squeezed. No matter how stressed or tired she was, she never got tired of hearing the word *Mommy* from her baby's lips. She couldn't say she'd done everything right, but this little girl—she had to be a reward for something. She was too good to be anything but that. There was nothing Cassie wouldn't do for her. Which was why it broke her heart to know she couldn't give Emma her biggest wish.

"So did you have fun today at the Sandpiper?" She watched the water level rise around her daughter, the bubbles forming softly scented mountains.

"Yup. I played with Murphy and ate brownies, and we saw a butterfly, and Mr. Nic pushed me super high on the swings."

Nic was Jillian's husband. He had bought the Sandpiper for Jillian just a few months ago, and the playground was one of the first things he'd added to the grounds. He and Jillian were hoping for a child of their own soon, but in the meantime the paying guests—and Emma—made good use of it. "That sounds like a real adventure."

"Uh-huh. And then Miss Jillian helped me make

my valentines. I made one for her, and you, and for a daddy. We just need to get one so I can give it to him."

Darn. The child hadn't forgotten, not that Cassie was surprised. Emma had perfect recall when it came to what she wanted. Now to figure out a way to let her down without breaking her heart. "Honey, I can't just go get you a daddy."

Emma frowned up at her.

Okay, that didn't work. "You are going to have a wonderful Valentine's Day. You're going to have a party at school with cupcakes and candy and everything. And then we'll go to the big dance. It's going to be great, you'll see."

"It would be better if I had a daddy. Then he could be our valentine. Like Mr. Nic is Jillian's valentine. I heard him say so."

Cassie blinked back the sudden sting of tears. She'd tried to be everything for Emma, to provide enough love for two parents, but the older Emma got, the more she realized something was different. Something, someone, was missing.

"A daddy would be nice," she conceded. "But you have me. And we're a great team, you and I. So if you don't have a daddy right now, that's okay, because we have each other, right?"

Emma looked thoughtful, her nose crinkling as she considered. "But why don't I get to have a daddy? Lots of kids at school have one."

The pounding behind Cassie's eyes returned with a vengeance. Rubbing her temples, she tried to explain to her daughter what she still didn't understand herself. "That's just how it is sometimes. Some kids have mommies, and some kids have daddies, and some kids have both."

"Oh, and some kids don't have a mommy or a daddy, right? That's why we get to have the Share the Love party, to help them, right, Mom?"

Cassie sighed in relief. "Right, honey. Those kids are in foster care with people that take care of them until they get a new mommy and daddy. Every family is different, and we just have to be happy about the one we have."

Her face falling, Emma nodded slowly. "Okay."

Watching her daughter's solemn expression, Cassie felt like she'd kicked a puppy. The guilt sat heavy in the pit of her stomach, reminding her of how her choices had led to this. Her impulsiveness, her recklessness, had created this situation. For the millionth time, she fought the instinct to regret ever meeting her lying ex. But of course, without him, there would be no Emma. And that was simply unthinkable. Being a single parent was hard, but it was worth it.

That didn't mean that she didn't sometimes wish she had a partner in all of this. As she toweled Emma off and got her ready for bed, she wondered what it would have been like to have a man to talk to once her daughter was asleep. Instead of eating ice cream out of the carton, she'd have someone she could talk things out with, someone to share her fears and frustrations with.

But letting someone into her life, relying on him like that, was too big a risk. She'd let her emotions carry her away once, and look how well that turned out. No, she needed to keep doing what she was doing and leave the idea of romance alone. She wasn't any good at it, and she couldn't afford to make that kind of mistake again.

Chapter Three

Alex was still shaking his head over Mrs. Rosenberg's sign-up shenanigans ten hours later. And puzzling over the intriguing veterinarian, despite the way she'd blown him off. She was fire and ice, and definitely not interested, but he couldn't quite get her out of his head. Between her and Mrs. Rosenberg, the island definitely had its share of headstrong women.

He'd spent the long night patrolling the quiet streets of Paradise and the connecting highway across the bridge, alone except for Rex and his own thoughts. He was grateful for the lack of crime, but the slow shift gave him too much time to think, too much time to remember the chain of events that had brought him here. Not that this was a bad place to be.

When he'd accepted the position with the Palmetto County Sheriff's Department, he'd expected to be working at the county headquarters in Coconut Bay. Instead he'd been assigned to the small substation serving Paradise. The island was too small to support a city police force, so it, like some of the rural ranching areas across the bridge on the mainland, was under county law enforcement.

As dawn approached, he made a last loop along the beach road to catch the sunrise over the ocean. Stopping in one of the many parking spaces that bordered the dunes, he got out and stretched, his neck popping loudly. At Rex's insistence, he opened the back door as well, snapping the dog's leash on and walking him to a grassy area to relieve himself. When the dog had emptied his bladder, they strolled together to one of the staircases that led down to the sand.

Here he had an unobstructed view of the water and the already pink sky that seemed to melt along the horizon, the water turning a molten orange as the fiery sun crept up to start the day. Sipping from the lukewarm coffee he'd picked up a few hours ago at a gas station on the mainland, he let himself enjoy the quiet. No jarring static from the two-way radio, no traffic, just the soft sound of the waves rolling on the sand and Rex's soft snuffling as he investigated the brush along the stairway.

Alex had made a habit of doing this since he moved here. In the clear morning light, he could feel good about himself, his job, the direction his life was taking. The fresh start to the day was a reminder of his own fresh start, one that he hadn't asked for, but probably needed.

He was over thirty now, as his mother never failed to remind him. Maybe here he'd find a life beyond his work. He wasn't a family man; nothing in his background had prepared him for that kind of life, but a place like Paradise made him want to settle down a bit, make some friends, maybe join a softball team or something.

Chuckling at the image, he turned to go. Rex, trained to stay with him, uncharacteristically resisted the tug on the leash. Maybe he was tired, too.

"Here, boy! Come on, it's quitting time. Let's go."

The dog stood his ground, whiskers trembling as he stared into the dark space under the steps.

"What it is it, boy?" Alex found himself lowering his voice, catching the dog's mood. He was no dog whisperer, but obviously there was something under the stairs. Something more than the broken bottles and fast-food wrappers that sometimes got lodged there.

"Is somebody there?"

There was a scrambling sound, but no answer.

Rex whined, the hairs on his back standing up in a ridge. Feeling a bit silly, but not willing to take a chance, Alex removed his Glock from its holster, finding confidence in its weight even as he sent a silent prayer he wouldn't have to use it. Crouching down, he aimed his flashlight under the wooden structure, his gun behind it. He couldn't see anyone, but there was an alcove under a support beam that was hidden from his light. He'd have to go around.

He circled around to the other side, leaving Rex pacing back and forth at the foot of the stairs. Repeating his crouch and waddle move from before, Alex inched up under the overhang, scanning the area with his light. Nothing.

Woof!

Alex jumped, rapping his head on the rough boards

of the stairway. A lightning bolt of pain shot through his skull as he quickly crab-crawled back out of the cramped space beneath the stairs. He heard Rex bark again and rolled the rest of the way out, careful to keep the gun steady.

"What is it, boy?"

A quick series of staccato barks answered him from the landing above.

"Stop! Sheriff's Deputy." The logical part of his mind knew that it was probably just a kid sneaking a smoke or a surfer who had passed out after too many drinks, but he'd had more than one close call in his career and wasn't going to chance it. Standing up, cursing the sand spurs now embedded in his skin, he followed the dog's line of sight.

There, clearly visible in the breaking dawn, was the menace that had his dog, and him, so worked up. A tiny kitten, barely more than a ball of fluff, was huddled against the top step.

"Rex, hush!" he commanded, not wanting the big dog to scare it back under the stairs. He was not going into those sand spurs again if he could help it.

The kitten was gray, its fur nearly the same shade as the weathered boards he was clinging to. If Rex hadn't made such a fuss, the kitten could have been directly underfoot and Alex would have missed it. Putting the dog into a down-stay, he dropped the leash and tucked away the gun and flashlight. Then he eased up the stairs as quietly as his heavy boots would allow.

The kitten watched him, eyes wide, but didn't run. A small mew was its only reaction, and even that seemed half-hearted. The pathetic creature looked awfully weak. The temperature was only in the mid-forties right now and had been significantly colder overnight. Plenty of strays did just fine, but this one seemed way too small to be out in the cold on its own.

Scooping the kitten up, he cradled it against his chest with one hand, then leaned down and retrieved Rex's leash with the other. The kitten was trembling, obviously cold if nothing else. Loading Rex into the car, he mentally said goodbye to the sleep he'd intended to catch up on. It looked like he was going to be seeing that pretty veterinarian again after all.

Cassie stared at the teakettle with bleary eyes, as if she could make the water boil faster through sheer force of will. She'd tossed and turned again last night. Maybe at some point she'd get used to the nightmares.

She often dreamed about the accident that had left her father in the hospital and herself with a mild concussion and a mountain of worry. At first, they'd feared her father's injuries were permanent, but he was home now and steadily getting better. She'd hoped that would be enough to stop the dreams from haunting her. But so far, no such luck.

But last night the dream had changed. The broken glass and screeching tires were the same as always, brought back in minute detail to terrorize her, but this time the sirens had triggered something new. Instead of the middle-aged deputy who was normally part of the nightmare, there was someone else. Alex Santiago, the new deputy she'd embarrassed herself in front of.

Suddenly, instead of ambulances and flashing lights, there had been stars and the crash of the ocean. They were alone on the beach, kissing as if there was nothing more important than the feel of skin against skin, tongue against tongue. She'd been unbuttoning his uniform when the blaring of her alarm had woken her up.

She had lain there, hot and trembling, for several minutes before forcing herself to shut the dream out of her head. There was probably some deep, psychiatric reason her subconscious was twisting her nightmare into something totally different, but there'd been no point in lying there, trying to figure it out.

So she'd forced herself out of bed and into a quick shower before throwing on her usual uniform of casual khaki pants and a simple cotton blouse. Now she was desperate for some tea and maybe a bite of breakfast. She had another thirty minutes before Emma would be waking up, and she intended to enjoy the quiet while she could.

The tea was still steeping in her mug when she heard a knock at the door. Dunking the bag one last time, she tossed it in the trash as she made her way to the front of the house. Peering through the wavy glass of the peephole, she could just make out the blue uniform of the Palmetto County Sheriff's Department. Her mouth turned dry, another flashback threatening her still drowsy mind.

Her heart thudded hollowly as she turned the lock. Why would there be a cop on her doorstep? Had something happened to her parents? The clinic? A neighbor? Her mind darted through possible scenarios as she opened the door. Surely this wasn't because of the accident? In the beginning, there had been what seemed like countless interviews and questions, but that had all ended months ago.

Taking a deep, cleansing breath, she swung open the door. There on the stoop was Alex, looking just as he had in her dream. The fear retreated, chased off by other, equally potent stirrings. Her cheeks heated in embarrassment, not that he could possibly know that she'd dreamed about him. Keeping her voice cool, she asked, "Is there a problem, Deputy?"

He smiled at her, all male energy and smooth charm. "I suppose it's too early for this to be a social call?"

"I'd say so." She noticed the shadows under his eyes and realized he'd probably just come off the night shift. "I'm assuming you have a professional reason for banging on my door at dawn. If you could share it so I can get back to my breakfast, that would be helpful."

Before he could answer her, she caught the weirdest impression of movement under his department-issued windbreaker. "What on earth?"

At that moment, a tiny, gray head squirmed out of the neck of the jacket and nuzzled his chin. Darn. Now she had to let him in.

"I know it looks strange, but the little guy was shivering. I thought I could keep him warm in my jacket, but he doesn't want to stay put." He grabbed hold of the kitten as it wriggled its way farther out of the coat.

"Well, come on in. Let's take a look at him." She motioned for him to continue back to the kitchen, then shut the door behind him. "Where did he come from and how long ago did you find him?" She kept her tone and actions professional, using her clinical manner to maintain some emotional distance. He might look like a Latin movie star, but the Palmetto County Sheriff's Department logo on his shirt was a glaring reminder of the chaos she was currently embroiled in. She'd help the kitten, then send him on his way, before he or the animal got too close.

Alex followed her, his large stature making her cozy cottage feel small. "Rex found him under one of the beach access staircases. We'd stopped for a few minutes and he refused to leave. Somehow he knew the little guy needed help."

"Is Rex your partner?" The name didn't ring a bell.

"Yeah," Alex answered distractedly as he attempted to remove the kitten's claws from his uniform shirt. "He's waiting out in the car."

"He didn't want to come in?" Had the animosity toward her gotten that bad?

"Oh, he wanted to, but I figured it was better not to totally overwhelm you at this hour of the morning."

Right. More likely his partner just wanted to avoid her. Well, too bad. She was tired of feeling like a pariah in her own town. "It's going to take me a little while to check the kitten out, so you might as well tell Rex to come in. No reason to sit out in the cold."

"You're sure?"

"Of course."

While he fetched his partner, she went to the hall closet to retrieve her medical bag. It was on the top shelf, wedged next to a box of random sports equipment. And a bit too heavy to snag one-handed. She was on her toes, the kitten snuggled firmly in one arm, when she heard the front door open behind her.

Giving up, she turned around to ask for help. "Hey, could one of you hold the kitten while I—"

Her voice died in her throat. Standing directly in her path was the largest German Shepherd she had ever seen, taking up most of the limited real estate in her tiny foyer. Suppressing a completely unprofessional squeal at the sudden intrusion, she cautiously observed the behemoth before deciding the doe-eyed canine meant no harm. Probably. Intuition and years of experience gave her the courage to edge around him, keeping the kitten out of his reach, just in case.

She was relieved to find Alex in the foyer, apparently not eaten by the mammoth canine. "You aren't going to tell me Rex found that guy under a staircase, too, are you?" No way was this regal giant a foundling.

"What?" Alex's eyes narrowed in confusion. "Found who?"

She waved her arm toward the dog. "Him. Where did he come from? Obviously your partner didn't find him when he found the kitten."

Alex's full-throated laugh filled the air, erasing the tired lines that had creased his face a moment before. Unable to resist smiling along with him, she rubbed the kitten's head with her free hand and waited to be let in on the joke.

"Rex is my partner." When she only raised her eyebrows, he continued, "I mean, the dog is Rex. My partner."

Understanding belatedly wound its way through her sleepy brain. "You're a K-9 officer?"

"Yeah. I just assumed a local veterinarian would have known that."

She thought back. She *had* heard rumblings of a new K-9 unit, but she would have sworn the idea had been tabled when it was determined there wasn't enough money in the budget. "I thought the department couldn't afford a K-9 unit? Trained dogs have to cost a fortune."

Alex ruffled the big dog's fur, a wry smile on his face. "He's worth every penny, but you're right. He's way outside Palmetto County's price range. The department was able to get federal and state grants to cover the purchase cost, and Miami-Dade County let me train with its K-9 unit on my off time before I came. The department still has to foot the ongoing costs for veterinary care and our continued training, but that's less expensive than paying the salary for another officer. In the long run, having a K-9 on staff should save the department manpower and money."

Watching Alex's eyes shine with pride in his job and his dog had her swallowing hard. She'd been too quick to think she was being avoided, to assume she was being treated badly. Had she gotten so cynical that she assumed the worst of everyone?

If so, she needed to stop. That wasn't who she wanted to be or what she wanted to teach her daughter. Which meant she needed to bite the bullet and at least try to be open-minded, try to be friendly. Even with the sexy cop standing in her living room.

If Alex had been a little less tired, maybe he would have picked up on Cassie's confusion earlier. As it was, the look on her face when she'd found the hundred-plus-pound dog in her house had been priceless. He gave her credit, though; she'd stood her ground without flinching. She'd correctly read Rex's body language and known he wasn't a threat, despite his size. Heck, even some of his fellow officers were skittish around Rex.

Tough and beautiful. A dangerous combination. He'd once described his ex, a fellow cop, the same way. Then she'd dropped him for an assistant DA and he'd shifted his assessment from tough to cold-hearted. But Cassie, although she'd been less than friendly when he'd first met her, didn't seem to have the calculating nature that had doomed his relationship with his ex. Cassie tried to hide them, but her emotions were right there on the surface, reflected on her face like the rays of the sun off the ocean.

She had her eyes closed as she felt her way over the kitten's body from head to tail. Watching her slender but capable fingers skim the soft fur had him wondering what her touch would feel like. Her husband, if she did turn out to be married, was one lucky bastard.

Who probably wouldn't be happy to find a stranger staring at his wife this way.

Not that she'd even noticed. She'd all but forgotten Alex. Her brows knit in concentration. All her focus was on her small, purring patient.

Better take it down a notch. Focus on the issue at hand. "Is he going to be okay?"

Cassie made a noncommittal noise, then slid the earpieces of a stethoscope into place. A few tense minutes later, her face relaxed into an easy smile. "Lungs sound good, no evidence of any kind of infection, and his heart sounds great. At least, what I can hear over the purring." She nuzzled her face against the now ecstatic creature. "He seems none the worse for wear, just hungry and cold. It's lucky you found him when you did—the forecast is calling for another cold front to roll in by the end of the day."

He suppressed a shudder, despite the warmth of Cassie's cozy kitchen. An image of the kitten, all alone in the cold, flashed through his head, and he made a mental note to pick up one of Rex's favorite chew bones at the store later. The big dog deserved a reward, for sure.

As if reading his mind, Cassie opened a whitewashed cupboard and pulled out a box of dog biscuits.

"Can the hero here have a treat?"

"Of course. He's off duty, and he's definitely earned it."

"What about you?" She tipped her chin toward the kettle on the stove. "I've got hot water for tea, or I can make a pot of coffee. If you have time, I mean."

"Tea would be fine, thank you." He normally stuck to coffee, but there was no point in her making a whole pot just for him. Maybe the coffeepot was strictly for her husband, although it didn't look as if it had been used yet this morning. Her mug, purple with pink paw prints on it, sat alone on the empty counter, smelling of peppermint and flowers.

Come to think of it, there'd only been one car in the driveway. Her husband could have left for work already, but there was nothing in the kitchen to indicate a male presence. Surreptitiously, he scanned the room. No dirty breakfast dishes, no mugs other than hers. Even more telling, the decor ran to pastels and flowers. The evidence was circumstantial, but certainly enough to introduce reasonable doubt as to the existence of a Mr. Marshall.

Accepting the tea, he told himself it didn't matter one way or the other. She'd made her opinion of him, and his profession, perfectly clear when they first met. But as he sat across from her in the cozy kitchen, his dog at their feet and a kitten in her lap, a new, friendlier relationship seemed possible. Which didn't explain why he cared if she shared her home, or her bed, with another man.

He'd obviously been up too long. That was all. Sleep deprivation could mess with your mind. Everyone knew that. After a few hours' sleep, he'd remember all the reasons he wasn't looking for a relationship, especially with the firecracker of a redhead sitting across from him. For now, he'd drink his tea and enjoy a few minutes of company before going home to his empty apartment.

When he'd first taken the job in Paradise, he'd suggested he and his mother share a place, but she'd just chuckled and said he would need his own space for "entertaining." Right. He'd had only one other person in his apartment since he moved to Paradise, and that was the cable guy. Between the new job and the extra training sessions he'd signed up for with Rex, he hadn't had the time or energy for dating. Which was fine by him.

Although right now, enjoying the morning light with a beautiful woman, he wondered if he wasn't missing out after all.

Unwilling to explore that thought, he finished his tea and stood, the chair scraping against the terrazzo floor.

Startled by the noise, the kitten leaped onto the table, nearly overturning the china cups.

"Sorry about that. I'll get this guy out of your hair and be on my way." He scooped up the kitten with one hand. "Thanks for checking him out—I didn't know where else to take him."

Cassie stood to escort him out. "What will you do with him now?"

Good question. One he hadn't thought through yet. He'd been worried about the little guy making it. "I'll have to keep him for a few days, I guess, while I ask around, try to find him a home." Frustrated, he rubbed his eyes with his free hand. "Guess I'd better stop and pick up some food for him first." He nearly groaned with frustration. His tired body was crying out for a bed, but he couldn't let the little guy starve.

"The stores won't even be open for another hour." Cassie's eyes went from man to kitten. "I can take him to the office with me, get him fed, wormed and cleaned up, and then you can pick him up before you start your shift tonight. How does that sound?"

"Like you're my guardian angel. Thank you."

She blushed, the pink accentuating her soft coloring. "I'm not doing it for you. I'm doing it for him." Her firm tone was a contrast to the camaraderie they'd shared in the kitchen. The friendly interlude was over, it seemed.

"Either way, I appreciate it just the same. What time do you need me to come get him?"

"The clinic closes at six, so any time before then is fine."

He could get a solid stretch of sleep and still have time to get food and the cat before his shift started. Thank heaven for small favors. And the angels who delivered them.

Cassie had spent way too much time thinking about Alex today. Really, any time thinking about Paradise Isle's newest lawman was too much. But between Emma's incessant questions over breakfast and the knowing looks and suggestive remarks from her staff, she'd found her attention forced to him more times than she could count. Not that it took much forcing. The sight of the rough-around-the-edges deputy cuddling an orphaned kitten had triggered something inside her, reminding her she was still a woman, not just a mother and veterinarian.

She eyed the gray bundle of fur that had triggered today's chain of events. "You're a troublemaker, you know that?"

The kitten in question was currently exploring her office after being evicted from the patient care area by Jillian. "He hates the cage and his crying is getting the other patients upset," she had said when she'd deposited him on her desk an hour ago.

Absently, Cassie balled up a piece of paper and tossed it in front of the cat. Thrilled, the tiny predator pounced on it, rolling head over heels in his enthusiasm.

Once upon a time, she'd been that carefree, that eager to chase adventure. But she'd been knocked down too hard to be willing to risk tumbling end over end again. She almost envied the kitten its bravery. He'd nearly frozen to death last night and yet he still seemed fearless. Meanwhile, she was afraid of her own shadow most days.

Having her ex leave her had made it hard to trust people, but the aftermath of the car accident she and her father had been in certainly hadn't helped. Naively, she'd assumed that the drunken deputy who hit her would face jail time, that he would pay for his actions. Instead, he'd gotten what seemed like a slap on the wrist. She'd tried to push for more, pointing out Jack's obvious alcoholism, but the department had closed ranks around him. According to them, he'd made a simple mistake and she was just stirring up trouble. A few people had even suggested the accident might have been her fault, despite all evidence to the contrary. Logically, she knew they were wrong, but that didn't make the nightmares or the guilt any better.

"Hey, Cassie?" Mollie, her friend and the clinic receptionist, spoke over the intercom. "Emma's here."

Cassie glanced at her watch. How was it already five o' clock? "Send her back and let her know her little friend is still here." Her daughter had fallen in love with the kitten when she saw it this morning. She'd be thrilled it hadn't been picked up yet.

"Mommy!" Her daughter flew into the tiny office, tossing her backpack down to give Cassie a big hug. "Mollie said he's still here! Where is he?"

Cassie laughed and pointed to the wastebasket in the corner of the room. "Look behind the trash can. I think he'd hiding back there."

Emma, always excited by a new visitor to the clinic, scrambled out of Cassie's lap to check it out. "Found him!" she whooped, clutching the kitty to her chest.

"Careful. Don't squeeze him too hard."

"I know that, Mom. I'm not a baby." The indignation on her little face was better suited to a teenager than a preschooler, but she did have a point. Emma had grown up with foster animals and convalescing pets around the house and knew how to handle them.

"Well, this one is a bit of a troublemaker, so just be careful." Even as she gave the warning, the little guy was trying to climb out of Emma's arms and to scale the mini-blinds over the window. Delighted at his antics, Emma gently untangled him.

"You sure do get into trouble," she scolded the kitten. "That should be your name—Trouble."

Cassie laughed. "I think you're right. That's the perfect name. I'll have Mollie put that on his chart."

"Will the policeman mind that we named the kitten without him?"

"I'm sure he won't mind." Time for a change in subject. "So did you have a good day at school?" Emma had started half days at the preschool affiliated with their church only a few months ago.

"Oh, yeah! John Baker brought a snake into school today for show-and-tell."

"A real snake?" She shivered. There was a reason she hadn't specialized in exotic medicine, and that reason was snakes. Professionally she knew they were legitimate pets, but personally she found them cringe-worthy.

Her daughter nodded with glee. "Uh-huh, a baby one. He had stripes and was really pretty. Can we have a snake, too? I'd take really good care of it."

"Absolutely not. No snakes."

"But you said we could get a pet ages ago and we still don't have one." She stuck her lip out in a perfect pout.

"We will when the time is right."

"When will that be?"

When? When her father was able to work again? When the nightmares went away?

"Soon."

Emma shot her a disbelieving look and went back to snuggling the kitten.

Great, just one more way she'd let her daughter down.

Alex had overslept, then cut himself in his hurry to shave and shower. Now he was standing in the pet food section of Paradise's only grocery store, still bleeding, and confused as heck. Was growth food the same as kitten food? Or should he get the special indoor formula? Or sensitive? What did that even mean, sensitive? And then there were all the hairball options. By the looks of it, half of America's cats were fighting some kind of hair trauma he had no desire to understand.

Dabbing again at the cut on his jaw, he decided on

the bag marked Growth, mainly because it had a picture of a kitten on the front. That had to be a good sign.

Taking the smallest bag, he added it to his basket, which already contained a box of protein bars, new razor blades and the chew bone he'd promised Rex this morning. Thankfully, the checkout line was short, and he was in the car and tearing into one of the protein bars in a matter of minutes. He washed down the makeshift meal with some bottled water and nosed the vehicle south on Lighthouse Avenue. A few quick blocks later and he was pulling into the small parking lot.

Rex woofed hopefully.

"All right, you can come in." He got out and then let Rex out, snapping on his leash. The dog trotted at his side, nose working the breeze. The K-9 was probably picking up a full buffet of smells from all of the pets that had been through there recently.

Once inside, Rex honed in on the treat container in the reception area, sitting prettily directly in front of it.

"Hi, handsome!" The pretty brunette behind the counter, Mollie, according to her name tag, smiled at the panting dog, then turned to Alex. "You must be the man that rescued the kitten this morning, right?"

"Guilty as charged. Although really Rex was the one who found him. He deserves all the credit."

"I'm not sure *credit* is the word." She made a wry face. "Maybe *blame* would be more accurate. That little guy has been driving everyone nuts all day. They had to move him into Cassie's office because he was getting the other patients all worked up with his yowling."

Alex winced. "Sorry. I probably should have taken him with me, but I wasn't exactly prepared for a surprise kitten at six this morning."

"Don't be silly. It's not your fault he's so rambunctious. And Dr. Marshall's daughter is in love with him. She's back there playing with him now."

"Emma's here? Surely her mother doesn't bring her to work every day?"

The receptionist tipped her head, studying him. "I didn't realize you'd met Emma already. Her grandparents dropped her off a little bit ago. They watch her in the afternoons."

He nodded. "Emma and I met at the Share the Love meeting the other day—she asked if I was going to take anyone to jail. She's quite the character."

Mollie laughed. "That she is. Not a shy bone in her body, that's for sure. Have a seat. I'll let them know you're here."

Alex chose the seat farthest from the door, across from an older man snuggling a Persian cat. Rex ignored the cat, preferring to keep an eye on the treat jar.

Only a few minutes later, he was called into an examination room. He was surprised to recognize one of the owners of the Sandpiper, Jillian, waiting for him, dressed in scrubs.

"Deputy Santiago, good to see you again." She offered a wide smile, then crouched down to pet Rex. "And nice to meet you, Rex. I hear you're quite the hero."

"He's going to get a swollen head from all the compliments the women in this place give him. And call me Alex."

"Okay, Alex. Well, Dr. Marshall should be with you in just a minute. She was checking on the kitten's lab results, but he seems plenty healthy."

"Yeah, I heard he's been a handful. Sorry about that."

"Please. If we can't handle a two-pound kitten for a few hours, we're in trouble."

"Well, thank you anyway. I have to admit, I'm surprised to see you here. I thought you ran the Sandpiper?"

"Oh, no, I'm one of the owners, but my husband's the one who really runs it. Nic grew up in the hotel business, so he handles all the day-to-day stuff. I've been working here in the clinic since I was in high school. I can't imagine doing anything else."

He nodded in understanding. He could respect that; it was how he felt about being a cop.

The door opposite the one they came in from opened and Cassie entered, her daughter behind her. In Emma's arms was the kitten.

"He looks better," Alex commented. "Jillian said he's doing okay now."

"He's doing more than okay," Cassie told him. "He's got a belly full of food and has been given more attention today than he's probably ever had in his life."

As if to prove her statement, the kitten began purring, his throaty rumbling surprisingly loud given his small size.

"That's good, because he's going to be on his own tonight. I did stop and get him some food. And I can make him a bed up, with towels or something."

"Good. What kind of litter did you get?"

Uh-oh. "Um, well..."

Cassie watched his face, then burst into laughter. Her shoulders shook as she spoke. "You've never had a cat before, have you, Deputy?"

Her laughter was almost worth the embarrassment. Almost. He had a college degree and had solved numerous criminal cases, yet he couldn't figure out how to take care of a simple cat? She must think he was an idiot.

Still chuckling, she put a hand on his arm. "I'm sorry I laughed. I should have given you a list this morning or at least told you what to get."

Her hand on his arm was warm, the casual touch sending a jolt of heat through his body. Pulling away, he cleared his suddenly dry throat. "You did more than enough. This was my fault." He rubbed a hand over his jaw. "I don't suppose you sell that stuff here? I've got to be on patrol in a bit, and, well—"

"Why don't we take Trouble home with us, Mommy?"

Alex looked from the bright-eyed girl to her mother. "I don't think—"

"Please, Mommy? You said we would get a pet. And this one needs a home. And he loves me so much, I know he'd miss me. And," she said, pointing at Alex triumphantly, "he doesn't know how to take care of a cat. He doesn't even have a litter box."

Put in his place by a child. So much for making a good impression. He'd be offended, except she was right. He had no idea what to do with a cat. He'd grown up with dogs, but cats were a new experience. Still, he didn't want to put Cassie out more than he already had.

"I'm sure I can figure something out for tonight, and I'll pick up a book at the library tomorrow. It can't be that hard, right?"

Cassie nodded slowly, but her eyes were on her daughter. Remembering her earlier conversation with Emma, she gave Alex a half-hearted smile. "I'm sure you could figure it out, but Emma's right. I did promise her a pet." And since she couldn't give her a dad, she might as well give her a cat. Because that made sense. Not.

"Really, Mommy? Really-really?"

"Really-really. But you'll have to take care of him yourself. He'll need to be fed and his litter box scooped. It won't just be about playtime and snuggles." Her lecture was lost on the girl, who was already whispering into the kitten's ear. No doubt they were planning all sorts of adventures.

"You didn't have to do this. I would have managed."

Alex looked uncomfortable with the change in plans. The poor guy probably wasn't used to being overruled by a four-year-old.

"I'm sure you could have handled it, but Emma's right. I did promise her a pet. I've been saying it for a while now, and since we aren't fostering any pets right now, it's a good time to do it. And a kitten's better than a snake."

"A snake?" He arched an eyebrow.

"It's a long story." A thought struck her. "You didn't want to keep him yourself, did you? I really should have asked before basically catnapping him from you."

He grinned at her pun, one side of his mouth tipping up higher than the other. The crooked smile made him look boyish and devious all at once. A potent combination that had her pulse tripping faster. "No, I wasn't planning to keep him. Between the new job and Rex, I'm not looking to take on any more responsibilities."

Her libido cooled as quickly as if he'd dumped a bucket of ice water on her. Avoiding responsibility was a definite turnoff. "Right, well, it's good you know your limitations. Too many people don't take that into account until after the damage is done."

"I just want to do right by the little guy. If you and Emma are willing to give him a good home, well, I can't imagine a better place for him." He paused. "Do you need to run this by your husband before bringing a new pet home? I don't want to cause any problems."

She fumbled with the stethoscope around her neck. "No, that won't be necessary."

"It's just Mommy and me at home," Emma piped up. "We're a team."

Cassie was used to looks of pity when people found out she was a single mom, but Alex's eyes showed only admiration.

Turning back to Emma, he crouched down so he could look her in the eye. "Well, then. Do I have your word that you're going to take good care of him? Feed him and clean up after him and whatever else your mama says?"

Her eyes wide, she nodded solemnly. Then, without warning, she ambushed him with a hug, nearly knocking him, the kitten and herself to the floor. "Thank you for finding Trouble, and for giving him to me! He's the best present ever!"

No one could resist Emma when she turned on the cute, not even a hardened lawman like Alex. He hugged the girl right back. Then, once she released him, he stood and called Rex to his side. "Rex here is the one who found your kitty."

Awed by the massive dog, she asked quietly, "Does he like little girls?"

"Of course he does. Little girls are his favorite kind of people."

That was all the encouragement Emma needed. She wrapped her arms around the giant dog's neck, burying her face in the thick fur. Cassie started forward, visions of police dogs and bite suits flashing through her mind.

Alex stopped her with a touch. "They're fine."

He was right. Rex had his tongue lolling out of his mouth, panting in the way of happy dogs everywhere.

"I'm sorry. I normally wouldn't worry, but I haven't had much experience with police dogs. I wouldn't want—"

"No need to explain, I get it. Honestly, I wouldn't suggest she try that with most K-9s, but Rex really likes kids. I've even done some demonstrations at the school. He was chosen for our department partly because he's so social. He's the first dog here, and if he gets a bad reputation, that would be the end of the Palmetto County K-9 unit."

As she watched the dog, her instincts agreed with Alex's words. Rex did seem as comfortable with Emma as any family pet.

"You take Rex to schools?" Emma had lifted her head to speak, but kept her arms around the dog.

"Sometimes." He winked, then stage-whispered, "I think he likes to show off."

Oh, my. The combination of the wink and the dimples, not to mention the low gravel of his voice, had Cassie clutching the edge of the exam table. This man was so potent he needed a warning label.

"Could you bring him to my school for show-and-tell? That would be even cooler than John Baker's silly snake."

"Well—"

"Emma, Deputy Santiago is a busy man. He and Rex have a very important job to do."

"That's right, we do."

Emma's face fell.

"But show-and-tell sounds pretty important, too. And Rex sure would love to see you again."

Sexy, confident, good with dogs and kids. If she hadn't had a hang-up about the Palmetto Sheriff's department, she would have said he was perfect.

Why couldn't he have been a doctor or a lawyer, or even a mechanic? No, he had to be part of the good old boy network that passed for law enforcement in this area. Yeah, she was cynical. But for good reason, darn it.

Pasting a smile on her face, she remembered this wasn't about her. It was about her daughter. "Thank you, Deputy Santiago. I know the kids will love having you come. I'll have her teacher contact you about the details, if that's okay."

"Sure, no problem at all." Patting Emma's strawberry-blond curls, he extended a hand to Cassie. "Thank you again for taking the kitten. Let me know if it doesn't work out, and I'll figure something else out."

His hand was warm on hers, firm but gentle. Letting go abruptly, she stuck her tingling hand in her pocket. "We'll be just fine, Deputy. Thank you."

As Alex passed by the receptionist's desk, Cassie caught Mollie checking out his rear end, and who could blame her? The deputy said he didn't want to cause trouble, but from where she stood, he was exactly that.

Chapter Four

Alex stood in front of the double doors of All Saints School, feeling as if he was eight years old again. He'd gone to an elementary school very similar to this one and had spent more than his fair share of time in the principal's office. But that was a long time ago, and he was no longer a messed-up little kid in trouble for fighting. He was a grown man; there was no reason to be intimidated.

Rex whined, looking between him and the door. Sometimes having a dog so in tune with his emotions wasn't a good thing.

"It's okay, boy. They invited us. You'll show them your tricks, and then we can go home." He'd scheduled this visit for his day off and was looking forward to a nap and then maybe stopping by his mom's place for dinner. Just the thought of her empanadas had his stomach grumbling.

"All right, let's go." He squared his shoulders and opened the door, stepping into the relative warmth of the building. It even smelled like a school, of crayons, newly sharpened pencils and that odd industrial soap all schools seemed to use.

Rex's nails clicked on the industrial linoleum floor as he walked to the door labeled Administration. An older woman with a neat bob of silver hair sat behind a massive oak desk. Spotting him, she stood as he came in. "Deputy Santiago, I'm Eleanor Trask, the assistant principal. I want to thank you for coming. Our pre-schoolers are really looking forward to this."

"I'm happy to do it."

She stepped past him through the door, motioning him to follow. He walked beside her down the wide hall, then down a side passage with doors every few feet. Paper-plate snowmen with children's names on them lined the walls. He smiled, knowing that most of the artists had never seen a single flake of snow.

"You like children, Deputy?"

"Yes, ma'am, I do. Children are honest, and I don't see much of that in my line of work."

She paused and then nodded. "I've never thought of it quite that way, but you're right. They are honest in a way refreshing to most adults. I find that people who don't like children usually have something to hide."

He thought of his own childhood and agreed. "I suppose that's true."

They stopped in front of a door toward the end of the corridor. "This is it. We decided to bring in the other two preschool classes as well, given the exciting nature of this particular show-and-tell. You should have quite the audience."

Swallowing, he let her open the door and introduce him. From the doorway, he could see about thirty small children seated in rows on the brightly-colored carpet. After Ms. Trask reminded the students to be on their best behavior, she left, leaving him wondering what he'd been thinking. He'd faced hardened criminals less intimidating.

"Hi, Rex!" The familiar voice carried over the whispers of her classmates. Rex woofed in return, setting all the kids into fits of giggles. Emma was front and center, her red-blond curls in pigtails and her face alight with joy. Smiling back, he felt a heavy tug on his heartstrings. It seemed both the Marshall women knew how to get to him.

Alex spent the next half-hour telling the students a bit about police dogs before moving on to some demonstrations. Rex did his various obedience moves, then used his nose to find a hidden object in the room. He determined which of two pencils had been held by Alex. Delighted by the dog's tricks, the children all begged to pet Rex. He let them, one by one, monitoring closely. Rex might like kids, but that many children could overwhelm any dog.

Emma's excitement was contagious. By the end of his talk, all the kids were in love with Rex, and half wanted to be K-9 handlers when they grew up. Definitely a success. Before leaving, he handed out shiny sheriff's deputy stickers, hoping they would keep the kids distracted enough for him to make his getaway. He was just slipping out when Emma stopped him.

"Deputy Alex?"

"Yes?"

"Do you have anyone to be your valentine yet?"

Where on earth did that come from? "Um, no, I guess not. Other than Rex here."

She rolled her eyes at him. "A dog can't be your valentine. It has to be a people."

"Oops, sorry. I guess I don't, then."

"Would you like one?"

Was he being propositioned by a four-year-old? "Um, sure, I guess. I hadn't thought about it much yet."

"Perfect. I'll tell her you said yes." Flush with success, she waved goodbye and ran back to her friends.

Had he just agreed to something? And if so, what?

Cassie managed to snag one of the few open parking spots; maybe that meant her luck was changing. The school secretary had called an hour ago to tell her that Emma had forgotten her lunch again. Stuck in surgery, she hadn't been able to leave until twenty minutes ago, only to find the abandoned Hello Kitty lunchbox on the backseat of her car, tucked under a sweater. And after baking in the hot car all morning, the contents were less than edible. It might be January, but in typical Florida fashion the temperature had climbed twenty degrees in the past few days. Then, what should have been a quick trip to the corner store for more food had stalled out when the person ahead of her paid with loose change—counting and recounting three times.

But she was here now, and lunch period didn't start for another ten minutes. Slamming the car door closed, she made for the main entrance, only to have the door open as she reached for it. Off balance, she did a stutter step to keep from falling.

"Whoa, sorry. Are you okay?"

Alex Santiago and his dog were staring at her, concern showing in both their gazes. How could she have forgotten today was the show-and-tell thing? "I'm fine, really. I just have a habit of tripping over my own feet, that's all."

"Are you sure?"

His deep voice set off tingles in all the right places. Stomping down on her libido before she said something stupid, she held the lunch box out in front of her like a shield. "I'm good. Just going to drop off Emma's lunch. She forgot it this morning. How about you—how was show-and-tell?"

He winced. "Loud. Very loud. I'm not quite sure how such small people make so much noise. But other than that, I think it went well. And Rex put on a good show."

"I'm sure he did." Awkwardly, she ducked past him into the building. "I'll see you around, I guess."

"Oh, you will. Mrs. Rosenberg was helpful enough to sign me up for every committee there is for the Share the Love dance. We're bound to run into each other."

"Mrs. Rosenberg is a force to be reckoned with." Shaking her head at the image of the elderly lady pulling a fast one on the tough cop, she suddenly realized something. "Does that mean you'll be at the decorating committee meeting tomorrow night?"

"So it seems. And you?"

"Yes, that's the only committee I signed up for."

"You've got plenty on your plate already with Emma and the clinic, I'm sure."

"You're right, I do." And yet she'd been standing there making small talk when it was almost time for Emma's lunch. "Speaking of which, I'd better get this to Emma."

"Of course. See you tomorrow." He exited via the door she'd just come through, Rex trotting at his side.

Shaking her head to clear her thoughts, she went to the front office to sign in and get a visitor's pass, then headed for her daughter's classroom. She should have just enough time to say hello before getting back for afternoon appointments. Her own lunch would have to be a protein shake between patients, but that wasn't anything new.

Emma was lining up at the front of the room with her friends, but ran for a hug when she saw Cassie walk in. "Thanks, Mom. Sorry I forgot it."

Cassie guided her back into line and walked with her toward the cafeteria. "You know, one of these days I'm going to just let you starve." Rolling her eyes, Emma reached for her hand as they walked.

They both knew that wasn't going to happen, mainly because Cassie was just as forgetful, if not worse. If she didn't have Mollie to keep her on track at work, she'd be in deep trouble. Sticky notes and alarms on her smartphone were a big help, but it would be a few years before Emma could make use of those. "Just try to be more careful. Okay?"

"I will. I was just so excited about seeing Rex and Deputy Alex that I couldn't think about anything else."

Another shared trait—a fondness for handsome men and good-looking dogs.

"Oh, and Mommy, guess what?"

"What?"

"Deputy Alex is going to be your valentine!"

"What?" Several heads had turned at Emma's enthusiastic statement. No doubt there would be talk in the teacher's lounge later.

"I asked, and he said he doesn't have a valentine. And you don't have one, either. So you can be each other's. It's perfect."

Emma's innocence made Cassie's heart squeeze. "Oh, honey, it's not quite that simple. Just because we're both single doesn't mean we're going to be valentines with each other."

Emma frowned. "Why not? Don't you like Deputy Alex?"

"Of course I do." More than she should. "But someday, when you're a grown-up, you'll understand that things like valentines are more complicated than just liking someone."

"I don't ever want to be a grown-up. It makes everything complicated."

No kidding, kid. No kidding.

Cassie gave Emma a quick hug at the cafeteria door, then headed back out to her car and her very grown-up, way-too-complicated life.

Back at the clinic, Cassie had little time to dwell on her lack of a valentine or her daughter's ridiculous matchmaking. A terrier with kennel cough had one exam room shut down until it could be fully disinfected, causing the rest of the appointments to be delayed. She'd soothed the last cranky client of the day only a few minutes ago and was going over the day's receipts when Jillian knocked on the open door.

"Got a minute?"

Cassie stretched her arms over her head, her vertebrae popping at the movement. "Sure, what's up?"

Her friend pushed her dark curls off her face, fidgeting, her eyes looking everywhere but at Cassie.

Gut clenching, Cassie put down the stack of papers she'd been reading. "What is it? What's wrong?" Jillian was her best friend, the closest she'd ever gotten to having a sister.

Jillian's big brown eyes filled with tears, which she quickly wiped away. "Nothing. I mean, nothing's wrong. It's just…well…" She placed a hand on her flat belly and met Cassie's gaze. "I'm pregnant."

"Oh, my goodness, really?" Jumping up, Cassie stared at Jillian's hand, as if she could see through it to the baby growing underneath. "That's amazing! But why are you crying? I thought you and Nic wanted to have kids right away?" A horrible thought hit her. "The baby's okay, right? And you're okay?"

"We're both fine. I saw the doctor on my lunch hour and she says everything is perfect."

"Oh, thank goodness." She sat back down. "And Nic's happy about the baby?"

"He's over the moon. He was drawing out plans for the nursery when I left."

That sounded like Nic. The former hotel magnate had recently discovered a latent talent for carpentry. "So then why are you crying?"

Laughing through her tears, Jillian shook her head. "I don't know! It just keeps happening."

Relief sang through Cassie. Embracing her friend, she found her own eyes filling. "Hormones will make you crazy, but who cares? You're going to be a mommy! You have to let me throw your baby shower, promise?"

"Of course you can. So you aren't upset?"

Cassie pulled away. "Upset? Why on earth would I be upset?"

"Because of all the inconvenience. I'm not going to

be able to take X-rays, and I think I'll have some limits on lifting, and it's just going to make more work for everyone," she finished with a sob.

"Oh, sweetie, don't worry about all that. Mollie can cross-train some and help out in the back, and you can help her up front. We're all in this together, right?"

A fresh round of tears soaked Jillian's smiling face. "Right. Thanks. And I am happy. I just didn't think it would happen so soon, you know?"

"I've seen the sparks between you and Nic. Honestly, I'm surprised it took this long."

Jillian grinned through her tears. "Speaking of which, I've seen the way that new deputy looks at you, the one with the Shepherd. Anything going on there?"

"Hardly." She turned her gaze back to the paper printouts on her desk.

"Well, why on earth not? He's hot, single and likes dogs." She ticked off the traits on her fingers.

"And works for the sheriff's department. No thank you."

"Cassie, the entire sheriff's department is not against you. Besides, Alex wasn't even working there when all that happened."

"It doesn't matter." She forced a smile. "I've got my hands full anyway, with work and Emma and the charity dance. And on top of all that, I've got a baby shower to plan. Who's got time to think about men with all that going on?"

"Right." Jillian didn't look convinced, but good friend that she was, she dropped the subject. "If you don't have anything more for me, I'm going to go. Nic wants us to call and tell his family about the baby tonight."

"Go, then. I'm almost done here anyway. And congratulations again. You're going to make a wonderful mother."

And she would. Despite Jillian's lonely childhood, bouncing from one foster home to another, or maybe because of it, she would be an excellent mother. And her baby would be lucky enough to grow up with a father, as well. He or she would have two stable, loving parents, the kind of family Emma was so hungry for and Cassie would never be able to offer.

Chapter Five

Alex parked his department SUV in the gravel lot of the Sandpiper and tried to psych himself up for the scrutiny and pointed questions he knew were coming. It wasn't that he disliked socializing, but being the new guy in a small town meant everyone thought they had a right to his life story. Thankfully, so far the gossips had been too well-mannered to press him, but his luck couldn't hold forever.

"Come on, boy. Jillian said you can come in as long as you're nice to her dog."

Rex woofed, nearly toppling Alex in his eagerness to get out and explore. The inn billed itself as pet friendly, and no doubt there were a myriad of smells for the big dog to enjoy. Not to mention, letting him amble a bit on the way in meant a few more minutes before he was put under the microscope by the committee ladies.

Rex was intently sniffing a coco-plum hedge when his ears suddenly pricked up. A moment later, the sound of footsteps on gravel signaled someone coming up the path behind them. The dog's frantic tail wagging indicated a friend, so it was no surprise when Cassie came around the bend. "He remembers you."

"He remembers the treats I gave him, don't you boy?"

Woof.

"Sorry, I don't have any on me right now. But don't worry, I bet Emma will sneak you some out of Murphy's stash."

"Is Emma with you?"

"My mom dropped her off here after dinner, so I wouldn't have to make an extra trip to pick her up."

He angled his steps beside hers as they headed for the main building. "It must be a big help, having your family around."

"I couldn't have done it without them. My dad is a vet, too. He owns the clinic, in fact. But he hasn't been able to work since the accident, leaving me with longer hours. It's a bit better now that Emma's in preschool, but that's only part-time. Knowing she's with family or with a friend like Jillian after school keeps me from going totally insane."

Accident? He was about to ask her about it when the front door swung open. A tall, dark-haired man stepped out and embraced Cassie, nearly sweeping her off her feet.

"Can you believe it? Jillian said she told you today."

Cassie laughed and gave him a peck on the cheek. "Yes, she told me, and of course I can believe it. You two are meant to be parents." She turned back. "Nic, this is Alex Santiago. Alex, meet Nic Caruso, proprietor and father-to-be."

Alex's offered hand was enveloped in a very enthusiastic handshake. "Thanks for letting us use your place for the meeting. It's very generous of you."

"That's all Jillian. She's the one in charge."

Cassie grinned. "And don't you forget it."

"I won't. She won't let me. In fact, I'd better go see if she needs anything else before the meeting starts."

Alex watched him duck through a swinging door into a private hallway. "He seems like a nice guy."

"He is. They're really lucky to have each other."

At her wistful smile, an ache started deep in his chest. Her vulnerability triggered all his protective instincts. Someone had done wrong by this woman, and he wouldn't mind a few rounds alone with whoever it had been.

Breaking the silence, Cassie indicated the French doors that were the rear entrance. "We'd better get started before they get it all done without us."

He followed her gaze across the casual yet elegant room. Overstuffed furniture was arranged around a native coquina-stone fireplace. Beyond that, large windows were open to the crisp night air. Over the sound of the sea came the rise and fall of voices; it seemed everyone else was out back.

As soon as they stepped outside, they were greeted by a chorus of welcomes. Mrs. Rosenberg was there, of course, and she nodded approvingly when she saw them. Jillian was seated next to her at a large picnic-style table, and a number of other women filled the deck chairs scattered along the wide whitewashed porch that wrapped around the building. As expected, he was the only male member of the decorating committee. Well, except for Rex and Murphy, Jillian and Nic's dog. The border collie had been sleeping under the table, but at the sight of Rex had bulleted through his mistress's legs to greet his new playmate.

"Murphy, don't make a pest of yourself. Rex is a serious working dog, not your new partner-in-crime," Jillian admonished. She smiled up at Alex. "Sorry, he means well, but he's still stuck in the puppy phase. Possibly permanently."

"No problem. Rex likes other dogs and could do with a buddy." Rex held still as the younger dog sniffed him all over, then returned the favor. Canine introductions over, they both looked up at Alex, as if waiting for permission to play. "Is it okay if I let him off his leash? I don't want him to get tangled with Murphy."

"Of course. Maybe Rex's good manners will rub off on him. Either way, I've got the gate to the yard closed off, so they can't go far."

At the click of the lead unsnapping, both dogs bounded off for the far end of the porch, away from the crowd. Keeping one eye on the dogs, Alex settled onto a white bench next to Cassie and across from Jillian. "I hear congratulations are in order."

The mother-to-be blushed. "Yes, we just found out. We're both a bit overwhelmed."

"Understandably. I'd be quaking in my boots, but fatherhood never has been on my radar. Nic seems to be taking it in stride, though."

"You didn't see his face when I told him. I thought he was going to pass out right in front of me."

Mrs. Rosenberg patted her hand. "They all get a bit jumpy when they find out. I know my Marvin did. But before you know it they're passing out cigars and acting like they're the first person to ever make a baby."

Next to him, Cassie fiddled with the edge of her sweater. Most of the women he knew loved baby talk, especially the experienced mothers. Cassie, however, looked as if she'd sooner face a firing squad than swap maternity tales. Jillian must have seen it, too, because she took one look at her friend's face and changed the subject.

"Cassie, can you and Alex work on the banners? Mrs. Rosenberg and I are going to go inside and put together the centerpieces."

"Sure." Cassie looked to Alex. "Does that sound okay to you?"

Alex nodded. "Sure, as long as there are some instructions somewhere. I'm kind of clueless with arts and crafts."

Mrs. Rosenberg pointed to the stacks of paper and craft supplies on the table as she stood up. "Cassie knows what to do. Just stick with her and you'll be fine."

He looked expectantly at Cassie. "I hope you're a patient teacher. I'm afraid I failed cut and paste in school."

That got a grin from her. "Well, big guy, you're going to get a crash course in it tonight. Not to brag, but as a surgeon, I'm an expert at precision cutting. All you have to do is watch me."

No worries there. Seeing her there, bathed in moonlight, he couldn't have taken his eyes off her if he tried.

Cassie never would have imagined she'd enjoy spending an evening cutting out hundreds of construction-paper hearts. But talking with Alex had made the time fly by. He'd entertained her with stories of growing up

Puerto Rican in Miami, teasing her when she couldn't pronounce the name of his favorite food. She'd shared some of the funnier animal encounters she'd had over the years, and then they'd both cracked up when Murphy ran in with an entire string of pink twinkle lights wrapped around his body.

After they untangled the dog, he had been banished to Jillian and Nic's private quarters, where he'd kept Emma company watching cartoons. Rex, worn out by the younger, more rambunctious dog, had curled up under the table with his head on Cassie's feet.

In fact, the only awkward part of the evening had been when Jillian and Mrs. Rosenberg were comparing stories about their husbands. They hadn't meant any harm, but remembering her own early pregnancy was hardly a pleasant experience. Nic might have been over the moon about the new baby, but Cassie knew too well that not all men got past the initial shock and fear. Certainly her ex never had. He'd called her a liar, then suggested the baby wasn't his after all. Learning that he'd walked out on her had been almost a relief after the awful things he'd said.

His reaction might have been extreme, but it wasn't all that uncommon, in her view. Even Alex had commented on how frightening the idea of fatherhood was.

Thankfully, once the subject was changed, the rest of the evening had been more pleasant than she'd expected. Now it was probably time to get going. She finished stringing one more heart on the banner in front of her and reluctantly stood up. "It's late. I need to get Emma home and into bed."

He looked down at his watch. "Wow, it is late. She must be exhausted."

"Actually, she's probably passed out on Jillian's bed. She can fall asleep anywhere."

"Seriously?" His eyebrow cocked in disbelief. "We haven't exactly been quiet out here."

"I'm telling you, she could fall asleep in Times Square. The clock strikes eight and she's out for the count. She's been like that since she was a baby. Come, I'll show you."

She grabbed his hand, pulling him up to follow her. Awareness snaked up her arm like heat lightning on a summer's night. Dropping his hand, she stumbled back as if she'd literally been shocked.

Alex stared, the heat in his eyes a match for the surge she'd felt in his touch. All she had to do was lean forward and he'd kiss her, and it had been so long since she'd been kissed.

But a kiss wouldn't be enough, not by half. Accepting that and knowing it couldn't be more, she drew a deep breath and turned away. She wasn't running away. She was being sensible. So why did the sound of his footsteps behind her have her increasing her pace?

She stopped just inside Jillian and Nic's private suite, taking a moment to calm herself before waking Emma up.

"Wow, you were right." Alex's husky whisper sent a shiver down her spine.

Emma was passed out in a heap on the floor, her head resting on Murphy's snoring form. "She's always fallen asleep easily, but she's a bear when you wake her up."

"Then let's not wake her." Alex stepped past her and gently scooped Emma into his arms. Cassie meant to stop him, to insist that she could handle things, but the way his jeans molded to his body when he bent over left her temporarily speechless. Oblivious to her ogling, he effortlessly carried the girl past her and toward the front of the inn. Scrambling after him, she rushed to open the door while waving a hasty goodbye to her friends. Jillian's lips quirked up at the sight, but she thankfully didn't comment.

Outside, the cooler air calmed her senses and her libido. There was no need to get all worked up. Alex was just being chivalrous. But all her rationalizations didn't stop her heart from aching at the sight of her daughter cradled in his strong arms. This was the kind of thing Emma had missed out on by not having a father around.

In the parking lot, Alex silently slid Emma into her car seat, then managed the buckles like a pro.

"Thanks."

"Anytime."

Right. One time was more than was smart, if her jumping pulse was any indication. If she wanted to protect her heart, she was going to have to stay far away from Alex Santiago.

Chapter Six

"So, I hear you met the new K-9 officer?"

Leave it to her dad to touch on the one subject she was hoping to avoid. He'd had a knack for that all her life.

"I've run into him a few times. And he found an abandoned kitten that Emma talked me into keeping." Across the kitchen table in her parents' home, her father watched her carefully.

"Emma told me about that. She's taken quite a shine to him."

"Well, kittens are pretty hard to resist."

"I was talking about the man, not the cat."

Well, he was hard to resist, too. But that was more than her father needed to know. Turning her eyes back to the laptop in front of her, she chose her words carefully. "He seems very nice."

Her father looked over his glasses at her. "Very nice?"

"Yes, he seems nice." No way was Dad going to get her to admit to more than that. She'd come over so they could go over the clinic books together, not so he could play matchmaker.

He leaned over her shoulder and tapped at the keyboard, printing out the most recent month's statistics. "Well, that should make things easier."

"Make what easier?"

"I'm getting to that. You see, before the accident, I'd agreed to help the sheriff's office with the new K-9 unit. Nothing major, just routine checkups and some help with the training runs."

She closed the laptop. Obviously that wasn't why her dad had called her over anyway. No, he had something else up his sleeve.

"So anyway, with me still not up to par, that leaves you."

She stared at him. "Leaves what to me, exactly?"

"Like I said, routine medical care. And some training."

"Medical care, sure. But training? You want me to put on a bite suit or something?" What on earth had her father gotten her into?

"No, nothing like that. But they want the dogs to do search work and need some volunteers. I'd planned on doing it, but as it is…" He pointed to his injured leg.

"Fine. I'll do it." Darn him, he was actually smirking. "You know, you don't have to look so pleased about the whole idea."

"Who, me?" He winked at her. "I really do feel bad about backing out, so I'm glad you're going to take my place. But yes, I am also happy about you spending some time with a young man. A very nice young man, I believe you said."

"Who just so happens to work for the sheriff's department. You know, I wouldn't think you'd be so eager to help them after everything that happened."

"Cassie, honey, we've been over this. You can't hold the whole department responsible for what happened. And this Alex fellow wasn't even here back then."

Logically, she knew her father was right. But that didn't keep her from breaking out into a cold sweat at the sight of the blue sheriff's uniform or jumping every time she heard a siren. She'd made some progress, thanks to a therapist recommended by the ER doctor who had treated her. And it was true that Alex didn't trigger the usual panic. But he caused a whole different kind of emotional overload, one she wasn't up for dealing with.

"I said I'll help. Don't push for more, okay?" She was agreeing at all only because she still felt guilty about the accident. No, she hadn't caused it, but she'd been the one driving, and she couldn't help but second-guess herself. Especially when she saw the pain her father was still in.

"How's the physical therapy going?" She gestured to his knee, now supported by a brace.

"Good." He beamed. "I should be back at work in another week or so."

"Is that what Jen said?" Jen Miller was her father's physical therapist and an old schoolmate.

Her father rubbed the knee absently. "It's what I'm saying. You're doing a tremendous job, but you can't run that clinic on your own forever. That's why I asked you to come over. I can at least start doing the paperwork." He ran a hair through his still-thick gray hair. "If I don't do something, I'm going to go crazy."

"He's right, much as I hate to admit it." Her mom walked in, a load of laundry in a basket on her hip. "I know he enjoys spending time with me and helping with sweet Emma, but if he doesn't get back to the clinic soon, he's going to drive both of us crazy."

Her father snaked out a hand and pulled his still-trim wife into his lap. "Lady, I'm already crazy, over you." He planted a loud kiss on her lips, then let her up.

Cassie turned back to her computer, never sure what to make of her parents' affectionate displays. She was glad they were so happy together; plenty of her friends growing up had come from divorced or unhappy homes. But she couldn't help wonder what was wrong with her, that she had never found that kind of happiness herself.

Clearing her throat, she tried to bring the conversation back on track. "I get that you're frustrated, and yes, I'm happy to have you take over the bookkeeping. But please, follow Jen's advice." Veterinary work was often physically difficult, and as much as she felt crushed under the workload, she didn't want her father having a relapse, either. She'd have to talk to Jen and get the real prognosis, and if Dad was rushing things, she'd have a heart-to-heart talk with her mom. Her father might be bull-headed, but he would listen to his wife. Love had that effect on a man, or so she'd been told.

Cassie waited in the cool, casually decorated lobby of the Paradise Physical Therapy clinic, watching the minute hand tick its way around her watch. Stopping by without an appointment had been a mistake; it seemed the practice was much busier than she'd expected. It wasn't that she didn't have the time—Emma wasn't due to be picked up for another two hours and Mollie had cleared the rest of her appointments for the day—just that she hated waiting.

Flipping through an out-of-date magazine filled with celebrities she had never heard of, she wondered when she'd lost track of pop culture. Probably about the time she became a single mother. Between work and childcare, there hadn't been much time for movies or concerts, and her television habits had been reduced to educational cartoons. Although if half of what the magazines said was true, she hadn't missed much.

"Cassie?"

Her childhood friend looked the same as she had in high school, trim and athletic with curly brown hair pulled back in a neat ponytail. "Hi, Jen. Thanks for seeing me on such short notice."

"No problem. Thanks for waiting. Come on back. I'm going to grab some coffee in the break room before my next appointment."

Jen led her down the hall to a small but tidy room, then offered her a drink.

"Water would be great, thanks."

Jen handed her a bottle from the refrigerator, then poured a cup of coffee. "So what brings you by here? Is there a problem with your father?"

"No. Well, sort of. I'm just worried that he's pushing too fast. He says he's going to be back in the office in a week or two, and although I'd love the help, I'm afraid he's going to end up hurting himself worse."

Jen sipped her coffee. "I can't discuss his medical records with you. You know that. But I can say that, professionally, I don't see a problem with that plan. He'll be sore, but it shouldn't set his recovery back, if that's what you're worried about."

What felt like a hundred pounds of dead weight lifted from her shoulders. "Really? You think he's doing that well?" He'd been in such bad shape after the accident, it was hard to imagine him finally back at work. But she trusted Jen's opinion, so if she said he was up for it, then he was.

"Like I said, I can't release details, but since you are business partners, I can tell you the same thing I would put in a note for an employer. He's still got some hurdles to overcome, but yes, he should be clear for light duty in a few weeks if he feels up to returning."

"That's wonderful. Thank you, Jen. I know you're the reason he's done so well."

Jen dumped the last bit of her coffee in the sink and rinsed the cup. "I've done the best I could for him, but the truth is, your father is a strong man with an incredible work ethic. He gets full credit for his success."

Cassie laughed. "I think what you are trying to say is that he's tough and a bit bull-headed."

"You said it, not me," Jen replied, a grin on her face. "But really, it was good to see you. We should get together soon."

"I'd like that. Maybe once Dad is back up to speed, I can meet you for lunch or something."

"Sounds good. Just give me a call." Jen looked down at her watch. "Sorry to rush off so fast, but I've got another patient."

"No problem. I can see myself out." She gave Jen a quick hug goodbye, then navigated the twisting hallway back to the front lobby. Outside, the bright sunshine echoed her mood. Her father's recovery had been so long in coming, it was amazing to see the finish line after so many months of therapy.

"How come you never smile like that for me?"

Cassie startled, then saw it was just Alex, carrying a white prescription bag from the pharmacy next door. "Sorry, I didn't see you there."

"No apology needed. You just looked so happy I had to ask why."

"Well, I just talked with my father's physical therapist, and he's doing really well. In fact, he's going to be able to come back to work in a few weeks, if everything goes well."

"That's great news—in fact, how about I buy you a hot chocolate to celebrate?"

She did have a bit longer before she had to get Emma, and the only thing waiting for her back at the office was a stack of paperwork. She'd told herself Alex was off-limits, that getting involved was a bad idea. But it was just hot chocolate, not really a date. And when the choice was a sexy man with dimples to die for or writing up charts, there wasn't much of a decision to make.

"Hot chocolate sounds great."

Walking down Paradise's Main Street, she could feel everyone's eyes on her. They probably were wondering what she was doing with the new hot deputy when she hadn't been on a date in known memory. Small towns were great most of the time, but they didn't allow for much privacy. Luckily, the Sandcastle Bakery was only a few blocks away and served all sorts of hot beverages.

Inside the bakery, she stepped up to the glass display counter where Grace was sliding a tray of cinnamon scones onto a shelf. Normally, the pastries were a favorite of Cassie's, but right now she was too focused on the man beside her to care about food.

"Well, Cassie and Alex, what a surprise to see you two here...together." She winked at Cassie, no doubt remembering their earlier conversation about the good-looking deputy. "What can I get for you?"

"Two hot chocolates, please." Alex pulled out his wallet and paid for both, a move that had Grace raising an eyebrow in surprise.

"We're just celebrating Dad's recovery. Alex bumped into me as I was leaving the physical therapy clinic, and when I told him the good news, he suggested we come here."

"Well, that's very sweet of you, Alex." She handed him his change and then passed over the two cups, each with a hefty dollop of whipped cream on top. "You two have fun, now."

Alex held the door for her, and they walked back onto the sidewalk, Grace no doubt peeking out after them. This was why she didn't date. Well, one of the reasons why. The minute you said hello to a man, the entire town was all up in your business, watching your every move. She loved Paradise, but sometimes it felt like living in a reality show. Although having Alex as a costar in their own little romance was pretty tempting.

He was in khakis and a polo shirt today, looking strong and sharp and altogether too good for her. Not that he seemed to realize it. He hadn't taken his eyes off her since they ran into each other, his heated gaze warming her core faster than the hot drink in her hand. Desperate to change the subject, she tried to come up with a topic of conversation.

"So, my dad told me you need some help with Rex's training."

"We do. The department's been trying to find some volunteers. I guess the original plan was to have your father help, but even with all the progress your dad is making, I can't imagine he's going to be up to traipsing through the woods for quite a while."

"No, he's not." Again the guilty voice in her head reminded her that even though she'd been driving, her dad was the one in the brace. "But since he can't do it, I told him I would. Just tell me when and where you need me."

Alex stopped walking, his hot chocolate nearly sloshing over the side of the cup. "Really? You'd do that for me?"

"I'll do it for my father," she clarified. "I'm just filling in for him. That's all."

He grinned, his dimple winking at her. "Of course, and I appreciate it. Can you meet me at the wildlife refuge Saturday afternoon, around four o'clock?"

"I'll be there. Do I need to bring anything?"

"No, I'll have a pack for you and supplies. All you have to do is show up and enjoy yourself. It's really pretty straightforward."

Right. A day in the woods, purposely getting lost, while trying to avoid her growing feelings for a man she had no business falling for. What could possibly go wrong?

Chapter Seven

Alex ducked his head farther into his hooded sweat-shirt. The relative warmth of the last week had broken this morning when a cold front blew in. Yesterday afternoon had been a balmy seventy-five degrees; today the mercury had stopped in the low forties and was expected to drop further at dusk. All over the island, people were putting sheets over prized rosebushes and bringing their potted plants indoors in advance of the expected freeze tonight. He'd thought about resched-uling the training session, but being able to work in all weather was part of the job description. Training only in perfect conditions wouldn't create a reliable dog, and with lives possibly in the balance, that was unacceptable.

"So tell me again. What do I have to do?" Mollie squinted up at him, shading her eyes from the bright but cool sunshine. She'd shown up with Cassie, a last-minute surprise volunteer. She seemed eager to work and hadn't complained once about the weather, which earned her points in his book. Right now, she was bouncing on the balls of her feet, waiting for instruction.

"You're going to wander away and find a place to hide. Spend about fifteen minutes or so walking before you stop. If you have any problems, you can use the radio, but otherwise try to keep quiet if you can. I want Rex to use his nose, not his ears."

"And he'll really be able to find me just by my scent?"

"That's the idea. He's going to be smelling the rafts of cells that fall off your body. Sometimes those fall right where your footsteps are, but sometimes they're blown around, pooling in invisible eddies of air. My job is to help interpret the wind patterns, as well as any terrain or temperature issues that might affect where the scent pools."

"I'm not sure if I'm fascinated or intimidated." Mollie's pixie-like features grinned up at him. "But I'm curious to see how well it works."

"Well, go hide, then, and we'll see how he does." Mollie gave a mock salute and started out across the scrubland that made up much of the Paradise Isle Wildlife Refuge. A few minutes later, she disappeared into a more densely wooded area shadowed by thick oaks.

With nothing to do but wait, he turned to Cassie, who'd been mostly silent since they arrived. "Sorry it's so cold out. I thought about canceling, but I'm not sure when my next day off is going to be, and Rex needs the practice."

"No, it's fine. I mean, you can't exactly choose the weather during a real search."

"Exactly. And I really want to get him up to speed. Police dogs don't usually do search and rescue, but with the nearest search group a few hours away, it makes sense to try to cross-train him."

"Really?" She cocked her head. "I thought all police dogs did that kind of thing—you know, tracking down bad guys and such?"

"Not all K-9s. And even then, not all scent work is the same. There's tracking, where they stay right along the footprints of the person they are following, and then there's air scenting, which is more what we are doing today. Rex will search in a zig-zag pattern to find the scent, then triangulate in. It's similar to how a police dog might clear a building. And then of course some dogs are also trained to detect drugs, or explosives, or even cadavers."

She shivered, and he had a feeling it wasn't from the cold this time. "That's kind of creepy."

"Well, sure. But at the same time, being able to provide closure for grieving families is pretty amazing."

"You're right. I'm sorry."

"No need. I'm just glad you came. Like I said, Rex needs the practice. He's doing well so far but hasn't made the jump yet to longer, aged tracks."

Cassie leaned down and ruffled Rex's fur. "I've got faith in you, buddy. You'll find her."

Energized by the attention, the dog bounced into a deep play bow, wiggling his butt in the air. "This cool weather has him acting like a puppy. We'd better let him burn off some energy while we're waiting or we won't be able to keep up with him on the trail." He pulled a tennis ball out of the backpack at his feet and tossed it to Cassie. "See if you can wear him out a bit while I double-check the map."

Cassie's face lit up at the challenge. She whipped the ball across the field and Rex tore after it as if it was the last ball on earth. Then, rather than waiting for him to bring it back, she chased after him, initiating a canine version of tag.

Crouched over his maps and log book, Alex couldn't help but notice how much more relaxed she seemed while playing with the dog.

"You should do that more often," he called out after watching them play for a while.

"Do what?" She walked back, the dog panting at her side.

"Smile."

Her back straightened stiffly. "Sorry, didn't realize I was such a downer usually."

Crap. "No, I just meant—well, you looked so happy just now. Not that you seem depressed otherwise, but you do seem a bit more weighed down most of the time." He shrugged a shoulder. "It was nice to see you just having fun. That's all."

"Oh." She bit her lip, an innocent act that had his mouth watering. "Well, I don't get a lot of time to just run and play. So thank you for inviting me out here."

"Hey, you're the one doing me a favor. But I'm glad you're not hating it."

She ducked her head. "Actually, I thought I would. In fact, I only agreed to help because my dad guilted me into it."

"Is it me? Have I done something to offend you? Or is it just the cop thing?"

"It's not you." She gave a wry grin. "I don't have a good relationship with the sheriff's department, that's all."

Well, at least it wasn't him; that was progress. "Anything I should know about? I'm too new to have heard much gossip, so I'd consider it a public service if you'd fill me in."

She smirked. "Public service? That's an interesting way to spin it."

Chuckling, he shouldered his pack. "We should get started now. And seriously, if it involves the department, I'd like to know, but if you're not comfortable sharing, that's fine, too. I didn't mean to put you on the spot."

She fell into step beside him. "It's not exactly a secret. I'm surprised you haven't heard all the details by now. I'll fill you in while Rex finds Mollie."

"If he finds Mollie. Remember, he's pretty new to this." He opened a small Ziploc bag that held a T-shirt of Mollie's and held it down for the dog to sniff. "Search, Rex. Search."

The dog snuffled the bag, then started sniffing around. Working back and forth in front of them, he covered an amazing amount of ground. Soon, his tail flagged up and he started moving in the direction Mollie had taken.

"Now what do we do?"

"Watch him and try to keep up."

Cassie watched the dog work, fascinated at the way he seemed to follow invisible signposts only he could see. Or, more accurately, smell. Alex was tracking each turn in his logbook, and he occasionally called out encouragingly to Rex. His love and pride in the dog and his dedication to his job were obvious. She respected that. And yet she'd treated him badly when they first met without provocation. He deserved to know why.

"Several months ago, my father and I attended a professional lecture over in Orlando. He drove on the way over, so I volunteered to drive home. It was late by the time we hit the Paradise Isle bridge, not much traffic at all. We were so close to home, and then, going through the intersection there at the base of the bridge, we were sideswiped. He didn't even slow down. I don't think he saw us at all, or the red light." She paused and turned to Alex. "The who that ran that light and hit us was an off-duty sheriff's deputy. He was drunk. He kept saying he was sorry over and over, and I could smell the booze on his breath. My dad had to be cut out of the car and still isn't back to work or able to walk without a brace. Jack, however, is just fine." Bile rose in her throat. "So yeah, I'm not a fan of cops right now."

Alex looked concerned, but to his credit he didn't exude sympathy like some people had. She hated pity.

"Jack? Jack Campbell? Older guy, real skinny?"

"Yeah, that's him. Paradise Isle's resident alcoholic. He was suspended, but because it was his first offense, he won't serve any jail time. His lawyer said he was a dedicated public servant going through a hard time, that it was a one-time mistake." Sarcasm coated her words. "No one is willing to acknowledge that he has a real problem. Least of all the Palmetto County Sheriff's Department."

"Wait, so you're saying the guys at the department are covering for him?" The disgust on his face made her like him even more.

"Maybe not covering for him exactly, but definitely

in some serious denial. Several of his friends accused me of exaggerating Jack's drinking, saying I was just trying to make trouble. Maybe they're right about it being the first time he's been caught, but given how frequently Jack closes down the only bar in town, I can't believe it was the first time he has driven under the influence. He needs more than just a slap on the wrist, but no one is willing to do anything about it. They act like I ruined his life, like he's the victim in all of this."

"Well, if it matters, I didn't know about any of it. I've been mainly working night shifts since I got here, so I'm a bit out of the loop."

It did matter. Reaching out, she squeezed his hand. "Thanks for listening, and thanks for believing me. I think that's been the worst part of this whole thing, having people not believe me."

He kept hold of her hand, tracing over her skin with this thumb. She shivered, and not from the cold.

"I do believe you. I'm not sure what I can do to help, but you can bet I'll keep my eyes open. Loyalty to fellow law enforcement is one thing, but I've been doing this long enough to know that not everyone lives up to the responsibility of the uniform. And when they screw up, they drag us all down with them."

His eyes had gone cold, as if locking down whatever pain that lesson had cost him. She could try to find out what had happened, but that seemed too personal just yet. Being here, walking hand in hand through the crisp air—that was enough for now.

Ahead of them the dog was getting more animated, making shorter zigs and zags as he narrowed in on the scent. The oaks were thicker here, the branches forming a living canopy of green above their heads. With the trees blocking some of the wind, it was quieter, the only sound the rustle of old leaves at their feet. It was hard to believe that this quiet oasis of green was only a few hundred yards from the beach and a short drive from the shops of downtown Paradise.

The quiet was broken by Rex's excited bark. "Sounds like he found her." He checked his watch and made a notation in his log. "Now he's supposed to make his way back to us so he can lead us to her."

At his hip, the radio crackled. "Hey, Rex was here, but then he ran off again."

Alex grinned, and spoke into the radio. "Yeah, he's supposed to do that. It's okay. He's coming to get us. We'll be there in a minute."

As he finished, Rex came bounding up, barking at Alex.

"I hear you. Bring me to her. Let's go." Alex broke into a jog behind the dog, and Cassie followed. The excitement of the moment was contagious; it was like being a kid on a scavenger hunt, racing to the next find. They crashed through some low-hanging branches and came into a clearing. Rex was waiting on the far side, getting petted by Mollie.

"Good boy, Rex. Good boy." Alex took a tug toy out of his bag and tossed to it Rex, who caught it in mid-air, then pranced around the clearing with it, shaking it gleefully.

"He's awfully proud of himself," Cassie commented, watching his antics.

Mollie stood and brushed the dirt from her jeans. "He should be. He did a great job. I didn't think it would be that quick."

"He was pretty incredible." Cassie had known in an

academic sense how amazing a dog's sense of scent was, but seeing it in action was another thing entirely. "Do you think he's up for another round?"

"I think so. He needs the practice, and he certainly doesn't seem tired." He handed her one of the printed maps. "Take this, just in case."

Cassie shoved the map into her pack, then patted the radio on her belt. "I'll take it, but if he doesn't find me, I'm calling for help. I can't navigate my way out of a paper bag without a GPS."

"Hey, I know. How about I go with you? I'm good with a map, and it will be more fun to hide together," Mollie suggested.

Alex quirked an eyebrow, but after a moment agreed. "I guess that would work. Lost hikers are often in pairs, so it would be worth trying. Just stay close to each other to keep from spreading the scent too far. Oh, and ladies?"

"Yes?" Mollie asked.

He winked. "No talking about me."

"What the heck was that about?" Cassie demanded as soon as they were out of earshot. "And don't give me that line about being good at reading a map. I've been on road trips with you, remember?" Mollie's sense of direction was even worse than her own.

"How else was I supposed to get a few minutes alone with you? So spill it. What's going on with you and Deputy Sexy-Pants?"

Cassie tried, and failed, to hold her laughter in. "You are awful. And nothing. Nothing is going on."

Mollie rolled her eyes. "Please. He can't keep his

eyes off you. And you keep checking him out when he isn't looking. Admit it. You think he's hot."

"What are you, twelve?"

Mollie grinned and stuck her tongue out at her. The girl had no shame.

"Fine, yes, I think he's attractive."

"Hot," Mollie corrected her.

"Okay, he's hot." There was no point in denying it; just the thought of his hard body and those bedroom eyes had her temperature rising. She grinned. "Total eye candy."

Mollie smiled in triumph. "And he likes dogs, rescues orphan kittens and is sweet to your kid." She ticked off each trait on her fingers. "In other words, perfect for you. You need to go for this."

Cassie shrugged. "I don't think there is anything to go for. I can't imagine he's looking to hook up with a ready-made family a few weeks after moving here."

Mollie rolled her eyes. "I'm not saying you have to marry the man. But you could go on a date or make out or something. Anything. Do you even remember how to kiss?"

"Mollie!" She smacked her friend on the arm. "And just when am I supposed to do this? While I'm covering my work and my father's at the clinic, or during the preparation for the charity dance, or maybe while I'm attempting to be both mother and father to a four-year-old girl?" It wasn't as if she hadn't thought about dating. But moving from the thinking stage to the action stage took time and energy. And it seemed as if there was never enough of either.

"You have friends and family to help with Emma.

And you weren't dating even before the accident, so it's not about that. Your real issue is that you're afraid."

She wanted to argue, but the truth was, she *was* afraid. Afraid of messing up again. Of falling for the wrong guy. Or worse, falling for the right guy and him not feeling the same way. As upset as she'd been when Tony left her, her heart hadn't been broken. He'd been an adventure, not the love of her life, and even then, it had still hurt. How much worse would it have been if she'd really had her heart on the line?

Annoyed, she tromped off through the leaves, angling east toward the ocean. Mollie stayed a few steps away. As they left the shade of the oaks, the landscape changed back to the saw palmettos and sand pines that were typical of the coastal scrub habitat. Picking her way through, Cassie made sure to avoid the sharp teeth of the saw palmettos, keeping an eye out for any other hazards. This area was home to a large number of native gopher tortoises, and stepping in a burrow would be a quick way to get a twisted ankle. They had walked almost to the edge of the boundary marked on Alex's map when she found a burnt-out log, the remnant of some long-ago brush fire. "This looks like as good a place as any to stop."

Resting against the damaged tree, she watched two bright blue scrub jays search for their evening meal as tension seeped from her shoulders. Her dad and Mollie were right; she had needed to get away from her responsibilities, at least for a few hours. And they were right about Alex, too, at least partly. He did seem like a good guy, and it wasn't right to lump him in with the likes of Jack Campbell. That didn't mean she was going to date him or anything like that. But maybe they could be friends, have some fun. What would be the harm in that?

Chapter Eight

Alex kept his focus, checking wind currents, watching Rex for signs of a find. But a part of his brain was stuck on how Cassie's hand had felt in his. He wanted to touch her again. Hell, he wanted to do a lot more than touch her. But she wasn't the type for a quick romp in the sack. And he didn't date women with children. Emma was ridiculously cute, but he knew he wasn't cut out for fatherhood. His own dad had failed spectacularly in that department and he had no desire to repeat those mistakes.

Growing up with a father more interested in his next score than his family had left its mark. He'd been ten before he gave up expecting his dad to show up at his Little League games or school parent nights.

He'd been twelve when his father went to jail for the first time.

His dad tried to say it was a bum rap, but the truth was, he'd been busted for possession. He'd sworn he'd get straight, and for about six months after his release, he did. Or at least, he'd seemed to. But then he started missing work and disappearing for days at a time. When the cops finally locked him up for good, Alex had been glad to see him go. Better no father than one who broke his promises as fast as he made them. Drugs or no drugs, he'd never been happy as a family man. He wanted more adventure than a wife and kids and mortgage could offer.

Alex had vowed never to be like him. He'd chosen law enforcement instead of a life of crime, but weren't those just two sides of the same coin? Working the streets of Miami was an adrenaline rush as addictive as any drug. Maybe he'd found a better way to channel his need for adventure, but that didn't mean he was any more suited to family life than his father had been. And unlike his dad, he wasn't willing to start one if he couldn't stick around for the long haul.

Which meant there was no way he could get involved with Cassie. "Look but don't touch" would be his motto.

He could do that. He would do that. He'd wanted to get more involved with the community, to let his guard down a little and make some real friends. Spending time with Cassie could be the first step in that direction.

Rapid barking broke him from his thoughts. Rex was just beyond the tree line, impatiently looking back at Alex as if annoyed with him for taking so long.

"I'm coming. Some of us only have two legs, you know." To pacify the dog, he eased into a run. Breaking through some low-hanging moss, he spotted the women up ahead. Mollie was taking photos of something with a camera she must have stashed in her pack, and Cassie was just standing there, waiting for him. Locking eyes with her, he felt energy crackling between them. Not daring to move closer, he stopped a few feet away.

"You found us," Cassie finally said, moving toward him.

"The dog did all the work." She was almost close enough to touch, but before he could make a move, Rex pushed into the space between them, nosing Alex for the tug toy he knew he'd earned. Nothing like a slobbery dog snout to cool off sexual tension. Tossing the toy to the dog, he marked down the details of the find, then took a swig of water.

"I think that's enough for today. If we stay out much longer, we'll be searching in the dark."

Cassie looked up from playing with Rex. "Can't he search in the dark?"

"Theoretically, yes. But we haven't practiced that yet, and I'd rather end on a high note and a successful find, just in case. When we move to night searches, I'll make it really easy for him at first, then gradually build to longer searches."

"That makes sense." Mollie chewed a granola bar, then stuck the wrapper in her pocket. "Besides, I'm hungry."

"You're always hungry," Cassie said. "It kills me that you can eat all day long and you never gain an ounce. I'm probably gaining weight just watching you eat."

"What can I say? Good genes, I guess."

Alex ignored the friendly banter. He'd learned long ago that there was nothing to be gained by entering into this kind of argument. Not that Cassie had any reason to be concerned. Her athletic curves were in perfect proportion. She must look amazing in a bikini.

Picturing her in one wasn't part of his "just friends" plan, and his body's quick reaction to the mental image was anything but platonic. Hoping to keep anyone from noticing his predicament, he turned to head back. He'd only made it a few steps when the chorus of "Cat Scratch Fever" blasted his ears. Turning, he saw Cassie grab her phone out of her pocket while shooting Mollie a dirty look.

"I change her ringtones every now and then," Mollie explained. "The last one was 'Who Let the Dogs Out.' Cassie isn't always as appreciative as she should be."

"What? When?" Cassie's face went white as she fired off questions. "Did you check under the beds? In the garage? The yard? Wait, what? Oh, my God." She sank to her knees, a look of pure pain on her face.

Crossing the ground between them in two strides, he took the phone from her limp hand. "Hello? This is Alex Santiago. What's the situation?"

He listened carefully. "We'll be right there, and I'll call for backup. Stay by the phone in case they need to reach you."

He turned to Mollie, who had an arm wrapped around her panicked friend. "It's Emma. She's missing."

Chapter Nine

Alex risked a glance at Cassie as he navigated the rapidly darkening streets of Paradise. She was staying strong, but he'd seen the tears that she'd silently wiped away. He couldn't imagine how frightened she must be. From what Cassie's father had told him, Emma had accidentally left the back door open and her kitten had escaped outside. They'd looked for it, but after an hour with no luck, the Marshalls had made Emma come in for dinner. Distraught over her pet, the little girl must have snuck back outside when she was supposed to be washing her hands.

Dr. Marshall wasn't mobile enough yet to do much searching, but Mrs. Marshall had searched the yard and house with no luck before calling Cassie. Their house backed up to the wildlife refuge with its acres of undeveloped land. The only good news was that the area he'd chosen for Rex's training session today was less than five miles from the Marshalls' neighborhood.

"I shouldn't have let her take the kitten with her," Cassie said.

"You had no way of knowing this would happen." They'd replayed this conversation several times already, but none of his assurances made a difference. Nothing would, other than finding her daughter, safe and sound.

A crackle of the radio pulled his attention back to the logistics of the situation. Backup was coming, but it would be a while. The deputy assigned to Paradise today was dealing with a serious traffic accident on the other side of the bridge and would be tied up for who knew how long. The main sheriff's office was almost an hour away, and the nearest trained search team was double that. Had the girl wandered off in the daytime he might not be so concerned, but given the remote location and the weather, he was calling in every person he could. In the meantime, he'd scour every inch of those woods himself if need be.

He pulled into the driveway only a few seconds ahead of Mollie, who was driving Cassie's car. Together they approached the house, where a large man with a cane was waiting on the porch. *He must be Cassie's father.*

Taking charge, he held out a hand. "Dr. Marshall, it's good to meet you finally. I'm sorry it's under such circumstances. Can we go inside?"

"Yes, sorry, come in." He led them through the door and back to the rear of the house into a large, comfortable kitchen. "I made some coffee. I didn't know what else to do. My wife's out looking for her, but I'm stuck in here with this damned leg like some kind of invalid." He slammed his cane on the ground, punctuating his words.

"I understand your frustration, sir, but trust me, you're going to be needed right here. First, I need you to get me something with Emma's scent on it. An article of clothing, a favorite stuffed animal—anything like that would work. While you're doing that, I'm going to take a look at my maps and maybe have some of that coffee you made."

The distraught man limped off toward another part of the house, the sound of his cane marking his progress. Alex wished he could offer more comfort, but the best thing he could do right now was work on finding Emma. Pulling out the maps he'd used during the training session, he located the Marshalls' neighborhood on the edge of the refuge. Marking it, he tried to figure out where Emma could have gone. The only road was the one they'd driven in on, and they had seen no sign of her. Which meant she most likely was somewhere in the refuge.

Cassie paced behind him, watching him work. She didn't ask any questions, probably because she was afraid of the answers.

Mollie shoved a cup of coffee in her hand, then placed one on the table next to the maps. A few minutes later, a sandwich joined it.

"Thanks." He took a bite and washed it down with the strong brew. When Cassie didn't join him, he looked up at her. "Eat. I can't afford you getting weak out there because you've got low blood sugar."

She looked as if she might argue, but Mollie steered her to the table and pushed her into a chair. Cassie picked at her food, but did seem to get some down. Good. There was no telling how long this was going to take; they all needed to be as strong and prepared as possible.

Dr. Marshall came back into the kitchen with a small stuffed bunny just as the back door opened. A tall woman with a noticeable resemblance to Cassie walked in, holding the missing kitten in her arms. "I found the cat, curled up in the shed, but Emma isn't anywhere." Her voice cracked. "I'm so sorry. I'm never going to forgive myself." Sobs shook her shoulders.

Cassie embraced her mother. "You didn't know. And we're going to find her. We have to find her."

Watching the two women cry was more than Alex could take. Shoving away the rest of his food, he stood and shouldered his pack. "Dr. Marshall, can I borrow that stuffed animal? And maybe a plastic bag to put it in?"

"Of course." He pulled out a bag from a cupboard, and placed the small, worn toy into it. "Here you go. It's her favorite. She's had it since she was a baby."

Alex could tell the man was trying to be strong for his family, but the strain was etched into the lines on his face. "Thank you, sir. I'm sure she'll be happy to have it when we find her."

Cassie let go of her mother. "You're going to have Rex search for her?"

He nodded grimly. "It's the best chance we have right now if we want to find her quickly. Once backup arrives, we can start a grid, cover more ground. But until then, with our limited manpower, I think it's our best option."

Mollie broke in, "But you said he wasn't ready for night searches. And Emma's been gone nearly an hour.

That's a lot longer than the tracks you had us making for him."

She was right, but there wasn't a better option. "I've been following the rule book with him, but he doesn't care about the rules. He does care about Emma. He'll do what he has to to find her."

Dear Lord, let that be the truth.

Cassie gripped a flashlight and waited on the back deck for the rest of the group. She'd stepped outside while Alex talked with the deputy team headed in their direction. It seemed the county search team was already deployed farther north and wouldn't be available until morning.

Acid swirled in her stomach at the thought of her little girl alone all night. She'd been wearing only a long-sleeve T-shirt and jeans, no jacket, when she snuck out. The weather was expected to drop below freezing in a matter of hours. Emma couldn't wait until morning. They had to find her now.

As if responding to her thoughts, Alex came through the French doors onto the patio, Rex at his side. Ignoring the hot tears burning her eyes, she knelt down and hugged the dog. "You have to find her, Rex. Please."

"Cassie, he'll find her. But we need to get started. The sooner we go, the easier it will be for him."

What he wasn't saying was that the odds were already stacked against them. Rex would be working a trail aged longer than any of the ones he'd practiced on and under new, nighttime conditions. Alex had assured her on the way over that search dogs worked just fine at night, but they both knew his lack of experience was working against them. He wasn't even a certified search-and-rescue dog, but he was all they had.

Alex opened the bag with Emma's toy in it and offered it to Rex to smell. The dog sniffed the toy, then started moving back and forth across the deck, his nose quivering. Instead of going down the steps to the yard, he circled back to the railing at the north side, where it met the house.

"That's where Emma likes to climb down from. She can reach the ground from that spot if she ducks under the rail." She started to scramble over the rail when Alex grabbed her arm.

"We'll take the stairs. He knows not to get too far ahead of us. He'll wait. And you won't be any good to your daughter if you end up with a sprained ankle."

Her face heated. He was right, of course. She took the stairs two at a time, needing to see what direction Rex was headed in. Alex's flashlight beam found the dog first, his reflective collar a beacon of hope. He was waiting at the edge of the yard, scenting the wind.

"The wind should make searching easier," Alex assured her.

And increase the risk of hypothermia. Damn it, what had Emma been thinking? The wildlife refuge took up almost half the island; there were a thousand places to get hurt or lost. "Emma!" Her voice lodged in her throat, her call coming out a raspy croak. Alex glanced at her, but kept his focus on the dog. Rex was moving quickly now, angling back and forth as he'd done in the training session earlier. In the distance, over the sounds of lovesick frogs, she could hear Mollie calling for Emma, as well. Mollie had chosen to walk the street, in case Emma had chosen to follow it. She'd knock on doors, as well, to get the neighbors in on the search. Everyone was doing what needed to be done. She needed to focus on that.

"Watch your step." Alex pointed to a broken branch she'd been about to trip over. "I know you're worried, but keep your head in the game."

She nodded. She would focus, for Emma's sake.

They were on an old walking trail, one that Cassie had taken many times in her life. Hopefully Emma had stuck to it. She'd be easier to find if she was on the path. "Do you think he knows where she went?"

"Definitely. See how high he's carrying his tail? He does that when he's got the scent."

Alex's confidence gave her the strength to start calling again. "Emma! Can you hear me, Emma? If you can hear me, say something, sweetie."

She strained her ears until she thought they would bleed, but there was no response. So she called again and again. Every step, every minute took an eternity.

"He's leaving the trail. You'll need to stay closer now, single file."

The dog had no trouble negotiating the thick press of wax myrtles and slash pines, but it was slow going for Cassie and Alex. Had her daughter really pushed through this kind of brush? "I can't believe Emma would have climbed through all this."

"She might have if she thought the kitten did. Or she could be on the other side of it. Remember, Rex isn't limited to following her exact path. He's scenting the air for her. He's going to take the shortest route to where she is right now."

Rex's shortcut had her arms covered in scratches, but she kept moving forward. At least in the trees it wasn't quite as cold. They trudged through for several minutes. Then suddenly they were back on the walking path again. Rex was picking up speed, his zig-zags getting tighter. Could he be narrowing in on her? Frantic, she called again. "Emma! Emma, it's Mommy. Can you hear me?"

Again, Rex veered off into the brush, this time angling down an embankment toward a creek that ran through this part of the refuge. Sliding down after him, she and Alex tried to keep up. "Wait, do you hear something?" Alex asked.

She paused, finding it hard to hear anything over the pounding of her heart. At first, there was nothing, but then she heard a whimper. "Emma?" Rex barked, then whined. Letting go of the root she'd been grasping, she slid down the rest of the way on her bottom. Alex was right behind her, his flashlight joining hers as they scanned the area.

There. Rex was nosing something on the ground a few feet away from the creek bank. Was it Emma? Dear God, were they too late? A sob ripped through her as she ran. Falling on her knees, she pushed the dog aside. There, curled up in the roots of an old oak, was Emma, white and motionless.

"Don't move her!" If the girl had any serious injuries, movement could make them worse. Cassie flinched at his words, but didn't pick her daughter up. Instead, she lay down in the mud beside her, murmuring something to her.

"Mommy?"

The child's voice sounded weak, but coherent. Thank God. As Cassie continued to soothe the girl, he swung his pack off his back and rummaged for an emergency blanket and the Thermos Mrs. Marshall had given him. "Here, put this on her."

Cassie tucked the flimsy metallic sheet over Emma, but the girl kicked at it, pushing into a sitting position. "Careful, honey, we need to make sure you're okay. Does anything hurt?"

"No. But I can't find Trouble. I looked and looked, and then I couldn't find me, either. I think we both got losted. Can Rex find Trouble like he found me?"

"Your grandma already found Trouble," Alex said. "He's waiting back at the house for you. I bet he's real worried about you." He placed a disposable thermometer strip on her forehead as he spoke and was relieved to see she was cold, but not yet hypothermic. "You're sure nothing hurts?"

She shivered, but shook her head. "My tummy's hungry. I didn't get any dinner."

Cassie hugged the girl, holding her tight. He could see the emotion in her eyes, but her voice was calm and upbeat. "I'm sure Grandma saved you a plate, but first we have to get you back up there. Can you walk?"

"I think so. I walked a really long time, but then my legs got tired and I sat down to take a rest."

"How about I give you a ride instead?" Alex could get her back to the house and medical attention faster if he carried her.

She nodded.

"All right. Why don't you have some of this hot chocolate your grandma sent while I call everyone and tell them you're okay? Then we'll all go back to the house and warm up. Oh, and here, your grandpa thought you might like this to keep you company." He handed her the stuffed rabbit he'd used for a scent article. Delighted, she snuggled the worn toy and curled up closer to her mother.

Satisfied the situation was in hand, he radioed in their status, then called Cassie's parents with his cell phone. They promised to relay the good news to Mollie and alert the neighbors, leaving him able to focus on getting Emma out of the woods, literally.

The cocoa seemed to have put a bit more color in her cheeks, the hot drink raising her spirits along with her body temperature. "You ready to go?" he asked her.

"Yes, please. I want to see Trouble."

Alex shook his head at the girl's tenacity. "All right, I'm going to pick you up, and you just hold on and enjoy the ride." Cassie helped the girl stand. Then he scooped Emma into his arms. She weighed nearly nothing, and he once again was reminded of what a close call she'd had.

Cassie led the way, using her flashlight to illuminate the path for both of them. This time, they stayed on the trail, trading the longer distance for easier going. Every so often, Cassie would lay a hand on Emma, as if to reassure herself the girl was safe. He didn't blame her. He was still shaken, and it wasn't his kid. Rex seemed to be the only one unaffected by the ordeal. He was enjoying the nighttime hike, sniffing trees and marking his territory. Just being a dog.

Cassie was watching him as well. "He gets free vet care for life. And anything else he wants. He's amazing."

"I think he wanted to find her as much as we did. He adores her."

"There they are!" Mollie's voice had Emma scrambling to get down. He tightened his grip. "Hold on there, sweetie, we're almost there."

They met up with Cassie's parents, Mollie and a paramedic team in the backyard.

"Is she okay?"

"She's fine, Dad, but you shouldn't be out here. You're not supposed to be doing stairs yet."

"Right here is exactly where I should be," her father replied gruffly, then planted a kiss on his granddaughter's head.

Cassie rolled her eyes, but Alex didn't blame the man. He must have been out of his mind not being able to help with the search.

"Just be careful going back up, okay?" Cassie asked.

"I will. You just get that girl inside and warmed up. I'll take my time, now that she's safe."

"You can all take your time," Alex said. "She's going to get checked out by the paramedics before anything else."

Emma spoke from his arms, still wrapped in the shiny emergency blanket. "What's a purple-medic?"

Cassie pointed to the waiting medic team. "These are paramedics. They're kind of like doctors, but they come to you instead of you having to go to Dr. Hall's office. They just want to give you a quick check-up."

Emma's eyes were wide, but she nodded. By the time Alex made it across the yard and up the steps, she was chatting about kittens with the medical team, winning them over with her charm. Inside, she proudly showed off a few new scratches, which turned out to be the extent of her injuries. Her body temperature was rising, as well, and the paramedics left her with a few neon bandages and instructions to drink lots of fluids and get a good night's sleep.

Once the paramedics were gone, everyone sat down to a late supper in the cozy country kitchen. Even Rex got his own plate of chicken stew. Emma cleaned her plate, but was rubbing her eyes by the end of the meal.

"I think I'd better get her home and into her bed," Cassie said, standing to clear her plate.

"Leave the dishes on the table. I'll get those later," Mrs. Marshall insisted. "And you don't have to go anywhere. You're welcome to spend the night here."

Cassie gave a weary smile. "I appreciate that. But honestly, I think we both need our own beds more than anything right now."

"I'll drive them home." Alex wasn't going to be satisfied until Emma was home, safe and sound. "And Mollie can bring you your car tomorrow sometime. The clinic is closed on Sundays, right?"

"Yes, but—"

"That's a great idea. You just give me a call tomorrow when you're ready for me to come over," Mollie gave her friend a hug, then left with Cassie's keys in her hand.

Alex said his own goodbyes, then escorted Cassie and Emma to the car. Mollie had left Emma's booster seat on the front porch, and he installed it in the backseat of his personal SUV, thankful he hadn't driven the department-issued vehicle today—there would have been nowhere for Emma to sit. "Your chariot awaits."

Giggling, the little girl let him buckle her in, her laughter a balm after the panic of the evening. For such a tiny thing, she stirred up big feelings, ones he didn't have a clue how to handle.

Chapter Ten

The drive home was a complete blur for Cassie. All she could think about was how close she'd come to losing her little girl. She tried to do all the right things, to live her life as carefully as possible, and yet she'd almost lost her daughter. Over and over in her mind, she saw Rex lying beside Emma on the cold ground. What if they hadn't gotten to her as soon as they had? What if Rex hadn't been trained so well? What if Alex had never moved to Paradise?

"We're here. I'll get Emma if you'll get the door."

Digging in her purse, she remembered Mollie had her keys. No matter. She kept an extra in a green ceramic frog by the front door. Retrieving it, she ignored Alex's raised eyebrow and opened the door for him.

"Remind me to discuss home security with you later," he whispered, carrying a sleeping Emma cradled in his arms.

She rolled her eyes, but knew he was right. One more thing to fix, to be responsible about. "Her room's down here." Keeping the lights off, she led him to the end of the short hall and into her daughter's pink-and-white room. Watching Alex gently lower Emma into her bed, as if he'd done it a thousand times, took her breath away. This simple moment was the kind of thing other families took for granted. Turning her back, she dug through the small white dresser for a nightgown. "I'll get her changed and be right out." She needed a minute to collect her thoughts, and she couldn't do that with him standing so close.

Once he left, she changed Emma out of the dirty clothes and into the clean nightgown. The exhausted girl never even stirred. Tucking the covers over her, she kissed her now warm forehead.

Alex was waiting in the living room, inspecting the various photos hanging on the walls. "She looks just like you did as a kid."

"Thanks. I think so, too. Listen, about tonight—"

"You don't have to say anything."

"Yes, I do. Emma means everything to me. If you hadn't been there, if we hadn't found her..." Her throat constricted, the sobs she'd been holding back finally breaking through.

Alex pulled her into his arms. "Hey, don't cry. I was there, and we did find her. She's going to be fine."

She sniffled. "What she's going to be is grounded for the rest of her life." With her head resting on his chest, she could feel his deep chuckle as well as hear it. "You think I'm kidding. I probably have a head of gray hair now."

He stroked her hair gently, caressing her. "Still looks as beautiful as ever," he whispered against her ear. Shivers of awareness danced across her skin, waking desires long buried. "I thought I was going to lose it out there. I don't know how you held it together."

"I had you." And that was the truth, she realized. He'd been there for her, giving her strength, making her stronger than she was on her own. Even now, she could feel the power radiating off him. Just once, she wanted to feel the full force of him.

Rising up on her toes, she looked at him, gave him a chance to pull away. When he didn't retreat, she pushed forward, taking his mouth with her own. He hesitated, then gave in with a moan, running his hands down her body, then back up again to tangle in her hair. He smelled like hot chocolate and pine trees and felt like heaven. Maybe this was wrong, but every fiber in her body was screaming for more.

She ran her hands up under his shirt, reveling in the hard planes of his body. Needing to see him, she tugged at the fabric, and he released her just long enough to strip it off. Panting, he rested his forehead on hers. "Are you sure this is what you want? Maybe I should go."

This was her out. Her chance to stop this madness and play it safe, by the book, the way she always did.

Screw that. Playing it safe hadn't kept her daughter from being lost or her dad from being injured. And it was one night. One night to break all the rules and just let herself feel. She deserved that. She needed that.

"Please, stay."

Alex had never been so turned on in his life. He'd tried to do the right thing; he'd given her a chance to kick him out. But no way was he strong enough to leave while she was begging him to stay, not when she was tearing off his clothes and kissing him as if he was the last man on earth. He'd seen her fragile and upset; he'd seen her patient and gentle. Now he was seeing her passion, and it was more than he could take.

The most primal part of his brain wanted to take her right there on the living room floor. But with Emma in the house, that wasn't an option. Lifting Cassie, he carried her to the hallway. "Which room?" he managed to grunt as she rubbed against him.

"First door," she said in between nibbles on his neck.

He somehow made it to the bed, where they stripped each other in record time, barely stopping long enough for him to grab a condom from his wallet. Then Cassie was pulling him down on top of her, arching up to meet him. He tried to take things slowly, but she sped him on, urging him with her body to give more until they came together in one final moment of ecstasy.

Rolling, he pulled her against him while he tried to catch his breath. He could feel every heartbeat clear down to his toes, and instead of feeling spent, he felt more alive than he ever had before.

They shouldn't have done this, but he was glad they had. In fact, he didn't want to leave; he wanted to do it all over again. But he only had the one condom. Grabbing a tissue from the box on the nightstand, he went to dispose of it and froze.

"Um, Cassie?"

"Mmm-hmm?"

He tossed the offending latex in the trash and looked her in the eye. "The condom broke."

"Cassie, I'm so sorry. I've never had this happen before."

She had. Once. And the evidence was sleeping in

the room at the end of the hall. Alex reached out to brush her hair out of her face, and she jumped as if he'd burned her. She couldn't think when he was touching her. Pacing, she tried to comprehend what had just happened. Five years without sex, and this happens the first time she lets herself feel something? "Can you sit down so we can talk about this?" His voice was soothing, the way you might talk to a scared animal or child. But it didn't help.

"No, I'm trying to think. I pace when I think."

"Well, then, can you at least put some clothes on? Because I'm trying to think, too, and you're a bit distracting right now."

"What?"

He gestured at her still-naked body.

"Oh, yeah. Sorry." Turning her back, she grabbed a robe from the hook on the back of the door.

"No need to apologize, I was enjoying the view. We moved too quickly for me to get a good look before. You're gorgeous, you know."

"Thanks, but not helpful."

He sprawled out on the bed, making no move to cover his own nudity. Not that he should; his body was beyond impressive in every way. But unlike him, she was too worked up to be distracted by anything, even him.

"Is the timing…well…right? Do we need to be worried?"

She tried to do the math in her head. "I don't know. I need to get my phone." She crept out to the living room as quietly as possible. The last thing she needed right now was to wake up Emma. Her phone was in her purse in the middle of the floor. She took it and Alex's discarded shirt back to the bedroom, then pulled up her calendar app. "I think we're safe." She set the phone down and collapsed on the edge of the bed. She was going to be on edge until she got her period, no matter what the calendar said.

"I meant what I said. I've never had anything like this happen before. So you don't have to worry as far as diseases go. I'm healthy."

Her laugh was brittle. "Yeah, I'm healthy, too." If you didn't count the stress-induced heart attack she'd just almost had.

He put an arm around her shoulder, and she let herself lean against him. "So, are we good?"

She swallowed hard. "Yeah."

"Good enough to go again?" he teased, his hand stroking up and down her back.

She ignored the way her body reacted even through the thick robe and stood up. "I don't think that's a good idea."

He ran a hand through his sex-rumpled hair. "I know. I guess I should go, then."

"Probably." She tossed him his shirt and left him to dress.

She was waiting at the door when he came out. "Thank you again for finding Emma. And, well, everything."

He leaned down and planted a chaste kiss on her lips, igniting a slow burn that worked its way south. "Thank you for an amazing night. Sleep well."

She closed the door after him and leaned against the cool wood, hoping to douse the heat he'd raised. Sleep? He'd saved her daughter, rocked her world and then scared her to death in the space of one evening. She'd experienced more emotion tonight than she had in years.

Of course, he had no way of knowing that. He didn't have kids, didn't want kids, so although he'd been a rock tonight, he couldn't know how she'd felt. As for the sex, she very much doubted that was an unusual occurrence. He could have his pick of women in Paradise and probably did. He'd been too much of a gentleman to say so, but she knew a one-night stand when she saw one.

She still couldn't believe she'd attacked him like that. Her only excuse was the lingering trauma of nearly losing Emma. Her emotional control had been stretched too thin for too long, and he'd been around when it finally snapped. He'd been convenient, and she'd been overwhelmed. That was all.

Any other emotion she thought she felt could be chalked up to the drama of the night. She wasn't looking for a man, and he definitely wasn't looking for a family.

So why was she crying?

Chapter Eleven

The smell of coffee and frying bacon greeted Alex as he stepped into his mother's town house. She'd heard about the search last night and had called to invite him for breakfast. Mom's cooking or a bowl of cold cereal? He'd been half out the door before hanging up the phone.

"I'm in the kitchen," his mom called from the direction of all the good smells. "Make sure you wipe your feet."

Busted, he backed up a step and carefully wiped his shoes on the mat. All these years, and he still couldn't get away with anything when it came to her. Once he was sure he wouldn't track in any dirt, he found her standing over the stove. She set down her wooden spoon to give him a hug, then stopped and gave him a long, hard look. "So, who is she?"

"What are you talking about?"

"You tell me." She waved the spoon as she talked. "You've got that look on your face, the same look you had when you mooned over Rebecca Stutz in the sixth grade. And every girl since." She poured him a cup of coffee and handed it to him. "So, who is she? Is it that pretty animal doctor?"

He nearly choked on a mouthful of coffee. "How do you know about her?"

"What, you think you're the only one who can put a few clues together? Everyone knows. This is a small town, *mi hijo*. There are no secrets. So tell me about her."

"Sounds like you already know everything." She raised an eyebrow, and he capitulated. "She's great. Beautiful, smart, fun—"

"But?"

"But she has a daughter."

"And you don't like her little girl?" His mother's tone warned him he was on shaky ground. She'd been a single mother herself for many years.

"No, that's not it. Emma's a great kid. I really like her."

"So what's the problem? Is this doctor lady not a good mother?"

"Her name's Cassie. And she's a fantastic mother. She was beside herself last night when Emma was lost. She tries so hard to do the right thing by her girl. You'd really like her." She would, he realized. They were both strong women who'd made the best out of the hands they were dealt.

"But getting involved means I'd be involved with the daughter, too. And if the relationship progressed, I'd have to step into a role I can't fill. I don't have the first clue about how to be a father." He sat down on a stool and stared at the floor. "She deserves better."

"Please. There is no better. You are a good man, and you'll be a good husband and father someday. Not like—"

"But what if I am like him?" He stood, nearly knocking over the stool. "What if I'm exactly like him? I'm sure he didn't think that he'd turn out the way he did, that he'd put his own selfishness ahead of his family, but that's how it ended up. I'm used to being on my own, not having anyone to answer to. What if I can't change? What if I try, and then years from now, I can't handle it and I ruin their lives?"

His mother drew herself up and gave him the same look she'd given him when he brought home a bad grade in elementary school. "If you want something badly enough, you'll make it work. You always have. You've never been afraid of hard work, and a relationship is work like any other. It's all about putting in the time and effort. But only you know if it's worth it to you."

His mother's words made a kind of sense, but acid still boiled in his belly. She was his *mami*—of course she thought the best of him. If she was wrong, he'd be hurting innocent people.

Not that he'd been thinking about that last night. He hadn't been thinking at all. The minute Cassie had pressed her lips to his, he'd been working off pure instinct. Normally he trusted his instincts, but could he now?

His mother passed him a plate with bacon and eggs and put a tray of *mallorcas*, a sugar-topped pastry, on the table. The comforting smell awakened his appetite, and he dug in, chewing as he thought. There was no reason he had to make a decision right now. For all he knew, Cassie wasn't even interested in anything long-term.

"You think too much."

"What?" What kind of comment was that?

"You. You're thinking about everything that can go wrong from now until the day you die when you haven't even been on a date yet."

His face heated, and he shoved more food in his mouth, trying to avoid his mother's gaze.

"What? You've been out with her already?"

Damn. He swallowed carefully. "No, not exactly. But last night we spent some time together after all the excitement with Emma."

His mother narrowed her eyes at him. "I'm not going to ask because I don't think I want to know. But all the more reason you should take her out, do something nice. Behave like a gentleman."

"Yes, *Mami*."

"Now finish up so you can give me a ride to Mass. If we hurry, you'll have time for confession first."

This was why he usually avoided his mother's house on Sunday mornings. But darn it if the food wasn't worth it.

"Thanks for bringing me my car." Cassie swung into the driver's seat as Mollie scooted across to the passenger side. Emma was already buckled in in the back.

"No big deal. But I have to say, I'm surprised you're up so early. I thought you and Emma would sleep in after last night."

Cassie rubbed her eyes. "Yeah, I thought so, too. But

she was up at the crack of dawn, just like always. So since we were up, I figured we might as well be productive. We can pick up the rest of the decorations for the dance and be back in time for a nap. Hopefully."

"And you're okay with Emma going back to your parents' house so soon?"

"Honestly, Mom and Dad are as traumatized as anyone. They won't take their eyes off her for a minute. And seeing her bright-eyed and bushy-tailed will make them feel a bit better. We rushed out of there pretty quickly last night. Besides, taking Emma shopping for party supplies is like taking an alcoholic shopping for booze. She'd want to buy everything in sight."

"Whatever you say, boss."

They dropped Emma off with her grandparents, who were, as expected, eager to see she hadn't suffered any ill effects from her adventure the night before. And it seemed Emma wasn't the only one who'd gotten up with the sun. Cassie's father had already been to the hardware store and was installing small sensors on all the doors.

"These will alert us every time the door is opened and they'll keep buzzing if the door isn't shut all the way. She won't slip out unnoticed again."

Touched, she gave him a hard hug. "Thanks, Daddy."

He returned the hug, then spoke around the nail he had clenched in his teeth. "I've got another set of these for your house. Thought I'd drop by and install them when I'm done here."

"I'd love that. Thank you."

"Got to take care of my girls. Now, you and Mollie go shopping and don't worry about things here. You deserve a bit of fun."

Cassie turned away before her father could see her blush. She'd certainly had her share of fun last night, but she wasn't about to tell her father that. "Okay, I'll see you later. Bye."

She walked as quickly as she could to the car, then pulled out of the drive. As soon as they were on the road, heading to town, Mollie started in on her.

"So spill it. What happened with Deputy Sexy-Pants last night?"

She coughed, trying not to laugh. "What makes you think anything happened?"

Mollie rolled her eyes. "Because you know better than to wake me up this early just to go shopping. So there must be something you're dying to tell. So tell me everything, and include lots of detail."

She couldn't stop the grin she felt splitting her face. "You mean, besides sleeping with him?"

"What?" Mollie shrieked. "You had sex with him? Last night? I thought you'd maybe made out, a good-night kiss, that kind of thing."

"Well, we did that, too."

"Who cares about that now? Go back to the sleeping together part. Is he as gorgeous naked as I think he is?"

She thought of his hard, tanned body and nodded. "Oh, yeah."

"So does this mean you guys are dating, or what?"

"I don't know. I don't think so. I mean, we didn't discuss it. Things got a bit complicated, and then he left."

"Huh? I mean, it's been a while since I've engaged in that particular activity, but I don't remember it being very complicated."

Cassie eased into a parking space behind the stationery and party goods store. Turning off the car, she stared out the window. "The condom broke."

"Are you kidding me?"

She covered her face with her hands. "I know. I still can't believe it. One minute I'm coming on to him, and the next I'm pacing the room, panicking that I'm pregnant."

"Well, are you?"

"I don't think so. I'm pretty sure the timing wasn't right."

"Wait, did you say you came on to him?"

"I totally did. I didn't even know I had it in me, but hell, Mollie. I've spent so long trying to do everything right, and bad stuff still happens. I figured I might as well do something I wanted to do for a change. So I went for it."

"Well, good for you. I mean, not for the whole birth-control fiasco, but still, it's nice to know you still have some life in you. But what are you going to do now?"

"I have absolutely no idea."

"Well, I do. We're going to shop. I don't mean just party stuff. This kind of news calls for at least a new pair of shoes, if not a whole new outfit. Actually…" she said, tapping her fingers on the door handle. "We can look for a new dress for you to wear to the dance. Something that will knock his socks off. When I'm through with you, he won't know what hit him."

Cassie sipped carefully at her hot tea and eyed the pile of bags and packages on the coffee shop chair beside her. Had she really bought all of that? They'd probably still have been shopping if she hadn't distracted Mollie with the promise of caffeine and baked goods.

She wiggled the shoe box out of the stack and snuck a peek under the lid again. "I'm going to break my neck walking in these."

Mollie set down her café con leche and broke open a chocolate-filled croissant. "No, but Alex might, tripping over his tongue when he sees you."

The sharp-heeled shoes were higher than any others Cassie owned, but they were incredibly sexy. As was the dress Mollie had talked her into. And the lingerie that was so barely there she'd blushed when the checkout girl rang it up, much to Mollie's amusement. She didn't even know why she'd bought it. She wasn't planning on a repeat of last night—was she?

"So when do you think you'll see him again?"

"I honestly don't know. I guess at the dance, if not before."

"That's almost two weeks from now. You've got to see him before that! You should call him."

"And say what, exactly? 'Thanks for the most passionate night of my life. Were you interested in having coffee sometime?'"

"Most passionate night? You cannot let this guy get away. If you won't do it for yourself, do it for all of us who barely remember what a good man is like."

"You really think I should go for it?" She wanted to believe that he *was* a good man, but she'd been wrong before. Really, really wrong.

Mollie straightened in her chair, a devilish look in her eye. "I definitely do. And I take it back. You don't have to call him."

"What? Why not?"

"Because he just walked in."

She turned, and sure enough, there he was. Heart

pounding, she ate him up with her eyes. He was wearing snug jeans and a black T-shirt, the uniform of bad boys everywhere. But he was one of the good guys. He'd proved that to her, over and over. So why was she so scared?

"Hey, Alex, over here." Mollie waved him over with all the subtlety of a Great Dane. She wasn't afraid of anything.

"Hey, Mollie." His gaze shifted to Cassie. "Hello, Cassie. How are you?"

"I'm good." Good? That was her version of witty conversation?

He smiled, that long, slow smile that made his eyes crinkle just a bit and brought out his dimples. "I'm good, too. Great, actually, now that I've seen you. I was going to call you when I got home, but this is even better."

Mollie pulled out a chair for him. "Have a seat."

"Well, I was going to get some coffee—"

"I'll get it. My treat. You and Cassie sit and chat."

As if realizing he had no choice in the matter, he sat down and watched Mollie dart to the counter to place an order. "So she knows, huh?"

Cassie chewed her lip. "Well."

He placed a hand on hers where it rested on the table. "I'm not mad. In fact, I might be a bit flattered."

"Flattered?" That was much better than angry.

"Well, I figure, if you thought it was awful, you might be too embarrassed to share."

His thumb was tracing little patterns across her skin, short-circuiting her brain. Mollie saved her from responding by plunking down a coffee cup next to their joined hands.

"Well, aren't you two cute."

Cassie smacked her with her free hand.

"What? You are. Anyway, you two enjoy. I'm going to run over to the library and pick up some books I reserved. Whenever you're done, you can just pick me up over there. Bye-bye." She breezed out with a wink, bumping the pile of bags as she went.

Alex grabbed them, but not before several of them spilled their contents to the floor. Of course, the lingerie box had ended up on top, the store name emblazoned on the lid for anyone to see. He tapped a finger on it. "So, doing some shopping, I see."

Her face was on fire. She might actually die of embarrassment right here in the town coffee shop.

He grinned, then put everything back in the bags. "Sorry, but you're driving me crazy here."

"I am?" She was?

"Yeah." His deep voice sent flickers of awareness down her spine. "But I also know that we kind of got things out of order, and I'd like to make up for that, if I can."

"Out of order?" Had she messed something up last night? It had been so long since she'd had sex, maybe she'd done something wrong.

"Yeah, I realized that we haven't actually been out on a date. And I'd very much like to take you out and get to know you a bit. What do you think?"

"What about Emma?" Damn it, she hadn't meant to blurt that out. "I mean, does it bother you that I have a child?"

His face turned serious, and he ran a hand through his hair. "I'll be honest. If you'd asked me that a month ago, I would have said yes. But Emma's a great kid. Of course, it probably helps that she's out of the diaper stage. Anyway, what I'm trying to say is, I'm not willing to walk away from whatever's happening between us. I don't think I can."

Alex waited, his heart pounding, for Cassie to say something, anything. He'd taken a chance; now it was up to her. He couldn't take it back now—and he didn't want to take it back. But if she wasn't willing to try, there was nothing he could do.

"What did you have in mind? As far as a date, I mean."

He let out the breath he'd been holding and resisted the urge to kiss her. He'd said he wanted to take things slowly, and he meant it. At least, he did when he wasn't actually this close to her, smelling the mango-scented body lotion she wore. Reeling in his libido, he focused on her question. "I was thinking dinner, Friday night. How does that sound?"

She nodded. "I'll get someone to watch Emma."

"I'll pick you up at seven?"

"That sounds perfect." She gathered up her packages and stood. "I really should get going, but I guess I'll see you Friday."

"You can count on it." He got the door for her, then took his coffee and strolled back to his car. Grabbing one of the *mallorcas* out of the bag on the front seat, he munched it while sipping the strong brew. Rex raised his head hopefully. "Sorry, buddy, these are for people only." The big dog sighed and lay back down on his blanket, content to snooze through their shift. At least one of them would be caught up on sleep.

Not that he was complaining. Every moment spent with Cassie last night had been amazing. He only wished they'd had more time together. Once with her was definitely not enough. He'd lain awake the rest of the night, his body unwilling to calm down. He hadn't felt this worked up since he was a teenager. And seeing those lingerie boxes hadn't helped.

Cassie in lingerie wasn't something he should be thinking about if he wanted to keep his promise about starting over and moving more slowly. Jumping into the deep end had made his hormones happy, but that kind of plan wasn't fair to Cassie or her daughter. He was venturing into unknown territory, so slow and steady was the way to go. Until he knew he could make things work, he needed to keep himself under control.

Checking traffic, he pulled out onto the street carefully. Sunday afternoon was a busy time for downtown Paradise, with the after-church crowd hitting the shops and restaurants before heading home. Families of various sizes strolled up and down the sidewalks, giving him a good view of what his future might look like if he and Cassie ended up together.

Watching a man with a toddler on his shoulders, he wondered if his own father had ever done anything like that. He certainly didn't remember any father-son outings. All of his memories were of disappointments and broken promises. He'd die before he'd put Emma through that kind of pain.

But for the first time, he found himself wondering what it would be like to be one of the good fathers. To have someone look up to him, want to be like him. Would he be strengthened by that kind of love? Or would he feel stifled by the responsibility, the way his father had? Being a parent meant being there all the time, forever. He'd never even managed to keep a plant alive for more than a month, let alone commit to a human for the long haul. Maybe he didn't have what it took. But the way he felt about Cassie, and Emma, made him wish he did. Maybe that was enough for a first step.

For now, he needed to keep his mind on work. He was due in for a staff briefing at the top of the hour, and the chief deputy had asked to speak to him afterward. Luckily the Paradise Isle substation was only a mile away from the café. He was able to park, change and make it to the conference room with time to spare. The meeting itself was uneventful, mostly covering the new forms the county had started requiring and a reminder about the free bike helmet program now in place. Deputies were to keep a few in their vehicles to hand out if they saw a child violating the helmet law. Alex had already handed out several since he'd started the job. He'd rather hand out helmets than tickets any day.

Meetings like this used to bore the heck out of him. He'd never seen a need to sit around talking about things when he could be out actually doing something. But lately he'd found himself looking forward to the briefings. The information he gained made him more effective when he was out on patrol, and he liked having a view into the big picture. Funny how a bit of time and experience could change your perspective. Maybe there was hope for him yet.

Chapter Twelve

Cassie stripped off her dress and threw it on the bed with the other five she'd tried and discarded. A knock at the door had her scrambling for her robe. "I'm coming." With her luck, Alex was here early, and would find her half-naked with no babysitter. Holding the terrycloth together, she peered through the peephole.

It was Mollie, thank heavens. Turning the lock, she let her in.

"I got your message and came right over." She eyed Cassie's ugly orange robe. "And none too soon. Shouldn't you be dressed by now?"

"Yes, and I would be, but Mom canceling kind of threw off my schedule."

"Is she okay?"

"She will be. It's just strep throat. But she's contagious until she's been on the antibiotics a few days, so—"

"So I'm here to save the day. No problem. Emma's

easy. You're the difficult one. Have you even picked out what you're going to wear?"

She thought of her torn-apart closet and winced. "Not exactly."

"And when is he picking you up?"

She checked the clock. "Any minute."

"Well, I'm hardly one to give fashion advice, but I'm pretty sure anything would look better than that robe."

She had a solid point. "Emma's—"

"Emma's handled. I'll make her some dinner, and then we'll watch movies and drink hot chocolate. Don't worry about her. Just go take that thing off before your Prince Charming shows up and thinks you've turned into a pumpkin."

Mollie always did have a way with words. Retreating into the bedroom, she heard Emma's squealed greeting for her favorite babysitter. Gratified that her daughter would have a good night, she braved the closet again. It would help if she knew where they were going to eat, but Alex hadn't said when he'd left her a message confirming the date, and she hadn't had a chance to call and ask. More to the point, her stomach had clenched up in nervous knots every time she thought about picking up the phone to call him. Which was ridiculous; she wasn't an awkward teenager anymore. There was no reason to be nervous about a simple date.

And no reason to be so worked up over what to wear. Telling herself to stop acting like a lovesick schoolgirl, she chose a simple but attractive sweater and a black pencil skirt. A pair of strappy black heels that she'd purchased on a whim last year finished the outfit.

She'd just finished her makeup when Mollie poked her head in the room. "He's here. And he's gorgeous.

If you don't hurry up, I'm going to go out with him myself."

"I'll be right out." Luckily her hair didn't require much work. A quick brushing and she was as ready as she was going to get.

In the living room, she found Alex sitting on the floor, coloring with Emma. Relaxed, lounging in her living room with her daughter, he looked like a dream come true. What would it be like to have this kind of scene every night?

Whoa. Tonight was about dinner, not happily-ever-after. She was going to scare him off before they got out the door. "Sorry you had to wait."

He looked up and grinned. "No problem. Emma was an excellent hostess. She even gave me first pick of the coloring books."

Those dimples were going to be the death of her. "I'm happy to hear it."

Mollie came in, licking a wooden spoon. "Mac and cheese is ready, so I'm going to steal my dinner date away from you folks."

Emma jumped up, nearly knocking over the crayons in her excitement for her favorite meal. "Bye, Mom. Bye, Deputy Alex." Whizzing past, she raced into the kitchen.

"Well, I guess she's okay with you leaving, huh?"

Cassie shrugged. "I guess so. Although a kiss good-bye might have been nice." She grabbed her purse and checked that she had her cell phone and keys. "So where are we going?"

"Actually, that's up to you."

"Um, okay."

"You have two options. If you're up for it, I'd love to make you dinner at my house. I picked up some food and wine, and I am fairly certain I won't set the house on fire. But if you'd be more comfortable, we could go out. I've got reservations at Isle Bistro, just in case."

He cooked? She wanted to say yes to that, but could she trust herself to be alone with him? The restaurant was a safer choice, but it would be loud and crowded on a Friday night. Not exactly the best atmosphere to get to know each other.

"If you do let me cook for you, I want to be clear— it's just dinner. I'm not trying to trick you into anything else."

She believed him. That he'd thought to give her another option showed he wasn't trying to manipulate her into something. Besides, she was dying to see what he could do in the kitchen—no guy had ever made her a meal before. "You're really going to cook?"

"Absolutely."

"Well, let's go, then."

Yelling a goodbye to Mollie and Emma, she followed him out to his car, where he held the door and offered a hand to help her climb up. Ignoring the thrill of awareness that his touch sparked, she settled into the SUV. How was she going to survive an entire evening with him if just the touch of his hand got her all worked up? And why did he have to smell so good?

"Are you okay over there?"

She realized she was gripping the seatbelt like a lifeline and relaxed her hands. "Fine."

"You know, I meant what I said. I'm not trying to seduce you or anything. I don't want you to be worried about my intentions for tonight."

"No, I trust you." And she did. She was the one she didn't trust.

* * *

Alex parked in front of his apartment. He'd chosen a ground-floor unit that had a small yard in a newer building just a block off Main Street. He'd barely opened the door before Rex barreled into him. Spotting Cassie, the big dog darted off, returning to drop a rather damp tennis ball at her feet. "Sorry, big guy, but I don't think you're supposed to play ball in the house."

"Definitely not. He knocked over a lamp the last time."

She gave the disappointed dog a scratch. "Can I help you in the kitchen?"

"No need. I already made the salad, and everything else is going right on the grill."

"The grill. I should have known. Somehow I couldn't picture you standing over a hot stove."

"Grilling counts as cooking." At least he hoped it did, because she was right—he wasn't much use in the kitchen otherwise.

"I suppose it does. Besides, I'm too hungry to argue."

He was hungry, too, but not the way she meant. He'd been trying not to stare since he picked her up. She was sexier in her ladylike skirt and sweater than any bikini-clad beach bunny. Tearing his eyes away before his body betrayed the direction of his thoughts, he opened the refrigerator and found the platters he'd made up earlier.

"Can I help carry something out, at least?" She'd followed him into the tiny kitchen, unaware of the effect she had on him.

"You could bring the wine. It's on the counter by the stove." Hefting the trays of meat, he let her open the door to the patio. "While the grill heats up, I'll get the table ready. You just sit and relax."

Inside, he found the plates and silverware, and a stack of cloth napkins he didn't remember buying. Stacking everything up, he grabbed the salad bowl with his free hand and headed back outside.

He'd expected Cassie to be sitting at the table sipping her wine. Instead, she was out in the yard, playing tug of war with Rex. She'd kicked off her shoes and was barefoot, laughing in the grass. And she was beautiful.

She saw him and paused. "I hope you don't mind. He really wanted to play."

Mind? He couldn't think of anything he wanted more than to see her laughing and happy like she was right now. "Of course not. Have fun. I'll let you know when the food's ready."

Loading up the grill, he watched her play in the moonlight. He'd never met anyone like her. She was dedicated and driven, and if he hadn't looked closely, it would have been easy to think that's all she was. But he'd seen the softer side, the playful side that he had a feeling she didn't often let show. He admired how seriously she took her work and family responsibilities, but everyone needed some downtime. He had a feeling she didn't allow herself nearly enough of it.

He was just turning off the grill when she came back and collapsed into a chair.

"I hope you worked up an appetite out there. The food's ready."

Reaching for the wine glass he'd filled for her, she took a sip. "Perfect. I'll just go wash up."

"Past the living room, first door on the right."

"Thanks."

He had the food on the table when she returned. "Wow, that looks amazing."

"So do you."

She blushed at the simple compliment. He got the feeling she wasn't in the habit of hearing them. Obviously, she'd had at least one prior relationship, but maybe she wasn't as experienced as he'd thought. One more reason to back up and slow down. And maybe do some damage control while he was at it. "Listen, about the other night. I want to apologize."

She looked up, eyes wide. "Apologize?"

He rubbed the back of his neck. "Yes, apologize. I shouldn't have taken advantage of the situation. You were vulnerable, and I should have realized that."

She crossed her arms against her chest, and her chin jutted up. "You know, I'm a grown woman, and I make my own decisions. I don't need you to look out for me."

"No, I didn't mean it that way. But I also don't want to be a reason you look back and regret anything."

She paused, her fork midway to her mouth. "Do you regret it?"

"Absolutely not."

Her face relaxed. "Good. Me, either."

Time to change the subject. "It was good to see Emma so happy today, after everything."

Cassie swallowed and nodded. "She's bounced back like nothing ever happened. Out of all of us, I'm pretty sure she's the least traumatized."

"She's a lucky girl to have so many people who care about her."

"She does have that. My parents are nuts about her, obviously. And Jillian and Mollie both help out when I need them to. They're great friends, and Emma's really comfortable with them."

"What about her father. Does he spend much time with her?"

Her lips pressed together in a hard line.

"I'm sorry. If that was too personal a question…"

"No, it's fine. I'm actually surprised you hadn't heard the whole sad story already."

"I'm new in town, remember?"

"True, but once people find out you're interested in me, it will come up. Trust me."

"Well, if that's the case, it's probably better I hear it from you."

Cassie folded and then refolded her napkin, finally setting it down next to her plate. "I met Tony right after I graduated from veterinary school. I'd spent the last months—years, really—working my butt off, and I thought I'd earned a bit of fun. So I went with some girlfriends on a gambling cruise, one of those boats that goes out into international waters for a few hours."

He nodded. "A booze cruise."

"Yeah, basically. Tony was there with some buddies and we kind of hooked up. He was older and a first mate on a yacht docked in Port Canaveral. He was fun and so completely different from anyone I knew. Later he took me dancing, and to clubs, all the things I'd missed out on holed up in my room with my books." Picking up her glass, she drained the last of the crisp wine. "I thought he loved me. Even so, we were careful, except for the first time. But you know what they say. It only takes once." At the tightening in his jaw, she said a silent prayer that history wasn't going to repeat itself. "Anyway, when I found out I was pregnant, I still thought everything would be okay. I was about to start work at the clinic, he had a decent job, and we'd have our own little family." Looking back it was hard to believe she'd ever been that naive. "As I'm sure you can imagine, he had a very different reaction."

"Was he angry?"

"Not exactly. He just said he needed some time to think about it. That was about five years ago. I haven't seen him since."

"What? What happened to him?"

She shrugged and started stacking the plates. "Last I heard, he was in the Bahamas. He had some friends who worked boats down there. Honestly, I haven't tried too hard to track him down. Let sleeping dogs lie and all that."

Alex took the plates from her hand, setting them back down with a *thunk*. "But what about child support? Even if he doesn't want to stick around, he could still be sending money."

"The money isn't worth it. If I tracked him down, made him pay, he might fight me on custody. As far as I'm concerned, he lost out on that chance when he left, and I'm not going to let him come back and screw up her life. I've seen what that does to kids—having dads who come and go, breaking promises, forgetting birthdays. I'm not going to put Emma through that, not over money. Having no father must be better than having one who doesn't really care."

Chapter Thirteen

Alex thought about all the times his dad had left him waiting, all the baseball games he'd been too drunk to remember, the school award ceremonies he didn't bother to show up for. Alex's heart had been broken more times than he could remember, and he had the emotional scars to prove it. "You're right. Nothing's worse than waiting for a parent who never shows up."

She sniffed and nodded. "So you see why I have to be careful. I can't mess up like that again."

His head spun. "Wait, what? How is this your fault? He's the one who ran out. That's all on him."

"But I let it happen. I went out with him. I believed him. I went to bed with him. If I'd been smarter—"

"Stop it." He took her by the shoulders. "You were young, and maybe you made a mistake. Guess what? Everyone makes mistakes. The difference is, you did everything you could to make things right. You've been an amazing parent to that little girl, and that's what counts. He could have done the same. Hell, even if he didn't want to stick around, he could have at least made an effort to help support you and the baby financially." He looked her in the eyes. "Don't blame yourself for his failings."

He wanted to kiss her until she believed what he was saying. He wanted it so much that he let go and took a step back. So this was why she'd looked so upset when Jillian and Mrs. Rosenberg had been talking about proud fathers handing out cigars. This Tony person certainly hadn't stuck around to celebrate or do anything else, for that matter. Angry at a man he'd never met, he worked to calm himself. Getting upset wasn't going to help anyone, least of all Cassie.

Calling Rex over, he stroked the dog's soft fur, feeling the tension seep away. "Your Tony sounds a lot like my dad. Lots of fun, but not someone you can count on when things get tough. The difference is, my father stuck around, at least for a while. He'd hold down a job, pay a few bills, buy a few groceries, then get fired for coming in drunk or not showing up at all. Even when he was working, he was more likely to spend his paycheck on drugs than pay the rent. We moved around a lot until my sister was old enough for school and Mom could get a job. Things got better when she stopped relying on him for anything."

"Oh, Alex, I'm so sorry. That had to be so hard."

"It wasn't great. By the time I was in middle school, he was pretty bad off. He went from using to selling and got busted."

"He's in jail?"

"I don't know. Probably. He's been in and out so many times, he probably has a cell named after him. I stopped keeping track years ago."

"Is he why you volunteered for the mentor program?"

"I guess, yeah. I know what it's like to grow up without a man around to look up to. And I know how easy it is to head in the wrong direction. I had a teacher who took an interest in me, got me thinking about college instead of easy money. Otherwise, I could have ended up just like my old man."

Cassie came over to where he stood and wrapped her arms around his waist. Tipping her head back, she met his gaze. "But you didn't. You're hardworking, dedicated and caring."

"You forgot sexy."

Her eyes twinkled up at him. "That goes without saying."

This time he was the one to initiate the kiss, capturing her mouth the way he'd wanted to all night. Her lips were warm, her tongue hot as she opened for him. Pulling her against him, he forced himself to go slowly, to draw every second of enjoyment out of this. It would be so easy to pull up her skirt and take her right there on the patio. The little moans she made told him she wouldn't tell him no. But he'd made a promise. Holding himself in check, he gentled the kiss, smoothing her hair with his hands to soothe himself as much as her. Sensing the shift, she pulled away and looked up at him, questioning.

"If we don't stop now, I'm not going to be able to stop." Just watching her, with her lips swollen and her cheeks flushed, made him want to pick her up and cart her off to his room. But after what she'd been through with her ex, that wasn't an option. He needed to prove to her he wasn't going to turn and run when the going got tough. Hell, he needed to prove it to himself, too. Until then, he had to keep things from getting too intense too fast. And sex with Cassie was nothing if not intense.

She swallowed, understanding showing in her eyes. "So, now what?"

"How about a drive before I take you home?" At the mention of a drive, Rex came bounding over, nearly tap dancing in his excitement.

Cassie laughed. "Rex certainly thinks it's a good idea. And I do, too. A drive would be nice."

He took the dishes into the house, leaving them in the sink for later. At the front door, Rex waited impatiently, his leash in his mouth. Alex never should have taught him that trick. "You know, I don't have to bring the dog along. He'll be fine here."

"Oh, bring him. I'm sure he's used to going everywhere with you."

Outnumbered, he snapped the leash on Rex. "Fine, you can come. But she gets to ride shotgun."

"Mommy, I'm bored." Emma's pouting had started within minutes of her arrival at the clinic and was giving Cassie an epic headache.

"Honey, I'm sorry, but we can't go home yet. I've got a patient coming in later, and I have to finish up some paperwork."

"Then I wanna go to Grandma's house like I always do."

Cassie sighed. Emma was usually so good, but today she was really out of sorts. Her dad had what was hopefully his final visit with the orthopedist today, and her mom had wanted to be there to ask some questions. Once her father was back at work, Cassie could spend more time with Emma in the afternoons, but until then Emma was just going to have to cope. They all were.

"Do you have any puppies or kittens for me to play with today?"

"Honey, I already told you we don't. I know. Why don't we go up front and get some paper and crayons, and you can color for a while?"

"I guess." Emma started down the hall, scuffing her feet. It really was pretty boring at the clinic today. Normally there were clients in and out who would show Emma some attention or pets to play with. Today was slower than normal, and even Cassie felt a bit restless. The weather outside wasn't helping, either. Today was the first day of really warm weather and everyone had a bit of spring fever.

"Mommy! Come look. Rex is here!"

Rex? He didn't have an appointment; she'd just checked the schedule a few minutes ago. Coming around the corner, she saw Mollie tossing Rex a treat, the phone at her ear, and Alex leaning on the counter, looking exactly like a man in uniform should look.

"Is Rex okay?"

"He's fine, just a bit bored. I thought we'd stop in and pick up a few of those dental treats you told me about and pay a visit to a pretty lady." He looked down at Emma and smiled. "Seems we got a two-for-one deal on that."

Relieved there was nothing wrong, she ran a hand through her hair, trying to smooth it. It was always a mess by this time of day. "How have you been?" It had been a few days since their dinner, and she had missed him more than she'd expected. Not that she thought he'd been avoiding her, but they both had busy schedules that didn't seem to overlap much.

"I'm good. Better now that I've seen you. I hope you're ready for the dance this weekend?"

She felt her cheeks warm. "Definitely."

"That's good because I'm looking forward to dancing with a particular volunteer."

Emma looked up from playing with Rex, her eyes wide. "Are you taking Mommy and me to the dance?"

"Oh, no, honey, Alex didn't mean—"

"I'd be honored to escort you and your mother to the dance." He winked at Cassie. "In fact, that's really why I stopped by. To formally invite you to be my dates."

"Yes!" Emma pumped her little fist. "I told Mommy you were going to be our valentine."

Alex raised his eyebrows. "Is that right?"

"Uh-huh." Features falling, she scuffed the toe of her shoe across the tiled floor. "I wish the dance was right now. Then I'd have something to do."

"I'm afraid it's been rather slow here this afternoon," Cassie explained. "It's not much fun for a little girl."

Alex scratched his chin. "Well, maybe I could help out with that a bit. I'm not on duty for another hour. Think I could convince you two to take a break and get some ice cream with me? On a sunny day like this, it's practically against the law to stay cooped up inside."

"Can we, Mom? Can we? You don't want to break the law, do you, Mom?" Emma was practically vibrating in excitement.

"How can I turn down an offer like that? Let me grab my phone in case there's an emergency, and we'll go."

Heading back to her office, she realized she was

nearly as excited as Emma. Not over the ice cream, but just from seeing Alex. Whenever she was around him her senses were heightened and her mood lifted. He made her feel good, happy with herself and her life. Just his presence, and his smiles at her daughter, were enough to have her walking on air. It was as if he was the final piece to a puzzle she'd been trying to figure out all her life. Scary, but exhilarating, too. And unlike her previous relationship, this time she would take her time and just enjoy things as they happened.

Grabbing the phone, she stuck it in her pocket and rejoined Emma and Alex. "Mollie, want me to bring you back something?"

The petite receptionist nodded at Alex. "If you run into another one of him, that would be perfect. Otherwise, a strawberry milkshake would be great."

Cassie rolled her eyes. "I'll do my best. Call me if you need me."

"Will do, boss. Have fun."

They walked outside into the kind of weather that made Florida famous. Blue skies, puffy white clouds and enough sunshine to remember that soon enough it would be summer again. The Sugar Cone was a couple of blocks down near the middle of town, an easy walk on such a nice day. She and Alex strolled hand in hand, Rex heeling beside them while Emma skipped ahead. Soon enough they were in front of the old-fashioned ice-cream parlor.

Cassie looked down at the dog; he wouldn't be allowed inside. "If you know what you want, I'll get it for you so you can stay out here with Rex."

"Two scoops of rocky road in a waffle cone. And thanks."

She nodded and followed Emma, helping her with the heavy glass door. "Do you know what you want?"

Emma pressed her face to the glass-fronted case, examining her choices. "Chocolate chip, please. In a cone."

Cassie joined her, scanning the brightly colored options. "I think I'll have mango. In a bowl, so I don't drip all over my work clothes."

"A good choice." Woody, the owner of the shop, started scooping. "Anything else?"

"Actually, yes. I need a double scoop of rocky road in a waffle cone and a strawberry milkshake, please."

"Coming right up."

Outside, they sat at one of the sidewalk tables, silent except for the occasional woof from Rex when someone he knew passed by.

"I swear, I think that dog knows more people on the island than I do," Cassie remarked after yet another person stopped to pet him.

"He's my secret weapon. I use him to get people to like me."

"Is that so?"

"Hey, it worked on you, didn't it?"

Watching him, sitting next to her daughter, eating ice cream together, she could only nod. She liked him, all right, more than she knew how to handle.

Getting into his patrol vehicle, Alex wondered how long it had been since he'd had such a simple, pleasant afternoon. A year ago, he never would have believed that watching a little girl eat ice cream would be life-changing. But watching her smile as she licked up the last bit of ice cream had made him realize that as much as he'd missed out on having a father, his father had missed out, too. Whatever demons drove him had cost him the joy of seeing his children grow up.

Alex headed away from town toward the beach road, the vastness of the horizon a counterpoint to the new view he'd stumbled upon. He'd always thought that his father had chosen adventure over the mundane, that the drab ordinariness of family life just couldn't live up to the lure of the streets. But these past few weeks with Cassie and Emma had been anything but ordinary. Being around them made everyday things better, more intense, more exciting. There was nothing boring about the way a child interacted with the world. If anything, Emma gave him a chance to see the world through new eyes, to find the fun in things that had become commonplace.

He'd worried that he couldn't be a family man because of his adrenaline-junkie ways. But the highs and lows of the past few weeks had been more intense than any he'd had on the force.

So why did men like his father and Cassie's ex leave? What made them give up what should have been the best part of their lives? The only thing he could think of was fear. The night Emma had been lost, he'd thought he might die himself. Loving a child was like having your heart out there walking around in the world, where anything could happen. From skinned knees to broken hearts, there were so many ways she could be hurt and only so much he could do to protect her. But surely the good times, the Christmas mornings and Father's Day brunches, made up for that, right?

His feelings for Cassie were just as intense. She made him want to be better than he was, to be the kind of man she deserved. She'd been through so much; just hearing about the way her ex had treated her made him sick inside. She deserved better. Emma deserved better. They deserved a man who would be there; instead, Cassie'd had to make do on her own, all while worrying that the loser might show up and demand custody one day.

Not that that seemed likely. In Alex's experience, men who abandoned their families weren't likely to show up years later, wanting to play house. Besides, wouldn't he be responsible for all that back child support? That would be a tidy sum by now, and more than enough incentive to stay lost rather than start coughing up money. Not that playing the odds was enough to calm Cassie's mind. She would have that fear hanging over her head as long as he was out there.

Alex would like nothing better than to go back in time and handle the deadbeat, man to man. He hated that the creep could still upset Cassie, and selfishly, he didn't want anything standing in the way of them building a family together.

A family. Was that really what he wanted? Pulling over, he let the car and his mind idle. Images of Cassie flashed through his head. Her gentleness with the orphaned kitten, her strength when Emma was lost, her passion and fire when they were alone together. Meeting her had changed everything, and he never wanted to go back.

He wanted to be there when she had a bad day, to find ways to make her smile or share in the laughter of a bad joke. And he wanted to be there for Emma, too. That little girl had wrapped him around her little finger the first time he saw her, and there was no pretending he didn't love her. Hell, he loved both of them.

He wanted both of them in his life, and damn it, he was going to make that happen. He'd never failed to accomplish anything he'd set his mind to and wasn't going to start now. He just needed to convince Cassie that it could work, that he could make things better for her, not worse. He needed to convince her that he was worth the risk and help her let go of the past and all the pain that had gone with it.

And he had a pretty good idea of how to start that process. He just needed to make a few phone calls to the right people.

Pulling out his personal phone, he located the number he needed and dialed.

"Ramsey, Rodriguez and Cates. How may I direct your call?"

"Ms. Cates, please. Tell her it's Alex Santiago." Now to hope that the time they'd spent working together when she was with the district attorney's office had earned him a favor. Kris Cates had a reputation for being harder than the criminals she put away, but like him, she had a soft spot for kids who'd gotten a bad rap. If he could get her to listen, she'd help.

"Alex?"

"Kris, I've got a problem, and I think you might be able to help."

Chapter Fourteen

"So are you excited about tonight?" Jillian took her lunch out of the break room microwave and stirred the spicy gumbo.

Stomach turning at the sharp smell, Cassie just nodded. Suddenly the tuna sandwich she'd packed didn't seem so appetizing.

"Are you okay? You look a bit pale."

"Just a little bit queasy. Nerves about tonight, I guess." She forced a smile and reached for a package of crackers to have with her water. Maybe the saltines would settle her stomach. Jillian had taken to stashing them around the clinic in an attempt to conquer her morning sickness.

"Oh—my—God." She stared at the package still in her hand, trembling.

Jillian's mouth dropped open as she looked at the

crackers and made the connection. "No, you don't think? I mean, could you be?"

"I didn't think so. I can't be, right? I mean, what are the odds? This is just nerves. That's all."

"Well, are you sleeping with him?"

Cassie's cool cheeks heated. "Yes, but just the one time. We decided to slow things down."

"It only takes once. You know that."

She did know, only too well. Her stomach twisted, remembering. "No way. I can't be pregnant. Alex is still getting used to the idea of Emma, and she's older. Not in diapers is what he said." Head whirling, she clutched her stomach. "Oh, God, I think I'm going to be sick."

Racing for the bathroom, she made it just in time to empty what little was in her stomach. Flashes of morning sickness with Emma came racing back, bringing on another round of retching. Behind her, the door opened a crack.

"Are you okay? Can I get you anything?"

"Um, no, I don't think so, unless you have a pregnancy test handy." Straightening up, she moved to the sink. Luckily she kept a toothbrush there for days she had garlic for lunch. Brushing her teeth and splashing some water on her face helped, but the only thing that would make her feel really better would be knowing she wasn't pregnant.

Not that she hadn't dreamed of giving Emma a sibling one day. But not like this. Not now, when she and Alex were just getting started. If he'd been cautious before, he'd be petrified now. And who could blame him?

Mollie crowded in behind Jillian. "Hey, what's going on? Why's everyone in the bathroom?"

"Cassie threw up."

So much for keeping this on the down-low. "I'm fine. I must have eaten something that didn't agree with me, that's all."

"But you didn't eat anything," Jillian protested. "You started to open those saltines I brought in, but you didn't eat any yet."

"Wait, she wanted your saltines? And she's throwing up?" Mollie turned back to Cassie, eyes wide. "Oh, my God, are you pregnant?"

"No." Having intuitive friends was really a pain sometimes.

"Maybe," Jillian countered. "You did sleep with him. You need to take a test. I have some at the inn. I can run home and get one."

"Wouldn't it be faster for me to just run to the drugstore?" Mollie asked. "If anyone asks, I'll tell them it's for a dog or something."

"You can't use them on dogs," Jillian pointed out.

"I know that, but they don't."

Cassie felt her lips twitch. Even with her world crashing down, her friends could still make her smile. "Fine. Mollie, take some cash from my purse and go get a test. And maybe some ginger ale for my stomach. All this crazy talk about pregnancy is making it worse. Then once you both see that it's negative, we can move on with our day."

Two lines. That couldn't be right. Maybe they'd changed the tests since she'd taken that one five years ago. With shaking hands, she grabbed the box back out of the trash and read the instructions again. And again.

Deflating like a balloon, she slid down the wall, landing in a pile on the floor. She was pregnant. And just like before, she was going to have to figure things out on her own. At least this time she knew what to expect. She wouldn't be scared by Braxton Hicks or looking up the symptoms of colic online at 3:00 a.m. She knew how to take care of a baby. What she didn't know was how to tell Alex.

She needed to do it now before he started getting any more pie-in-the-sky ideas about a relationship with her. She grimaced. If she'd wanted a surefire way to scare him off, she'd found it. Breaking the news on a second date should pretty much guarantee there wouldn't be a third, not after he had made such a big deal about wanting to slow things down. Having a baby together was pretty much the opposite of that.

But before telling him, she had to face her friends. From her spot on the floor, she called them. "You can come in."

Both women squeezed into the tiny room. Jillian went to Cassie, but Mollie dove for the test on the sink. Holding it up, she squinted, then passed it to Jillian. "You're pregnant. You must know how to read these things."

Jillian took one look and started crying. "Oh, my goodness, you're pregnant—we're going to be pregnant together!" Taking the Kleenex a bewildered Mollie handed her, she blew her nose. "I'm sorry, honey. I know you're more upset than excited. But really, it's going to be wonderful. Just think, our babies will grow up together."

Okay, so maybe she wasn't alone this time. She'd have her friends; that meant something. And it would be fun to be pregnant together; she'd never had a mom friend before. Sniffling, she took the tissues from Jillian. "Look what you did. Now I'm crying."

Mollie looked from one crying woman to the other. "Hell, if this is contagious, I'm getting out of here."

Laughing through her tears, Cassie shook her head. "Trust me. That's not how it happens." Sobering, she stood up, pulling Jillian with her. "Seriously, though, what am I going to do?"

"For starters," Mollie said, "we're all going to get out of this bathroom. This is getting weird. Then, Jillian's going to put the Closed sign up—you planned on closing early anyway because of the dance—and cancel whatever appointments are left. Then we can all go have some ice cream or a pedicure or whatever it is girls are supposed to do when bonding. We'll figure out everything else together."

Jillian nodded, tears forming again. "She's right. No matter what happens with Alex, you and that baby are going to be loved to pieces."

Looking from one woman to the other, Cassie had to smile. Her luck with men might be lousy, but she sure knew how to pick her friends.

Alex nailed the last board in the makeshift bandstand into place. In a few hours, this place would be transformed, and it felt good to know he'd played a part. Smiling, he pictured himself dancing with Cassie in front of the bandstand later tonight. He couldn't wait to get his hands on her, even if it was in the middle of a crowded room.

"What're you grinning about?" Nic wiped the sweat off his face with the bottom of his T-shirt. "We've been working like dogs for hours, and you're grinning like a fool."

"No. I'm not. I'm just picturing what it's all going to look like when it's done."

Nic smiled knowingly. "You're picturing Cassie all dressed up in something slinky. That's what you're thinking about."

"Hey, watch it."

Nic held his hands up. "No harm meant. Seems like you're pretty serious about her, huh?"

Alex dusted his hands on his jeans, then met the other man's gaze. "I think so, yeah. I don't know that she's ready for anything serious, but I'm hoping I can convince her."

"And you're okay with her having a kid? Not every guy wants to take on a family all at once like that."

"I'm more than okay with it. I thought I wouldn't be. My dad wasn't exactly father of the year, and I just didn't want to even get into the whole family thing. But Emma's great. Kids are great. Heck, I don't have to convince you. You're having one of your own soon."

Nic took a swig from a bottle of water, swallowing hard. "Yeah, it's kind of terrifying, but in a good way, you know? I mean, there are so many ways to screw up, but still, I can't wait to have a son to teach things to, do things with, you know?"

"Wait, it's a boy? You found out already?"

Nic grimaced. "Uh, yeah. But can you pretend you didn't hear that? Jillian wants to wait a bit before we tell people, so she can do a big announcement or something. She'll kill me if she finds out I told you."

"Hey, no problem, man. I don't want to get you in any trouble. In fact, I'd appreciate it if you didn't say anything about my intentions with Cassie. I don't want to scare her off by moving too fast."

"Intentions? What exactly are you thinking here? Marriage?"

"I know it sounds crazy, but yeah, eventually. I think it will take some time to get her to trust me, but I'm in this for the long haul." Just saying it made him feel as if he'd won the lottery—how much better would the real thing be?

"Congrats, man." Nic slapped him on the back and handed him an unopened bottle of water. "Here's to new beginnings."

"I'll drink to that."

Taking a deep drink, he realized Nic was becoming a real friend. He'd made a few buddies in the department since moving here, but it was a different kind of friendship. He relied on them to watch his back, but he couldn't see talking to them about his relationship problems or anything like that. That was likely his own fault; after what had happened in Miami, he'd kept to himself, afraid to let his guard down. Maybe it was time to work on that, too. After all, he'd told himself Paradise was going to be a fresh start, the place where he put down some roots. Cassie was part of that, but if he was going to build a life here, he'd need to put in the effort and meet people halfway.

"You going to stand there looking dreamy-eyed all day or get some work done? We've still got to hang the lights and set up the tables."

"Yeah, I'm going to help, but let's hurry, okay? I want to swing by the florist before I pick up Cassie and Emma." He was going to make sure tonight was a night they'd never forget.

Chapter Fifteen

Cassie nervously twisted her hair around a finger, checking her image in the mirror. Did she look pregnant? Would everyone be able to tell? Would Alex be able to tell?

"You look fine." Mollie took her hand and led her away from the mirror. "Better than fine. You look amazing. Alex is going to flip when he sees you. If he's not in love with you already, he will be when he sees you in that dress."

"I don't think a dress is going to do any such thing." Although she did look good in it. The red material clung to her curves, draping nearly to the floor. The neckline showed just a hint of cleavage, but the back was cut away nearly to her waist, and a slit exposed her thigh every time she took a step. If seduction was a dress, it would be this dress. Too bad it would go to waste tonight. Seduction was what had gotten her into this predicament.

"Where's Emma? She's usually in here underfoot when I'm getting dressed."

"She's making up another batch of Valentine's Day cards in the kitchen. Don't worry. I told her, no glue, glitter or paint."

"Thank you." It had taken forever to get Emma to choose a dress; if she ruined it, they would never get her in another one.

"So, are you going to tell her about the new baby?"

Cassie checked to be sure the bedroom door was still closed. "Not yet. I'll have to eventually, especially if the morning sickness keeps up. But I want to talk to Alex first. I need to figure out where things stand before she starts asking a zillion questions."

"So you're definitely going to keep it?"

"Absolutely." There was no doubt in her mind about that. She'd had her crying fit this afternoon, but her maternal instincts were already kicking in. "It's going to be hard, but I've done the single mom thing before, and I can do it again. Besides, this time I have you guys to help."

"You know, it might not be like that, not this time. Alex isn't Tony. He's not going to take off. He's too responsible for that."

"Maybe. It would be nice if he was part of this baby's life. But I'm not going to count on it." She'd been burned before. And selfishly she dreaded the idea of working out a visitation schedule. She'd heard horror stories about ugly custody battles and didn't want to fight over a baby as if it was a prized toy instead of a family member. Of course, given Alex's feelings on children, it might not come to that.

Mollie tugged at the hemline of her dress. "Well, I'll be there for moral support if you need it. Although I'm not sure how long I'm going to last. Why couldn't we have had a casual fundraiser, like a fish fry or something? I could wear shorts to a fish fry."

"You look gorgeous. And you're going to be too busy fighting off eligible men to even think about what you're wearing."

Mollie rolled her eyes. "I doubt it. Besides, I'm going to be hanging out with Emma so you and Alex can have your talk. Unless you aren't going to tell him tonight? You could always wait a bit before you say anything."

"No, I have to tell him before he starts getting any more ideas about us. No use putting off the inevitable. Besides, once Emma knows, everyone in town will know. She can't keep a secret for more than a millisecond."

"I see your point."

A knock at the front door ended the conversation and sent Cassie's pulse skyrocketing.

"Want me to get it?"

Cassie nodded. "Please." Taking a few deep breaths, she reminded herself that everything would be okay. Alex might be angry, but she could handle that. She just needed to get through the night; then she'd worry about everything else.

Forcing herself into the living room, her heart jumped at the sight of him. He always looked good, but wow, could he rock a tux. He would have fit right in on a red carpet somewhere in Hollywood. For a moment, she let herself pretend that nothing had changed, that they were just two people having a romantic evening. Maybe she could wait just a little longer before she ruined it all.

But the longer she held on, the harder it would be to let him go. Better to do it and get it over with. But not here—she'd wait until they'd finished with their duties at the dance. The kids were counting on everyone to make the dance a success, and her personal problems shouldn't stand in the way of that.

Alex turned and saw her standing in the hallway. "You look amazing. I'm going to be the envy of the island tonight with you on my arm."

"And me," Emma added, twirling to show off her dress.

Kneeling, Alex slipped a tiny corsage over her wrist. "Of course. In fact, I think you'll be the prettiest one there."

Enchanted, Emma examined the flowers while Alex crossed over to Cassie. "I got one for you, too. Here, let me." She held still while he pinned a tasteful white orchid spray to her dress. Could he feel how hard her heart was beating? The scent of his cologne teased her, making her want to forget everything and just bury her head against his chest.

"Are you okay?" he asked, a concerned frown on his face. "You seem awfully quiet."

"She's just worried about getting there on time, that's all," Mollie interjected. "In fact, we really should be going. Mrs. Rosenberg will have a fit if we're late."

"She's right." Cassie nodded, grateful for her friend's quick thinking. "Let's hit the road." The sooner they left, the sooner the whole night would be over, and she could start finding a way forward.

* * *

Alex carefully buckled Emma's car seat into the backseat of his SUV, then helped the little girl climb in.

Emma sat up straight as he adjusted the straps, then surprised him with a kiss on the cheek. "Thank you for being my valentine."

Swallowing past the lump in his throat, he smiled. "No, thank you." He'd always considered himself a tough, masculine kind of man, but he was no match for a four-year-old in a party dress. Cassie had already let herself into the car and was ready to go, so he climbed in and started the engine. Mollie was going to follow in her own car. "So, which one of you do I get to dance with first?"

"Me! Pick me," Emma called from the back.

"All right, you got it. But you have to let me dance with your mommy, too."

"I know that. She's your valentine, too, so you have to dance with her."

Cassie just nodded while looking out the window. She'd been awfully quiet since he picked her up. Was she worried about the event? Or had he done something wrong?

"Hey, everything okay?" he asked in a low voice, mindful of Emma in the back.

"Hmm? Oh, sure, everything's fine. I just have a lot on my mind."

"Mommy didn't feel good earlier. She had a tummy ache. I heard Mollie say so."

So much for keeping the conversation private. "Are you sick? You don't have to go if you aren't feeling well. I can explain to everyone."

"No, I'm fine. Just a minor case of nerves, or maybe

something I ate. I'm fine now. Besides, Emma would be heartbroken."

"I could still take Emma—"

"I said I'm fine."

Taken aback by her sharp tone, he let it drop. Maybe she didn't trust him to take Emma by himself, which kind of stung. Or maybe she really was fine, although her color seemed a bit off. Either way, he was going to keep a close eye on her tonight. If she started feeling bad, he'd insist on taking her home.

She was quiet the rest of the way to the Sandpiper, but Emma kept up a constant chatter to fill the gap. It seemed she was most looking forward to the cupcakes and seeing Mrs. Rosenberg, whom for some reason she adored. He was half in awe, half terrified of the woman himself.

Soon enough he was pulling into the packed parking lot. Not spotting any open spaces, he idled for a minute. "Why don't you ladies get out here, and I'll go find a spot on the street."

Once his passengers were safely on their way, he circled back out and found a parking spot a block away. It seemed most of the town had come out early to be sure everything was ready. Luckily the kids were coming by bus, so they wouldn't have to walk too far. Hiking back, he wondered if expanding the parking lot was in Nic's renovation plans.

Up at the main entrance, the streamers he'd helped hang were blowing gently in the wind, illuminated by twinkling white lights. Mrs. Rosenberg stood sentry at the front door, decked out in a fluorescent-pink sequined dress and a corsage the size of a dinner plate. Waving her clipboard, she flagged him down. "I need you to help fill the coolers with ice. And then after that, the ladies in the kitchen will need some help carrying the food trays out."

"Yes, ma'am." He hoped she didn't keep him running all night; he had a few dances to claim.

As if reading his mind, she winked at him. "And then go find Cassie and her girl. Enjoy yourself. You've earned it."

Letting out a breath, he thanked her and made a beeline for the kitchen before she thought of any other projects for him to do. On his way he passed Jillian, looking radiant and starting to show. "You look beautiful. Nic's a lucky man."

She blushed and put a hand on her belly. "Thank you. I'm afraid I feel a bit oversize at the moment. My scrubs at work are a lot more forgiving than evening wear."

"Like I said, beautiful." And he meant it. He thought of how Cassie must have looked carrying Emma and was sorry he'd missed it. Maybe someday they'd have a child of their own. That thought would have terrified him a few months ago. Now it just seemed the natural way of things. They'd date, get to know each other better, and down the road, who knew? The future was wide-open.

He'd moved ten bags of ice and carried out more baked goods than he'd seen in a lifetime before he was able to look for Cassie. He checked the lobby, which seemed to be the gathering spot for the island's senior set, then moved to the back porch. Parents and children sat eating cake at tables covered in pink-and-white tablecloths. Winding his way through them, he was stopped every few feet by people he'd met while volunteering or out on the job. It struck him that he'd made more friends in his short time in Paradise than he had in a lifetime in Miami. Not because the people in Paradise were so much different, but because he was different. He'd grown up protecting himself from being let down, but what he'd really done was isolate himself. For whatever reason, being forced to start over had helped him get past that.

"Deputy Alex, come see!"

Emma was at a smaller, child-size table set up on the part of the patio that wrapped around the side of the building. Covering the table were markers, paper and various odds and ends. Several other children were huddled around the table with her, studiously working on what must be some kind of Valentine's Day craft. "What did you make?"

"It's a Valentine's Day spider! See, it's red and has candy stuck in its web instead of flies."

Trying not to laugh, he picked up the paper. "Wow, that's really creative."

"Thank you. Now can we dance? I've been waiting forever."

"Absolutely. I promised, didn't I? And I always keep my promises."

Cassie watched Alex and Emma walk onto the makeshift dance floor and felt another piece of her heart break. Emma looked so happy, gazing up at Alex as if he was the father she'd never had. How would she take it when she found out there was going to be a baby that really was Alex's? Would she be jealous if he turned his attention from her to the baby? Or worse, if Alex wasn't willing or able to be there for this child, would it shatter the dreams Emma had built up about what a father was?

Cassie would have given anything to fix this for her little girl, but it was out of her hands. Once Alex knew, it was up to him. And he'd been perfectly honest with her about his issues around fatherhood. He'd asked to take things slow, and she was throwing them both into the fast lane.

Jillian stepped up beside her and followed her gaze. "You know, you might be wrong about him. That doesn't look like a man who is afraid of children. In fact, he looks pretty smitten with your little girl."

"I'm sure he likes Emma, but—"

"Cassie, Alex isn't Tony. You need to stop expecting him to act like Tony. Give him a chance. Go talk to him." She gave Cassie a little push. "And if you need me, I'll be over at the refreshment table, loading up on key lime pie. Just look for the lady eating for two. Now stop standing here staring and go get your man."

Not having any better ideas, Cassie started down the stairs toward Alex and Emma. Spotting her, Alex waved. "Honey, I think it's your mommy's turn for a dance. Why don't you go find some of those cupcakes you were talking about?"

Energized at the thought of the treats, she darted off in a blur of pink lace.

Alex shook his head. "Where does she get her energy?"

"Well, I think it helps that she still gets an afternoon nap."

He chuckled. "I'll have to try that sometime. How about you? Are you feeling any better?"

She nodded, not wanting to open that can of worms

just yet. "Didn't you promise me a dance?" One dance couldn't hurt, right? And he looked so good in his tuxedo, she just couldn't resist. She'd be strong later; right now she just wanted to lean into him and let the music carry her away. Taking his hand, she let him lead her onto the floor and pull her close enough to melt against him.

"Have I told you how beautiful you look in that dress?"

She shook her head, not trusting her voice.

"Well, you do. You're absolutely stunning. Of course, you always are."

In a few months, he might not think so. Soon she'd be too big around for anyone to consider her stunning. Choking back her sob, she forced herself to try to enjoy the moment.

"I've been thinking." Alex's deep voice resonated through her body. "I know I said I want to take things slowly, but I think you should know how I'm feeling. The truth is, I'm crazy about you."

Looking up, she kept her voice in check. "And what about kids? You said you weren't sure you'd ever be ready for them."

"I know, but the more I'm around Emma, the more I'm crazy about her, too. And it's not like you're talking about a houseful of kids. It's just Emma, and she's wonderful, like her mother."

Wonderful. Except in about nine months, it wouldn't be just Emma anymore. Screwing up her courage, she stopped dancing. "Listen, Alex, we need to talk."

"I thought that's what we were doing." Confusion filled his eyes.

"Oh, there you are, Alex." Mrs. Rosenberg appeared at the edge of the dance floor. "I'm afraid I must pull you away for just a moment. We need someone strong enough to move some crates in the kitchen, and I can't find anyone else."

Cassie stepped back, dropping her arms from his shoulders. "Go. I should go check on Emma, anyway."

Hesitantly he walked away, leaving her alone on the dance floor.

"Hey, there's my girl. Did you save a dance for your old man?" Her father smiled, and she felt tears prick her eyes.

"Sure, Dad." Placing her hand in his, she let him lead her slowly around the floor. He was still a bit stiff, but he did remarkably well, given that he'd stopped using the cane only a few days ago. Soon he'd be back at the office, a godsend, considering the circumstances. Her parents had given her so much support when she'd had Emma, and they would again. That was one thing to be grateful for.

"What's going on, sweetie? Are you crying?" He offered her a freshly starched handkerchief from his suit pocket.

Hastily wiping the tears away, she smiled. "I was just thinking how lucky I am to have you and Mom." It was the truth; she did have the best parents. She just hated to disappoint them again.

"Well, I'm not sure what brought that on, but thank you. We're pretty proud of you, too. But speaking of your mother, I'd better go rest this leg before she catches me down here and makes a scene."

Giving him a quick squeeze, she smiled and watched him limp up the stairs to the patio, where, sure enough, her mother was watching, concern on her face. Her parents had that rare kind of love usually found only in romance novels and love songs. She'd always assumed she'd have that kind of relationship one day, but so far she hadn't even managed a long-term boyfriend, let alone a successful marriage.

Heading for the back of the inn, she tried to smile and be polite to everyone, while inside all she wanted was to go home and curl up in her bed until morning. But first she needed to tell Alex about the pregnancy. She'd never be able to sleep otherwise. She found him in the kitchen, holding Emma up to the sink so she could wash her hands. Such a simple thing and a reminder of what might have been.

"Hi, Mommy. I ate two cupcakes!"

"That she did, although how much she ate versus how much was on her hands, I'm not sure. I figured we'd better get her cleaned up before she got chocolate all over her pretty dress." He set Emma down and handed her a paper towel.

"Thanks. I appreciate it."

"Can I go play with the other kids now? Miss Jillian said there were going to be games on the side porch."

"Sure. I'll come watch in a little bit."

Once Emma was out of earshot, she turned back to Alex, her hands clenched in front of her.

"We need to talk."

Chapter Sixteen

Alex carefully finished drying his hands, taking the time to fold the dishtowel he'd used and hang it back up on its hook. He was in no hurry to hear what Cassie was about to say; the look on her face made it clear this wasn't good news. Besides, he'd dated enough women to know that "we need to talk" was relationship speak for "I want to break up." He should have realized something was off when she was so quiet earlier. But he'd been so caught up in how he was feeling, he hadn't stopped to think if she was in the same place.

No, he'd just come out and told her that he was crazy about her, basically said he loved her, and then left her standing there while he played pack mule for Mrs. Rosenberg. Not exactly the most romantic way to handle things. He must have scared her, read the signals wrong.

"If this is about what I said earlier, if I came on too strong—"

"No, it's not that." She looked over her shoulder nervously. "I'd rather talk somewhere more private, if that's okay."

This was definitely not good. But he needed to hear what she had to say before he could come up with an argument, so he just shrugged. "Sure. Nic and Jillian are outside supervising the games. We could use their office."

She didn't say anything, just went down the short hallway that led to the private suite of rooms separate from the public side of the inn. A small, comfortably-furnished office doubled as a sitting room and had a thick oak door that Cassie closed behind them. "You might want to sit down."

"I'm fine, thanks." He'd stand on his own two feet and handle this like a man.

"Well, when Emma said I wasn't feeling well, that was partly right."

"Wait, are you sick? Is it something serious?" Words like *cancer* and *multiple sclerosis* cluttered his head.

She managed a sad smile. "No, I'm not sick, not really. But there is something serious going on." She twisted her hands, her knuckles turning white. "You remember our night together after Emma was lost?"

"Of course I do. It was the most amazing night of my life." What on earth did this have to do with her feeling sick? Unless... But she'd said the timing wasn't right. That couldn't be it. "You're not saying you're pregnant, are you?"

"I'm sorry." Her voice cracked, but she kept her head up and her shoulders straight. There was fear in her eyes, but strength as well. "I just found out today. I didn't know how to tell you, or if I should tell you—"

"If you should tell me?" Voice rising, he tried to keep his temper in check. "How could you even consider not telling me?" Another thought intruded. "Are you even sure? You said you didn't think it was the right time."

"Do you think I'd be having this conversation with you if I wasn't sure? Do you want to see the test with the two lines?" Her eyes narrowed. "Or are you questioning if it's yours?"

Was he? No, not really. They'd never said they were exclusive, but he didn't think she was the type to be dating multiple men. Which meant, if she was right, all his doubts about becoming a father didn't matter. He was going to be one, ready or not.

Sweat pooled along his back as the full impact of what she was saying hit him. He opened his mouth, then closed it again, not wanting to say the wrong thing. Finally, realizing he hadn't answered her question, he shook his head. "No, I believe you. I just don't know what I'm supposed to say. I don't know what to do."

Silent tears marked her face. "Well, the good news is that you don't have to do a damned thing. I've done this on my own before, and I'll do it again."

"Cassie, no, I didn't mean that. Of course I'm willing to do whatever I need to—"

She threw her hands up, determination written on her face. "No, stop right there. I don't want my baby to have a father who's there just because he thinks he's supposed to be. You made it very clear how you felt about fatherhood and having kids. I'm not asking you for anything. I just thought you should know before anything more happened between us. Now, if you'll excuse me, I'm feeling tired and I'd like to go home."

He ran a hand through his hair, too confused to argue. "Fine, I'll go get the car."

"Don't. I think it's better if I have Mollie drive Emma and me home." She was openly crying now. He wanted to go to her, to comfort her, but she would surely push him away. So he just stood there, helpless, while the woman he loved walked out the door.

Half blinded by tears and emotion, Cassie nearly ran Jillian over on her way down the hall. "Oh, my God, I'm sorry, Jillian. Are you okay?"

"I'm fine." She reached out and steadied herself against Cassie, assessing her friend. "More to the point, are you okay?"

Cassie sniffed and rubbed at her eyes. "Not really, but I will be. I just need to get home and have some space to figure things out."

Jillian's eyes filled with sympathy. "So you told him?"

"I did. And he was shocked, and confused, and doesn't know what he wants to do. Which is a luxury he gets to have, being a man. I, however, know what I need to do. I need to get my child and get home, and then start rearranging my entire life to accommodate a baby that *is* coming, like it or not."

Jillian's jaw dropped open. "He didn't say you shouldn't keep the baby?"

"No, nothing like that." Thank goodness. That might have really sent her over the edge. "He just really didn't have much to say at all."

"Well, he probably needs some time to process everything. Even Nic was a bit overwhelmed when I broke the news to him."

"The difference is, Nic wanted a baby. You two were actively trying, so you knew he would come around. Alex and I were definitely not trying. He once said fatherhood wasn't even on his radar. So I don't think I'll hold my breath."

"I don't know if he's lying to you or to himself, but something isn't right here. I've seen him with Emma. He adores her. And don't forget, he was the first one to sign up for the new mentor program. And he's spent hours of his personal time helping to make this dance a success so that those kids get what they need. He even came and helped make those silly heart decorations, remember? Does that sound like a guy who shirks commitment? I'm telling you, you need to give him a chance. Don't you remember how upset you were when you found out today? And you had Mollie and me there with you to support you. So maybe just give him some time, okay?"

That all sounded logical, but in her experience men seldom were logical in this kind of situation. Still, she'd at least think about what Jillian had said. "Fine, he can have time. Nine months, in fact. But for now, please, I just want to go home and go to bed."

"Why don't you go wash your face and freshen up a bit? I'll find Emma and Mollie and meet you out front in a few minutes."

"Thanks."

In the bathroom, she scrubbed off her ruined mascara and tried to finger comb her hair into some semblance of normalcy. No need to scare Emma—not that her rambunctious daughter was likely to notice after all the excitement. Thankfully it was a clear shot to the front door from here, so she wasn't likely to run into many guests. Taking a deep breath, she checked that the coast was clear and made it outside without seeing anyone. Emma and Mollie were already waiting on the stairs, looking through the party favors in Emma's goody bag.

"Hi, guys, ready to go?"

"Do we have to go already?" Emma protested with a yawn.

"Yes, sleepyhead. It's way past your bedtime, and mine, too."

"Then why isn't Deputy Alex taking us home? He brought us here. Shouldn't he drive us back?"

"He wanted to, but he has to stay and help clean up," Mollie said brightly. "That's why I'm taking you home. I don't like to clean up."

"Me, either." Emma let herself be buckled in without any more protests or questions and a few minutes later was softly snoring.

"Thank you for the ride, and everything."

"Hey, that's what friends are for. That, and babysitting. All I ask is first dibs on baby snuggles."

A baby. She was going to have a baby. She'd been so busy freaking out about it she hadn't let herself think about the good parts. First smiles and the smell of baby powder, things she'd treasured with Emma and was going to get to do all over again. Her heart might be broken, but a baby was a pretty amazing thing. She needed to remember that and focus on the good things to come.

At the house, she gave Mollie a hard hug. "Keep reminding me about the baby snuggles, okay?"

"Anytime. Now go to bed and get some sleep. You look like hell."

Mollie's smile tempered her words, and anyway, she was right. Exhaustion didn't begin to describe the level of tired Cassie was at right now. Lifting Emma out of the seat, she managed to carry the sleeping girl inside without waking her. Helping her use the potty and change her into a nightgown was a little trickier, but soon she was tucked into bed, looking too sweet to be real. On impulse, Cassie bent down and gave her an extra kiss, saying a silent prayer that no matter what happened, they'd all come out of this stronger and happier. Because no matter how her heart hurt, her children were counting on her.

Alex stacked the last of the folding chairs, leaving the Sandpiper's wide, whitewashed porch looking oddly deserted after the chaos of the evening. Since Cassie's big announcement, he'd been on autopilot, mindlessly moving from task to task. Stacking chairs, taking down decorations, sweeping floors; those were things he knew how to do. How to handle the situation with Cassie? He didn't have a clue. Obviously, considering she'd left in tears.

He still didn't know what to think, let alone what to do. So he grabbed the chairs and carried them to the storage building. As long as there was still work to be done, he could avoid everything else. Maybe that would give his shell-shocked brain time to start working again.

He was on his way back when Nic stepped out from the darkness, walking Murphy on a long leash. "I'm surprised you're still here. Jillian told me what happened with Cassie."

"What happened is, I let my hormones override my common sense. It's not like I'm a dumb teenager. I know how to use protection. I let her down, and now she's furious with me."

Nic stared at him. "That's what you got from your talk with her? That she's mad at you for getting her pregnant?"

"Well, yeah. Hell, I'm mad at myself. But I'm not the one who has to go through the whole labor and delivery thing."

Nic shook his head. "You, my friend, are an idiot. She's not angry—she's terrified."

"She sure seemed angry."

"Well, maybe she was looking for some support from you. Some kind of solidarity, given the situation."

He thought back. He hadn't really offered any support; he'd been too busy asking questions. Questions that, in retrospect, made him sound like a jerk. "Right. Man, I messed up. She must hate me. First, the condom broke. Then, when she tells me she's pregnant, all I can do is ask stupid questions."

Nic chuckled and slapped him on the back. "I think that's a pretty normal male reaction. But you've got to move past that. She's going to need you."

Cassie was so strong, it was hard to imagine her needing anyone, but Nic was right. She was carrying Alex's child, and that meant she was going to have to accept his involvement in her life, no matter how upset she was with him. She was carrying his child, and that gave him rights.

His child. *Dios mío*, he was going to be a father. Knees buckling, he leaned against a tree and tried to breathe normally. He'd sort of come to grips with the idea of someday, maybe, being a stepfather to Emma. But that was far in the future; this was happening now.

Or sometime in the next nine months, anyway. Besides, Emma was older. Babies were different; they had floppy heads and you could break them if you held them wrong. And they couldn't tell you what they needed—they just cried. How on earth was he supposed to know how to take care of a baby?

"It's scary stuff, huh?" Nic asked, grinning.

How could he just stand there with that stupid look on his face? "Scary? It's terrifying. I'm not qualified for this."

"None of us are, my friend. But you'll learn. Look at it like a new assignment. You'll study up, maybe do some on-the-job training, and whatever you don't learn ahead of time, you'll figure out as you go. At least Cassie's done this before. Jillian and I are both rookies. Now, that's frightening."

Despite himself, Alex smiled. He did have a veteran partner—if she was still interested in being his partner. That he might have permanently ruined his chances with Cassie was more frightening than the idea of becoming a father. Which meant he needed to fix things. The baby, he'd figure that out. But letting Cassie go was unthinkable.

Pushing himself up from the tree, he broke into a jog toward his car.

"Hey, what are you going to do?"

"Whatever it takes."

Chapter Seventeen

The coffee and stress of the past several hours were wearing a hole in his stomach, but Alex wasn't ready to quit yet. Night shifts were nothing new, and although he preferred footwork to computer searches, he wasn't going to complain. He'd spent the night reaching out to contacts down south, working his way along a web of information. Thankfully, many of them kept the same odd hours he did and worked quickly and discreetly. A few minutes ago, he'd found what he thought was his target, and now all he could do was wait. If his information was right he'd know soon.

Too keyed up to sleep, he checked a few sports stats and then, feeling foolish, found himself searching for baby-care websites. Close to an hour later, he had a half-page of notes in front of him and more questions than when he started. It seemed he'd underestimated the number of ways one could injure or maim a baby. Everything from what position they slept in to when they had their first bite of food seemed to be imbued with the potential for danger. And that was just in the first year of life. What the websites didn't say was that there would be bullies and book reports and bad dates, and no way to protect them from it all. How could he ever have thought parenting would be boring?

And before that even started, there was the pregnancy to get through, and after that the birth itself. He hadn't been brave enough to watch any of the birth videos he'd come across, but he'd read enough to freak himself out. Of course, Cassie was the one dealing with that, but he didn't intend for her to face it alone.

He couldn't carry the baby for those nine months, but he could try to make Cassie's life easier, handle what could be handled. Which was why he'd been on his laptop all night when he should have been sleeping. If he could track down Cassie's ex, find out where he was, if he was coming back and what his intentions toward Emma were, maybe he could ease some of the burden she'd carried for the past five years.

Of course, there was the chance he would stir something up and make more trouble. That's why he hadn't followed up yet on the information his lawyer friend had sent over. He hadn't wanted to risk making things worse. But the stakes were different now. If he was ever going to have a chance at a real family with Cassie, he needed to know where he stood, and so did she. Always looking over her shoulder was keeping her from looking ahead, and they'd never be able to plan a future together that way. And if he was going to be in Emma's life, he needed to know everything he could about her, and that meant knowing about the man who had fathered her.

Getting up to refill his coffee mug, he nearly tripped over Rex. The big dog had sensed something was up and had been at his side all night. "You need to go out?" Rex thumped his tail and rose, stretching leisurely the way only animals and small children seem to do. He let the dog out and then filled his mug with the overheated dregs from the pot. If he hadn't heard anything by the time he finished this cup, he'd try to get some sleep.

As if on cue, his email alert chimed. Straddling his chair, he clicked on the newest message and quickly scanned the text. Got him! It seemed Tony Williams was now a first mate aboard a sport-fishing boat in the Bahamas. Alex's contact over there said the boat was operating out of Nassau, less than two hours away by plane. He could shower, drop Rex off, catch a flight out of Orlando and be there by lunchtime. And after that? It was anyone's guess.

Cassie woke at dawn to a kitten purring in her ear. Pushing the little gray monster away did no good; the kitten was relentless when it came to food. Her eyes shut, she tried to ignore the cat climbing onto her chest, his sharp nails pricking her skin as he kneaded her with his front paws. She didn't want to wake up. As long as she was asleep, she didn't have to think about Alex, or the baby, or the million other things demanding immediate attention. At least the clinic was closed. She'd anticipated spending her Saturday recuperating after a late night at the dance. That she'd be dealing with morning sickness and a broken heart had never occurred to her.

Sensing she was awake, Trouble began meowing.

Not a quiet, demure mew, but a full-blown meow that made it sound as if he was in danger of actually starving to death. Giving up, she lifted him off her and sat up, petting the cat to keep him quiet. She could really use a few minutes of quiet before Emma woke up. "Keep the volume down, and I'll feed you, okay?"

She pulled on her robe and shuffled into the kitchen, the kitten darting between her legs and generally being a nuisance. He was really lucky he was cute. Putting the kettle to boil, she opened a small can of cat food and dumped it into a saucer on the floor. Delighted, the roly-poly critter pounced, nearly upsetting the dish. Grinning at his antics despite herself, she leaned on the counter and waited for the water to boil.

Once she'd made her tea, she eased open the sliding door and settled into her favorite chair on the patio. The hot mug warmed her hands, and she tucked her feet up under her robe against the early morning chill. Dew clung to the leaves of her orchids, and in the distance, a woodpecker was drilling for his breakfast. This was her happy place, her personal oasis from the bustle of everyday life. Right now she had half a dozen different plants in bloom, and on the breeze there was the first hint of the season's orange blossoms.

Alex had never been out here, never seen this little corner of her world. There were a million little things about each other they didn't know. But when she was with him, that hadn't mattered. They'd shared the important things, the things that made them who they were. She knew about his father and his fears for his own future. And he knew about Tony, and the accident, and the pressure she was under. She'd thought that had been enough.

"Mommy, where are you?"

"I'm on the patio, sweetie."

Emma's face peeked around the door, her eyes still glassy from sleep. "It's cold out there."

"Then I guess I'd better come in, hadn't I?" Getting up, she took a last look at her flowers, then scooped Emma into her arms and carried her to the kitchen. Setting her on a stool, she rinsed her mug in the sink. "So, what should we do for breakfast today?"

"We should have pancakes and bacon. I love bacon."

Cassie's stomach flip-flopped. Bacon didn't sound so good to her right now. Actually, cooking suddenly sounded like more trouble than it was worth. "What if we go out for breakfast instead? We could pick up some muffins and then take them over to the Sandpiper and have a picnic in the yard. How does that sound?"

Emma pumped her little fist. "Yes! Muffins and juice?"

She ruffled the little girl's strawberry-blond curls, so like her own. Would this new baby look like her or like Alex? "Yes, juice, too." In fact, juice and plain toast sounded like the perfect breakfast to settle her queasy stomach. "We'll go as soon as you're dressed and ready."

The lure of blueberry muffins had Emma dressed in record time. Cassie didn't take much longer, not bothering to do more than walk through a quick shower and throw on jeans and a T-shirt. She really needed to spend the day doing laundry and catching up on housework, but she was as eager to get out of the house as Emma. Some fresh air and time with Jillian would help clear the fog from her head. Then she could focus and start working on a plan.

Emma kept up a one-sided conversation about last night's festivities as they drove to and from the bakery, stopping only when they pulled into the gravel lot of the Sandpiper. "Can we have our picnic now, right away?"

Cassie freed Emma from her seat and grabbed the bakery box full of muffins. "Let's go up and say hello to Miss Jillian and Mr. Nic and see if they want some muffins. Then you and Murphy can have a picnic together."

Not bothering to reply, Emma tore off toward the front door. Following more slowly, Cassie was just turning off the path when not one, but two dogs came running up. "Hey, Rex, what are you doing here?" Stalling, she stopped and petted both dogs. She wasn't ready to face Alex yet. She was barely able to face herself. But Emma was expecting a picnic, which meant there was no going back.

Squaring her shoulders, she followed the path up to the inn, where Emma was waiting on the stairs for her. "Did you see, Mom? Rex is here, so he can come to the picnic with Murphy."

"So it seems." Unless she was lucky and Alex was just leaving. Why would he be here, anyway, and so early in the morning? Pounding up the stairs to the front door, she held the door for Emma and her four-legged buddies. Not finding anyone at the front desk, she headed back to the kitchen, where Jillian was mixing up some kind of batter at the counter.

"Are you making pancakes?" Emma stood on her toes, trying to see into the bowl.

"I sure am. With blueberries in them. Do you want some?"

"Yes, please." Emma nodded, eyes wide. "I wanted

pancakes, but Mommy took us to get muffins instead. Now I can have muffins and pancakes on my picnic."

Familiar with Emma's little adventures Jillian didn't bat an eye. "Then I'll make sure to pack some up for you. Just don't let Murphy eat them."

"Or Rex," Emma added.

Jillian stirred harder, not looking up from the bowl. "Right, or Rex. Listen, Emma, why don't you take a muffin out to the yard, and then I'll bring you some pancakes when they're ready?"

"Okay." Emma carefully extracted an oversize muffin from the bakery box, then headed out the open back door, Rex and Murphy at her side.

"So, why is Rex here, Jillian? And where's Alex?"

Jillian wiped her hands, coming over to sit next to Cassie at the old oak table that dominated the kitchen. "We're dog sitting. But listen, it's not what you think."

What? Where the heck was Alex that he couldn't take Rex with him? They went everywhere together. "What do you mean? Is he having some kind of work done on his apartment or something?" That would make sense.

Absently rubbing her growing belly, Jillian sighed. "No. He had to go out of town and wasn't sure how long he'd be gone, so he asked us to take care of Rex for him."

Cassie's stomach dropped. It was just like with Tony. She broke the news, and he left town the next day. It was happening all over again. Clutching the table, she felt the little bit of juice she'd managed to get down curdle in her stomach.

"No, Cassie, it isn't like that. He's not running away. He said he had some business to take care of, that's all.

He's coming back." She scooted closer and grabbed Cassie's hand, squeezing it in reassurance. "Listen, you have to be logical. Even if he wasn't in love with you—and I know he is—his job, his apartment and his mom are all here. He's not going to just walk away from all that, right?"

Breathing carefully, Cassie worked to calm herself. Jillian was right. He had to come back. Alex had responsibilities here that he wouldn't abandon in the middle of the night. He had an apartment full of stuff and a job that expected him. Of course, he could be out looking for a new job and a new apartment. Just because he was coming back didn't mean he was planning to stay. "Did he say anything about what he was doing, or where he was going?"

"No, he didn't. He said he couldn't say anything yet. But Cassie, you're going to make yourself crazy if you keep imagining the worst. Alex is a good man, and you know it. You've got to give him some slack, give him a chance to prove himself to you."

Could she do that? Could she put aside her trust issues and hope for the best? Or would she just be setting herself up for even more heartbreak?

Alex's flight landed right on time, setting down on a small runway in what seemed like the middle of the ocean. Grabbing his carry-on bag from the overhead compartment, he made his way off the surprisingly small plane and stood in line at the customs checkpoint. Traveling from Florida to the Bahamas was commonplace, and the whole procedure took only a few minutes. Outside, he entered the first car in a line of

waiting taxis and instructed the driver to take him to
the Harbor Bay Marina.

His sources had indicated the charter boat Tony was
working on operated out of that marina. The charter
company's website said it specialized in half-day trips,
morning and evening, which meant it should be docked
for the next hour or so between sessions. That should
be plenty of time to have a one-on-one chat with the
deadbeat dad. He didn't want to waste more time on
this guy than he had to.

Paying the driver with American dollars wasn't a
problem, since Bahamian dollars were pegged to the
American dollar, so both were equal in value and accepted everywhere in the small country. Finding the
right boat was a bit more difficult. His information
didn't include the slip number. He did have the boat's
name, though, and hopefully someone would be able to
point him in the right direction. Otherwise, he'd have
to wander around hoping to find it, and with hundreds
of vessels docked in the marina, it could be back out
on the open ocean long before he finished his search.

Turning slowly, Alex scanned the marina in an attempt to get his bearings. Five long wooden docks
stretched out into the turquoise water where boats of
different sizes and shapes were docked. Set back from
the water was a cluster of buildings. There was what
looked to be a restaurant with indoor and outdoor seat-
ing, a store selling tourist-style clothing, and another,
smaller shop that looked to be more of a bait and tackle
store. He headed for that one, assuming that a fishing
charter would at least occasionally need to buy supplies from there.

A buzzing fluorescent bulb and large open windows

lighted the store. Narrow aisles offered a dizzying array of equipment, some of which he knew to be top-of-the-line. Striding toward the back of the store, he noted that it seemed clean and well kept, despite the lingering smell of salt and fish. At the rear counter he found an elderly man with dark, weathered skin and close-cropped silver hair playing solitaire.

"Need some bait?" he asked while slapping down cards.

"No, but I could use some help. I'm looking for a boat, the *Marlin's Lair.* Do you know where I could find it?"

"You looking to charter a trip?"

"Something like that."

The old man's bushy eyebrows narrowed. "Maybe you could explain why you're lookin' and then maybe I can tell you where to look."

Deciding honesty would work better than a lie, Alex nodded. "I'm looking for someone. Do you know a Tony Williams?"

"I do." His tone implied he wasn't happy about the fact.

Sensing an ally, Alex laid it out for him. "He's got a little girl. She's four and has never met him, never gotten any support from him. Her mama seems to think that's for the best, and the look on your face tells me she's right. If that's the case, I'm here to find out if he's willing to keep staying away and put it in writing. If he's not, then I need to know that, too."

The shopkeeper's gaze was sharp and assessing. "I'm thinking the girl and her mama mean something to you, yes?"

Alex swallowed hard. "They mean everything to me."

"I thought so." He smiled and shuffled his cards while he talked. "If Tony's working today, and with that one you never know, he'll be at slip fifty-six. He's blond, kind of skinny, probably looks hungover."

Grateful for the help and the silent vote of confidence, Alex said goodbye and walked back out into the blazing sunlight. Even in mid-February, the temperature was nearing eighty degrees, although the ocean breeze kept it from feeling too warm. Making his way down the seawall, he kept his eyes on the slip numbers. The second long dock held slips fifty to one hundred, and a few spots down he could see a fishing boat matching the description of the *Marlin's Lair*.

Shading his eyes, he watched for signs of anyone on board as he walked down the rough wooden planks toward the boat. No one was in sight, but there was a radio blaring from somewhere below deck. Now what? Go aboard and see what happened, or wait for someone to come out? Time wasn't his friend, but boarding a strange ship unannounced probably wasn't the smartest move.

Movement near the bow of the boat caught his eye. Someone was coming around from the far side, a rag and cleaner in his hands. He was tall and lanky with sun-bleached hair falling in his eyes. He fit the description, but was it Tony? Only one way to tell.

"Tony Williams?"

"Yeah, I'm Tony."

"Mind if I come aboard?" Not waiting for an answer, he stepped onto the deck.

Setting down the rag in his hand, Tony flipped the hair out of his eyes and squinted at Alex. "Do I know you?"

"No, but we do have a mutual acquaintance. I'm a friend of Cassie Marshall's."

Shock and then panic flashed across the man's face. "What the hell? I haven't even talked to her since—"

"Since you found out she was pregnant?" Alex stepped in closer and caught the familiar scent of old booze and desperation. He'd smelled that same ugly combination on his father more times than he could count. Pity mixed with the anger already churning in his gut. The guy had abandoned his daughter, and for what? To drink and party his way into an early grave?

As Tony shuffled backward, his eyes darted back and forth, no doubt looking for an escape route. "What, you looking to run away again? You seem to be pretty good at that. What I want to know is, are you going to stay lost? Or does Cassie need to get her lawyer working on Plan B?"

"Plan B? What the hell is that?"

Alex smiled, his thumbs in his belt loops. "It's where she adds up all the child support you owe, and you start paying it."

"You gotta be kidding me. Listen, I was young. I couldn't take care of a kid—"

"You were older than Cassie, and she still had to do it. Without you. And she'll keep doing it without you, but she's worried you're going to show up one day and decide to play daddy dearest."

"What? What the hell would I do that for? I haven't bothered her yet, have I?"

Bothered? How about hadn't paid child support, helped out, or made any effort to bond with his daughter? "I guess she thought you might want to get to know your daughter at some point."

Tony shook his head. "She doesn't need a guy like me screwing up her life. And I don't have a lot of time, you know, for stuff like that. I'm fine just doing my own thing, and they can do theirs."

"I can see that, but legally, it doesn't work that way."

"What do you mean?"

"What I mean is, in the eyes of the law, you're her father."

"No, man, I'm telling you. I'm not cut out for the father thing, you know?"

"Unless you sign away your rights, it doesn't matter if you're cut out for it or not."

"Wait, I can sign something, and that's it? I don't have to pay anything or do anything?"

"If that's what you want. It would mean you agree you have no more rights as her father. No custody, nothing."

Tony's face blanched. "Custody? I don't even know where I'm going to be staying half the time. I don't want any kind of custody. You tell Cassie to give me the papers and I'll sign them. I just want to be left alone."

Chapter Eighteen

Cassie tucked Emma into her bed, smoothing sheets that would inevitably end up tossed on the floor by the morning. "I was thinking we might go by Grandma and Grandpa's tomorrow after church. Would you like that?"

Emma nodded and snuggled farther down under the covers. "That will be fun."

Fun for Emma. Not so much for Cassie. Having to tell them she was pregnant again wasn't on her top-ten list of ways to have a good time. But it had to be done. Her father was scheduled to come back to work on Monday and it wouldn't take him long to figure it out, considering she couldn't take X-rays while she was pregnant. And she'd need to be a little more careful of lifting, as well. With her dad not fully up to par and both her and Jillian pregnant, things were going to get interesting pretty quickly; in fact, they'd probably have to hire some extra help. Nothing about any of this was going to be simple, but then, nothing ever was.

Except her love for Emma. Leaning down, she pressed a kiss to Emma's forehead, smelling the baby shampoo she still used. "Good night, baby. Sleep tight."

"Night, Mommy," Emma mumbled, her eyes already closed. After spending a good portion of the day at the Sandpiper playing with the dogs, her little girl was worn out. Someday they'd get their own dog, but not now with a baby on the way. Housebreaking a puppy and changing diapers with only a four-year-old to help didn't sound like a very good plan.

Leaving Emma to sleep, she wandered the house, feeling lost. Laundry was piling up in the hampers, the dishwasher was ready to be emptied and there were bills to pay. All the normal things she'd neglected this weekend needed to be done, and she didn't have the energy or motivation for any of it. But avoidance wasn't a valid strategy, not even for housework. Grabbing a basket, she started with the laundry. Her scrubs and Emma's school clothes went into the washer, then the fancy smelling detergent she splurged on. Everyone said the generic stuff worked just as well, but when your job entailed blood and bodily fluids, it was nice to know your clothes smelled pretty.

She'd just closed the lid and turned the machine on when she heard a knock at the door. It was half past eight; who on earth would be stopping by on a Saturday evening? Mollie, maybe; she sometimes came by when she needed help with her college chemistry class. But usually she called first. More curious than concerned, Cassie set the basket on top of the washer and went to look.

More knocking had her gritting her teeth. Whoever

it was, they had better not wake up Emma. She normally was a sound sleeper, but still, there was no need to pound like that. Throwing open the door, she started to say so, and froze. Alex. Now, that was unexpected.

He looked like hell with bloodshot eyes and wrinkled clothes and somehow still made her knees weak. "Can I come in?"

Wordlessly, she let him pass, closing the door behind him. She wanted to go to him. It would feel so good to just lean into him, let him carry some of the worries that weighed her down. Instead she stood her ground, hands on hips, and waited.

"How are you? Are you feeling okay?"

Damn it. Staying strong was hard enough without him being all nice. "I'm fine. I have to admit, I was surprised to see Rex at Jillian's today. I wasn't sure what I was expecting from you after last night, but you leaving town wasn't it. Although, given my limited experience, maybe I should have."

Alex winced as if she'd dealt him a physical blow. "I'm so sorry. I thought I'd be back before you even knew I was gone."

"No, it's fine. You needed some space or something." At least he came back.

Fiddling with the manila envelope in his hands, he took a step toward her. "Actually, I just had something I had to take care of. Something that involves you and Emma." He handed her the envelope. "I had an attorney friend of mine draw these up. I hope that's okay. She's good. I trust her."

An attorney? Was he filing for custody already? She took the paperwork, hating that her hands shook. "Maybe I should just have my lawyer look this over later."

"I'd really like you to read it, please. It's important."

Giving in, she sank onto the couch, tucking her feet up under her. In front of her, Alex paced with the nervous energy of someone who had passed exhaustion hours ago. Whatever this was, he seemed to have put a heck of a lot of effort into getting it. Unfastening the little metal clasp, she slid out the stack of papers inside. Most of it was a jumble of legalese, but the purpose of the forms was clear. At the top, printed in bold letters, were the words Petition for Termination of Parental Rights. Tears blurred her vision, obscuring the rest of the document, not that she needed to see more. He was abandoning this baby, just like her ex had abandoned Emma. With more class, maybe, but in the end, the result was the same.

"You didn't waste much time, did you?"

"When something needs to be done, I do it. I thought you'd be grateful to have things wrapped up, finally."

Finally? It had been only one day. He'd found out she was pregnant and found a lawyer to write up papers to rid himself of the problem in one day. And on a weekend, no less. He couldn't even wait until Monday, when the offices would be open. No, he went God knows where to track down someone who could do it on a Saturday. So much for giving him the benefit of the doubt or thinking he was too responsible to walk out on his own child. She should have been listening to his words, not her heart. He'd told her he wasn't ready to be a father and now he wanted to put it in writing.

Shoving up from the couch, she threw the papers down, resisting the petty urge to stomp on them. "You can take your damn papers, Alex. I'm not signing anything."

* * *

"What?" Alex stood amid the papers scattered on the floor and tried to figure out when the woman he loved had completely lost her mind. Her face was flushed with anger and if looks could kill, he'd need his Kevlar vest. Was she upset that he'd gotten involved in her private life? Or had she been wanting her ex to come back, after all? "I thought this was what you wanted."

Her eyes grew wider as she stared at him, tears streaming down her face. "What? Why would you think I wanted this?"

"Well, when we talked about Emma and her father, you said you worried he'd come back one day—"

"So you decided to make sure I never had to worry about that with you?" She stomped off to the kitchen and he followed at a cautious distance. Knives were in the kitchen, after all. She'd filled the kettle and set it on the stove before her words penetrated his brain.

"Wait, what? What do you mean, worry about it with me? What does this have to do with us?"

She slammed her mug down so hard, he half expected it to crack in her hand. "Signing away your rights to this baby has everything to do with us. How on earth can you think otherwise?"

His rights? "I'm not signing anything away."

Exasperated, she pointed back at the living room. "Then why did you get the papers drawn up? Are you just messing with me? Because it's not funny."

His sleep-deprived brain finally started to make the connection. "You think the papers are about our baby?"

"Who else would they be for?"

Rounding the counter, he put his hands on her shoulders, steadying her. "Tony signed those, not me.

I tracked him down, and he's willing to give up his rights, permanently."

Cassie went boneless under his hands, nearly collapsing. Propping her up, he led her to a stool at the counter before letting her go to turn off the now-screeching kettle.

"You found Tony? When? How?" Blinking rapidly, she stared at him. "And more than that, why? Why would you do that?"

"One thing at a time." He poured the water into her mug and added a tea bag from the canister on the counter. Pushing it toward her, he sat down on the other stool. "I started looking for him a little while ago. I have some contacts down south, private investigators and such, and I thought they might be able to track him down. And I talked to a woman I know from the district attorney's office in Miami. She works for a private practice now and has a reputation for protecting kids. I wanted to find out what the options were—she's the one who drew up the legal forms. When you told me you were pregnant I decided to push forward."

Emma swallowed hard. "Don't you think you should have discussed this with me first?"

"Maybe. Probably. But at first I didn't know where he was. And then, last night—well, you weren't in the mood to discuss things. Besides, I didn't want to get your hopes up if I couldn't find him. But I did find him, working on a boat in the Bahamas. He's been there ever since he left, probably afraid that if he came back to the States, you'd make him pay child support."

"So that's where you were today? You flew to the Bahamas?"

He nodded.

She rubbed at her eyes, exhaustion showing on her face. She didn't look as if she'd slept much more than he had. "We can talk about it tomorrow," he said, "if you're too tired—"

"No. I want to know the whole story. What did you say to him? What did he say? What does he want?"

"I told him I knew you and his daughter, and you deserved to know if he was coming back. I also reminded him that he owed quite a bit of child support. As for what he wants, he just wants to be left alone. He has no interest in custody or anything else and said to tell you he'd sign whatever he has to sign."

"So that's it? He signed the papers and he's out of our lives for good?"

"Basically, yeah. I mean, the judge has to approve it, but given the circumstances it shouldn't be a problem."

"I know I should say thank you, but I can't even wrap my head around this yet. And the dumb thing is, part of me is sad. Not because I want to see him," she added quickly. "But it sucks that he couldn't pull it together enough to be there for her, that he doesn't even want to know her or anything."

"That's not dumb at all. It is sad, but from where I sit, he's the one missing out." He placed his hand on hers, stroking her soft skin with this thumb. "No man in his right mind could walk away from you and Emma."

Cassie's pulse pounded in her ears. Was he trying to say he wasn't going to walk away? This was way too much information way too fast, and she couldn't think straight with him touching her. Pulling her hand away, she stood up and headed for the patio. Maybe some fresh air would help her clear her mind so she could make sense of everything.

Behind her, she heard Alex let out a low whistle as he stepped outside. "This is amazing."

Smiling, she sat down on her favorite chair. "It is pretty wonderful, isn't it?"

"It's like something out of a magazine. You could charge admission."

She gave a mock shudder at the thought. "I don't think so. This is where I come to get away from everything. No tourists allowed."

"Well, then, I'm honored to be allowed into the inner sanctuary."

"You should be," she said with a grin. It was crazy how easy he was to be around. After all the stress of the day and the shock of his news, she should have been a basket case. But being near him somehow helped put her mind at ease. Which *was* crazy, considering most of her stress could be traced back to him.

"Are you okay? I know this was what you wanted, but like you said, it's still a big deal."

"I'll be okay. But I have to know. What made you decide to get involved? Why go to all this trouble?"

He pulled a chair over, the metal legs scraping across the concrete. As he sat down, his brown eyes shone with an intensity she hadn't seen before. "I didn't decide to get involved. I already am involved. Up to my eyebrows. But I knew you couldn't move forward—we couldn't move forward—if you were constantly looking over your shoulder, waiting for your past to show up and ruin things. I wanted to give us a fresh start."

"Us?"

He leaned closer, taking both of her hands in his.

"Yes, us. You, me, Emma…and the baby. Our baby. Whatever happens, I'm not running away. I'm not your ex, and I'm not my father."

"But…" Her brain stuttered and stalled. "I thought you didn't want children. You said you were scared—"

"I am scared. Hell, I'm terrified." He grinned and squeezed her hands. "But just because something is scary doesn't mean I'm going to turn tail and run. I've faced down drug dealers and gang bangers. I think I can handle an unarmed baby."

"Really?"

"Really. I admit the idea of being a father frightens me. But you know what frightens me more?"

She shook her head, emotion a lump in her throat.

"Losing my chance with you."

"You still want to be with me?" Maybe she'd heard wrong, misunderstood. She'd been doing a lot of that lately.

"If you'll have me." His voice was rough but sensual, like the ocean during a storm. Goose bumps dotted her arms as if he was already touching her.

"You're sure?" she whispered, afraid of breaking the spell if she spoke too loudly or moved too quickly.

Alex's words, on the other hand, were loud and clear. "I've never been more sure of anything in my life." He drew her into his lap, settling her against the hard planes of his body. "I'm not saying it's going to be easy. I don't know how it's all going to work, but I know that I want to try."

Curling into him, she let herself feel all the things she'd been denying. He was there, he wasn't leaving and he felt so very good pressed against her in the dark. Turning her head toward him, she looked for something in his eyes to tell her this was a mistake. But all she saw were sincerity, trust and a longing that matched her own. He'd made no promises for the future, but his pledge to try meant more than any declaration of love could. Honesty was what she needed, not pretty words.

"Would it be okay if I kiss you now? I've been dying to since our dance last night." His breath tickled her ear as he spoke, sending little sparks up and down her spine.

In answer, she reached up and brought his lips down hard on hers, kissing him with all the pent-up fear and hope and worry and love that had tangled her up in knots. He met her intensity with his own heat and passion. Everything she didn't know how to say, she said with her lips against his, her body molding against him. Only when she was afraid she might actually explode with need did she pull away, panting in his arms.

"Wow." His eyes had gone nearly black under the starlight, and she could feel his heart pounding through his chest. "If leaving town for the day results in that kind of treatment, I'm going to be gone a whole lot."

She smacked him on the arm. "Not funny."

He winced. "I suppose not. Chalk it up to my lack of sleep. I'm running on empty, and as good as that kiss was, I should get myself home before I'm too tired to drive."

He was leaving already? She'd pictured something much more...well...intimate happening. "You could stay."

"I can't. I called Nic when I landed and told him I'd be by soon to pick up Rex. Besides, there's Emma. I don't want our first conversation about us to be when she wakes up and finds me in your bed. That's not fair to her."

She sighed. "You're right. I don't want that, either. You just make me so crazy, I can't think straight."

"Good." He kissed the tip of her nose. "I love that you're just as affected as I am. Now, you're going to have to get out of my lap or I'm never going to be able to make myself go."

Sliding out of his lap, she could feel exactly how much he wanted to stay. "When will I see you again?"

"Is tomorrow soon enough?"

Alex watched Cassie's face turn serious. "Actually, we have plans tomorrow."

"Oh." Maybe he'd read her wrong and she was still mad?

"No, don't be upset. I do want to see you, but we are going to my parents' house tomorrow after church." She laid a hand on her still-flat belly. "I need to tell them about the baby."

"Tomorrow?" Heck, he'd just found out himself; he'd thought he would have a little time to get used to the idea before they started telling people. Not that he was ashamed, but he would have liked to have a plan, and ideally a ring, before that news got out.

Cassie grimaced. "I know. I'm not wild about everyone finding out, either. But my dad's coming back to work on Monday, and I won't be able to hide it. There are safety issues, with radiation and anesthesia and such."

He hadn't even thought of that. He'd been so wrapped up in his own baggage, he hadn't even considered how she would juggle the pregnancy with her career. "Is it safe for you to keep working? Because if it's about the money, I can—"

"Don't worry. I'll be safe. I just have to take a few extra precautions. Which means I have to tell my dad now, and he can't keep a secret from my mom to save his life, so I might as well tell both of them at once. I'm not exactly looking forward to it, but it is what it is. They need to know. Might as well get it over with."

"Then I'll go with you." This was as much his doing as hers, and if she was brave enough to face her parents, the least he could do was be there to support her.

"What? No, you don't have to do that."

"I know I don't have to, but I want to. I should be there for you. And your parents need to know that I'm going to be a part of this baby's life, and yours, if you let me. After Tony, I think I may have my work cut out for me."

She grinned. "They already love you. After you found Emma...trust me, liking you isn't a problem. I'm the one that they'll be disappointed in. Again."

"You've got to be kidding me. How could anyone be disappointed in you? You've raised an amazing little girl on your own and made an impressive career for yourself. I can't imagine they are anything but impressed by you."

Shadows clouded her eyes, but she nodded. "Maybe. We'll see, I guess. But are you sure you want to do this?"

Did he want to? Not exactly. But she needed to do this, so he needed to be there. They were a team now, whether she realized it or not. "I'll be there. Just tell me when and where."

"We'll go after the ten o'clock service, if that's all right. Emma doesn't want to miss Sunday school."

"I'll be there. I already arranged to have the rest of the weekend off."

"Well, okay, then." She looked at the door, then at him, as if trying to find another reason for him to stay. A feeling he shared, but couldn't give in to. But if he had his way, there wouldn't be too many more late-night goodbyes.

"Good night, Cassie." He gave her a soft, lingering kiss that only reminded him how much he wanted to stay. Still tasting her, he pressed a hand to her belly. "Good night, baby. Don't give your mama too hard a time, okay?"

Cassie bit her lip, tears shining in her eyes. He hated that she was so surprised by the smallest bit of affection from him. Knowing how hurt she'd been made him want to go right back to the Bahamas and feed Tony to the sharks. Giving her one last quick kiss on the forehead, he let himself out while he still could.

Outside the stars were shining as if they'd been polished, each a bright pinprick of light against the dark island sky. Getting in the truck, he wondered again at the circumstances that had brought him here. If his partner hadn't screwed up, if he and his fellow officers hadn't betrayed him, if the Palmetto County sheriff's office hadn't had an opening at just the right time, he might never have come to Paradise, never met Cassie or Emma. Now, driving through the quiet streets on the way to pick up his dog, he couldn't imagine living anywhere else.

Paradise had given him a place to lick his wounds, to start over. But the island was more than a temporary sanctuary; it had become a real home. Maybe part of that was meeting Cassie; it was hard to say. Both the woman and the place had seduced him, and he had no intentions of letting go of either one.

At the Sandpiper, he walked quietly up the stairs and through the front door. The front desk was vacant, but lying in front of the fireplace in the main lobby were Rex and Murphy, both passed out. In a similar state, Nic was sprawled on one of the loveseats, eyes closed and an open book on his chest. The dogs noticed Alex first. Rex stretched like a cat, then rolled over for a belly rub. "Wow, I'm gone all day and you don't even bother to get up and say hello?"

A rumble from the couch drew his attention back to Nic, who was now sitting up and rubbing his eyes. "So, how did it go? Did you find him?"

"I did. I even got a bit of help from a local. It seems he's not very well liked down there."

"Imagine that." Nic stood and stretched. "So, what did he say?"

"He signed away his rights. He'd do anything to avoid paying all the child support he owes. You know, he didn't even ask about Emma. Didn't want to know how she's doing or see a picture. Nothing." At least Alex's old man had tried. He'd cared, but it just hadn't been enough. "If nothing else, I can understand now why Cassie was so sure Emma was better off without him."

Nic nodded and walked to the kitchen, snagging a couple of sodas from the fridge and handing one to Alex. "How did Cassie take the news?"

"Not well at first. She saw the papers and thought I was giving up my rights to our baby."

"Oh, wow. Way to mess that up."

"No kidding. But once I explained, everything was

fine. Better than fine." He smiled, thinking of that amazing kiss on the patio.

"Hot damn, good for you. So, when's the wedding?"

Alex coughed, spewing soda down the front of his shirt. Nic laughed and handed him a towel.

"Don't tell me you haven't thought about it. Remember, I proposed to Jillian not long ago, so I know the signs."

No point in pretending. "Fine, yes, I'm thinking about it. But I don't know if she's ready yet. I want things to be right."

"Dude, she's in love with you and she's pregnant with your child. What else are you waiting for?"

Chapter Nineteen

Nic's words haunted him. Tossing and turning all night, he asked himself this: What was he waiting for? He loved her. He was certain of that. And he wanted them to be a family. Fatherhood hadn't been the plan, but if he was going to do it, he wanted to do it right. Part-time wasn't enough, not after all the time he'd missed out on with his own father. He wanted to be there when Cassie felt the first kicks, to rub her feet when they hurt or buy her ice cream when she craved it. And most of all, he wanted to make love to her every night and wake up to her soft body against his each morning.

Which was why he was up and knocking on his mother's door at what felt like the break of dawn. Scratching at his two-day beard, he waited for the door to open. Hopefully he'd caught her before she left for Mass.

"Alex?" His mother's worried face appeared at the open door. "What are you doing here so early? Is everything okay?"

"It's fine, Mama. I just needed to talk to you about something."

Relaxing, she accepted a hug and shooed him toward the kitchen. "There's coffee ready, and I'll make us some breakfast while you tell me what's so important."

"Just coffee, please. I'm not hungry."

She pinned him with a hard stare. "Not hungry? Are you sick?"

"No, Mama, I'm not sick. I'm fine, in fact. I promise."

She scrutinized him as if looking for some sign of illness before turning away to pour the coffee. "This is about your animal-doctor friend, then, yes?"

How did she always know? He accepted the cup of strong, rich coffee and took a sip, waiting for her to sit at the table with him. Instead, she stood over him, watching with the same sharp gaze that had intimidated him as a child. This time, however, he wasn't confessing some childish sin.

"So? What is it that has you so tied up in knots you can't even eat your mama's cooking? Did you mess things up with her? Because if you did, you need to face up to it and make it right."

There was no way to say this, other than just to say it. "She's pregnant, Mama."

His mother narrowed her lips, considering. "And are you the father?"

"Yes, ma'am." He was in for it now; he'd sat through enough lectures as a teenager to know her feelings about premarital sex and unintended pregnancies.

"Oh, Alex." Tears filled her eyes as she smiled. "A baby? I'm going to be a grandmother?"

Stunned, he nodded as she fanned her eyes. Wasn't she supposed to be yelling at him? "I thought you'd be upset. Because of what the Church says and—"

"The Church says babies are a blessing. And that's what this baby will be. Anything else is water under the bridge."

The knotted muscles in his shoulders released a bit. He hadn't quite realized how worried he'd been about her reaction until now. "Thank you for being so supportive. It means a lot."

She smacked his shoulder, tears still slipping down her face. "Don't be silly. I'm your mama. Now, are you ready for breakfast, or is there more?"

"Well, there is one other thing." He grinned. "I wanted to ask about Grandma's ring. I'm going to ask Cassie to marry me."

His mother wrapped her arms around him, nearly smothering him in her enthusiasm. "Mom, you're choking me."

She gave a final squeeze, then stood up, smiling as if he'd won the Nobel Prize and the World Series all on the same day. "A wedding and a baby. The ladies at the senior center are going to be so jealous."

"You're going to have to hold off on bragging for now. She hasn't said yes yet. And she doesn't want to tell people about the pregnancy right away, I don't think. We haven't even told her parents yet. I'm meeting her over there for lunch."

Her face fell a bit, but she nodded. "Then I'll wait. Oh, let me go get you the ring."

He finished his coffee while she rummaged in her

bedroom. Who'd have thought his strict, super-religious mother would have reacted so well? He knew he was doing the right thing, but it was nice to know he had her support.

"Here you are. Your grandfather gave it to your grandmother, and she gave it to me. Now you will give it to Cassie." She placed the small plain box on the table in front of him. Opening it, he found the ring as he remembered it—a brilliant round diamond resting in an antique setting. Hand-wrought scrollwork covered the elegant platinum band, and inside was inscribed the word *Forever*. He could buy a new ring, but somehow he thought Cassie would appreciate the significance of a family heirloom.

"Thank you. It's beautiful. She has to say yes now."

"She'll say yes because she loves you. I was trying not to pry, but I saw you at the Sandpiper the other night on the dance floor. She looked at you the way a woman looks at the man she loves."

"I hope so." He didn't know what he'd do if she said no. Which was why he wasn't going to ask until he'd had time to prove himself to her. He couldn't risk rushing her and pushing her away.

"Remember, don't say anything. We'll tell her parents today about the baby, but then she needs some time. I'm not going to rush her, so you're just going to have to be patient."

"I won't say a thing. Now go get cleaned up before you go over there. You look like something the cat dragged in."

"Gee, thanks." Between her and Nic, his ego was taking a beating. "You sure know how to flatter a guy."

She waved her finger at him. "You don't need flattery. You need a shower and a shave. Maybe a haircut, too. I can get my scissors—"

"No, no, that's okay. I'll take care of it." He put the ring in his pocket and gave her a hug goodbye. He was grateful for her support, but right now the woman he needed to see was Cassie.

Cassie bowed her head for the closing prayer, adding her "Amen" to those of the congregation. Once the organ belted out the final hymn, she made her way up the aisle to the main doors, dodging the line of people waiting to shake hands with the priest. Normally she would join the throngs that stood around chatting after the service, but today she was too keyed up.

Emma was just finishing up her snack when Cassie got to her classroom to pick her up. Her craft for the week, an angel with glittery wings, was drying on the table next to her. "Hey, sweetie, time to go to Grandma and Grandpa's house."

Emma sucked the last of her juice from the little cardboard box and nodded. After saying her goodbyes she walked out with Cassie, clutching her masterpiece, as if it were made of jewels instead of glue and glitter. "Can I give my angel to Grandma?"

"Sure, honey. I bet she'd like that." Loading her into the car seat, Cassie was careful not touch the glue on Emma's still-wet creation. "Oh, and Deputy Alex is going to be there, too. Is that okay?"

The little girl's eyes lit up. "Yay! Is he going to bring Rex, too?"

"I don't know. Maybe." Starting the car, she headed toward her parents' home on the outskirts of town. Butterflies flew a serpentine pattern in her stomach as she got closer, a combination of nerves, anticipation and hormones. Rolling her window down helped. The rush of fresh salt air settled her stomach and cleared her head, leaving just the excitement of seeing Alex again. She needed to know that what happened last night wasn't a dream. It had seemed real last night, but in the light of day it was hard to believe.

Turning into the driveway, she spotted Alex's SUV parked by the house. He was early—maybe he was as eager to see her as she was to see him. Pulse thrumming, she let Emma out of the car and headed up the walk. They were still a few feet from the house when a loud bark announced their presence.

"Rex is here!" Emma broke into a run, her paper project fluttering in her hand.

"Hey, there." Alex opened the front door and watched Emma fly by him to look for her furry friend. "I guess I know which of us she really wanted to see." He smiled at Cassie, his dimples doing dangerous things to her heart.

"Sorry. Don't take it personally."

"I won't." He leaned down and gave her a quick kiss, then took hold of her hand. "I missed you."

Her cheeks heated. "I missed you, too. I was afraid I'd dreamed last night."

He lowered his voice so only she could hear. "Honey, if last night had been a dream, it would have ended with us in bed, not with me leaving to pick up my dog."

Every nerve ending flared. How was she going to get through today with that thought tormenting her?

"Cassie, there you are. Come on back. Alex was helping me man the grill."

Startled, she tried to drop Alex's hand, but he kept a firm grip.

"I don't want to hide, Cassie. Especially given the circumstances. Unless you have some reason you don't want people to know about us?"

"No, it's not that. I'm just…surprised, I guess. I'm not used to thinking of us as, well, an *us*." He'd said he wanted to make things work, to be with her, but what did that mean, really? One minute she was rude to him, the next he saved her daughter, and now they were having a kid together. Where in all of that did holding hands fit in?

Apparently not as prone to overthinking as she was, Alex pulled her along with him to the back patio. At the far end, sweet-smelling smoke wafted from the grill. Down on the grass, Emma was playing some kind of elaborate game with Rex involving a half dozen tennis balls and a soccer net.

Her father turned from cooking the food when they came out, his eyes widening a fraction when he saw them holding hands. Looking from one to the other, he raised an eyebrow. "Elizabeth, why don't you come out here and join us?"

Her mother stepped out onto the patio, wearing a striped apron over her jeans and blouse. "What is it, David? I'm not done with the coleslaw yet."

He reached into his wallet and pulled out a ten-dollar bill. "I just wanted to pay up on our little bet."

"Bet?" Cassie glared at her father. "What bet?"

Her mother took the money and tucked it into her apron pocket. "Your father was being hardheaded and wouldn't listen when I told him you two were falling for each other." She shrugged. "Anyone could see it."

Cassie's mouth dropped open. They'd bet on her love life?

"Sorry I cost you a bet, sir," Alex said with a grin.

"No worries. You making my daughter happy is worth more than all the money in the world. Just take good care of her."

Alex cleared his throat and squared his shoulders. "I fully intend to, sir. Her and the baby."

"Excuse me?" Her father's shocked tone matched the look on her mother's face. "Baby?"

Stepping forward, Cassie met his gaze head-on. "I'm pregnant, Daddy. I'm sorry."

"Sorry. What do you mean, sorry?" Her mother waved away the apology. "You've always said you wanted a sibling for Emma someday. And we've always wanted more grandchildren, haven't we, David?"

At her mother's heated look, he quickly capitulated. "Of course we have. I was just surprised a bit, that's all. You two haven't known each other that long and—"

"And nothing, David Andrew Marshall. Love has its own timing, doesn't it, honey?" She held out her arms and Cassie accepted the hug, her eyes filling. "Now, when is this little bundle of joy going to make an appearance? We have so much to plan—a baby shower, your registry—"

"A wedding," Alex said.

"What did you say?" Cassie asked. She couldn't have heard that right. Except her parents looked as stunned as she felt.

"A wedding." He moved directly in front of Cassie, his gaze never wavering from hers. "I was planning to ask you later, when things calmed down." He shrugged. "It kind of slipped out."

"It slipped out? What on earth is that supposed to

mean?" She heard the hysteria in her voice, but didn't particularly care. What did he expect with an announcement like that?

He ran a hand through his hair and took a deep breath. "It means that I messed up and got everything out of order, again." He turned to Cassie's father. "Sir, I'd planned to talk to you and Mrs. Marshall and ask for your blessing. Heck, I wanted to talk to Emma, too, and feel her out on the idea."

"And when was all this supposed to happen?" Cassie asked. Everything was happening so fast. Just last night she'd thought he was running out on her; now he wanted to marry her?

"Not for a while. I thought you needed some time to adjust to the idea of us being together, to learn to trust me."

"I do trust you. I know I haven't acted like it, but I do."

"Well, then, maybe it's better this way. I know it's fast, but Cassie, I don't want to wait. I know what I want, and I want you."

Dumbfounded, she watched him pull a small box out of his pocket and get down on one knee.

Behind him, Emma climbed up the steps to come lean against Cassie's side. "What's he doing, Mommy? Did he fall down?"

Alex smiled at her. "I did fall, for you and your mommy. In fact, I'm head over heels in love with both of you."

Emma tilted her head, looking for injuries. "Are you going to be okay?"

"Well, that depends."

Heart thumping wildly, Cassie let him take her hand.

Everything was happening in slow motion; even the birds seemed to have stopped chirping. "Cassie Marshall, you've already filled my heart and changed my life. I don't want to ever give that up. Please, will you marry me?"

"Mommy, say yes," Emma said in a stage whisper, her eyes like saucers.

Cassie hugged the little girl and whispered back, "I don't know. You think he might make an okay daddy?"

Emma nodded. "The best, and he'll bring Rex, too!"

Laughing, Cassie looked back down at Alex. "In that case, yes, Alex Santiago, I'll marry you." She winked at Emma. "But you have to bring Rex with you."

Chapter Twenty

Cassie pulled the last pin from her hair and breathed a sigh of relief. The fancy updo her mother had talked her into had turned out gorgeous, but she felt more herself with her curls loose around her shoulders. Across the room, Alex watched, his eyes smoky with desire. Sprawled on the bed, his bow tie long gone and his tuxedo shirt open at the neck, he was the sexiest man she'd ever seen. And as of a few hours ago, he was her husband.

She'd wanted a small, quiet ceremony, but between her mother and Alex's mom, who was possibly the sweetest woman on the planet, she'd been outvoted. Almost half the island had ended up in attendance. At least she'd gotten her way with the location. They'd been married in her parents' backyard, only a month after Alex had proposed. Tomorrow, they'd be leaving for their honeymoon, a trip to Puerto Rico to meet some of Alex's relatives. But tonight Emma was with her grandparents, and she and Alex were finally alone.

"Think you could help me take off my dress?"

"I thought you'd never ask." In an instant, he was behind her. But before he had a single button undone, there was a knock at the door.

"Don't answer it."

"I have to. It could be my mom—something could be wrong with Emma. I'll be right back, I promise." She started for the front door, the silken skirt of her dress swishing as she walked.

Alex followed, padding barefoot down the hall. "Whoever it is, they had better be quick."

Silently agreeing, Cassie opened the door, then nearly slammed it shut again. Heart pounding, she stared at the man on the doorstep.

Behind her, Alex stiffened. "Who is it?"

Cassie opened the door the rest of the way, making room for Alex to stand beside her. "Jack Campbell, the man I told you about from the accident." Her voice shook, but she stood tall. She was not going to let him frighten her.

Alex stepped forward, positioning himself in front of Cassie. "You shouldn't be here, Jack."

Swallowing, Jack nodded, taking in Cassie's wedding dress and Alex's tux. "I'm sorry, I didn't realize... Well, I mean, I'd heard Dr. Marshall was getting married, but I didn't know it was today."

"Well, it was, and you're interrupting our wedding night. So if you would just go—"

"I will. I just need to say something to the doc first."

He peered around Alex to make eye contact with Cassie. "I just wanted to tell you I'm sorry—"

"Jack, I don't think now is the time—" Alex moved to close the door.

"No, it's okay." She'd spent too long thinking about this; she didn't want to bring it into her new life with Alex. "Let him have his say." Maybe then she could put it behind her.

Jack twisted his hands together. "I came to say I'm sorry about the accident. I'd been drinking that night. Hell, I drank every night. But I'm not drinking any-more—I'm in a program now. One of those twelve-step programs. And one of the steps is to admit my mistakes and try to make things right where I can. I admitted everything to the department, and they put me on a leave of absence." His voice cracked and his shoulders started to shake. "I can't fix what happened to you and your dad, but I'm going to make sure I don't hurt any-one else. I promise you that."

Cassie listened, waiting for the familiar surge of anger she felt whenever she even thought of Jack Camp-bell. She'd spent months convincing herself she hated him. Here he was, and all she felt was pity. "Thank you, Jack. That means a lot to me."

Alex wrapped an arm around her in support. "Stick with it, man. You have a family that needs you."

"I know, and I'm going to do right by them. Anyway, I'll leave you folks alone now. Oh, and congratulations." Backing down the walk, he grabbed an old bicycle and hopped on. Watching him ride off, she felt free. His con-fession had given her permission to move on.

"Are you okay?" Alex closed the door, checking that it was locked securely.

"I'm better than okay." She pressed her body against his, feeling the hard muscles of his chest against her breasts. "Now, are you going to make this marriage official or what?"

She barely had the words out before Alex stilled her lips with a kiss. Hungry for her, he teased at her lips, needing to taste her. She moaned into his mouth, pulling at his clothes. Without ending the kiss, he stripped his clothes off, giving her busy hands access to his body. Gritting his teeth against the throbbing need to take her, he pulled back.

"Let me undress you." Slowly, one by one, he undid the long line of pearl buttons, teasing himself with each peek at the skin beneath. As the last one gave way, the dress slid to the floor in a puddle of silk and lace. Dear Lord, she was completely nude underneath. "If I'd known you weren't wearing anything under this, I don't think I would have made it through the ceremony."

She turned, smiling, and his heart skipped a beat. This beautiful, sexy woman was his wife. The soft swell of her belly was his child. "Cassie…"

She came to him, pulling his head down to hers for a soft but sensual kiss. He couldn't wait any longer; she felt too good and he needed her too badly. Sweeping her up into his arms, he carried her down the hall to her bed—their bed now. Afraid of hurting her or the baby, he eased her down on top of him, letting her take control. The first time they'd made love, it had been frantic and out of control. This time, there was no rush, no fumbling, just her body and his, skin to skin and soul to soul until they melted together in a single moment of pure pleasure.

* * *

Near midnight, after yet another round of lovemaking, Cassie collapsed against Alex, loving the way her body fit perfectly against his. Tracing her fingers through his chest hair, she decided now was as good a time as any to ask the question that had been in the back of her mind ever since he proposed. "Alex?"

"Again?" he mumbled, half asleep.

"No. I mean, not now." She sat up, letting the covers fall away. "I wanted to ask you something important."

Rousing himself, he propped himself up on the pillows. "What is it?"

"There's something I've been wondering, and I haven't known how to bring it up."

"Just say it. You can ask me anything."

She took a deep breath, not wanting to spoil the mood but needing to know. "What would you say to the idea of adopting Emma? It wouldn't have to be now, but maybe you'd consider it? She's always wanted a father, and with the baby coming—"

Alex put a finger on her lips, silencing her. "I'd say that, as long as Emma wants me, too, I'd like nothing better. And that I already have an appointment scheduled with my lawyer for the day after we get back from our honeymoon."

Tears filled her eyes. "Have I told you lately what a good husband you are?"

He grinned and pulled her back down on top of him. "No, but I can think of a really fun way for you to show me."

* * * * *

SINGLE FATHER: WIFE AND MOTHER WANTED

SHARON ARCHER

Thank you to Anna Campbell, Rachel Bailey
and Marion Lennox—for your honesty when I
asked for your opinion, and for fun, friendship
and tons of encouragement.

Thanks, too, to my ever-patient medical friends,
Judy Griffiths and paramedic Bruce.

To Rhonda Smith, friend and neighbour, who
read this in an early draft and liked it!

To the members of Romance Writers
of Australia for support, above and beyond.

And to Glenn: husband, hero and believer!

CHAPTER ONE

GHOSTLY gum trees loomed in the fog then slid away to the side as Matt Gardiner drove cautiously through the deserted countryside. With visibility reduced to metres, the route looked unfamiliar. No chance of using the craggy peaks of the Grampians as a point of orientation this morning.

Beside him sat his ten-year-old son, uncharacteristically quiet. Nicky Gardiner was in big, big trouble. Matt suppressed a shudder at the thought of the dangerous game Nicky and his friend had devised to entertain themselves. At this point, grounding for life sounded good.

Finally, Matt spotted the hazard-warning triangle he'd put out earlier at the site of Jim Neilson's accident. He pulled onto the verge behind a tiny sports car.

The vehicle's driver was crossing to the fence where Jim's truck and horse float had ploughed through into the paddock beyond.

As he unbuckled his seat belt, Matt watched a figure pick a path across the green swathe that the runaway truck had slashed through the frost. An elegance of movement suggested the person could be a woman. Bundled up in a huge padded black jacket and hat, she looked more like the Michelin Man.

Seven-thirty. He felt like he'd been on the road for hours. Between yesterday morning's delivery of a slightly premature baby and last night's acute asthma attack in one of his younger patients, he was beyond tired. With the respiratory emergency resolved, he'd been on his way home more than an hour ago only to discover the sometime horse breeder's latest debacle.

Nothing had been straightforward. Poor phone reception had meant a trip into town to organise the tow truck instead of a simple phone call. Which, as it had happened, had worked out well since he'd been close by to deal with the fallout from the boys' adventure. An overnight stay with a mate had ended with a sword fight with real machetes, for heaven's sake. He tamped down another shiver at what could have happened to the would-be elf lords.

Matt glanced at his son, stifling the fresh words of censure that threatened to bound off his tongue. Instead, he managed to keep it mild. 'Stay in the car, Nicky. I'll be back in a minute.'

'Sure, Dad.' At least he sounded subdued. Like he might have realised he'd pushed his father too far.

Frigid air seared Matt's lungs when he stepped out of the warmth of his car.

Steady, rattling thumps were battering the foggy tranquillity. From the confines of the horse float, Jim's four-legged passenger didn't sound happy.

Matt rubbed his face, enjoying the momentary relief of chilled fingertips against the lids of his tired eyes. He wanted to go home to bed, snatch maybe a half-hour nap before starting work. He shrugged away thoughts of quilt-covered comfort. No chance of that this morning. Not now.

He tucked his hands into his pockets and trudged after the driver of the sports car.

Brittle spears of frosty grass crunched beneath his feet and his breath plumed in front of his face. Winter was reaching into the second month of spring to give inland Victoria one final taste of its power. Hard to believe another two months could see them sweltering in the heat of the Australian summer.

He saw Jim scramble out of the cab of the truck. Frustration was obvious in every movement of his barrel-like body as he stomped back towards the horse float.

As soon as he let the man know the tow truck would be at least two hours, Matt could take his son home. Take time to have a serious talk. His heart clenched tight. Didn't Nicky realise how precious every single hair on his head was?

Even Nicky's mother, a very absentee and uninterested parent, would take a dim view of their son getting stabbed.

Ahead, the newcomer paused by the tangled wreckage of the fence. 'Would you need a hand, then?' a husky female voice called into a small pocket of silence.

Matt's stride faltered and his breath caught at the sound of the lilting Irish accent.

Ridiculous. He must be even more sleep deprived than he'd thought if a woman's voice could have that sort of effect.

Suddenly, all the tension of the morning coalesced and unreasonable anger flared deep in his gut. Why had she stopped at the accident? The truck and float were thoroughly bogged down. No way was her tiny sports car going to be any use. She was only going to get in the damned way.

From the paddock, Jim shot a disgruntled look in their direction before opening the trailer door to heave himself inside.

Matt drew level with the woman. 'Unless you can morph into the Incredible Hulk or you're a certified fairy godmother, there's probably not much you can do,' he said, not even trying to curb his sarcasm.

But as soon as he began to speak, she turned and fixed him with direct smoky-grey eyes. He swallowed. Brown curls peeped out from beneath the hat, curved onto her sculpted cheekbones and disappeared beneath her padded collar. She was lovely.

The package screamed affluence.

And sex appeal.

His pulse spiked.

'Is that so?' Even her voice was seductive. Deep with that intriguing foreign burr.

His gaze settled on her mouth. The full lips were lightly covered with a tempting gloss. Matt's mouth and throat felt parched.

He hadn't kissed a woman for a long time. A very, very long time.

Matt blinked as he struggled to direct his thoughts in a less unnerving direction. An apology. He was being obnoxious. She was a passer-by trying to do the right thing. He had no right to take his accumulated ill-humour out on her.

He twisted his mouth into a smile as he tried to dredge up the right words. The apology froze on his tongue as she tilted her head to look along the length of her perfect straight nose. Thick lashes swept down, narrowing her eyes to a dismissive glare. He felt as though someone had paralysed his rib muscles, trapping the air in his chest.

A frantic whinny and a shout from the stranded vehicle shattered the moment. The woman swivelled back to the trailer and his lungs resumed functioning.

He wanted her to look at him again. To speak again. 'Of course,' he said, as he walked beside her towards the horse float, 'a horse whisperer could be just as good as a fairy god-mother.'

'I might surprise you, now, mightn't I?' But she didn't bother to glance his way.

Jim shot through the door, backside first, as the float rocked under the impact of several solid thumps. It sounded as though the horse inside was trying to kick its way out.

After slamming the door, Jim turned to scowl at their approach.

'Problem?' said Matt.

'Uppity mare. Tried to take my arm off.'

Matt glanced down to see blood seeping between the man's fingers where he clutched his forearm.

He sighed. Home just got further away. 'You'd better let me have a look.'

The messy red fingers shook as they uncurled. Matt grimaced

when he saw the wound; large tooth marks scalloped the edges. 'Nasty. You'll need stitches.'

'It'll mend, I've had worse.' After a quick peek at his arm, Jim's florid cheeks turned an unhealthy grey. 'No need to fuss. I'm not one to see the quack unless I have to.'

'And a tetanus booster.' Matt was aware the woman followed as he escorted Jim to the flat tray of the truck. An occasional hint of her floral perfume tempted him to breathe deeply.

'Sit. Do you feel faint?'

'Of course not.' Colour washed back into the man's face.

'I need to get my bag.' Matt turned his head to look at the woman. 'If he feels faint, get him to lie down.'

'I don't need a nanny.' Jim set his jaw.

Silvery eyes slanted up to meet Matt's in a flash of unexpected communion. One brow arched expressively. 'I will.' Her lips twitched and he found his own curving in response.

He was left with the impression she'd be firm and efficient if Jim required her ministrations.

'What would be the problem with your mare, then?' the woman asked as Matt turned away. He heard Jim mumble a response.

As he made the return journey a few minutes later, having reassured Nicky that he wouldn't be long, Matt could see she still stood guard, arms folded. He gave in to temptation and ran an appreciative eye over her slender legs, feeling a sneaking regret that the warm jacket hid the rest of her.

She looked around at his approach and he found his pulse bumping all over again as the impact of her features hit him afresh.

He set his bag beside Jim, his fingers on the catch fumbling, oddly uncoordinated. How long since the proximity of a member of the opposite sex had affected him so badly? He couldn't remember.

'I didn't have the opportunity to play Florence Nightingale, more's the pity.' Her smoky eyes sparkled with humour.

'Better luck next time.' Good grief. It wasn't just his hands that fumbled at her nearness, it was his wits as well.

'Do you need a hand?' she murmured.

'What? Oh, no. Thanks.'

She stepped back. Half relieved, half disappointed, he snapped on a pair of latex gloves and turned his attention to the mangled forearm. After irrigating the area with saline, he probed the torn flesh, pleased to see no sign of foreign material in the wound.

He dried the surrounding skin after applying antiseptic then closed the ragged edges as tidily as he could with steri-strips. Digging around in his bag, he found a packet of sterile gauze dressing and a crêpe bandage.

The sounds from the float were quietening, he noted peripherally as he worked. At least that aspect of the problem seemed to be settling down.

With practised efficiency, he bound the gauze pad into place. It wasn't going to be pretty but at least it was cleaned and dressed. The chances of Jim coming into the surgery to have the thing seen to properly were minimal. He made a mental note to look up the man's immunisation status.

'If I haven't heard from you about the tetanus booster,' he said, as he taped the end of the bandage securely, 'I'll give Judy a buzz.'

'No need for that,' Jim said in a rush.

'No trouble.' Matt permitted himself a small smile as he stripped off the blood-smeared gloves. Jim's wife would make short work of any objections.

Bundling up the discarded gloves with the used gauze, he fastened the top of a small rubbish container.

Behind him, from the float, came a series of low gruff whickers and a few soft shuffling thuds. And the murmur of a soft feminine voice. He looked around.

Where was the woman? Surely she wouldn't…

He frowned at the curved perspex window of the trailer. It

was too scratched for him to see anything except the movement of blurred shapes. His gaze dropped to the black padded jacket draped over the drawbar. A sinking feeling chilled the pit of his stomach. 'Is she in the float?'

Without waiting for an answer, he set his teeth and spun towards the trailer. Did the woman have no sense? Now he'd have another patient for stitching…or worse.

Three long strides took him to the door. He was about to jerk it open when the significance of the soft noises from inside sank in. Forcing himself to calmness, he eased it back and looked inside. The smell of ammonia clogged his breath and he realised the floor was awash with urine.

Apparently unconcerned by the stench or the fact that her boots were getting wet, the woman was at the horse's shoulder, talking softly. The animal's long ears flicked in response to the soothing voice.

Without the bulky jacket enveloping her, the newcomer had a very nice figure. Matt froze, his feet rooted to the spot.

A *very* nice figure.

Naturally padded in all the right places.

The ribbing of her jumper accentuated a narrow waist and he could see the gentle curve of one breast.

Unaware of him, she bent, lifting the canvas rug, to look at the horse's belly. The way the black denim stretched across her rear had him drawing in a quick gulp of air.

'What's happening?' His voice sounded strained.

Two sets of eyes snapped around to look his way. The effect would have been comical except for the anxiety he could read on both faces.

'Could you open the back of the trailer, please? She's in labour.'

'She's in labour?' he repeated, his glance bouncing from the woman to the horse and back again. The words wouldn't form a reasonable picture in his head.

'You know…in labour? She's going to be a mother.'

'I know what in labour means. I'm a damned doctor.' He squashed a wave of dismay. So much for his hopes that the situation in the trailer had improved. 'I've just never had a patient with this many legs.'

'Isn't that a handy coincidence, then?' She arched a shapely, dark eyebrow at him. 'I'm a damned vet. Most of my patients have this many legs.'

And then she smiled. It was as though the sun had come out.

Matt blinked. She'd wanted him to do something…at least he remembered that much.

What was wrong with him?

CHAPTER TWO

DESPITE the seriousness of the situation, Caitlin Butler-Brown found herself smiling. As she watched the man absorbing this new crisis, the details of his face burned into her brain. Medium gold-brown hair, tussled as though he'd run careless fingers through the short thatch. Strong cheekbones and chin, stubbled jaw, slightly crooked nose. But it was his eyes that held her. An aston-ishing clear green and filled, right now, with naked disbelief.

With her hand on the mare's back, she felt as much as heard the shuddering groan, the restless shift to find a more comfort-able position. Her concern switched instantly back to her patient.

'Perhaps you could hurry. She needs to move around, find a spot for her birthing.'

'Right.' He pulled back and the latch snicked softly behind him. Caitlin turned to soothe the fidgety mare.

'There, then, sweetheart. At least he's not the sort to blather on when a girl's got urgent business.' She kept up a steady flow of patter as she reached for the hitching rope and untied the knot. 'We'll have you out of here in no time.'

A loud clunk at the back of the trailer told her that the man was doing as she'd asked.

'Here!' At a shout from the cab of the truck, Caitlin glanced through the grubby haze of the window. A blob moved rapidly towards the trailer and then, down the side, out of sight. 'What're you doing?'

'Your master's not best pleased, darlin'.' She caressed the sweat-damp neck. 'Let's hope our intrepid doctor is up to the task of overruling him.'

Conditions were already less than ideal—without any obstructions from a belligerent owner. Caitlin tamped down the unease in her belly, knowing the mare needed her to be calm.

'Your mare's about to deliver, Jim.' The second bolt clattered back. Their rescuer wasn't allowing himself to be distracted. 'She needs to get out of the float.'

'But—' The protest was cut off as the ramp lowered with a grinding squawk.

Caitlin ducked under the chest bar and moved to the back of the float. When the doctor caught her eye, she sent him a grateful smile. His answering grin made her heart skip a beat and her fingers fumbled with the chain looped behind the mare's haunches.

She blew out a small breath. The man was far too distracting. Best to concentrate on her patient, she told herself sternly as she encouraged the mare to back slowly down the slope, step by uncertain step.

Mentally, she ran through the stages of a normal delivery. Heaven help them if there was a problem. She had her bag in the car, but any serious intervention could require more specialised equipment.

'She can't foal here.' Jim reached for the lead rope. The mare's ears flattened against her skull in clear warning and he snatched his hand back.

'It won't be perfect.' Caitlin decided to act as though his concern was for his horse's safety. Moving methodically, she unfastened the canvas rug and slid it off. She ran a professional eye over the heavily pregnant belly. The membranes of the placenta were just visible beneath the arched black tail. 'But don't worry. She'll manage, Mr...?'

'Neilson. You don't understand.' He waved his arms and the mare sidled away, rolling her eyes. 'I'm taking her to stud.

She's supposed to have her foal there so she can be put to Johnny Boy.'

'You've left it too late for that,' she said keeping a tight hold on her temper. 'She's in stage-one parturition.'

'What?'

Ignoring his confusion, she handed him the folded rug. 'Would you have a longer lead, Mr Neilson?'

His shoulders sagged. 'There's a lunging rein. In the truck.'

Caitlin bit back a retort when he stood clutching the canvas, staring uselessly.

'Get it for us, Jim.' The masculine voice commanded, reaching Jim where hers had not.

'Eh? Oh, right.' He set off towards the truck.

Caitlin shut her eyes briefly and puffed out a small sigh. 'Thank you.'

'No problem.' He gave her a lopsided smile, moving broad shoulders in a faint shrug. 'You looked like you could've taken a chunk out of his hide and I figure he's had enough free medical attention from me this morning.'

Her gaze was caught, trapped by the appeal of his smile. He had a lovely mouth, the sort to turn a girl's head if she was foolish enough to let it. Just as well she wasn't so daft as to be tempted by such superficial things. Her parents' relationship had taught her the danger in that.

And yet, mesmerised, she watched the curve slowly straighten. Now that it wasn't stretched into a smile, the bottom lip was plumper.

Kissable and—

The mouth pursed.

Oh, God. He'd caught her staring. Her heart stuttered as heat rushed into her face.

Flustered, Caitlin jerked her eyes away as long loops of rope were thrust into her hands. Relieved to have an excuse to move, she stepped forward quickly to clip the lunging rein to the halter.

This raw awareness of a man was so alien that she felt self-conscious and uncomfortable in her body. Even simple movements seemed stilted, graceless. She struggled to understand what was wrong with her. Where was the reserve that invariably scuttled her relationships? This was a fine time for it to desert her.

She couldn't be vulnerable now. She had a mission to accomplish. No time for sightseeing or holiday flings…or to be distracted by a gorgeous face.

Caitlin loitered by the mare for a moment then reluctantly stepped back towards the men, leaving the rein loose to give the animal as much space as possible. As though sensing her limited freedom on the long rope, the mare moved restlessly, her head down as she pawed at the ground.

After a few minutes, the expectant mother folded her knees and, with a drawn-out groan, lowered herself inelegantly. Strong contractions rippled across the huge brown stomach and the membrane bulge grew larger.

'Just give her a minute here, Mr Neilson,' Caitlin said, stopping Jim with a hand on his arm as he started to move forward.

'She needs pulling.'

'Perhaps, but we should give her labour a chance to progress naturally first.' Everything so far seemed normal but any ill-considered human interference could easily change that.

Caitlin's senses went on high alert as the younger man moved to stand closer. The action seemed almost protective and she felt at once steadied yet even more unsettled by his presence. Impossible.

'You're in luck this morning, Jim.' The deep, mellow rumble of his voice played havoc with her bouncing pulse. 'You've got the services of a doctor and a veterinarian on hand.'

Caitlin forced her lips into a reassuring smile. This was not the moment to reveal that her experience was in small-animal practice.

Jim stabbed a nicotine-stained finger in the direction of the horse. 'That's my prize standard-bred mare. If anything goes wrong, I'll sue.'

Caitlin watched him stomp off in the direction of the truck.

'Jim Neilson at his worst, I'm afraid.'

'Hmm. He's worried.' And perhaps not without good reason since the largest animal she'd treated in the last few years had been a lanky Great Dane.

'I feel like I should offer a blanket apology for Australian men. We're not all obnoxious, all the time.'

She swivelled her head to look up at him. 'Just some of you, some of the time?'

'Quite.' He grinned at her, his green eyes glowing with open approval. Her heart fluttered uncomfortably. 'You haven't met me at my best either, have you?'

She swallowed.

'Matt Gardiner. Local doctor.' He held out his hand. 'And you *are* the horse whisperer. Much more use than a fairy godmother.'

'No horse whisperer, I'm afraid. Just Caitlin Butler-Brown. Itinerant veterinarian.'

Glancing down as her hand slipped into his, she was very glad she'd already introduced herself. Long fingers closed around hers, causing a warm tingle that had her utterly focused on his touch. The sensation intensified when his thumb brushed over her knuckles.

'Even better. Glad to meet you, Caitlin Butler-Brown.'

She couldn't have replied if her life depended on it.

A grunt of pain from the mare gave her the will to reclaim her hand…and her mind. She curled her fingers into a tight fist to quell the lingering fizz of the connection.

She forced her mind to the job at hand. 'If I do need to scrub, is there anywhere handy I can get soap and water?'

'I have water in the car. And I've got a bottle of alcohol hand sanitiser in my bag.'

'That'll do the job. Thanks.'

The scratch and hiss of a match announced Jim's return. She realised he was beside her, puffing on a cigarette in agitated gasps. The smell of smoke hung, unpleasant, on the crisp morning air, but Caitlin couldn't bring herself to complain. She was glad he was there, a defence of sorts against the man at her other shoulder.

Long minutes crawled by as they watched the mare.

'Dad?'

Caitlin's system jolted. *Dad?* She turned slightly, aware of Matt doing the same, to see a slim boy of about ten standing behind them. Except for his dark hair he was the spitting image of the man beside her. Matt had a child. He was married...or at least very committed. A surprising disappointment stabbed her square in the chest.

'I thought I told you to wait in the car,' said Matt.

'But I wanted to see the horse.' The boy stared at the groaning mare.

'Mmm. That makes all the difference, of course.' He ruffled the boy's hair. 'Caitlin, this is my son, Nicky. Nicky, this is Dr Butler-Brown. She's a vet.'

'Nice to meet you, Nicky.' Despite her disturbing reactions about his father, she didn't have to fake a smile for the boy—he was adorable. 'You can call me Caitlin.'

'Hi.' Anxious green eyes lifted to meet hers. 'What's wrong with him? Is he sick?'

'No, not sick.' Caitlin glanced over at the mare and smiled again, knowing Nicky needed reassurance. 'It's a mare and she's going to have a foal.'

'Wow. A foal? Like...now?'

She chuckled softly. 'Yes, very much like now.'

'Can I watch?'

She looked at Matt.

He shrugged. 'Sure.'

'Thanks, Dad.'

Matt's eyebrows came together sternly. 'This doesn't mean you're off the hook, sport.'

'I know.' Nicky looked both angelic and cheeky as he grinned up at his father.

The loving affection in the look the two exchanged brought a lump to Caitlin's throat. Instinctively, she knew Nicky would never doubt his place in Matt's heart.

Her eyes stung as she turned away. It was like getting a glimpse into the way a family should work, one where love was given unconditionally. The kind of family she would never be a part of. The insight was stunning. Powerful. Beautiful.

The mare moved restlessly. Another contraction and the membranes ruptured with a watery rush. Caitlin's focus sharpened. Spindly legs and a tiny narrow head were clearly visible. The delivery should proceed quickly now.

The minutes stretched and her instincts began to clamour. She drew in a deep breath and held it for several seconds. Something was wrong.

She licked dry lips then turned to Matt. 'I'm going to need that alcohol sanitiser after all, please, Matt. I need to check the foal's position.'

'Right.'

Jim fidgeted, pulling at the waistband of his grubby jeans. 'What's happening?'

'Your mare's not progressing as quickly as I'd like now that her waters have broken,' said Caitlin calmly. 'Did you have any scans done on her through the pregnancy?'

'Nope. She didn't need 'em.'

So, no clues as to what the problem might be. Caitlin prayed it was a straightforward abnormal presentation. Anything more complex could be hard to deal with under these circumstances. And with Nicky there, too.

'Have you got any clean cloths in your truck, Mr Neilson?'

The cigarette dangling from the corner of his mouth bobbed as he thought about it. 'There's a bunch of towels the missus forgot to take out yesterday.'

They'd do. 'Could you get them for me, please?'

Jim nodded, casting the mare a worried look as he headed to his vehicle.

Matt was back with his bag and a bottle of clear gel.

She stripped off her ribbed jumper, looked for somewhere to put it. Matt was one step ahead of her. 'Grab Caitlin's top for her, please, Nicky.'

'Thank you.' She smiled at Nicky as he held out his hands.

He clutched the jumper. She could feel his eyes following her every move as she squeezed out a generous handful of gel and rubbed her arm from fingertips to shoulder.

'Are you going to take the foal out now?'

Without stopping her preparation, she sent him a gentle smile. 'I'm going to feel how he's lying inside his mother, Nicky. I think the wee fellow might not be in quite the right position and that's making it hard for him to be born.'

'Will it hurt?'

'The mare? It might make her a bit uncomfortable but we need to help her so she can push her baby out.'

'What can I do?' asked Matt softly, as she dosed one of his gauze pads with the alcohol solution.

'I'll get you to hold her tail away for me.' She knelt at the mare's straining haunches and Matt crouched beside her. Frosty dampness from the grass seeped through the denim of her jeans, chilling her skin as she waited for a contraction to pass.

With one hand braced on the mare's rump, she threaded her other hand beneath the spindly front legs as the foal's nose slipped back. She felt the knobbly knees, the bones of the mare's pelvis and then... the problem. Another pair of hooves. The hind legs were engaged. They needed to be manoeuvred back down the birth canal before the forequarters could slip free.

A long contraction gripped her arm in a punishing hot vice. Caitlin closed her eyes and breathed through the pain. As soon as the muscles released she pushed the tiny feet with all her strength. No movement.

Another contraction. She couldn't suppress a tiny gasp as the powerful muscles clamped around her flesh. She felt a hand on her shoulder, opened her eyes to find Matt looking straight at her.

'You're doing great,' he murmured. His green gaze drilled into her eyes, as though he could transfer his strength to her. Unexpectedly, she realised she did feel a lightening, an ebbing of tension.

She nodded once, felt the contraction ease. 'This time.' She pushed. The feet moved. A tiny bit at first, before slipping back under the foal's stomach.

'That should do it.' She slid her arm out and sat back on her heels. The ache in her muscles slowly subsided. Out of the corner of her eye, Caitlin saw Nicky's runners tiptoe to a halt beside Matt's knees.

The mare gathered herself for another huge push and the foal slid onto the ground. Steam rose from the ominously still little body.

'Is it okay?' whispered Nicky.

'Yes.' Caitlin knew the declaration was reckless. But she felt compelled to make it. And there was no way she was going to let the foal be anything else. Later she might be able to analyse her need to shield this child she'd only just met.

For now she had work to do.

A promise to keep.

CHAPTER THREE

CAITLIN leaned forward to strip remnants of birth sac from the foal's perfectly formed face and clear the small nostrils. She placed her hand on the chest just behind the sharp little elbow. The fine ribs felt impossibly fragile as she felt for a heartbeat. Relief surged as a pulse fluttered against her palm.

'Matt, can I get you to raise her hindquarters, like this?' She flipped a towel around the haunches and lifted.

'Sure.' He moved to take her place. Back at the foal's head, she blocked one of the delicate nostrils and blew a breath into the other, watching as the chest inflated.

Come on, little one. You can do it.

After the ribs lowered, a second breath. Her mind willed life into the filly.

A moment later, she was rewarded with a quiver of movement. A tiny snort.

Caitlin sat back on her heels and took a deep breath, hoping the others wouldn't see the tears that were perilously close to the surface.

'Let's move back and give them a little space,' she said, taking refuge in practical details. 'If the mare's comfortable she'll stay down for a little longer. The less intervention, the better she'll bond with her bairn.'

'That was awesome, Caitlin,' said Nicky shyly, as they

moved back a short distance. 'You gave it mouth to mouth just like we learned at swimming…only different.'

'Clever boy, Nicky.' She smiled at him. 'It is different. Horses can't breathe through their mouths like we can. So the filly needed mouth-to-nostril resuscitation.'

The foal sat up, the small head lifted unsteadily, looking comically lop-eared.

Now that the emergency was over, Caitlin began to notice the cold air on her bare arms.

'Here.' Matt held out his windcheater. 'Put this on before you get a chill.'

'Oh, no. Please, it's not necessary.' She turned away quickly to reach for the jumper Nicky was still holding. The thought of wearing something of Matt's was more than she could cope with. Too much like an embrace from the man himself, all that warmth and the delicious smell from his body would surround her. He was disturbing enough just standing beside her. 'Thanks, but this will do. It's only, um, an old top.'

Matt shrugged back into his windcheater. A sharp sting of rejection at her sudden withdrawal was uncomfortable.

'Look, Dad. She's trying to stand up.'

Sure enough, the foal's long legs scrambled at the ground. It seemed to be a signal to the mare as she heaved herself to her feet. She turned to lick the coat of her newborn, intently checking her baby over.

Matt smiled, his heart squeezing. In an oblique way the scene reminded him of Nicky's birth. The precious moment when his son had been placed in his arms, tiny hands waving as the infant had yelled his displeasure.

The mare became more insistent, with nudges to the miniature haunches. Spurred on by the encouragement, the foal manoeuvred awkward limbs, pushing up with her hindquarters until she stood, albeit unsteadily. She looked all leg and large bony joints. A few staggering steps took her to the mare's flank where she nuzzled determinedly until she latched onto the teat.

'Congratulations, Mr Neilson,' said Caitlin softly. 'You've a grand little filly.'

'With a little help,' said Matt, determined that Jim should give Caitlin her due.

Jim cleared his throat. 'I'd have managed.'

Matt opened his mouth but Caitlin was there before him with a sweet smile for the cranky old man. 'Of course you would have, Mr Neilson.'

Matt had the satisfaction of seeing the older man's double take.

'Ah. Yes. Well, anyway, er, thanks. Just as well to have a vet here.' Jim's mouth snapped shut as though he was surprised by the words he'd just said.

'My pleasure.'

Matt stifled an abrupt urge to laugh. She'd handled Jim beautifully, better than he would have, wringing reluctant gratitude from the man with nothing more than a smile.

'She'll expel the placenta over the next couple of hours now her bairn's nursing. You'll know to leave that well enough alone, of course.'

'Of course.' Jim shuffled.

Caitlin was obviously unconvinced because she went on smoothly with her warning. 'Any pulling could lead to infection or prolapse of your mare's uterus. If the placenta hasn't cleared in a few hours, you need to call your vet.'

Bloodstains marred the sleeves of her pink top. The knees of her jeans were dark with dampness and there was dirt on the toes of her boots. Matt had never seen a woman look more beautiful than she was right now. She was marvellous. That willingness to get in and get her hands dirty, literally, without worrying about her appearance. No complaints. A practical woman.

She hitched a shoulder to rub her cheek. Matt suddenly realised her hands were still wet and grubby.

'I've got soap and water in the car, if you'd like to clean up.'

She hesitated and for a moment he thought she was going

to refuse. 'I would, yes. Thank you. Goodbye, Mr Neilson. I wish you well with your mare and foal.'

'Yeah.' He cleared his throat. 'Like I said, ah, thanks.'

Matt walked silently back to the car listening to Nicky chatter to Caitlin about how he was going to tell his class about the birth. Now that the excitement was over, Matt had time to wonder more about her. Who was she and why was she here? If she was a tourist, perhaps he could convince her that Garrangay was a good place to use as a base for seeing Western Victoria. What were her plans?

Not that it was any of his business…but for some reason he wanted to know.

At the station wagon, he got out the water bottle and liquid soap.

'Did you want to wash…?' He indicated her arm.

'No. No, just my hands. Thanks. I can have a shower later.'

He tipped liquid into her cupped hands, watching while she lathered her slender fingers.

'Have you got far to travel?' He congratulated himself on striking just the right note of casual interest.

'I haven't, no.' She was going to be staying locally? Anticipation tightened his gut.

'What brings you out this way?' There was an odd suspended second when her movements seemed to falter. 'Holiday? Work?'

She'd resumed scrubbing vigorously and Matt wondered if he'd imagined the moment.

'Secret mission?' he joked, when she didn't answer.

Wide, startled eyes, dark with some suppressed emotion, flicked up to his and away. Was it guilt? Surely not.

'Could I have some more water, please?'

Silently, he rinsed away the suds and handed her a cloth.

'I'm between jobs,' she said, finally. 'I thought…. It seemed like a good opportunity to see something of Victoria.'

The answer was reasonable. But her reaction told him it wasn't the entire story.

'Are you staying locally? I can recommend somewhere that makes a good base for sightseeing.'

'Thank you, but…no. I—I have…plans.'

The change from competent, compassionate professional to tongue-tied uncertainty seemed odd. The frown pleating her forehead, the tight line of her mouth, the agitated way she dried her hands all screamed, *No trespassing*. Had he unwittingly touched on something personal…painful?

His gaze drifted over the rapidly clearing mist in the paddock as he mentally replayed the conversation. Nothing he'd said seemed unforgivably insensitive.

She was about to disappear from his life. Bemused by the compulsion, he nevertheless wanted to say something to tempt her to stay. But he'd already stumbled in a way he didn't understand. Regret tugged at him, leaving him off balance. Perhaps it was just as well she was moving on.

A kookaburra began to laugh, the great whooping chuckles echoing into the air. Abruptly, the sound stopped, leaving a profound silence in its wake.

He forced his mouth into a smile. 'If you're ever out this way again, look us up. We'd like that, wouldn't we, Nicky?'

'Yes!'

'You're very kind.' She smiled gently at his son.

By the time her grey eyes transferred their gaze up to his, there was no trace of warmth left. She handed him back the cloth. 'Perhaps you could invite your wife. We could make it a family outing.'

No puzzle about his misstep here. 'Ex.'

'Sorry?'

'Ex-wife. I'm divorced.'

'Oh. I'm sorry.' Pink spots flared in Caitlin's cheeks, her eyes shadowed with vexation. 'I didn't mean…'

'Don't be.' Matt said, wanting to make sure she understood. 'It's old history.'

Caitlin's mouth opened, then closed, her teeth biting her full bottom lip.

'Mum lives in Melbourne,' said Nicky, with a complete lack of awareness of the undercurrents in the conversation. 'She hardly ever visits.'

'I…see. Well, I—I should be going.' She looked towards the paddock. 'Please, be sure to tell Mr Neilson he shouldn't trailer the mare and foal for at least a week.'

'I'll tell him. It'll be a while before the tow truck gets here to pull him out. He'll have a chance to get used to the idea.'

There was a brief silence, then Caitlin held out her hand. 'It's been an interesting morning, Dr Matt Gardiner.'

'It has, Dr Caitlin Butler-Brown.' He squeezed her hand gently, reluctant to let her go. 'Drive safely.'

'I will, yes.' She retrieved her hand.

'Goodbye, then.' She smiled at Nicky. 'You were great over there at the foal's birth.'

'All I did was hold your jumper.'

'That, too, but mostly you were cool and calm when things weren't going so well. That's a big thing.'

'Thanks.' Matt watched as his son all but wriggled with pleasure.

Caitlin turned and walked to her car, aware of a lingering regret to be saying goodbye.

Her fingers were still warm from the pressure of Matt's hand. She'd been prepared for the zing of his touch this time. And it had helped. Just.

Father and son were watching as she slid into the driver's seat. She winced about her embarrassing mistake—though who could blame her for thinking there would be a wife and mother waiting for them at home? What woman in her right mind would let such a darling pair go?

But, then, her own mother had demonstrated time and again how much more important research was when weighed against a husband's or a daughter's welfare. Only the dogged persistence of Caitlin's father, following his wife around the globe, had kept the family together.

She started the car, put it in gear and accelerated away.

A glance in the rear-view mirror revealed Matt was still there, one hand on his car roof, his head tilted slightly. He'd gathered Nicky to his side with his free hand.

A shadowy shiver surprised her as she took a final glance in the mirror. Matt and Nicky's figures were now tiny. She shook her head, irritated by the illogical trend of her thoughts. The feeling that the man was important to her in some way was plain daft. As was her wayward delight that he was single. Single didn't mean available. He certainly wasn't available to her. No man was. Especially not a family man.

She turned the corner, almost relieved to be able to dispose of the last tiny physical trace of them.

Matt's presence lingered in her mind, though. A secret mission, he'd suggested. He'd been joking but the words had held enough truth to tip her off balance. She *was* here for a reason. Not underhand but not straightforward and open either.

How do you introduce yourself to an aunt who doesn't know you exist? How do you tell a woman that her long-lost brother died with an apology on his lips?

'Da, you've left me in an impossible situation.'

Caitlin sniffed, blinking away the quick rush of moisture that blurred her vision.

She was here to gather information, to decide how to handle this delicate family matter. There was going to be pain, that was unavoidable in the circumstances, but she wanted to minimise the suffering if she could…for herself, for her unknown aunt, for whoever else might be involved.

The last thing she needed was a complication in the form of a man. Especially one with a child. Regardless of how charming they both were.

It wouldn't be fair to them. She didn't do relationships or family well.

She didn't know how to make them work, had no blueprint to guide her. Her mother hadn't wanted children at all. While Caitlin knew her father had loved her, his first priority had always been his wife.

A grey cloud of gloom settled over her. Because now here she was in rural Victoria to see if she could reforge the ties her father had cut with his family decades ago.

And experience showed she'd inherited her parents' inability to make family relationships work.

No, she had no business wishing she could see more of Matt and his precious son. None whatsoever.

CHAPTER FOUR

STRUCK out big time. Matt's mood dipped as the MG rounded a curve and disappeared behind a stand of scrubby bush. Once upon a time, he might have managed a phone number.

Nicky shifted. Stifling a sigh, Matt roused himself.

'She's nice.' Nicky looked up. 'I like her.'

'Me, too, mate.' Perhaps just a tad too much. He couldn't put himself on the line in a relationship again, leave himself vulnerable the way he had with Sophie. That had nearly destroyed him. If he hadn't had to pull himself together for Nicky's sake, Matt wondered how he'd have ended up.

Since the end of his marriage his interest in female company had been precisely zero. A chance meeting with a little Irish veterinarian had changed that.

Maybe his foster-mother was right. Maybe he did need to get out more. She was always encouraging him to find a *good woman.* A partner for him, a mother for Nicky. Prospects were trawled under his nose from time to time. Doreen made no secret of wanting more grandchildren.

He'd have to put Caitlin Butler-Brown down to experience, as the one that got away, and make more of a commitment to his social life. The thought of leaping back into the dating game made him shudder. But leaping anywhere with a certain veterinarian for some reason seemed outrageously appealing.

Which showed that the scars from his marriage hadn't completely killed his masculinity after all.

One look and his wary heart wanted nothing more than to plop into Caitlin's clever, caring hands. He should be looking for a nice country girl. Much more sensible. Though perhaps not. He grimaced wryly. His ex-wife, Sophie, had been a home-grown Garrangay girl. And their marriage had been a total disaster.

'Let's go and talk to Mr Neilson and then we can head home.' With one last glance along the empty road, he followed Nicky back towards the float and truck.

Jim was watching the foal's increasingly confident forays.

'Your mare and foal need to stay here for at least a week. Vet's orders,' said Matt.

'A week! I can't leave her here that long,' Jim gasped.

'You don't have a choice,' Matt said. 'You were a damned fool to try and move her so close to foaling. And you know it. Caitlin hasn't saved your mare for you to risk the animal's life again. Organising agistment here until she's fit to travel is a small price to pay.'

Jim coughed and spluttered before he nodded grudgingly. 'Here, you'd better take this. Your friend left it.' He held out Caitlin's black padded jacket.

Matt's fingers sank into the down-filled softness and warmed instantly. Her perfume wafted up, the floral tang bringing a sharp memory of clear, smiling, grey eyes.

Resolutely, he tightened his grip. It was an expensive garment, the sort that someone would want back.

'Thanks. I'll get it back to her. Come on, Nicky.'

Whistling softly, he tucked the coat under his arm and set off across the paddock. He had a cast-iron excuse for tracking her down without looking like some sort of unbalanced weirdo.

He knew her name. Knew she was a veterinarian with delightful hints of an Irish accent. How hard could it be?

Nothing she'd said gave him a clue where she was staying, except that it was somewhere in the area. He knew where he'd start. With his foster-mother and her contacts in the local accommodation industry. If he had to, he'd work his way through every motel, bed and breakfast, hotel and hostel in the district.

The Grampians loomed over her aunt's bed and breakfast. Remnants of fog clinging around the base did nothing to soften the daunting majesty. Despite the late morning sun, Caitlin shivered. The stark, craggy range glowered down at her, challenging her right to be there.

Her stomach clenched as doubts suddenly swamped her. Perhaps she should have written first. Prepared her aunt. How would the poor woman react to having a stranger drop into her life without warning?

Not for the first time, she wondered if her father had had other siblings. Was there a whole host of aunts and uncles and cousins lurking in Garrangay? She swallowed as her heart skipped uncomfortably.

As it stood, she was the only child of parents estranged from any family they'd had. Martin Brown and Rowan Butler. Her family was a tiny unit, even smaller now that her father had passed away.

Three hundred kilometres away, in the comfortable suburbs of Melbourne, this whole venture had seemed simple. But here, on her aunt's doorstep, it seemed fraught with complexity. Her usual calm detachment deserted her completely, leaving her mouth dry, a sinking sensation in her stomach. The urge to get back in the car and drive away was almost overwhelming.

She shut her eyes. Waiting behind her closed lids was a clear vision of brooding, green eyes beneath a dark gold thatch of hair. Her eyes snapped open. *Dr Matt Gardiner.*

There was an intensity about him—and her reaction to him—that was unnerving. She'd read the interest in his eyes, seen it turn to curiosity after she'd fumbled with answering his questions.

Her cheeks warmed at the memory of her gauche behaviour. Stupid. He'd even provided a ready answer for her—a holiday. All she'd had to do was say *yes*. Instead, she'd hesitated and that stark tension had sprung up between them.

'We hardly ever bite our guests.'

She spun around. A pleasantly plump woman smiled at her from a few feet away.

Her aunt? Caitlin stared, searching the face, the friendly blue-grey eyes.

'Mrs Mills? I'm Caitlin Butler-Brown,' she said, pushing the words past the constriction in her throat.

The welcoming smile faltered, replaced by a peculiar, almost stunned look.

Oh, Lord. *Was it recognition?*

It *couldn't* be. Da had said his sister didn't know he'd even married, let alone that he'd had a child.

Her surname was Butler-Brown, no reason at all for Doreen to associate the hyphenated name with Martin Brown.

And, besides, everyone said she favoured her mother in looks. Except for her eye colour. The silvery grey came straight from Doreen's brother…Caitlin's father.

Suffocating panic made her want to retreat, snatch open the door of her car and drive away. Maybe she wasn't ready for this after all.

'I—I have a booking.'

'Oh. A booking. Yes. Of course you do.' The woman seemed to shake herself mentally. 'I'm sorry, dear. Come in. Come in. Let's go around the back. Did you want to bring your bag in now or…?'

'Er, I might leave it until later.' If her courage failed her, she could still make that dash for Melbourne.

'I thought you might have come a bit earlier. Oh, but I expect you've been sightseeing.'

'Mmm, yes. I have.' That was one way of describing her long morning. She'd found a public bathroom so she could have a wash and change her top. Then lingered over cups of coffee while she'd debated whether she'd continue with her plans or retreat back to Melbourne.

'You don't mind using the tradesmen's entrance, do you? I've been gardening. That's what I was doing when I saw you.'

Now that the woman had started, it seemed as though the sentences gushed out.

'I'm Doreen Mills.' She gave a small, embarrassed laugh and her hands fluttered briefly. 'But you know that. Call me Doreen, of course. We don't stand on ceremony. I've not long taken some muffins out of the oven. I got so involved with the broad beans I nearly burnt them. The muffins, that is, not the beans.'

'I…see.' Caitlin bit back an urge to giggle lest it explode into full-blown hysterical laughter. She waited for her aunt to lever off her dirty boots at the step.

'I'll show you your room. Then we can have a nice cup of tea.'

The house smelled of the muffins and lavender and lemon polish. Everything was spotless and tidy without seeming intimidating. It was…homey and welcoming. *Settled* in a way that her family's houses had never managed, Caitlin realised with a small sense of envy. It beckoned to her but at the same time left her feeling like an outsider, as though she could never quite belong there.

'I'll put the jug on, then.' The flow of words stopped abruptly.

'Doreen?' Caitlin frowned. Was her aunt looking a little pinched around the mouth? 'Are you all right?'

'Oh, dear, yes. Nothing to worry about. I'd better just…' Doreen rummaged in a large bag then pulled out a box and shook out a blister packet '…take a tablet.'

Caitlin glanced at the label. Glycerol trinitrate. Her stomach swooped on a quick flood of anxiety. Her aunt had a heart condition. 'You're having chest pain? How bad is it?'

'Mild angina, dear. I'll be right in a minute.' But Doreen

allowed herself to be led over to the table and pushed gently into a chair.

'Sit here now and we'll see how you're feeling.' Caitlin slipped into the chair beside her hostess. To her critical eye, Doreen's colour seemed good. Better now, in fact, than it had been outside. 'Do you want me to call your doctor?'

'No, no. Heavens no. Silly me. I've overdone it in the garden, that's all. I'll be good as gold after we've had that cuppa.' Doreen grimaced ruefully, her eyes glinting with affectionate humour. 'And Matt will just growl at me.'

'Matt? Your doctor? That wouldn't be Dr Matt Gardiner, would it?' An odd sense of inevitability settled over Caitlin.

'My son. Well, technically my foster-son, of course.'

'Of course,' said Caitlin faintly. That would teach her to ignore her earlier shiver of premonition. She wondered what else might be in store.

Doreen made a small grimace, looking resigned. 'I'll tell him tonight when he comes home.'

'Comes home?' Shock numbed Caitlin's tongue, making her stumble over the simple words.

'Yes. He's—' Doreen broke off, her head cocked to one side. 'Oh, dear. I'm not expecting anyone. I wonder if that's him.'

Caitlin had been vaguely aware of the sound of the crunch of car wheels on gravel. Now a door on the other side of the house banged shut.

'Him? You mean Matt?' Her voice wasn't much more than a squeak. She was still grappling with the idea that he *lived* here. It was too much to think that he might actually *be* here. *No.* She couldn't meet him again. *Not right now. Not without some time to prepare.*

'Yes. He has an uncanny knack of…. Oh, dear. Please don't say anything about my little episode, will you, Caitlin?' Doreen shot a guilty look towards the door. 'He's had such a dreadful morning, I don't want to add to his load today.'

'But—'

'Mum?' The rich, deep voice jolted Caitlin to the core.

She swallowed hard, clasping her hands together tightly in her lap to prevent her fingers betraying her internal shudders.

'We're in the kitchen.' Doreen gave Caitlin a conspiratorial smile.

'Something smells delicious.' Matt came through into the large kitchen-dining area. The easy smile on his face froze as his whole body seemed to do a double-take. Caitlin's brain played the scene in slow motion so that it seemed to progress inexorably from frame to frame.

'You.' He was obviously having trouble believing his eyes. 'You're here.'

'Yes,' she managed. She felt barely able to string thoughts together, let alone put them into words to form coherent sentences.

'Oh, you two have met.' Doreen sounded intrigued.

'Yes. At Jim's accident this morning. This is the Caitlin that Nicky was talking about. She delivered the foal.' Matt's disbelieving eyes stayed focussed on her face. Almost as though he expected her to disappear if he looked away.

'Oh, my. Nicky's going to be so excited to see you,' said Doreen.

Caitlin smiled weakly.

'So staying here was one of those plans you were talking about earlier,' said Matt.

'Yes,' she croaked.

'Then you'll be here when I get home later?'

She stared at him. Escape to Melbourne beckoned.

'Of course she will be, dear,' said Doreen. 'She's booked in for a week.'

'Bookings can be changed,' he murmured, his eyes all too knowing. 'Caitlin?'

She swallowed hard. 'Yes.'

His mouth moved into a small smile and a spark of humour lit the green eyes. 'Yes, you'll be here? Or, yes, bookings can be changed?'

'Um. Yes. I'll be here.' Why did she feel as though she'd committed herself to more than simple accommodation?

'Good.' He nodded with satisfaction. 'Right. I'll be off, then.'

'Do you have time for lunch, dear?' said Doreen.

'Had some, thanks. I just called in to pick up these files.' He shifted and for the first time Caitlin noticed he was carrying a wad of papers. 'I'll take some of whatever smells so good back to work with me, though.'

'Muffins. I'll get you something to put them in.' Doreen slipped away from the table.

Compelled to break the small ensuing silence, Caitlin asked, 'How—how did Mr Neilson take the news about not moving the mare and foal?'

'He accepted it. You must have charmed him.'

'As long as he doesn't rush it.'

'Here you are.' Doreen was back, holding out a bulging bag.

'Thanks, Mum.' He kissed her cheek then looked back at Caitlin. 'I'll see you later.'

She hoped the smile she gave him didn't look as feeble as it felt.

After he'd gone, Doreen sat down again. 'Thank you so much for being discreet, dear. I feel a bit mean, involving you like that. But fancy it being you who was there to help this morning. I should have put two and two together earlier—Caitlin is an unusual name. But when you introduced yourself...I was so...' She gave an embarrassed laugh. 'Well, I'm just a bit muddle-headed today.'

Caitlin bit down on her lip, wondering what her aunt had been going to say. 'Sure, and don't we all have those days.'

'Some of us more than others.' Doreen smiled, but her eyes were thoughtful. 'Have you always worked with horses?'

'Never. I'm a small-animal vet.' Caitlin raised her voice to speak over the whistling of the kettle. 'You stay here. I'll fix the tea.'

'Oh, but you're my guest,' Doreen protested as Caitlin crossed to the kitchen to where all the tea things were laid out.

'You've got it ready, all I'm doing is the kettle,' said Caitlin, as she reached for the switch. 'Matt's practice is in Garrangay, then, is it?'

'Yes, he took over from Bert Smythe when he retired. Matt's built the practice up, modernised it,' said Doreen proudly. 'Poor old Bert had let things go a bit in his last few years.'

Having poured the boiling water onto the tea-leaves in the pot, Caitlin placed everything onto a tray and carried it across to the table. 'It must be nice for you, having Matt and Nicky living here with you.'

'Yes, it is, though, strictly speaking, I live with them, of course,' said Doreen. 'Matt bought the place when my husband's health deteriorated and organised renovations to make things easier for us. After Peter passed away, I was rattling around, wondering what to do with myself. Matt suggested turning it into a bed and breakfast. Milk for you?'

'Yes, thank you.' Caitlin accepted the proffered cup. 'It's a grand old building.'

'My great-great-grandfather, William Elijah Brown, built it. He and my great-great-grandmother, Lily, were early pioneers in the district.' She gave a self-deprecating laugh. 'Don't get me started or I'll have you looking at all my old photos.'

A sharp quiver ran though Caitlin's stomach. The man who had built this magnificent place, who had worked and, with his wife, raised a family here, was her ancestor, too. Longing and sadness tempered a feeling of pride.

'I'd love to see them—the photos.' A sudden fierce need to put faces to the names pulled at her. And maybe it would lead in to a way to tell Doreen why she was here. 'I've always loved old photos, wondering about the people in them, what their lives were like.'

Doreen fixed her with a quick searching look, which changed

to a delighted smile. 'Well, it just so happens I love showing them off. Let's take our cuppa into the lounge, shall we?'

Caitlin's legs felt rubbery as she followed her aunt.

'I've put the best of the best in this album,' said Doreen, patting the sofa beside her. 'If you're really interested in what their lives were like, I've got a collection of newspaper articles I can show you some time.'

Doreen flipped through a parade of sepia-toned photos, pointing out an ancestor here and there with an amusing story. The formality of the poses, women in long dresses, men in suits and uniforms, held Caitlin enthralled. If she'd been on her own, she would have taken much longer to look at them.

'Is this you?' she said, when they came to a candid photo of a young girl with a woman and toddler taken outside Mill House. The gardens around the house were much simpler and the verandah looked as though it had been enclosed.

'Yes.'

'So that's…' Caitlin's throat closed over.

'Mum and my brother, Marty.'

Caitlin was ambushed by a paralysing breathlessness. The toddler was her father. *Her father.*

Doreen stroked the photo lightly with a fingertip, her face suddenly etched with grief. Moisture prickled Caitlin's eyes in sympathy and she had to look away.

Oh, God. How stupid to think that the photographs might have created an opportunity to talk about Martin Brown's death. Sorrow clogged her throat in a painful ball. No way could she speak about her father's death right now, even if she'd wanted to. Her own emotions were too raw, too close to the surface. She needed to be better prepared, to have the words ready, practised.

Doreen cleared her throat. 'Anyway, that's enough for today.' She closed the album with a snap. 'Finish your tea and then I'll show you your room so you can bring your bags in and get settled.'

'Oh. But…. Are you sure you're up to having a guest after your angina attack? I can easily arrange to stay somewhere else.' She pushed aside her promise to Matt about being at the house when he returned. After all, he hadn't known about the angina attack when he'd pinned her down about her booking. If Doreen needed to cancel, Caitlin wasn't going to feel bad about leaving.

'I wouldn't hear of it. Please. I'll be so disappointed if you leave now.'

'As long as you promise to say if it does get too much,' said Caitlin, after a small hesitation. Perhaps she could ask Matt if Doreen's health was strong enough. But that would involve breaking her aunt's confidence. Her life seemed to be filling with all manner of deceptions.

Doreen clasped her hands together in delight. 'Wonderful. And why don't you join us for dinner tonight? It's just a casserole,' she said quickly, when Caitlin would have refused. 'I've had it in the slow cooker since this morning so it's no trouble. None at all.'

'Thank you, that would be lovely,' Caitlin said, responding to the apparent underlying plea. Was it real or was she hearing what she wanted to hear? Letting her own yearning for family colour her judgement? After all, Doreen didn't know she'd just invited her niece to share a meal.

Doreen's face lit up with pleasure and an answering glow settled in Caitlin's heart. Matt would probably be there but this time she had the advantage of being able to prepare for their next meeting. She'd be able to handle him and this inconvenient attraction.

She had to…he was a part of her aunt's life.

Matt puffed out a breath as he stacked the papers on the back seat of his vehicle. He felt like he'd been punched in the gut.

Caitlin was here. In Mill House. *In his home.*

Not that she was here to see *him.* With his system starting to settle, he could recognise that she'd been as disturbed as he'd been by the coincidence. In fact, her reaction had been closer to horror.

He'd been so completely thrown that he hadn't thought of any of the questions that crowded into his mind now. Especially about her strange reaction to his comments when he'd helped her wash her hands earlier. He'd had the feeling that she was hiding something, but he couldn't imagine what.

He slid into the driver's seat, the wadded black lump on the passenger's seat catching his eye. Caitlin's jacket. He'd completely forgotten about it.

In the end, the chance to return the jacket had arrived with minimal effort on his part.

Always assuming, of course, that Caitlin was still here when he got home.

She'd said she would be.

He hoped she would be.

Mostly.

CHAPTER FIVE

MATT GARDINER.

Caitlin froze on the threshold of the lounge, her fingers tightening around the spine of her book until she was sure something would break. It'd been six hours since he'd walked into the kitchen. Six hours that she'd used to prepare for this meeting. She'd convinced herself she was ready.

But she was so wrong.

What was he doing in this room? Doreen said he and Nicky lived in an apartment upstairs. Shouldn't he have been tucked safely up there?

But, no, his long body was sprawled in a recliner, head tilted back on the cushioned rest, eyes closed. Dark shadows beneath his eyes made him look oddly vulnerable. The difficult twenty-four hours of routine work and after-hours emergencies that Doreen had described earlier must have caught up with him.

His mouth was slightly curved, the bottom lip invitingly full. Caitlin frowned. She didn't usually notice these details about men. To be sure, she didn't want to notice them about this man in particular.

A moment later, his mouth moved. Her eyes followed the tip of his tongue as it made a leisurely pass over his lips, leaving them glistening.

Stifling the need to gulp in air, Caitlin retreated, one painstaking step at a time. But the door, having opened so quietly inwards, gave a tiny protesting squeak at her attempt to shut it slowly. She stopped, her gaze snapping back to Matt.

The brilliant green eyes were open, watching her progress with interest. He smiled slowly, as he levered the recliner into an upright position.

'Well, well. Caitlin Butler-Brown. We meet again.' Straightening to his full height, he stretched briefly. The movement made the fabric of his polo shirt hug his leanly muscled torso. His well-worn jeans rode low on narrow hips. He ran a hand over his hair, smoothing wayward tufts. 'Come in.'

'I didn't mean to disturb you.' She clutched the book in front of her, a flimsy defence against his physical appeal.

'Bit late to worry about that, Caitlin,' he said cryptically, slipping his hands into the pockets of his jeans.

The gleam in his eyes made her feel like succulent prey venturing into a predator's lair. Instinct made her want to run, but she could find no plausible reason to refuse to enter the room. Especially since that had plainly been her intention before she'd seen him.

'Can I get you something to drink?'

'Not for me, no. Thank you.' The last thing she needed was alcohol. The unfamiliar pull of attraction she felt around him left her feeling skittish and vulnerable. Even the smallest level of intoxication might give her the illusion that she could handle him.

She sent him a cool smile and chose a chair beside the wood-burning heater. Instead of returning to the recliner, he followed her across the room and sank onto the end of the sofa nearest her chair. The arrangement seemed uncomfortably intimate. In her peripheral vision, she could see his long legs stretched out, sock-clad feet pointing towards the flickering warmth of the fire.

'Mum tells me she had an angina attack while you were here this morning.'

'She did, yes.' Thank goodness Doreen had come clean, thought Caitlin. At least that was one deception off her conscience.

'Thank you.'

'For what? I didn't do anything.' Worse, she had a nagging concern that her arrival might have precipitated the attack. Though there was nothing concrete to confirm her suspicion. 'She had everything under control.'

'I know. But I like knowing someone was here with her.'

Caitlin hesitated a moment. 'Is she well enough to have guests? I'd rather not stay if you think it'll put her under too much stress.'

'She manages her condition pretty well.' He smiled wryly. 'Besides, I don't think I'd dare try to stop her running the bed and breakfast now. There's nothing she enjoys more than a houseful of guests to pamper.'

Guilt made Caitlin's smile feel strained. She wasn't *just* a guest, she was the bearer of bad tidings. Why had her father turned his back on his sister and this wonderful ancestral home for more than half a lifetime? He'd swapped the certainty of belonging for a nomadic life with her mother.

And yet, in the last days of his illness, it was this place and his sister that his thoughts had returned to—family that he'd left behind all those years ago. Would Doreen want to know the news that her younger brother was dead? Was she even well enough to handle it? No possibility now of reconciliation.

'So you staying here is a happy coincidence, isn't it?' Matt's voice rumbled into her musing.

'A happy coincidence?' she said blankly, trying to pick up the thread of the conversation. His comment, coming on the heels of her thoughts, jolted her badly. 'I—I'm sorry. What were you saying?'

Was he toying with her? Did he suspect there was more to her visit?

'I was wondering how I'd be able to track you down.'

'Why—why would you want to do that?'

There was a small, charged silence.

'I have something you'll want.' Laughter and something warmer lurked in his eyes as he leaned on the arm of the sofa and watched her.

Flirting. There was nothing sinister going on. He was just *flirting* with her, and her conscience had imbued his words with deeper overtones.

Just flirting? she mocked herself silently. A pulse thumped frantically in her throat and it was all she could do not to put a protective hand up to cover it.

'Is that so?' She swallowed, willing herself to relax. 'I can't imagine what it might be.'

'You can't imagine…anything?' His mouth tilted into a small teasing smile. 'I'm stricken.'

'Sure, and don't you look it,' she said, struggling to keep her expression bland.

'Perhaps if you tried harder, something might come to mind.'

'Matt, could you—?' Doreen's head appeared around the door. 'Oh, Caitlin. Sorry, dear, I didn't realise you were in here as well.' The older woman looked from one to the other and back again.

Did her aunt sense the tension in the room? Caitlin shivered. The interruption couldn't have come at a better time.

'Could you call Nicky in for dinner, please, Matt, dear? He's down by the creek.'

'Of course.' He got to his feet, sending a small smile Caitlin's way as he excused himself.

'That thing I have that you'll want.' At the door, he looked back at her. The small smile on his lips made her heart beat skitter. 'It's your jacket.' She looked at him blankly. 'From this morning. You left it on the towbar of Jim's float.'

'Oh. Yes. Thank you.'

She huffed out a sigh of relief as he left the room. She'd never felt this out of her depth with a man before. Was it just her private agenda making her so vulnerable…or was it the man himself?

'What are you hoping to do while you're here, Caitlin?'

Matt ladled casserole onto Nicky's plate before adding a scoop to his own.

'Oh, a bit of sightseeing. The usual tourist things. I've got a stack of brochures.' No sign of the hesitancy that had marked her answers this morning. Of course, she'd had time to prepare her answers. Or perhaps he was being overly suspicious because of his attraction to her…his instinct for self-preservation trying to find a flaw, a reason to reject the undeniable chemistry.

'You've come at a good time of year,' said Doreen. 'The wild flowers are out. And it's not too hot. It's a shame you're only here for such a short time. Maybe you'll come back again and visit for longer.'

Matt glanced at his mother. He'd never heard her use that wistful tone before with her guests. In fact, now that he thought about it, this was the first time a guest had been invited to the dinner table with the family on the very first night.

'Da-ad. I don't like broccoli.'

Matt was surprised to see a generous helping of the vegetable on the edge of his son's bowl.

'Oh, right.' After transferring the unwanted florets to his own plate, he reached for the beans and filled the newly vacant space.

Nicky wrinkled his nose in disgust but didn't protest.

'And after your holiday? You're back to work—in Melbourne, didn't you say?' He served some of the buttery beans for himself then glanced at Caitlin.

She looked serene, thick lashes hiding her grey eyes, cheeks lightly tinted with pink, as she broke open the roll on her side plate and reached for the butter. Why did he have the feeling that beneath the calm exterior she was weighing her answer, using the food as a delaying tactic?

'I'm between jobs.' She put down her knife and looked across at him.

'You've got something lined up?'

'Not yet.'

'What are you looking for?'

'Small-animal practice.'

'Carrots, Caitlin?' Doreen handed their guest the bowl.

'Thank you.' A tiny secretive smile crimped the ends of Caitlin's mouth as she took the dish.

'Not equine medicine, then?' Matt grinned at her as she switched her gaze back to him. He wanted to know more about her. It was sensible, he assured himself. If she was going to be spending time with his family, it was right to find out a few things. At least.

'Not equine medicine, no.'

'You've obviously had quite a bit of experience with horses, though.' Using his fork, Matt speared a chunk of meat. 'The way you handled the foal's resus this morning.'

'Dr Tonkin would be relieved to know he taught me something in his classes. That was my first solo as an equine midwife.' A mischievous gleam lit her eyes.

'In that case, Dr Tonkin can be proud of you,' he murmured, enjoying the irony of her confession. 'Just as well Jim Neilson didn't know.'

'It is.'

As the meal progressed Matt realised how thoroughly Caitlin charmed his small family. Nicky had already told him that he liked her. His son was beside himself with delight that she was staying here. And Doreen seemed very interested in her guest. Matt compressed his lips. *Interested* wasn't quite the right word. His mother's demeanour was closer to fascination.

'That was delicious, Doreen. Thank you,' said Caitlin.

'Oh, it was nothing special.' Doreen looked pleased and

flustered at the same time. To Matt's amazement a faint blush tinted his foster-mother's cheeks.

'That's where you'd be wrong,' said Caitlin. Matt shifted his gaze, catching the soft, unguarded expression on their visitor's face. The admiration between the two women was obviously mutual. But there was something else about Caitlin's look that made him curious…. What was it exactly? Hope? Longing? And maybe a touch of sadness. 'I've survived on my own cooking. Now, *that's* nothing special.'

'Well, thank you, dear.'

'Are you going to be here on Saturday, Caitlin?' Nicky's question diverted everyone's attention.

'I am, yes.'

'Maybe you can come to the show.'

'The show?'

'The Garrangay A and P Show. Agriculture and produce,' Matt added at Caitlin's blank look.

'What a wonderful idea,' said Doreen enthusiastically. 'Matt will be on duty, of course, but you can come with us. Can't she, Nicky?'

'Yeah. An' maybe you can watch me ride Sheba. If you want to. 'Course, you'll probably be busy.' The ultra-casual attitude didn't mask the underlying need in Nicky's voice. Matt tightened his lips, stopping the words of caution that lay on his tongue. His son's willingness to invite rejection, to take chances and stay open with people amazed him. And…shamed him, he realised. He toyed with his wineglass, waiting for her answer as acutely as Nicky.

'Now, that sounds really grand.' The smile she gave his son made Matt lift his glass and take a gulp of wine.

'And I'll be putting my jams in again this year,' said Doreen. 'As well as my roses.'

'There's usually not too much for me to do,' said Matt, beginning to feel cut out of the arrangements. Was that petulance he felt? How juvenile…and more than a little disturbing.

'Overdoses on fairy floss or the Ferris wheel, ice for bruises after the three-legged race, the odd stitch or two after the sponge-cake judging.'

From the glow of humour in Caitlin's eyes, he was sure she'd detected the faint peevishness in his voice. He wasn't at all sure he liked being so easy to read.

'Matthew! That's only happened once.' Doreen gave him a brief reproachful look. 'Agnes was so excited about winning the sponge section last year that she tripped on the leg of a trestle table.'

'Perfectly understandable.' Caitlin's mobile mouth twitched.

'Well, it was her first win. Anyway, I'm sure you'll enjoy the day, dear,' said Doreen. Oblivious to the undercurrents, she picked up the leftover casserole and went through to the kitchen.

Caitlin rose and gathered up the dirty plates. Matt let his gaze follow her across to the sink. Their guest was a pleasure to watch, moving with a natural fluid grace. Casual dark grey trousers clung to gentle curves and her tailored red shirt nipped in at the waist. The overall look was sex appeal without flaunting it.

On the other hand, he'd probably have found her close to irresistible in anything. Hadn't he been attracted this morning when she'd been up to her elbows in horse blood and after-birth?

Caitlin stopped beside his mother, who laughed at something she said.

He frowned as he watched them.

Caitlin Butler-Brown was a walking, talking, red-blooded woman, intelligent, good looking, the right age. All the attributes that would normally have had his mother's worst match-making instincts on high alert.

What was going on here?

Last year, she tried to fix him up with a date on show weekend and he'd been working then, too.

Perhaps it was because Caitlin was a guest. Or was his mother trying a bit of reverse psychology? He could tell her it wasn't necessary. He was already interested in Caitlin Butler-Brown. Though, if she was only here for a week, they could have nothing more than a flirtation. Perfect, because he'd been out of the dating scene for so long, he wasn't ready for anything more.

So, a nice, short flirtation. For a week, he'd enjoy her company. No strings attached.

'And you must see the Grampians while you're here, Caitlin.' Doreen came back towards the table, using oven mitts to carry a pie from the oven. As soon as she'd put the hot dish on the trivet, she pinned Matt with a brief, meaningful look. 'How about a nice family outing one day while you're here? What about Sunday, Matt? I can make up a picnic lunch.'

Ah, there it was, the unquenchable matchmaking spirit that he knew so well. Matt smothered a laugh. His foster-mother thought she was being subtle, bless her.

He cleared his throat. 'Sure, Sunday sounds good.'

'Oh, but you don't have to include me in your family plans.'

'We want to, Caitlin.' Another significant look from Doreen to Matt as she handed him a wedge of apple pie. 'Don't we, Matt?'

'Yes, that's right.' He grinned at their guest and earned a stern look from stormy grey eyes in return. His pulse surged. 'We want to, Caitlin.'

'It'll be so much nicer for you to go with someone who knows their way around. Won't it, Matt?'

Caitlin subsided into her chair with an odd helpless expression on her face.

'So much nicer.' Matt lifted a spoonful of dessert and met Caitlin's eyes over the mound of steaming fruit. It was perversely enjoyable to see someone else fidget under Doreen's well-meant manipulations. He might regret falling into line down the track when he tried to resist his mother's next matchmaking target. But for now he wasn't looking any further ahead than Sunday. 'Just say yes, Caitlin. It'll be so much easier.'

'Well, if you're sure…'

'We're sure.' He assured himself that he wasn't about to make the mistake of getting involved with someone who belonged in Melbourne. This was just a day out while Caitlin was here. It would be fun. And maybe he could indulge in that flirtation he'd been contemplating.

A bit of practice.

Keep it light.

Don't get in deep.

No one would get hurt.

'Hurry up, Dad! Caitlin!' Nicky called over his shoulder. 'Did you know possums only come out at night, Caitlin?'

'Yes, I did.'

Dusk was crisp with the promise of an overnight frost as Caitlin trailed Nicky across the yard. A wash of delicate pastels coloured the sky, leaving a lovely peach on the western horizon where the sun had just dropped below the Grampians.

Matt walked beside her. Out of the corner of her eye, she could see the torch swinging from his hand. She was glad of his silence while she turned over her thoughts.

She jammed her hands deeper into her jacket pockets. What was she doing here?

The short, simple answer was that Doreen had refused help with the dishes and Nicky had insisted that she should see the ringtail possum that he'd found earlier.

The longer answer was more difficult. The longing in her to be accepted, to be included, had made it impossible for her to decline Nicky's invitation. The way this family had swept her into their centre delighted her and terrified her in equal measure.

Dinner had been a revelation. Was it like that every meal they shared? Everyone's contribution was valid, encouraged.

Enjoyed. Including Nicky's. Nothing suggested that the warmth had been staged for her benefit.

The contrast to her family couldn't be more pronounced. Her mother's intense technical discussions with her fellow researchers had left Caitlin feeling isolated and lonely at the table.

She wondered if she felt it acutely with this particular family because she was related to Doreen. And because of her reaction to Matt.

'Penny for them.'

'Oh, I—I couldn't take your money.' She smiled to take the sting out of her refusal. 'You'd feel short-changed.'

She was glad when a few steps more brought them to where they were waiting to point out their find.

'Shine the light up there, Dad.'

Matt halted in the doorway and played the beam as directed.

'Come and look, Caitlin. She's still here.' Nicky grinned at her.

Matt turned his head, meeting her eyes. The small smile playing around his lips told her that he guessed exactly why she was hanging back. To see, she would have to move close, to stand at his side. Her heart hammered so hard she wondered what the statistics were on myocardial infarcts in twenty-nine-year-old females.

She swallowed and stepped forward, keeping her eyes on the finger of weak torchlight. A slim white tail hung down from a wooden beam and, after a moment, a pair of round eyes and a pink nose appeared on the other side of the upright.

'Oh, she's gorgeous.'

'Yes, she is.' Matt's soft murmur in her ear jolted all the way to her soul.

'Dad says they can have lots of nests. We found this one last week but this is the first time she's been in it when we've looked.'

'Well, thank you so much for showing me.' Caitlin moved

back. She needed to escape. Get away from the man standing beside her. Give her system time to recalibrate. 'I'll leave you to watch her. I'm going to…um, see if there's anything I can do for Doreen.'

She took care to make sure her gaze skimmed quickly over the pair, not letting Matt's eyes snare hers. If he thought she was running away…too bad.

CHAPTER SIX

MATT looked through the theatre-viewing window. The gloved and gowned local veterinarian worked on a cloth-draped hump. Bob Fryer's nurse, Haley, stood at the head of the table, monitoring the anaesthetic and checking her watch.

She glanced up, lifting a hand, and must have said something because her boss glanced at Matt over the top of his mask. Matt pointed to the door and Bob nodded briefly before turning back to his patient.

The pulse monitor's regular beeping was audible as soon as Matt pushed open the door. After tying a mask over his nose and mouth, he moved forward to look over Bob's shoulder.

'I can...feel.... Ah, that's got it.' Bob pulled a small mass from the cavity and dropped it into a kidney dish with a dull clunk.

There was something vaguely familiar about the object but, because of a coating of greenish slime, Matt took a moment to identify the foreign body as a shapely torso.

'A Barbie-ectomy.'

Bob chuckled his appreciation. 'This dog's got eclectic eating habits. Last time, it was a piece of plastic currycomb. It's a shame I can't put in a zip instead of sutures.'

Belying the grumbling words, the vet quickly closed the opening with a neat line of stitches.

'Okay, Haley, let's bring him round.' Bob peeled off his

gloves, pulled off his mask and slanted a resigned look at Matt.
'What brings you out this way? Thinking of changing the
shape of your patients?'

The comment zapped Caitlin back into Matt's thoughts.
He'd managed to banish her from his mind for the day…well,
most of the day.

'I was just passing.'

'Just passing.' Bob snorted his disbelief as he dropped the
used gloves into a bin. 'Yeah. Right.'

Matt watched as the stocky veterinarian walked over to the
cupboards at the end of the room and rummaged through the
contents.

'You cancelled your appointment today.'

'Too busy.' A moment later Bob re-emerged, a large clear
plastic arc in his hand. Back at the table, he clipped it around
the dog's neck to form a wide collar.

'If you'll get the door, Haley, I'll carry him through. Back
in a minute, Matt.' He lifted the groggy Labrador off the table.
'I'll just get young Rex here settled.'

'I'm not going anywhere.'

'I was afraid of that. Wait in my office if you like,' he said
as he manoeuvred through the door. 'We might as well be
comfortable while you read me the Riot Act.'

Matt wandered through to the office, collecting his medical
bag as he went. The room doubled as a tearoom so there were
several armchairs, cosy if a little threadbare, grouped around
a coffee-table in one corner. Putting his bag on the desk, he
relaxed into the swivel chair.

Posters of the life cycles of various parasites were pinned
around the walls. Egg to larva to adult, all depicted in vivid
colour. Worms in dogs and cats and horses.

His gaze stopped at an unpleasantly graphic photograph of
a dog's heart. The organ had been sliced open to reveal a tangle
of thin white worms. This was the sort of thing Caitlin would
encounter in her job.

Matt grinned. How would she react to knowing that a bad case of heartworm had turned his thoughts to her? Would she find it amusing? He rather thought she might. She seemed to have a quirky sense of humour.

Very different to his ex-wife. Sophie was serious. Always. She'd never had time for the light-heartedness that he'd tried to bring to their marriage. He suddenly realised how stifling that had been. Very commendably committed to her studies, then to her research and career…but not to their relationship.

He didn't want to think about that now.

Instead, he leaned back in the chair and looked up at the heartworm poster. What was Doreen's Irish guest doing today?

When he and Nicky had trooped downstairs to make their farewells that morning, she'd been in the kitchen having breakfast. Fresh-faced and impossibly young looking with that tumble of ringlets curling from a ponytail onto her shoulders. What would she have done if he'd given in to the impulse to kiss her goodbye? Not a peck on the cheek, as he'd done to his foster-mother. Oh, no. He'd tug off her fancy hair clip and plunge his fingers through those luxurious curls to tilt her face up. And then he'd press his lips to hers. Caress her, taste her.

Test her.

Straightening abruptly, he opened his eyes. Test *himself* was closer to the mark. If he didn't stop his mind straying off into these little fantasies, he'd be a basket case. At thirty-four, he was too old to be suffering an adolescent crush. But a bad case of the hots…now, that was something else again.

'Haven't you got better things to do than chase me around?' Bob's gruff voice jolted Matt back to the present.

'Business is slow.' Swivelling the chair to face his belligerent patient, he grinned unsympathetically. 'I'm having to run my more uncooperative patients to ground.'

'Must be.' Bob sank tiredly into the second office chair. 'I heard you dredged up a bit of my business the other morning.'

'I had help.'

'I heard that, too. To quote Jim Neilson, "a slip of a girl".' He chuckled. 'And all of about twelve years old if he's to be believed.'

'Caitlin's a bit older than that and a damned competent vet. Jim was bloody lucky she came along when she did.' Matt winced inwardly at the raw conviction in his voice.

'Jim did mumble something along those lines, too.'

In an abortive attempt to deflect the speculation he could see in Bob's eyes, Matt said the first thing that came into his head. 'She's staying at Mill House.'

'Is she indeed?'

Before he could dig himself any further into the hole he'd made, he snapped open his bag and removed the long metal case of the sphygmomanometer.

With a sigh of resignation, Bob rolled up his sleeve.

'Taking your medication?' Feeling more in control, Matt wrapped the inflatable cuff around the bare arm.

'Forgot this morning. Took it at lunchtime.'

'Checking your blood sugar regularly?' Matt hooked in the earpieces of the stethoscope. After locating the steady pulse beat, he pumped up the cuff and placed the diaphragm onto Bob's arm.

'I've been busy.'

'Uh-huh. So, have you been checking your blood sugar?'

The mercury dropped until the sound of the surging pulse started again and then a moment later stopped. Taking note of the reading, Matt released the air.

Bob swore softly. 'Sometimes.'

'How's it been?'

'Up and down.'

'You eating properly?' Matt looped the stethoscope around his neck and unwound the cuff.

'What are you? My mother?'

'No. Should I get her involved?'

'You wouldn't!'

Matt slipped his instruments back into his bag and sat down. There was a small silence while he examined his friend's face, noting the dull, tired eyes, the unhealthy greyish cast to the man's skin.

'How's Gary?' he asked softly.

'No change.' Bob's voice was rough with emotion.

Matt's heart went out to him. He knew that the bone-marrow transplant Bob was pinning his hopes on for his gravely ill son had had to be delayed because the donor had had an upper respiratory tract infection.

'Any chance of getting some relief so you can go down and be with Sally again?'

Bob snorted in disgust. 'Had a locum all fixed up but the silly bloke broke his leg. Compound fracture of the femur. Horse riding, of all things.'

'How about someone from Hamilton?' Matt rubbed his jaw as his thoughts raced ahead. *How about Caitlin?* She'd said she was looking for a small-animal practice. How would she feel about somewhere that covered large animals as well? The pregnant mare had presented no problems for her the other day.

'Someone's covering for a couple of days after the show.'

'They can't cover longer?'

Caitlin had only planned to be here for a week. Would she be prepared to stay longer to help out? His primary concern was for his patient, of course, but if she stayed he'd have a chance to get to know her better. Was that a good idea or not? He might want more than a flirtation. He might start to think about getting involved.

Getting to know her could be…complicated. She was a city person. Like Sophie had become. And look where that relationship had ended up. In the ditch. They'd fought over everything until Sophie's final betrayal.

'They're having their own staffing hassles at the moment with that gastric virus that's going around.' Bob grunted. 'So give me the bad news.'

'Your blood pressure is one sixty-four over eighty-six. Not good for a diabetic. Sounds as though your blood sugar isn't under control at the moment either.' Matt leaned back in the chair as he contemplated his patient. 'Do I need to paint the picture here?'

'No.'

'You'd be happy to have a locum if you could get one?'

'You're thinking of your little Irish lass?'

Bob's phrase made Matt want to wince. 'I'm thinking of Caitlin. Yes.'

'The thought crossed my mind when you mentioned she was staying at Mill House. You think she'd be interested?'

Would she? Did he want her to be? 'I'm…not sure.'

'No harm in asking, though, is there?' Bob grinned, looking suddenly more cheerful.

'None at all.' Matt put his personal doubts aside. Bob needed relief. 'Why don't you drop around tonight? Come for dinner. Mum'll enjoy an opportunity to feed you.'

'I'll be there.' He rubbed his hands together. 'I'm looking forward to meeting your Caitlin.'

Matt bit down on the urge to correct the impression that Caitlin was his. He had the uncomfortable feeling he'd revealed far too much already. Reaching into his bag, he plucked out a screw-top specimen jar and handed it to Bob. 'We might as well see what you're doing to your kidneys while I'm here.'

Standing alone in the room, Matt felt a chill pass over him. What had he done? Caitlin had been at Mill House for three days now. If she unsettled him this much in such a short time, what would the *little Irish lass* do to him after several weeks?

CHAPTER SEVEN

LAUGHTER carried down the hall from the study. Matt's lips curved. Homework? Enjoyable? That was a first.

Doreen said Caitlin had volunteered to help Nicky with a project on marine biology after accounting herself as something of an authority on the subject. An unusual string to the bow of a small-animal veterinarian surely.

The thought highlighted the fact that she was a stranger. A stranger he was about to invite to spend even more time in their lives.

He slowed as he neared the room, listening to Nicky's giggles and the lower-register chuckles from Caitlin.

The door to the study was ajar. He pushed it gently and absorbed the sight of the studious pair sitting at the desk. Caitlin's head was tilted towards Nicky's as they both focussed on the computer screen. Seeing them together gave Matt an almost uncomfortable feeling—part warm, part protective. The time she gave freely to his son got under his guard, disturbed him. As did Nicky's obvious response. He blossomed under Caitlin's attention.

Perhaps Doreen was right, perhaps he should be looking for someone. A wife and mother to complete their family unit. Unfortunately, it had been hard to want to cast anyone in the role.

Until Caitlin's arrival.

But what did he know about her apart from the fact that she was a veterinarian? And a city girl in Garrangay on holiday?

A city girl. Like his ex-wife. Though he knew it wasn't fair to measure Caitlin against Sophie's behaviour. Her infidelity had had nothing to do with location and everything to do with her lack of commitment to their marriage…to him.

He folded his arms and leaned against the doorjamb, trying to analyse the direction of his thoughts. Caitlin as flirtation practice for his rusty skills was one thing…sizing her up as mother material for Nicky was something else again. The idea had disaster written all over it.

And if she stayed longer, his son was going to get more attached to her.

He dragged a hand down his face. The idea of Caitlin working and living in Garrangay seemed suddenly, subtly threatening.

She leaned forward to point to an icon and murmured something to Nicky. Seconds later, a full-screen picture of a walrus appeared.

'Cool!' Nicky said, nearly bouncing with enthusiasm.

Matt watched a moment longer then, shaking off his forebodings, he said, 'I must be in the wrong house. This sounds like way too much fun to be Nicholas Gardiner doing his homework.'

Although his eyes were on Nicky, Matt still noticed a stiffening of Caitlin's posture. Intriguing. So, that feeling of reserve he got from her wasn't just his imagination.

'Dad!' Nicky swivelled on the chair and beamed at him. 'Caitlin's helping with my project.'

'So I heard.' He met Caitlin's gaze. The lovely grey eyes were guarded. No sign of the laughter she'd shared with Nicky only moments before. As he watched, a rosy glow tinted her cheeks. His heart bumped hard.

'Will you look at that? Time got away from us. Did you need the study?' She looked away, her hands fluttering over the pages of the book on her lap. 'We've nearly finished.'

'No need to hurry on my account,' he said, straightening up

and sauntering into the room. He propped himself on one corner of the desk. Her reaction surprised him, pointing to a vulnerability he hadn't seen since her first day here.

'See all these pictures, Dad. I'm going to use them to make my poster. We found heaps of stuff about marine mammals.'

'Great.' Matt looked at the papers, his heightened senses attuned to Caitlin's every move. He realised that the book on her lap was a black leather organizer, which she was now shutting.

Nicky grabbed a piece of paper off the printer. 'That's the last one, Caitlin.'

'So it is.' She succeeded in dragging the zip closed on the bulging pages. 'We need to find you some scissors and glue.' The smile she aimed at Matt was tight as she rose from the chair. 'There, now. The study's all yours.'

'Before you go, Caitlin, there is something I wanted to talk to you about.' Matt stood, feeling oddly as though he loomed over her.

She eyed him warily. The hand she rested on the back of the chair clenched, the knuckles pale.

'How about asking Nanna to get the scissors for you, Nicky? Caitlin and I won't be long.'

'Sure, Dad. See you in a minute, Caitlin.' Nicky flashed a quick happy grin at her before racing out of the room.

Matt crossed to the door and pushed it shut. The move created an unintended intimacy. Should he reopen it? Frustrated with his indecision, he left it closed and stalked back towards the desk.

'This looks dire. Should I be standing on the mat, then?' The lightness in Caitlin's voice sounded forced.

'What? Oh, no. It's nothing too serious.' He tried for a re-assuring smile but it felt stiff and unnatural. 'Grab a seat.'

She slid back onto the edge of the chair, her movements not as graceful as usual. The black case was clutched to her chest as though it might protect her in some way.

He suppressed a sigh. A witty quip might diffuse the tension but he couldn't think of anything with his mind clogged with acute awareness of her.

And now that he had her attention he wasn't sure how to begin. Perhaps she wouldn't appreciate him having semi-volunteered her services.

He pulled out the other chair and sat. The silence lengthened as he contemplated her knees, held primly together, so close to his. After a moment, she laid the organiser across her thighs and, abashed, he wrenched his gaze up to meet hers. She looked confused, anxious. And no wonder. He'd shut himself in with her and now he was ogling her legs.

'Caitlin—'

'I apologise, Matt.' She'd obviously decided to tackle him head on but he wasn't sure where she was heading.

'Pardon?'

'I should have asked you before I helped Nicky with his homework. Doreen didn't object when I offered so I thought… But you'd rather I didn't, then?'

'No. No, it's not that. I mean, I'm happy for you to help. But it's not much of a way for you to spend your holiday.' He was making a hash of this. 'Though, actually, that's what I wanted to talk to you about.'

'My holiday?'

'In a roundabout way. Do you like Garrangay?'

A frown pleated her forehead. 'Sure. What's not to like?'

'How would you feel about staying longer?'

'Longer?' She stared at him blankly. 'Well, it'd be grand but I can't afford to.'

'But if there was a job, a locum position?'

'A locum?' said Caitlin slowly.

'For the local vet.'

'I see.' Her eyelashes swept down, hiding her expression. Matt frowned. He'd have sworn she was working hard to suppress some fierce emotion. 'So…there's one available, then, is there? A locum?' she said, after a small pause.

'Yes. I don't know if I've done the right thing but I mentioned your name. You're under no obligation, obviously.'

He looked at her hands lying flat on the case. Were they pressing into the leather or did he imagine tension in the long delicate fingers? While he watched she began to turn the ring on the middle finger of her right hand. He really looked at the thick gold band for the first time. A man's wedding ring? Was it just an adornment or did it have particular significance for her?

'For how long?'

Matt dragged his mind back to the conversation as she stopped fidgeting to cup one hand over the other. The move hid the plain jewellery from view.

'Depends on you and our vet, Bob Fryer. He needs to spend some time in Melbourne. His wife's down there with their son at the Children's Hospital.' He hesitated a moment. The child's condition was no secret around Garrangay and Bob would almost certainly tell her about it when he asked about the locum. 'Gary has leukaemia.'

No mistaking the sincere sympathy in her eyes when they lifted quickly to meet his. 'Oh, that must be so worrying for them. What's the prognosis?'

'Very good if the bone-marrow transplant takes. Which it should. They've found a very compatible donor.' He paused. 'Look, Bob's coming for dinner tonight to discuss the possibility of the locum with you but I wanted to give you some warning.'

'Thank you.'

He should leave it at that, let her go away and think about the position. 'You did say you're between jobs just now, didn't you?'

Her eyes flicked back to his and he had the feeling she'd been so consumed by her thoughts that she'd almost forgotten his presence.

'I am, yes.' She was silent for a moment. 'Though that's not the only consideration.'

'I suppose you have commitments in Melbourne, people to go home to, a partner?' He nearly winced at his lack of subtlety but he was still interested in the answer.

'Not…really, no.'

What did that hesitation mean? Had she just broken up with someone? Or was there someone that she didn't consider important? The way Sophie hadn't thought he and Nicky were important. He had no right to an explanation but the urge to demand one was hard to suppress.

He tried another tack. 'Are you worried about the large-animal side of the practice?'

'It's a consideration, certainly. I haven't done any since university.'

'Bob's arranged for some limited cover from a Hamilton practice so I'm sure they'd be happy to consult. And cover any days that you need off. Like the weekend.'

'The weekend?'

'The show on Saturday, though you'll possibly need to work there if you take the position.' He watched her reaction.

'Oh, yes. Nicky's event. I hadn't forgotten. Just hadn't put the two things together yet.'

'Then, there's the Grampians,' he said.

'The Grampians?'

'On Sunday. Our trip.' She *had* forgotten that. Didn't that put him in his place? So much for his interpretation of her blush and apparent tension around him this evening. Just because he was suffering these inconvenient pangs of attraction, it didn't mean the feeling was mutual.

Still, she'd remembered her promise to his son about the show event and that was the most important thing. If his own ego felt a little battered, he'd get over it.

'Oh, of—of course.' Her fingers tightened around her folder briefly before she stood. 'Thank you for telling me about the job, Matt. I'll think about it. See you later, then.'

He smiled tightly. Would she accept the position? He was no closer to knowing.

And no closer to knowing if he really wanted her to.

* * *

Caitlin stood from the side of her bedroom window and watched Doreen picking beans for tonight's dinner. The quiet, methodical act seemed to epitomise Doreen's love for her home and family.

Each night so far, Caitlin had been invited to share the evening meal with them. She loved being a part of their unit. Even as an outsider, looking in, she could feel their warmth enveloping her. Something in her spirit was desperate to be steeped in that generous, unconditional acceptance and caring. It was so different from what she'd grown up with.

At the same time, she felt torn, as though her silence about her father's death meant she was enjoying something she didn't deserve.

She closed her eyes and sighed. She was no closer to breaking the news to Doreen. And her holiday was nearly half-over.

But what if she took the locum position Matt had suggested? It was almost too good to be true. She wanted to grasp the offer with both hands. If she stayed longer, she wouldn't have to spring the sad news about Martin Brown's death on her aunt in the next few days. She'd have time. Surely, the perfect opportunity to tell Doreen about her brother would present itself.

And she could get to know Doreen better. And Nicky, too.

And, of course…Matt. Though that was potentially dangerous to her peace of mind.

The whole man-woman attraction thing had never hit her like this before. Being near him, hearing his voice, watching him with his family. All these commonplace things left her weak and vulnerable. Afraid of the impact he had on her senses.

But surely familiarity would take care of that. She just had to keep control until her mind and body became accustomed to him. It would happen soon…she would make sure of it.

CHAPTER EIGHT

CAITLIN had decided to stay.

Good thing or bad?

On the morning of the show, two days later, Matt was still undecided. He rubbed soap into a grubby mark on Nicky's buff jodhpurs.

Doreen had deserted him to take her prize roses in for judging. Caitlin was still around somewhere; she'd drifted in for coffee and toast while he prepared Nicky's breakfast. He huffed out a sigh and looked up at the clock.

'Nicky? Are you nearly ready?'

'Da-ad! I can't *do* it.' Nicky stomped to the laundry door, bottom lip wobbling alarmingly. The bridle, so easy to take apart last night, was still a jumbled assortment of leather and metal dangling from his hands.

'Give me a minute to finish this.' Matt stamped on the urge to point out he'd been against dismantling the fiendishly complicated apparatus in the first place. But Nicky had insisted it needed to be cleaned *everywhere*. 'Then I'll see what I can do.'

As he rinsed the fabric free of suds Caitlin appeared, coffee-mug in hand,

'Here, now, let me see what you're about.' She put the mug on top of the clothes drier then crouched beside Nicky.

Matt watched his son's distress melt away as she wove the straps and buckles magically into order.

'Do you think you'll be able to come an' watch me today, Caitlin?'

'I do, yes,' she murmured as she slipped the last strap into place then handed the bridle to Nicky.

'It'll be harder for you now 'cos you're working an' you've got responsibilities an' stuff.'

He was trying to be so grown up about the possible disappointment that Matt's heart went out to him.

'I have, but I'm sure I'll manage.' She grinned at Nicky. 'Are you too old for a good-luck kiss, then?'

'Nope.'

She planted a kiss on each of the boy's pink cheeks. Matt was debating whether he could reasonably suggest he could do with some Irish luck, too, when she glanced at her watch.

'I must run.' She rose smoothly to her feet, bending quickly to pop a kiss on Nicky's forehead. 'For extra luck.'

'Caitlin?' Matt wanted her to look at him, too.

She paused with her hand on Nicky's shoulder. 'Yes?'

'Thank you.' Matt gestured at the bridle. 'You've saved us a major tantrum. Probably mine.'

'My pleasure.' Her smile temporarily erased the wariness she'd treated him with over the last few days. 'You'd have managed fine if it hadn't had a caverson noseband.'

'Er, right.' Matt watched her go, aware that Nicky was doing the same. The Gardiner males had it bad.

'She likes me.' His son beamed up at him when they were alone again.

Matt grinned. 'She does indeed.'

'She likes you, too, Dad.' The look Nicky had given him held a knowing gleam far beyond his years.

Was it against the rules of parenting for a father to interrogate a nine-year-old about a possible love interest?

'Why do you say that?' It was a struggle to sound uninterested, but Matt thought he managed fairly well.

''Cos.'

Nothing profound there. He was conscious of sharp disappointment.

Unfortunately, a handful of casual questions later he was no closer to understanding what Nicky had seen or felt.

Springtime in the Australian bush. Was there anything more beautiful? And for now she belonged, at least temporarily, as the Garrangay veterinary locum. Caitlin didn't want to pinch herself lest she *did* wake up and find that she wasn't assessing a patient at the local A and P show.

She loved it all. The smell of sweaty, snorting horses, the rhythmic pounding of hooves as they trotted and cantered by.

Sun warmed Caitlin's back as she suppressed a smile and watched the walking gait of a lean bay thoroughbred.

'He's certainly stepping short on that hind leg, Robyn.' She ran her hand over the hock down to the fetlock. No swelling or heat in the limb. With the hoof balanced on her thigh, she applied careful pressure to the sole with a pair of pincers. When she reached the toe, the animal pulled back, wrenching the hoof out of her grasp.

'He's very tender in the toe area. We need to get his shoe off to have a closer look.'

'I guess that's the end of riding him today,' Robyn said, resigned. 'What do you think the problem is?'

'Could be seedy toe or—' A flash of wild movement caught Caitlin's eye. She spun to see a solid grey hack galloping towards a large practice jump. Arms flapping, the rider urged on the heedless flight.

'Oh, no. He's going too fast,' gasped Robyn, confirming Caitlin's fears. 'That's John Meredith on his new horse.'

With its head carried so high, Caitlin wondered if the horse was even aware of the obstacle in its path. Her breath caught in her throat, she reached for the radio at her belt and waited the suspended seconds to see if disaster would be averted.

Suddenly, hindquarters bunched, the horse twisted and

swerved, pitching the rider headfirst into the poles. As the poles clattered to the ground Caitlin began running, the radio held close to her mouth.

'Dr Gardiner to the exercise area urgently. Possible spinal injury to adult male rider.'

'Be right with you, Caitlin.' Matt's voice was calm. 'Keep him as still as possible.'

The spooked animal scrambled away, dragging the boy's frighteningly inert body for several paces before his foot slipped free of the stirrup.

Other spectators that were closer began to unfreeze and converge on the victim.

'Don't move him,' Caitlin called as she reached them.

'I was just going to take off his helmet,' a woman said, her hand on the chinstrap.

'Let's leave it until we see how badly he's hurt.' On her knees, Caitlin leaned over and touched the boy's shoulder and spoke firmly. 'Can you hear me, John? I want you to open your eyes for me.'

After a moment the lashes fluttered and clouded brown eyes stared up blankly.

'That's good, John. I want you to keep very still for us. Can you understand me?'

Apart from blinking slowly, he made no response.

'Should we call First Aid or something?' said the woman opposite Caitlin.

'Dr Gardiner's on his way.' Caitlin smiled reassuringly at her then moved to kneel at the boy's head, placing her hands on either side of his helmet. 'The best thing we can do is keep John as quiet as we can until he gets here.'

'Is he going to be all right?'

'I'm sure he'll be fine. Do you know if he's at the show with anyone?'

'His parents will be here. I've seen their alpacas in the pavilion.'

'Could you find them? They'll want to know what's happened.' As the woman rose to leave, Caitlin added, 'Perhaps have them paged if you have trouble locating them.'

Turning her attention back to the boy on the ground, Caitlin was pleased to see his eyes were still open and he seemed to be breathing comfortably. She couldn't see any obvious injuries apart from his reduced state of consciousness.

'John, you've had a fall.' That slow blink again as though her voice was registering on some level. 'The doctor's on his way to see you. He'll not be long.'

The circle of onlookers shuffled back.

'Matt!' Try as she may, she couldn't quite stifle the relief in her voice. Collecting herself quickly, she described the accident. 'He obeyed when I asked him to open his eyes but other than that he's not responding.'

'Okay, good. And you've kept his head stabilized. Well done. I want to get him into a cervical collar before we look at anything else. If I hold his head, do you think you can ease the helmet off?'

'I can, yes.'

Matt positioned his hands on either side of the boy's face and neck, moving his fingers up as she slowly slipped the hard hat away.

'Great. I'll get you to hold him steady again.' He slipped the collar into place and fastened it.

Caitlin sat back on her heels and watched Matt work. Now that he was in charge she could acknowledge how shaken she'd been by the accident. But there was something steadying about the methodical way he assessed John, checking his vital signs, feeling for injuries. John moaned slightly as Matt removed his elastic-sided boots.

Caitlin realised the youth was looking up at her, his eyes much clearer. 'Hello, John. Are you back with us, then? I'm Caitlin and this is Dr Gardiner. We're looking after you.'

'Where…am I?'

Matt moved up alongside their patient. 'Hi, John. Do you remember what happened?'

'I remember going to the show.'

'That's right, mate. You've had a bit of a tumble. Have you got any pain?'

'My…back.'

Matt flicked his small torch expertly into John's eyes again. 'Is the pain up high around your chest or down lower?'

'Down…lower.' John gasped, his hands clenching into fists and tried to point to the area.

'Don't try to move.' Matt's voice was gentle. 'How bad is it?'

'Pretty bad.'

'Okay, hang in there. I'll give you something to help in a minute. Can you wriggle your toes for me?' When nothing happened, Matt reached down to rub his hand over each foot. 'Can you feel that?'

'Yeah.'

'That's fine, John. I'm going to give you something for the pain.' Matt's long fingers worked deftly to set up an IV cannula in John's arm. 'Can you hold this for me, Caitlin?'

'Got it.' She took the fluid bag.

Matt attached the line and set the drip rate. After popping open a morphine vial, he drew up the contents and then slowly injected it into the valve. 'This should help in a minute, mate. Is anyone at the show with you?'

'Mum…and Dad.'

'I've sent someone to get them,' said Caitlin.

'Terrific.'

'Here comes Cathy Meredith now,' said someone in the crowd.

Matt stood up. 'I want a quick word with her, Caitlin. Will you be right here for a couple of minutes?'

'Of course.'

His eyes smiled his approval. 'Yell if there's a problem.'

Caitlin looked down at John as Matt strode away. 'Did you hear that? Your mum's on her way.'

'Yeah.' The boy's voice was rough with emotion.

'It's okay, John. She'll be here soon. Just keep as still as you can now.'

A few moments later, Matt was back with a subdued-looking woman obviously trying to put a brave face on her anxiety. John's face crumpled and tears trickled out of the corners of his eyes as his mother knelt beside him and stroked his forehead.

'Hello, sweetie. Dr Gardiner tells me you've had a fall.'

'An air ambulance helicopter is on its way,' murmured Matt, coming to stand beside Caitlin. 'We're sending him straight down to Melbourne. Even if this is just spinal bruising I want him to be with the experts. Are you right to be here for a bit longer?'

'Sure.' She looked up. The glowing approval in his eyes filled her with warmth.

'Let's finish getting him set up.' Matt put his hand on Cathy's shoulder. 'Cathy? We need to get John strapped onto the board now. Can you hold his IV bag for us?'

'Oh. Yes. Of course.' Cathy scrambled to her feet and moved aside.

Caitlin smiled reassuringly as she handed her the bag.

'How are you doing, John?' asked Matt as he crouched. 'How's the pain now?'

'Okay. Better.'

'Great. We're going to strap you onto a board to hold you nice and still so we can move you.'

'Okay.'

For the first time, Caitlin realised two uniformed first-aid men were standing patiently nearby, holding a long board.

Matt signalled them into position and crossed John's arms over his chest. 'We're going to roll you onto your side, John. You might feel a bit uncomfortable but I don't want you to try to help us. Let us do all the work. Okay, mate?'

'Okay.'

Matt looked at Caitlin and the others. 'I want to check him for injuries once we've got him on his side. You're right to support his head, Caitlin?'

'I am, yes.'

'Okay, on my call. One, two, three, roll.'

Working together, they soon had John positioned on the board. As Matt fastened the straps Caitlin could hear the steady drone of an approaching helicopter.

'We'll have you on your way in a few minutes, John,' said Matt.

As Caitlin moved back, the radio at her belt crackled into life, asking her to report to the main pavilion.

'I have to go,' she said, putting her hand onto Cathy's shoulder and rubbing lightly. 'Good luck, John. I'll see you later, Matt.'

A couple of hours later, Matt made his way through the amusements area, enjoying the tinny carnival tunes, the clatter of mechanical pulleys, the screams of delicious terror. Perhaps he could talk Caitlin into a ride in the House of Horrors. The girls always squealed and clung to the nearest person when the skeleton swung out of the rafters. If Caitlin was made of sterner stuff, he'd happily cling to her.

Oh, yeah. He grinned. The thought of holding her close was *very* appealing.

He'd had a busy morning. Fortunately, nothing nearly as dramatic as John Meredith's fall. A call to the hospital had reassured him that John's scans showed no obvious fractures. He'd be kept in until he regained full mobility but it seemed likely that the boy had escaped with swelling and soft-tissue damage. Damage that would heal.

Caitlin would be pleased. She'd been brilliant at the scene, taking charge of the situation until he'd arrived, organising someone to fetch John's parents. He'd almost forgotten what a pleasure it was to work in a well-coordinated team.

He glanced at his watch.

Half an hour until Nicky's event. Would Caitlin remember her promise to be there? Part of him wanted to find her and make sure she didn't forget, didn't disappoint his son. He knew first hand the heartbreak of an adult's broken promises. Before Doreen had rescued him all those years ago, he'd had a steady diet of them from his own mother. He'd do anything to protect his son from that pain.

Matt grimaced slightly. Sure, his main concern was for Nicky, but there was a strong element of self-interest. He didn't want to be disappointed either, for her to be less than the person he wanted her to be.

There was something about her. Something that made him want to touch, be touched. Her hair, her skin, her slender curves. The urge was stronger than anything he'd felt before. Was it clouding his brain and maybe his judgement?

He and Sophie had been friends through high school, then medical school. Country kids in the big smoke. The drift into matrimony had been a mistake that had destroyed their friendship—Sophie's infidelity had crushed him.

Though now he wondered if he'd truly loved his ex-wife. He'd certainly never experienced the flood of sensations, physical and emotional, that Caitlin sent raging through him.

He knew the chemistry of what was happening. His blood stream was overdosed with adrenalin and testosterone. Dopamine and serotonin zinged along his neural pathways.

Unfortunately, knowing *why* he felt this way didn't help. He was powerless.

Was it mutual?

He stifled a sigh. Most evidence pointed to the contrary. Though there were a few intriguing times that he'd felt an edgy nervousness about her, a sense of...anticipation almost.

Perhaps he could talk her into a bout of wild, passionate sex, relieve his inconvenient lustful needs. Once he'd moved past this hormonal overload, she might see him as the sensitive new-age guy that he really was.

Yeah, right, Matthew Gardiner. That's going to happen in this lifetime.

He puffed out a resigned breath. Knowing his luck, a taste would only exacerbate the problem.

He wandered down the rows of horse stalls peripherally aware of the feverish activity. Of the metallic jangling of stirrups and bits, the smell of horse sweat and leather.

Nicky had been bursting with enthusiasm about this moment for weeks. He'd started hinting about getting a pony. Riding the school horses had sufficed until now. But Christmas was looming. No prizes for guessing what would top the wish list.

When he reached the stall Nicky had been assigned there was no excited child in sight.

Instead, Caitlin was there.

CHAPTER NINE

SHE'D kept her promise!

His rush of relief made him realise just how anxious he'd been. But too quickly that feeling ebbed, leaving a gut-wrenching ache of desire.

He braced an arm on the partition between the stalls and watched her work. Her long slender legs bent slightly at the knees as she held the pony's hind leg off the ground.

Black denim pulled tautly across her backside, large pockets flattened to the curve of each buttock. The knitted fabric of her bright red T-shirt had come away from the waistband of her jeans. He could see the shallow line of her spine in the expanse of exposed creamy skin.

A loose ponytail tamed her dark curls, leaving her nape tantalising bare. A sensitive area for her? Would she murmur encouragement if he pressed his lips to the milky skin, bit gently on the smooth flesh?

What would happen if he scooped her up and laid her on the stack of straw bales at the back of the stall? What would happen if he followed her down, matching his body to the length of hers? It was all he could do to stop himself from groaning aloud. He clenched his jaw, looking away for a few moments until he had himself under control.

Madness to think having her stay in Garrangay was a good idea.

Madness.

He ducked under one of the ropes that clipped the pony into the stall and moved closer.

'Caitlin?'

Her name snapped out, harsh and short. She jolted upright and spun to face him. Wide grey eyes met his as she stepped back into the pony's flank. The placid chestnut shifted its weight, catapulting her forward.

Matt reached out to catch her.

Caitlin gasped as her foot landed on a shifting surface. Lurching awkwardly, she looked down to see the grooming kit wrapped around her ankle. A split second later, she found herself plastered against the front of Matt's shirt, her hands clutching at the soft fabric as she tried to find her balance.

'Do you think we've got time for this, honey?'

She could hear the husky laughter in his voice, feel his chuckle rumbling in his chest, the warmth of his hands wrapped around her upper arms.

'Very funny, to be sure.' She tipped her head back so she could scowl at his grinning face. His body heat radiated into her, making her desperately aware of him and of her own turbulent response. 'Stop blathering like an eejit and help me up.'

'Of course.'

His hands shifted, wrapping snugly around her waist. A moment later she realised his intention and grabbed his shoulders as her feet dangled clear of the ground. The grooming kit fell off with a dull clatter. Instead of releasing her, he kept her close. She could feel her breasts flattened against his chest.

They were nose to nose, would have been touching if she hadn't arched her head back slightly. With their eyes level, she was trapped by his shimmering dark green stare.

'Is that better?'

She nearly gulped at the husky growl in his voice.

'No. Yes. No. That's not what I...' She swallowed, wrenching her gaze away from the emerald eyes to the strong, angular bones of his face. 'Um, not what I meant. Put…put me down, please.'

'Of course.'

Her relief at his ready agreement was short-lived. The slow slide down his torso tormented her already sensitised breasts, made her aware of his solid strength. Made her aware of her needs and vulnerability. The few seconds that it must have taken for her feet to touch the ground seemed endless. Delicious torture.

She could feel the slight bunching of her T-shirt at her solar plexus where it had been pushed up. *If she could gather her wits, she would move to straighten it.* As soon as she'd completed the thought, Matt's hands moved, his fingers brushing the unbelievably sensitive skin at her waist.

She closed her eyes, feeling her shallow gasping breaths, clutching at his upper arms, as an avalanche of sensations raced through her. Her heart pounded, the hard beats shattering all hope of composure. Surely he could hear them, feel them. With the way they were standing, how could he not?

Opening her eyes, she found her gaze drawn to his mouth. He wasn't smiling any more.

Her gaze slid down, away from his face, away from the shapely fullness of his bottom lip to the column of his throat. His carotid pulse was surging just as erratically as hers was. The evidence of his susceptibility was deeply moving. She lifted her gaze, compelled to meet his.

He was closer, intent plain in his half-closed eyes.

His head tilted, angling so his mouth could meet hers. There was plenty of time to say no. She didn't want to stop him, but some small spark of sanity insisted on making an attempt at protest.

'Is this wise, Matt?' The words came out low and husky, disturbingly unlike her normal voice. Her hands flexed around his upper arms, over the solid muscle.

'Wise? No. But I don't care.'

The whisper of his breath passed over her waiting lips. Her eyelids fluttered down as his mouth settled over hers.

She'd waited for ever for a kiss like this. A tantalising invitation to get to know him better. She was utterly lost in the gentle teasing contact, time was suspended.

But then…it wasn't enough. She wanted—no, *needed*—more. She moaned softly, sliding her palms up over his shoulders and running her fingers into his short thick hair.

Pressing closer, she felt him move back until with a small bump he reached the wooden partition.

The kiss deepened, his lips sliding over hers, warm and firm and confident. His hands on her back, arms wrapping around her ribs, small delightful points of pressure as his fingers pressed into her flesh. All the while the wonderful, moist caress continued, promising excitement, hinting at greater pleasure. Her entire body hummed to the thrill of it. She felt at once energised and on the verge of fainting with pleasure.

A sudden clatter, loud and metallic, from a nearby stall ripped her out of the moment. She pulled back, desperately sucking in a chestful of air. Lord, what was she *doing*? She scrambled away to stare dumbly at Matt. The shock she felt was reflected in his dark eyes.

He stood, his back to the wall, legs braced apart. His arms stretched out towards her, the gesture almost a plea. If she wanted to, if she was brave enough, foolish enough, she could step forward, fit back into his embrace. Press her lips back to his glistening mouth. But the heady, seductive moment was gone and in its place the dousing chill of sanity.

And a split second later came a child's shriek, then a strident neigh from further away.

His hands slowly returned to his sides.

'Oh, Lord.' She backed away another step as she raised unsteady fingers to her lips, feeling their fullness and sensitivity. 'We must be gone in the head.'

He looked at her blankly. 'Sorry?'

'Daft, we must be daft.'

Despite the balmy warmth of the day, he felt almost cold where her body had been pressed against him.

He grunted, straightening away from the partition as he ran his fingers through his hair and around the back of his neck. The kiss had exploded in his brain, leaving him dazed and barely able to string coherent thoughts together.

Should he apologise? He didn't feel like it.

Caitlin touched her mouth, then snatched her hand away when she realised he was watching her. She scowled at him. 'You—you must be wondering where Nicky is.'

'Of course,' he said, his voice gravelly.

Her speedy composure felt like an insult. He wanted to see if it would hold if he dragged her back into his arms.

'He lost his number. Doreen's taken him to find another. They should be back any moment...' She glanced around. 'Any moment.'

'I'll wait.'

She looked as though she'd have liked to suggest he wait somewhere else but in the end she said, 'Right. I'll—I'll finish Sheba's feet, then.'

'Yes.' He watched as she bent to gather the scattered grooming gear. Her hands were shaking. *Not so composed after all.* Elation thundered through him.

'Caitlin?' He crouched beside her and reached for one of the brushes.

'Yes?' She kept her face averted.

He covered her hands with his, stilling her agitated movements, heard her quick indrawn breath. 'We need to—'

'Dad!'

Matt felt Caitlin's start. He released her as she pushed forward to gather the hoof pick.

Rising smoothly to his feet, he turned to face Nicky and Doreen. His son's excited chatter washed over him, filling the awkward void, giving him something to concentrate on. An anchor in a world turned inside out.

* * *

That evening Caitlin listened to Nicky regale them again with his third placing in his riding event. His delight with his success was engaging…and a blessing. If the dinner conversation had relied on her, the table would have been uncomfortably quiet. Especially since Matt was hardly making an effort to contribute his share either.

She pushed a piece of pumpkin around at the edge of her plate then sneaked a quick look at him, only to find him watching her. His brooding expression sent a hard jolt through her system. Was he thinking about their kiss? If so, it seemed to give him no pleasure.

Heat crept into her cheeks as she slid her gaze back to her plate. What was wrong with her? She'd been kissed before, so why all this maidenly blushing and ridiculous tongue-tied silence? Annoyed with herself, she looked back at Matt and frowned. He smiled slightly and raised one eyebrow as though he read her frustration.

The shiver of premonition she'd had when she'd first met him came back forcefully. She'd felt that staying in control would be a problem around him. And the kiss had proved her point. As soon as she'd finished her meal she was going to escape to her room. Until then, she would ignore Matt Gardiner and his eyes that saw too much.

Wrenching her gaze away from him, she was just in time to catch the puzzled look that Doreen shot between Matt and herself. Did her aunt suspect something? That was the last thing she wanted.

'Doreen, would you pass me the potatoes, please?' said Caitlin, blurting out the first thing that popped into her head.

'Of course, dear.'

Accepting the dish, Caitlin added another spoonful of the mash to the pile still on her plate.

'I meant to thank you earlier for your help with John Meredith, Caitlin.'

'I was glad to.' Talking about the case? That she could deal with. 'Have you heard how he is?'

'They've done scans and there's no lasting spinal damage, no internal damage.'

'That's grand. He's a lucky boy.'

'Yes. He's especially lucky that you were there this afternoon.'

Her smile felt more like a grimace but fortunately no one seemed to notice. She felt like a fake. Sure, helping with the injured boy had been real enough, it was everything else that was out of kilter. Matt's appreciative look. Doreen's warm motherliness. The way his family had folded her into their embrace.

For some reason, Matt's kiss had underlined how unworthy she was to be so accepted. They didn't know she was here to bring them grief.

As she worked her way doggedly through her meal, she lectured herself on the folly of being sidetracked. She needed to take back control, keep Matt at a distance. And, with her up-bringing and nomadic family, wasn't keeping her distance in relationships something she was good at?

The snippet of self-awareness was so depressing.

She was torn. There was so much here in this home, in these people, that was warm, precious, enviable.

But once she told Doreen the news about her brother, would she still be as welcome?

And if she was, would she be brave enough to reach out and try to really fit in? Wanting to belong here was different from actually carving out a niche for herself. She was afraid.

More than that.

She was terrified.

CHAPTER TEN

MATT'S kiss was the first thought that slipped dreamily into Caitlin's mind the next morning. Half-awake, she rubbed her lips over each other, reliving his taste, the feel of his mouth.

A moment later, heart thumping, she blinked her eyes wide. Oh, Lord! What had he thought when she'd backed him up against the partition? She'd behaved like a wild woman. As soon as his lips had touched hers, she'd wanted to devour him. She pulled the pillow over her hot face and smothered a heartfelt groan. She'd never reacted like that to a kiss before.

Unable to bear the trend of her thoughts any longer, Caitlin threw aside the pillow and scrambled out of bed.

A broad-brimmed raffia hat hanging on the post at the end of the bed reminded her she was spending the whole day in Matt's company.

The whole day!

How was she going to handle it after that kiss? Perhaps there'd be an emergency at the clinic. Not that she wished an injury on some poor animal.

'Get a grip, you eejit. It's not as if you're going to be alone with him.' She frowned at her reflection. Eyes shadowed with smudgy dark rings stared back, testament to her long, restless night.

'And even if you are, you've a tongue in your head. You can

say no. If you're asked. Which you won't be. Not with his family and Nicky's friend around.'

She snatched up her clothes and stalked through to the en suite for a quick shower. After a vigorous towelling that left her skin tingling, she stepped out of the cubicle.

Matt was definitely a man who would respect a woman's wishes. She smoothed moisturiser over her face. Her fingertips lingered a moment on her bottom lip, his kiss vivid in her thoughts.

He wasn't the problem...she was.

She didn't *want* to say no.

'It was just a kiss, for heaven's sake. It meant nothing.' She yanked on lightweight green cargo pants and a cream singlet top. 'He took advantage of the moment, that's all. And what was he supposed to do, with you plastered all over his shirt and looking up at him with cow's eyes?'

She looked at herself in the mirror and scowled. 'All right. So it did mean something to you but there's no future in it. He's a man with commitments. You live in Melbourne, his place is in Garrangay. And you're not in the market for a quick fling.'

She stared at her reflection a moment longer. 'A bit of conviction wouldn't go astray.'

Smoothing on a layer of lip gloss, she continued her lecture. 'This locum has bought you extra time in Garrangay so put it to good use. Concentrate on finding a way to talk to your aunt. She's the reason you're here. Maybe, once you've done that, all these other complications will get untangled.' She looked herself straight in the eye. 'Or maybe not.'

A light tapping had her spinning to face the door, her breath frozen in her lungs.

'Caitlin?'

Blood pounded through her veins at the sound of Matt's voice. *Oh, God, could he have heard anything?* She pressed her hand to her mouth to stifle a bubble of hysterical laughter.

'Yes?' she gasped.

'Are you nearly ready? Breakfast's on the table. We should head off shortly.'

'Right. Yes.' She cleared her throat and breathed deeply to steady the quaver in her voice and tried again. 'I'll only be a moment.'

She grabbed Doreen's raffia hat, a long-sleeved cotton shirt and her bag. By the time she got down to the kitchen Matt was packing sandwiches and flasks and water bottles into knapsacks. Her treacherous heart skipped a handful of beats as her eyes drank in the sight of him.

'Caitlin, dear, did you sleep well?' Doreen didn't wait for an answer, which was just as well since the power of speech deserted Caitlin as soon as Matt's eyes met hers. Caitlin made a noncommittal sound as she crossed quickly to the table and slid into a chair.

'Try this marmalade. It's made with mandarins.'

'Thank you.' Caitlin took the proffered dish from her aunt and scooped out some of the chunky orange spread. 'Looks delicious,' she said, before biting into a slice of toast.

'It won first prize in the jam section at last year's show.' Doreen smiled and picked up her cup. 'Have you recovered from yesterday? You had such a busy day with Matt.'

Her aunt didn't know the half of it, thought Caitlin, coughing to dislodge a toast crumb that threatened to choke her. Though she tried not to let it, her gaze flicked back to Matt, to find him watching her with a slight smile. She swallowed and turned her attention back to her breakfast.

'I'll put these in the car and get Nicky and his friend David ready. There's an extra water bottle here for you, Caitlin.'

'Thank you.'

Caitlin hurriedly finished her last mouthful and walked out to the front porch with Doreen. The four-wheel-drive was parked in front of the house.

'Enjoy yourselves and take care,' called Doreen from the porch.

'We will.' Matt opened the tailgate of the vehicle and stacked the rucksacks on the floor.

'You're not coming?' Dismayed, Caitlin stopped at the bottom of the steps and looked up at her aunt.

'Gracious, no, dear,' answered Doreen. 'All that hiking is too much for me these days.'

'Oh.' Caitlin bit her lip. How thoughtless. She should have realised the day might be too strenuous for someone with angina. 'I could stay and keep you company.'

'Nonsense, I wouldn't hear of it. You'll have a lovely time with the boys.'

Caitlin looked over her shoulder. Matt stood at the side of the vehicle, watching and waiting.

Nicky leaned out of the back window. 'C'mon, Caitlin.'

She lifted a hand in acknowledgement. 'Are you sure, Doreen?'

'Absolutely. Off you go. I'll look forward to hearing all your adventures when you get back.'

Caitlin turned and walked around to where Matt held the door open. He moved slightly when she reached him and her footsteps faltered. She looked up to find his green eyes focused solemnly on her face.

'If I promised not to bite, would you relax?' His voice was pitched low so only she could hear.

She tightened her grip on the brim of her hat and looked at him steadily. 'As I recall, it's not your bite that's the problem.'

His gaze settled on her mouth and Caitlin's pulse jumped. 'If I promised not to kiss you, would you relax?'

'And *do* you?'

'Promise not to kiss you?' His eyebrow climbed. She could almost see the cogs turning in his mind. 'If I must.'

'You…must.' But a small thrill raced along her nerves. He sounded as though he wanted to kiss her.

'Then, I…will.' He gave her a teasing grin. 'Enjoy the day, Caitlin.'

She nodded, a confusing mix of emotion churning in her stomach. Relief. But surely it wasn't disappointment. How contrary could she be?

Once they were on their way, Matt set himself to be entertaining, regaling her with stories about the area. History, people, fauna, flora, activities.

The road undulated through the valley. Vegetation—gum trees, banksias and tea tree—grew close to the road, with breaks in the foliage affording glimpses of the towering rock buttresses of the Grampians.

'If you're feeling brave, we could try abseiling or rock climbing,' said Matt.

Caitlin turned to look at him. 'Are you joking?'

'No. Why?'

'No way will you get me to do such a thing.' She laughed and realised, with a sense of surprise, she was enjoying herself. 'It's a mystery to me why people do.'

'Not a thrill seeker, then?'

'Life dishes up enough thrills without having to look for them like that, don't you think?'

'It's good for us to get out of our comfort zone occasionally.' He looked at her, only the briefest glance as he was driving. His eyes were warm, sparkling with humour, enveloping her in a bubble of intimacy.

Didn't he realise she was out of her comfort zone right now?

'I don't need to dangle at the end of a flimsy rope to feel that way,' she muttered.

'Really?' He sounded intrigued.

'Is it something you enjoy yourself? Rock climbing?' she asked hurriedly.

'I…haven't done any for a long time but, yes, I used to enjoy it.' There was a wistful note in his voice and she wondered why he'd given it up.

'I'll watch from level ground with the boys if you want to

try some today.' Though she wondered how she'd feel seeing him swinging from a rope halfway up a dangerous rock face.

'Would you?' Pursed lips and a small frown suggested he was mulling the idea over. 'Another time perhaps. Today I'll settle for a walk before lunch.'

In a small car park, half an hour later, he handed Caitlin her backpack. 'We probably won't need these but it's always a good idea to be prepared. This walk will take us about an hour and a half.'

'We're going to earn our lunch, then.' She glanced up at him, her eyes shining and her beautiful lush mouth curved.

He'd promised not to kiss her—but he hadn't promised not to want to. He turned back to the vehicle, staring blindly into the back as he struggled to quell the sudden need to reach for her.

'Matt?'

'We can skip this if you'd prefer. There's plenty of other sightseeing to do.' The words came out harsher, more impatient, than he'd intended. He glanced at her.

There was a moment of silence and her face fell. 'Think I'm a wimp, do you?' Her voice was light but he detected a note of hurt beneath the banter. 'Don't think I'm up to a *wee* bit of a walk?'

He shrugged uncomfortably, lifting the boys' backpacks out and shutting the tailgate. 'It's a bit more than a wee walk, Caitlin.'

'There's a challenge if ever I heard one.' She lifted her chin slightly. 'Let's get to it, shall we?'

He watched as she slipped her pack onto her shoulders and set off. Nicky and David came racing back to him for their backpacks and scampered after her. Shouldering his own burden, he followed more slowly, his thoughts centred on Caitlin's words.

Was she right? Was he setting a task, a challenge for her? Sophie had only been here with him once. She hadn't been interested, hadn't understood his fascination with the mountain range, and after a while he'd stopped asking her to come. He'd rationalised the time apart as a sign of a healthy relationship. No jealousy or fretting. Of course, he hadn't realised that Sophie had found her own entertainment.

Perhaps, deep down, he did hope Caitlin would fail so he could find reasons to distance himself from her. Or was he hoping she'd succeed, so he could give himself permission to fall for her?

But getting involved again meant putting himself on the line, trusting his ability to make good choices. Was he ready to do that yet? He didn't know the answer.

Quick strides soon brought him close enough to appreciate the gentle sway of her hips as she walked easily along the track. The boys gambolled happily around her and Matt smiled at their antics.

He huffed out a small sigh. Permission to distance himself from her? Who was he kidding? He was well past being able to do that easily.

CHAPTER ELEVEN

'TELL me what a nice Irish girl like you is doing in a place like this.'

The question wrenched Caitlin out of her daydream. She pulled her attention from the bold magpie eyeing her from a few feet away back to the man lounging on the picnic rug beside her. Matt had moved even closer, she realised. Propped up on one elbow, he watched her, his eyes alight with curiosity.

Her heart began an uncomfortable jig.

'You invited me,' she said, hoping her voice didn't betray her sudden attack of nerves.

'So I did.' He smiled lazily. 'But I meant in general rather than today specifically.'

'I see.' Her mind spinning over a dozen different answers, she leaned forward to pour more coffee into her cup. A distraction was what she needed. 'Would it surprise you to know my birth certificate's as Australian as yours?'

'You were born in Australia?'

'I was, yes.' The tangent she'd chosen wasn't the diversion she'd have wished. Followed to its source, it was far too close to why she was in Garrangay in the first place. A Freudian slip perhaps? *Think of something else, a safer topic.* She lifted the Thermos again and gestured at his cup. 'Want some more coffee?'

'Yes, thanks.' He held out his mug, his long fingers wrapped around the dark blue acrylic. 'But you were brought up in Ireland?'

She watched the level of dark brown liquid rising as she poured carefully then screwed the lid back on the flask before answering. Bless the lingering traces of her accent. A much better direction for their conversation. 'I was brought up in many places. But I spent a lot of time in an Irish boarding school.'

'Boarding school? What was that like?'

A lonely, frightening banishment for a child's ill-conceived rebellion. But she couldn't say that and ultimately she'd thrived on the stability of it. 'Effective. It turned me out at the end with what I needed to study veterinary science.'

'How old were you when you first went there?'

'Ten.'

'God, that's so young. Too young.' His gaze scoured her face before moving away to search for Nicky. The unreserved love for his son was plain to see. So sweet it pierced her to her core. She couldn't imagine him packing Nicky off to boarding school under any provocation.

'I was allowed to go a year younger than usual because I was ahead in the curriculum.' And because her mother had put pressure on the board.

His eyes came back to hers, demanding her honesty. 'You didn't mind?'

'Oh, sure I minded. At the beginning.' She'd been devastated by her mother's decision. All her promises, all her begging, hadn't changed things. 'But it gave me a good education and it was for the best in the long run.'

He was silent for a long moment. 'You said you were brought up in different places…. Did your father's job move around a lot?' he asked.

Caitlin shook her head. 'My mother's. Da's job was looking after me when I was with them.' She could imagine the questions forming in Matt's mind. Family was not a subject she was ready to discuss yet, especially not questions about her father. But it would look odd if she said nothing. 'My mother is a marine scientist. She's quite well known. You might have heard of her. Rowan Butler.'

'Your mother is Rowan Butler?' he said, sounding stunned. '*The* Rowan Butler who does those underwater documentaries?'

Caitlin nodded, philosophical. She didn't want to talk about her mother either.

'You travelled with her?'

'Some of the time. You could say that I grew up with a snorkel in my mouth instead of a silver spoon.' She smiled slightly. 'I've swum with most of those marine animals I helped Nicky find for his project. And sharks, too.'

His eyebrows arched. 'You've swum with sharks and you have a problem with abseiling.'

'I could swim before I could walk but I've never been able to fly.' She slanted a teasing look at him. 'And they were very well-fed sharks.'

He chuckled. 'Oh, well, that makes all the difference.'

His gaze shifted back to where the boys were playing. 'You had an unusual childhood.'

'I did, yes.'

'Any brothers and sisters?'

She swirled the liquid in her cup. 'No. Just me.'

'It must have been lonely at times, always moving.' Had he leaned closer? The atmosphere seemed even more intimate.

'Yes.' She sipped her coffee. Her heart swelling at his unexpected understanding. 'Most people don't think of that, though. They see the glamorous parts. They don't see that there's no chance to put down roots.'

A small silence settled between them, broken by children's laughter and a distinctive bell-like native bird call. Why was she telling him all this? She didn't want his pity.

'But then I'd be the envy of everyone at boarding school

after the holidays when I came back with tales of exotic lands and fabulous sea creatures.' She set her half-empty cup aside and busied her hands gathering up the plates and utensils from lunch.

With the implements in her hand, she paused for a moment. 'I made some good friends at school, spent some holidays at their places. They had *normal* pets like cats and dogs and budgies. And horses, of course. That's where I started gathering my vast equine knowledge.'

He tilted his head. 'Jim Neilson would be impressed.'

'Wouldn't he, though.' She laughed softly, remembering her first day, her meeting with Matt. Only a week ago. It seemed hard to believe how much he'd become part of her daily existence. Even harder to believe she'd let that happen.

'You weren't tempted to follow in your mother's footsteps?' Matt's question interrupted her thoughts.

She tried for a casual shrug. 'She's…very dedicated. A tough act to follow.' She fiddled with the lid to one of the plastic containers. 'Nothing gets in the way of her work. The world needs people like her but they can be very hard to live up to.'

The lid finally snapped into place.

After a moment, Matt said, 'I'm sure she's very proud of you.'

She dropped the container into a rucksack, remembering the last time she'd seen her mother. *Proud* didn't describe the response to Caitlin's career choice. Not at all. 'I think I disappointed her when I chose to specialise in small-animal practice with domestic animals. There is so much endangered wildlife that needs to be studied, saved.'

Her words sat between them, more revealing than she'd intended. She glanced at Matt to find him looking at her, his eyes warm and sympathetic. Oh Lord, he *did* feel sorry for her.

'She sounds like Nicky's mother.' He sat up, resting his forearms on his knees, his hands loosely clasped. 'Sophie's in a research lab in Melbourne. I know she's doing important work, but sometimes I'd like her to put Nicky first.' His lips curved in a rueful smile as he lifted a hand to wave away a persistent fly. 'Nicky seems to take it in his stride. I'm the one that gets bent out of shape about it. I hate the idea he's so low on his mother's priorities.'

The far-away look on his face held sadness as well as resignation. It was all Caitlin could do to resist the urge to reach out and touch him. She picked up her coffee instead.

'He has you, Matt. And Doreen. People who love him without reservation, who do put him at the top of their priorities. I think that's the most important thing.'

He looked at her steadily as though considering her words. 'You had your father. Was it enough?'

There was a small, almost expectant pause.

'I had Da, yes,' she said slowly. 'But I wasn't his top priority. He was very much in love with my mother. And she was in love with her work. I didn't realise how much until he got sick. There was no suggestion that she would drop everything to be with him.' She tilted her head, scanning the cloudless blue sky visible through the leafy canopy of the gum tree behind them. Talking brought back the difficult months of her father's illness. But now that she'd started to bare her pain and turmoil she couldn't seem to stop the words.

'The sad thing is that Da didn't expect her to come back. I was angry for him.' She picked up a gum nut in her free hand, rolled it along her fingertips absent-mindedly. 'And maybe I was angry *with* him that he didn't expect it.'

Why had she said that? She'd barely admitted it to herself, she realised, flicking the seed pod away. Now she'd told someone else. Such unguarded confidences were uncharacteristic and…unnerving. She wondered what she might divulge next. Her father's death and her secrecy about it weighed heavily on her mind. So much so that she was compelled to this dangerous flirtation at the edges of her concealment, almost as though she was daring herself to go further.

She stared at the dregs of her drink.

'Caitlin—'

'Do you suppose Doreen put something in this coffee?' She spoke quickly to cut off whatever he'd been going to say.

He glanced at her mug, obviously confused by her change of subject. 'Like what?'

'Oh, you know…an enormous dollop of sodium pentothal perhaps? I can't believe I've blathered on like this.' She half frowned, half smiled at him as she tried to make light of their conversation. 'You're much too easy to talk to, Matt Gardiner.'

'Good.' He held her gaze for a long silent moment. Caitlin caught her breath at the unmistakable warmth she saw in the green depths. 'I want to know everything about you, Caitlin. I want to know what makes you tick.'

An odd thrill of fear and longing trickled through her. If he did know what made her tick, would he like what he found?

'Sure, and why would you? There's precious little to know.' She began stacking the used picnic utensils and containers. 'I'll pack up here if you want to go and kick the ball around with Nicky and David.'

'Trying to get rid of me?'

'Not at all,' she said, determined to ignore the pout that made his mouth look so tempting. 'I—'

'Somebody, help! Please!' Screams shattered the afternoon quiet. Caitlin looked towards the end of the picnic ground as a girl ran out of the bush. 'My boyfriend's been bitten by a snake.'

Matt rose swiftly to his feet, scooping up his knapsack as he moved. He loped towards the hysterical girl as two youths staggered into the open area behind her, one obviously supporting the other.

Caitlin followed a bare second or two later, aware of Nicky and David running over as well. As she approached the group, Matt was settling the victim on the ground in the shade.

'Where were you bitten?' Matt's voice was calm as he took

stock of the situation. Both the youths looked to him for guidance but the girl was still agitated.

Now that Caitlin was closer, she could see the victim's extreme pallor and the sheen of sweat on his skin. She hoped that was reaction to his fright and not a sign that he'd walked a long distance with venom pumping through his system.

The boy lifted one hand and flapped vaguely towards his feet.

'On his leg. On his leg. By the ankle. See?' gasped the girl, her voice rising with each word as she pointed to the expanse of bare athletic legs between the bottom of the board shorts and a pair of rubber thongs. 'Oh, God. Andrew, please don't die.'

Matt turned the leg slightly and Caitlin could see two red lines, more like shallow grazes than puncture wounds. He opened his rucksack and took out two rolls of crêpe bandage.

'Please help him. Don't let him die.'

'Jodie!' The boy groaned a faint protest.

'Andrew, is it?' asked Matt. The boy nodded. 'I'm Matt Gardiner. I'm a doctor. You're going to be fine.'

Matt's concentration was focussed on his patient and he continued speaking in a soothing tone. 'I'm going to strap your leg. I want you to sit quietly, concentrate on relaxing. Deep breaths now.'

'Why aren't you putting on a tourniquet? What are you doing? What's he doing?' Jodie was nearly screaming. 'Oh, God, we need a tourniquet.'

Her hysteria flowed out in a swamping tide, raising everyone's tension. Matt had his hands full with the bite victim.

Caitlin grasped Jodie by the shoulders, turned her so her back was to her boyfriend.

'Jodie! Look at me!' Caitlin pitched her voice to a hard, no-nonsense edge. Tremors ran through the body beneath her hands but it stopped trying to pull away. 'Jodie. Listen to me. Andrew is *not* going to die.' The panicked gaze focussed on her and the hiccuping sobs quieted for a crucial moment. 'Dr. Gardiner is putting on a pressure bandage.'

'Your—your husband's a—a doctor?' she said, between gulps.

'He is, yes,' said Caitlin, not bothering to correct the mistake about her relationship to Matt. 'Andrew's in good hands. Once the pressure bandage is on, we'll get him to hospital.'

It would have been better if they hadn't moved their friend. The mad dash into the picnic area might have increased the danger considerably.

'I need you to take a deep breath now, Jodie, and keep calm,' said Caitlin, keeping steady eye contact and continuing to speak in a no-nonsense manner. 'You can help by answering some questions for us. Can you do that for us?'

'Y-yes.'

'Good girl.' She rubbed the still quivering shoulder. 'How far do you think Andrew walked after he was bitten?'

'Not—not far. We were just over there.' She turned and pointed to the nearby bush.

'Only about ten feet,' said the second boy, confirming Jodie's story. 'That's why Andy was trying to pick the snake up. Because it was so close to the picnic area.'

Caitlin suppressed a sigh. The boy's intention had been commendable but the outcome predictable. Most snake bites happened when people interfered with the naturally shy creatures. 'Do you know what type of snake it was?'

'It was dark brown,' said Andrew, through lightly chattering teeth.

'Any stripes, colour variations?' asked Matt.

'I don't know,' said Jodie, when Andrew shrugged. 'I didn't really see all that clearly. Andy was the one closest to it. Is it important?'

'Should we go and look for it?' asked the second boy.

'No!' Caitlin spoke at the same time as Matt. She shared a quick, speaking glance with him.

'No, don't worry,' said Caitlin more calmly. The snake was probably long gone but they didn't want to risk a second bite victim. 'The hospital can do a kit test. Jodie, why don't you hold Andrew's hand while I help Matt?'

Jodie wiped her cheeks and sniffed before going to sit beside her boyfriend to stroke his arm. If the girl's smile was a little shaky she at least held her tears at bay.

'Do you need something for a splint, Matt?' Caitlin examined the neat bandaging.

'I've got a couple in the back of the car. Could you grab those?' He tore open the next packet and continued strapping the limb.

'Keys?'

'In the front of my rucksack,' he said, pointing with his chin. 'Bring some more bandages, too, please. You'll find them in the grey box. And a blanket. And put a call through to Emergency Services while you're there, please, Caitlin. Let them know they'll need to test for the toxin. We don't know what sort of snake but the bite area hasn't been washed.'

'Sure.'

Though they were wide-eyed and fascinated with proceedings, Nicky and David managed to tear themselves away to follow her back to the vehicle.

'He looks real sick, Caitlin. He's not gonna die, is he?' asked Nicky in an awed voice, when she'd made the phone call.

'I'm sure Andrew will be just fine. Your dad knows what he's doing.' She unlocked the back door. 'Andy's had a nasty fright so he's probably suffering from a wee bit of shock.'

'Oh,' they said in unison, sounding half relieved and half disappointed.

Caitlin suppressed a grin. She'd had very little experience with small boys but she suspected that a ghoulish fascination with injuries was probably normal.

'Would you be able to give me a hand here, boys?'

They stepped forward eagerly as she handed them each a blanket. Their sense of importance at doing something to help was almost tangible.

'What's going to happen to him?' asked Nicky, as she gathered the bandages and splints for Matt.

She locked the back of the vehicle and set off back to the group, a boy on each side.

'Well, we've got an ambulance on the way and we'll send him off to hospital. They might have to give him an injection of anti-venin,' she said. Though that came with its own set of risks. The unfortunate Andrew would probably be kept in hospital under close observation for at least twenty-four hours to see if the injection was necessary.

'That's to stop the poison, right, Caitlin?'

'It is, yes.'

A short time later the ambulance she'd called arrived and Caitlin stood to one side with Jodie and the boys while Matt handed over to the paramedics. With her arm around Jodie's blanket-covered shoulders, she watched Matt help transfer Andrew onto the stretcher.

Matt turned back to ask if Jodie wanted to ride in the ambulance. A beam of late afternoon sunshine slanted through the treetops, shining at an oblique angle directly into his eyes. Spokes of clear green radiating out from black pupils held Caitlin oddly transfixed. Her heart squeezed painfully, her breath shallow and fast.

A snapshot of the moment was imprinted on her mind. The sound of the idling ambulance engine, kookaburras laughing in the distance, the smell of eucalyptus oil in the warm air.

Then he smiled, the corners of his eyes crinkling appealingly.

A shock of hot recognition ran through her, leaving her breathless and shaken.

Numb, she helped Jodie into the back of the vehicle, accepting the return of the blanket after the paramedic had replaced it with one of theirs. She seemed to see herself from a distance, looking normal, going through the motions of accepting Jodie's thanks, wishing them luck. No sign of the sick panic she could feel building in her chest, her stomach.

With a final, strained smile she turned away and walked back to the picnic blanket, her legs feeling disjointed and rubbery.

She was lost.

How could she resist this man? In that peculiar charged moment, she'd felt there was nothing she wouldn't do to stay with him.

How could that be?

CHAPTER TWELVE

HAD it been like this for her father? No sacrifice was too much?

Caitlin began mechanically packing the picnic utensils into the basket before stowing it into the back of the vehicle.

Da had nurtured his marriage with a deep love, a giving spirit. So proud of his wife's accomplishments, he'd never questioned the demands her work had put on him, on their family unit.

Leaves and twigs flew as she gave the tartan picnic rug a vigorous shake. She folded and rolled it up.

Her parents had had such a lopsided relationship. Something she would never tolerate for herself...or so she'd thought. How woefully naive she had been to vow never to give more than she was given. As if emotion could be parcelled out that way.

A tug on her sleeve snapped her out of her thoughts. Nicky was looking up at her. His eyes, so much like Matt's, were filled with concern. She realised he must have spoken to her several times while she'd stood staring into space, the blanket clutched to her chest.

'Sorry, Nicky. I was away with the fairies.' She moved her mouth into a smile of reassurance. 'What was it you wanted?'

'Can we have a drink, please?'

'Of course.' She rummaged in the esky then handed them each a small fruit juice. After a hurried thank you, they darted away to continue their ball game.

She watched Nicky laughing and wrestling with his friend. He was so happy and secure. Matt, Nicky, Doreen. A real family that played and laughed together. And talked.

Today, she'd talked. Blurted out things about herself, her past, her feelings. Things that she hardly acknowledged to herself. Now she felt almost exposed, raw.

Perhaps that's why she reacted so strongly to Matt. All she needed to do was back off a little, pull herself together and she'd be okay.

Happier that she'd found a reasonable explanation for that peculiar moment of shock, she risked another look at Matt.

He stood watching the ambulance move off as he talked on his mobile phone. Probably updating the staff at the emergency unit in Stawell. Caitlin gave a small sigh of relief. There, then. She was fine. She could look at him and everything stayed where it should. No little shocks.

He was just a nice-looking man. Gorgeous, in fact.

The call finished, he slipped the phone back into his pocket and strode towards her. His body moved easily, with an economy that was a pleasure to watch.

He looked up and caught her eye, his lips curving. And everything spun out of control.

She had to find another way to handle this.

Or she was in deep, *deep* trouble.

The temptation to make her excuses, run back to Melbourne, write Doreen a letter was overwhelming. She hated being a coward. But sometimes retreat was the only sensible option.

Thankfully, she didn't need to make conversation when they got back on the road. The boys filled in the silence with their chatter in the back seat.

She concentrated on the scenery. Banksias with distinctive yellow cones, tea tree, correa. She *would* stifle the turmoil that threatened to swamp her, even if she had to identify every single plant they passed on the way home. All she needed to do was apply a bit of common sense to the situation.

That shattering moment earlier had been an aberration. She hadn't slept well last night. No wonder, with Matt's kiss playing over and over in her restless dreams. It would pass…it *had* to pass.

All they needed was some normal interaction. Though not too much of that either. He was a dangerously attractive man— someone who *would* be too easy to fall in love with. And she wasn't ready for the sort of sacrifices that would mean. She had her life mapped out. And love and commitment were comfortably down the track. Not here. Not now.

'You're very quiet.' Matt's voice jerked her out of her thoughts.

'Am I?' For the life of her she couldn't think of an intelligent response.

'Tired?'

'A little. I was thinking…' She couldn't possibly tell him what was really on her mind. A burst of laughter from the back seat gave her a safe escape. 'Thinking it'd be good to harness the boys' energy.'

Matt chuckled. 'Hard to believe they've run around all day.'

'Yes.'

'Nicky should sleep well tonight.'

'So should I,' said Caitlin, then immediately wished she could unsay the words. They seemed to reverberate in the conversational lull, reminding her again of why she was so tired. 'Not that I'm saying I didn't sleep well last night.'

That was *worse*. Cheeks burning, she turned to look out the window.

'I didn't,' Matt murmured. She darted a quick look at him and caught his cheeky smile. 'Sleep well, that is.'

'Really?' *Matt in bed.* Just what she didn't need to think about. She cleared her throat. 'Well, um, you should tonight.'

'Perhaps.'

'Are we nearly home, Dad?' Caitlin was glad of Nicky's interruption.

'Not far.'

'Can Davey come back and play?'

'Not tonight.'

'Ple-ease?' He stretched the word out as though that might make it harder to resist. Caitlin hid a grin.

'No. It's getting late and you've both got school tomorrow.'

'But, Da-ad.'

Matt stifled a sigh and hoped this wasn't going to turn into a protracted argument. 'No, Nicky.'

'Not even for a little while?'

'Not even for a little while,' said Matt firmly.

The boys made their reluctant farewells at David's house a short time later. Matt looked at his son's glum face before glancing at Caitlin. Her eyes held a mixture of sympathy and laughter. He smiled wryly. It was nice to share the little parenting moment.

He restarted the car and headed for home. Today had been…great. A companionable silence filled the vehicle and his thoughts centred comfortably on the woman beside him. She was *fun*, fitting in with him and Nicky in a way that Sophie had never wanted to.

He slowed and moved to the left as a large articulated truck approaching them strayed over the centre line. A flash of white shot beneath the wheels. Matt instinctively jammed on the brakes. Hands gripping the steering-wheel, he waited for a thump.

Nothing happened.

He checked the rear-view mirror. The only vehicle on the road was the disappearing truck.

'Everyone all right?' He slowly pulled over to the side of the road then reached for his seat-belt buckle. 'Nicky? Caitlin?'

They both nodded, eyes wide.

'What happened?'

'I'm not sure. Something ran out from under the truck. We don't seem to have hit it but I just want to check.'

'I'll come, too,' said Caitlin.

'Thanks. Nicky, wait here, okay? We'll just be a minute.'

Nothing on the road. Matt was beginning to wonder if it had been a sheet of paper when Caitlin pointed. 'I've found the culprit.'

A dog peered at them from behind a small bush. One paw in the air and a mixture of hopefulness and fear plain on the little spotted face. Matt walked forward but the animal slunk a short distance away before turning to look back at them.

'Let me try.'

Caitlin approached the pup slowly, her voice soft and coaxing. Moments later, she crouched, holding out her hand for it to sniff.

'Well done. Is he hurt?'

'No, I don't think so. He's got a bit of dried blood on his back leg but it doesn't look serious. I'll wash it and check again when we get home. His condition's a bit poor.' Caitlin was checking the dog as best she could while the squirming form tried to lick her hands and face. 'I wonder how long he's been out here.'

'What do you think? Dumped?'

'Hard to say. No collar. Probably. I'll take him into the clinic and check for a microchip. He's still very young.' She sounded distracted and he could tell her mind was on the pup.

'Can we keep him, Dad?' Nicky materialised by his side. 'We can call him Spotty.'

'We'll see, Nicky.' Matt looked down into his son's hopeful face. The pup had found a champion. 'Someone might claim him.'

As soon as they arrived home, Nicky was out of the car. Caitlin smiled as she watched him heading towards the house with an armful of wriggling pup.

'We need to wash him before he gets the run of the house, Nicky,' Matt called. 'And Caitlin needs to check him again.'

'Sure, Dad.' Nicky flashed her an easy grin.

'Mum's going to be thrilled. What's the bet the laundry will be awash by the time we get inside.' Matt's voice was filled with amusement and, though she wasn't looking at him, Caitlin could tell he was grinning.

'Nothing surer.' She gathered her gear quickly and prepared to follow Nicky.

'Caitlin.' Matt's hand settled on her upper arm, stopping her escape. 'I had a good time today.'

'I—I did, too. Thank you.' She could feel the warmth of his hand through the light cotton of her shirt. She stared at his mouth, suddenly remembering the heat of their kiss. The firm, warm confidence of his lips on hers, the faint abrasiveness of his chin.

'I'm sorry we were interrupted when we were.' At her blank look, he added, 'The snake bite.'

'Oh. Yes. Well…' She shrugged. 'I—I guess it's part of your job.'

'Of both our jobs, yes. We've had a busy day.' His grin turned to something more intimate, warm and inviting. 'But I'm still sorry. I enjoyed our talk.'

Caitlin could hardly think straight with his thumb rubbing the sensitive area on the inside of her arm. How much more potent would it be on her bare skin?

'Listening to me blather on, you mean. Way too deep and meaningful.' Her voice sounded breathless and shaky to her own ears. 'I thought men avoided stuff like that.'

She knew she wasn't being fair. He was a doctor committed to his community, a loving and active father, a loyal and protective foster-son. No, not a superficial person by any yardstick.

He gave her a well-deserved look of reproach. His hand slipped down her arm to her hand.

'I'm interested in you, Caitlin.' The words came out quickly as though, if he didn't speak this minute, he might change his mind. Caitlin's heart skipped with a peculiar mix of excitement and trepidation as she waited to see what he'd say next. 'I'd like to find out where this could go. We skipped a step or two with the kiss yesterday but we're both adults, single and un-attached.'

Should she invent a convenient boyfriend, someone to protect her from herself? A buffer to Matt's attractiveness? Oh, Lord, how desperate was that?

'Well, I am, anyway.' He sent her a lopsided smile. 'You're definitely an adult…'

'And single and unattached,' she said, slowly. She shouldn't encourage him but felt oddly helpless to resist knowing more. 'Where…where do you think this could go?'

'From my point of view, anywhere we want it to.' He sighed. 'As long as it's in Garrangay.'

Of course, he needed to stay here. What would he say if she told him that it had already gone much too far? Whether it was in Garrangay or anywhere else.

For a split second she was tempted to throw herself into his arms, to confess everything she was hiding. To ask him how to approach Doreen without causing pain.

To beg him to let her stay in his life.

To see if she could be open and loving.

She wanted to dive in but her innate caution kept her mute for long seconds.

And then his hands moved on hers. She looked down to see him rubbing the gold band on her middle finger. Her father's wedding ring. Sanity swiftly returned. Everything was going to change once she told them about her father.

No matter how much she wished otherwise, she knew she'd never be the giving person that Matt's family deserved. She was her mother's daughter—good at keeping people at arm's length.

She'd come into their lives, accepted their wonderful hos-pitality while holding a secret that would cause Doreen pain. Caitlin knew, with her continued silence, she was also deceiv-ing Matt. It didn't matter how well intentioned she was.

She had to push him away, at least try to minimise the harm she was doing.

'You don't know me,' she said harshly.

'I like what I do know very much.' His expression was so inviting, so hard to resist.

She pulled her hand away, feeling his reluctance to let go, missing the warmth as soon as he did release her. 'Maybe I think you're looking for something I can't give you.'

'Can't...or won't?' A muscle flexed along his jaw.

'Does it matter?'

'Yes. Are you saying the feeling between us is one-sided?'

She paused, unable to lie. If he had any idea of how deeply he affected her, he'd be even harder to deflect. Already she'd been foolish to kiss him. But a woman would have to be strong beyond belief not to be tempted by a man like Matt Gardiner.

'You know it's not. But a relationship...it's not that easy.' She shook her head as she slipped her hand out of his grasp. 'We can't always have what we want. And you're right—you do need to stay in Garrangay. I don't know if I can.'

Matt watched as she walked away. He felt flat and tired. She'd withdrawn. There had been a moment when he'd been sure she'd wanted to agree. He'd almost been able to see the struggle in her mind. But then she'd shut him out again.

Did that mean she wasn't interested...or that she was? The chemistry of their kiss, the heat between them was undeniable. But she'd wanted to deny it.

In fact, she almost seemed to be warning him off. If that's what she was doing, he didn't want to hear it. Even knowing there was a good chance she would go back to Melbourne, he still wanted to try.

And it wasn't just a flirtation that he was after any more either.

Did that make him a fool?

CHAPTER THIRTEEN

PASSING on good news was a treat, Matt reflected as he hung up the phone a couple of days later. The laboratory results on Laura Bennett's breast tumour showed it was an adenoma. Benign, no further treatment required. He'd been fairly sure it would be. The lump had been discrete and mobile on palpation but the confirmation from the biopsy was still a relief for all concerned.

He dropped the file back in the cabinet.

Time to head home.

Home. Matt sighed. Since Caitlin had moved out the previous day, *home* hadn't felt quite right. Bob's house had been empty, even if it was in the middle of renovations. And she'd claimed it'd be easier if she was there in case there was an emergency.

But he couldn't help wondering if he was the real reason she'd gone. He and his pushing for some acknowledgment of their chemistry.

Just as well she couldn't know his preferred method for dealing with his attraction to her. The one that involved them making wild, passionate love and *then* getting to know each other better.

He knew how these things were supposed to work. Friends first, then lovers and maybe, just maybe, spouses later.

But with Caitlin he'd be more than willing to fast-track the first step and to hell with all the caution that past experience had taught him.

More than willing.

Caitlin was at Mill House.

Bless Doreen and her love of feeding anyone who'd sit still long enough.

He found Caitlin sitting cross-legged on the floor of Doreen's hobby room, folders spread out around her.

He felt his mood rise as he leaned against the doorjamb and watched her for a few moments. Engrossed as she was in a newspaper cutting in her hand, she hadn't heard him come in.

Her hair was loose across her shoulders. The lustrous curls made him want to sink his fingers into her hair, to see if it was as silky as it looked. Her slender legs folded easily into the semi-lotus position. Matt grimaced. He hadn't been able to achieve that posture since primary school and never with Caitlin's apparent degree of comfort.

'You're back,' he said, sliding his hands into his pockets to stop the temptation to touch her.

Her head whipped up and she pinned him with a wide-eyed stare. 'I—not really. Just a visit.' She sounded breathless. 'Doreen invited me for dinner.'

'Sorry, I didn't mean to disturb you.' He suppressed a smile at the words as they tripped automatically off his tongue. A psychologist would find all sorts of layers of meaning in his words. The truth was he *would* like to disturb her. A lot.

She ducked her head.

He frowned. Was that moisture on her lashes?

'Caitlin? Is something wrong?'

'Nothing, no.' Her fingers began busily slotting papers back into the folder in her lap. 'Why would you think that?'

'Well, looking at other people's family trees always brings tears to my eyes,' he joked, after a small pause.

She slanted him a narrow eyed look. 'Sure, and I believe that.'

The glitter on her eyelashes must have been a trick of the light. He grinned, angling his head to see the folder she held.

'What were you reading?'

'Your mum's articles on Garrangay's pioneers, among other things,' she said vaguely.

'You're interested in all that?'

'I am, yes. Why shouldn't I be?' She sounded defensive but he couldn't imagine why she would be. 'You're not interested?'

He shrugged. 'True family doesn't always have much to do with biological links.'

Why had he said that? It stopped Caitlin's agitated movements but now she looked at him with an expression of soft sympathy, a file clutched to her chest. Pity was the last thing he wanted from her.

'I suppose not, no,' she said softly. 'Doreen said she was— that you were—that is…'

'Doreen told you that she's my foster-mother?' he said blandly.

'Yes. I'm sorry, I didn't mean to pry.' A delicate pink crept across her cheekbones as her eyes slid away from his.

'It's common knowledge.'

'In Garrangay, perhaps, but that doesn't mean you'd want me to know.' She looked back at him, her eyes dark with uncertainty.

Perhaps it was a good time to lay it all out, tell her about his inauspicious childhood. Something tightened in his chest. Sophie's attitude to his background had been subtly condescending.

What would Caitlin's be? He realised he wanted to take a chance and find out.

Before he could change his mind, he crossed to the sofa and sat down. He leaned forward and sifted through a pile of photographs until he came to one of himself and his biological mother. It was the one Doreen had framed for him to have in his bedroom until, one day, he'd decided he didn't need it any more. Even then, she'd kept the picture for him. After all these years, it was a shock to see the facial features he'd inherited from this stranger, his mother.

In silence, he held it out.

Caitlin took the photograph and studied it for a long moment. The woman's face was stunning, with beautiful green eyes and high cheekbones. The hollows beneath those bones were more pronounced than seemed healthy. 'Your birth mother?'

He nodded. 'She'd taken me down to Melbourne for the weekend.'

'You—you spent time with her, then?' Caitlin handed the picture back.

'Some. When she'd detoxed.' His eyes were sad. Caitlin longed to reach out, to hold and comfort. 'Till the next time she couldn't resist a fix.'

There was no bitterness in his voice, just philosophical acceptance. Matching his tone, she said, 'It must have been difficult.'

'It was. My mother, like most drug addicts, was always making promises she couldn't keep.'

'Is she…? Do you still see her?'

'She passed away years ago. Complications from hepatitis B.' He looked back at the photo and his lashes shielded his eyes, hiding his emotions. But Caitlin wondered if she could see a residue of his grief in the straight line of his mouth.

'Matt. I'm so sorry.'

His gaze lifted, the piercing green looking directly, deeply into her eyes. 'Thanks. I was lucky, though. I had Doreen and Pete, people I could rely on. Doreen gave me stability, loved me the way my mother couldn't,' he said, with touching simplicity.

The praise for her aunt made Caitlin feel at once proud and confused. What had happened between Doreen and Martin? What had been so bad that he'd turned his back on his only family? So bad he'd never mentioned his sister until his illness had been in its end stages? The words that he'd spoken with such difficulty in the days before he'd died, the apology that Caitlin was here to deliver, indicated a deeply painful trauma. Yet Doreen wasn't an unforgiving woman who held bitter grudges.

So why hadn't her father come back to Garrangay to sort things out years ago?

'Caitlin?'

She jolted back to reality and covered her start by straightening the folders on her knee. 'Yes?'

'Where did you go?'

Again the urge to confide was nearly overwhelming. She shrugged. 'Nowhere.'

'You looked sad.' He tilted his head, giving her a considering look. 'I didn't tell you this to make you sad. I told you because I don't want any secrets between us.'

Her heart squeezed sickeningly. She felt shaken, as though he'd touched her with an electric prod. Right this minute she was living a concealment and this wonderful man wanted to be open with her. She didn't deserve his trust.

'I meant what I said yesterday, Caitlin. I want to know you. And I want you to know me.'

She swallowed, wondering how she could bear this peculiar rawness that he made her feel. The words of caution she knew she should speak stayed locked in her mind.

Four days later, Matt tossed his keys onto the hall table and briefly studied his reflection in the mirror. His eyes looked as tired as they felt.

'Matt, thank goodness.'

He spun around at the sound of Doreen's breathless voice. She was hurrying down the hall towards him with a large flat box and a teetering stack of towels in her arms.

'I was just going out to set up the car but now you're home, you can take him.'

'Take who?' Matt frowned as he moved forward to take the load from her.

'What?' Her face creased with apparent confusion as she hovered beside him. 'Oh. Spotty. To Caitlin. I've just rung so she's expecting us. I don't know what's wrong with him. Oh, dear. Nicky's going to be so upset.'

'Where is he?'

'At soccer practice.'

Matt was beginning to feel as though he'd dropped into a farcical sitcom where he hadn't been told the story line. If it weren't for Doreen's obvious agitation he'd have been tempted to laugh.

'I meant, where's Spotty?' he said gently.

'In the laundry. He must have eaten something poisonous, but I can't imagine…. Nothing's been left out.'

When she turned and scurried along the hall, Matt tucked the burden under one arm and strode close behind, wondering what he'd find. Whatever it was wouldn't be good if Doreen was talking about poisoning.

'He's been so sick that I shut him in there while I got everything ready.'

Matt opened the door. It only took the briefest glance to see how ill the young Dalmatian was. Mucus drooled from his blunt black muzzle and his gangly spotted body heaved several times with the effort of trying to vomit.

'Right.' He took one of the large towels and handed the box back to Doreen. 'Put that in the back of the four-wheel drive, Mum. I'll carry him out.'

Matt wrapped the towel around the trembling dog and lifted him carefully. The robust bouncing creature of the past couple of days was gone, leaving a fragile trembling frame.

As he walked out to the car park, Matt could feel heat radiating through the thickness of the towel. *Too much? What was the normal body temperature of a dog?*

After laying Spotty in the makeshift bed, he shut the door and turned to face Doreen. She stood, her hands clutched to her chest, looking drawn and shaken.

'Have you got chest pain?' he asked sharply.

'What? Oh, just a little.' She looked away guiltily. 'It's nothing to worry about.'

'Come back inside.' Matt grasped her elbow and turned her towards the house. 'I'll get your medication.'

'No, Matt. Please. Take Spotty to Caitlin.'

'As soon as you've taken your medication and you're looking better.'

'You always were a stubborn boy.'

A few minutes later, Doreen reassured him that she was feeling fine. 'Now, go. Please.'

'You'll stay by the phone and ring if it happens again?'

'Yes, dear.'

'And rest?'

'But dinner needs—'

'I'll organise dinner when I get back.'

'But—'

'Promise me you'll rest or I won't go. Spotty will have to take his chances,' Matt said, with what he hoped was convincing ruthlessness.

'I promise. Please, hurry.' Doreen sent him an anxious look. 'Nicky's so attached to him.'

'I know. Try not to worry.' Matt dropped a quick kiss on her forehead. 'He'll be in good hands with Caitlin. I'll call you as soon as I get there.'

Her words still ringing in his ears, Matt drove towards the veterinary surgery. Nicky and the pup had become inseparable since the stray had decided to adopt them.

Doreen had become very fond of spotty, too. Matt sighed. And if he was honest, so had he. So much for the idea they were only minding the animal until someone came to claim it. He may as well get used to it—they were now a family with a dog.

Caitlin was hovering on the porch as he pulled into the veterinary clinic drive. She met him at the back of the vehicle. Moving forward as soon as the door was open, all her attention focussed on her patient.

Matt watched, feeling helpless. He was used to being the one in charge.

'There, now, puppy,' she murmured as she peeled back the woebegone dog's top lip and pressed her thumb to the gum. 'He's very pale. Any sign of bloody discharge?'

'Not that I've seen. Mum didn't say anything when she rang?'

'She didn't, no.'

Grabbing a handful of loose skin from the back of Spotty's neck, she pulled it up slightly. When she released it, the hump stayed in a bizarre deformity.

'See the way his skin stays up? Dehydration.' Her grey eyes were guarded as she stepped back to look up at him. 'Haley prepared the isolation area before she went home. Let's take him in and I'll finish examining him there.'

Matt scooped up the box and followed Caitlin around to the back door. The words 'isolation area' sent a chill of foreboding through him.

Caitlin ushered him into a small room just off the entrance hall.

Matt took a quick glance around, noting the stainless-steel table in the middle of the room. On a stand at the table's corner hung a fat plastic fluid bag, the drip line looped over the hook. A collection of instruments was laid out on a metal tray. At one side of the room stood a cage, its large grilled door open. A thick layer of newspapers covered the floor.

'On the table?'

'Thanks.'

He lifted Spotty onto the spotless surface. 'I need to make a quick call.'

'Sure.'

Matt held the pup's collar with one hand and punched the numbers into his mobile phone with the other.

The pup stood passively, head drooping, as Caitlin lifted his tail to insert a rectal thermometer.

'Mum. How are you feeling?'

'Good as gold, dear. How's Spotty?'

'Caitlin's looking at him now. Are you resting?'

'Yes, dear.' The sound of long-suffering patience was plain in her voice. 'Though I do think I could peel a few potatoes.'

'No, no potatoes,' he said firmly. 'Consider yourself grounded. I'll see you shortly.'

Concerned grey eyes met his as he disconnected and slipped the phone back into his pocket. 'Doreen's not well?'

'Angina.'

'Is—is she all right?'

'She will be if she does as she's told,' he muttered.

'You can leave Spotty with me.'

He hesitated briefly. 'I'll stay until you've finished the examination.'

She nodded and glanced at the thermometer. Matt didn't like the pensive expression on her face as she wiped the cylinder and slid it back into a fluid-filled jar. Meeting his eyes as she rested her hands on the dog's shoulders, Caitlin said, 'I'd like to run a test to confirm it but Spotty has classic symptoms of Parvo.'

'And that's bad?' He could tell by the sombre look on her face but he had to ask the question anyway.

'It is, yes. I vaccinated him on Monday when I brought him in for a check over but it's too soon for him to have developed effective immunity.' One of her long, delicate hands stroked the dog's short coat.

Matt watched the gentle rhythmic movements as he considered her diagnosis.

'We'll start him on a fluid drip and a course of antibiotics,' she said, breaking into his thoughts. 'The virus damages the intestinal wall and we don't want to risk a secondary infection.'

'How bad is it?'

The hypnotic strokes slowed and then stopped. In a detached way, Matt realised the action of her hand seemed to be an answer in itself.

'Do I need to prepare Nicky?' he said. And Doreen. And himself.

'I won't lie to you, Matt. It's a very serious illness. The next twenty-four to forty-eight hours are critical. If we've caught it early enough, he might survive. I'd like to be more positive but at this stage his chances are about fifty-fifty.'

He swallowed. The feeling of helplessness returned in double measure. 'Is there anything I can do?'

She hesitated. 'Could you hold him while I put in the drip? It'll be a lot easier.'

He nodded then waited while Caitlin collected the instruments she needed from the tray. When she was ready, he gathered Spotty in a firm but gentle hold. The lack of resistance from the pup was sobering. No struggling at all, not even with the loud buzz of the clippers Caitlin used to shave the front of one thin foreleg.

'Could you hold his leg here, like this?' She demonstrated by wrapping her thumb and forefinger around Spotty's upper leg in a makeshift tourniquet. 'I'll get you to tighten in a moment.'

After tearing open a sterile pack, she swabbed the skin thoroughly with antiseptic.

'Okay, I'm ready.'

Matt tightened his grip. He watched Caitlin's long, slender fingers expertly slide a cannula into the vein. With it taped into position, she reached for the line from the waiting saline bag. Her eyes were intent as she took a few moments to check the drip rate.

Holding the pup's over-warm body, he watched Caitlin wrap

gauze around the leg with neat, efficient movements. The bright red crinkled bandage she finished off with looked inappropriately jolly against the stark white of the pup's coat.

She fastened a wide collar to his neck. 'Let's get him into the cage.'

Taking care not to touch the bandaged leg, Matt did as Caitlin asked, aware of her moving beside him with the saline bag in hand.

After she'd hung the bag above the cage, she closed the door and turned to face him.

'Try not to worry, Matt.' She reached out to touch his arm, her fingers light and warm against his skin. 'You got him here quickly. He's young and strong and the symptoms have only just appeared.'

'Thanks.'

With her eyes still on his, she smiled slightly, 'You know I'll do my best for him.'

'I know.'

When she removed her hand, he felt a disproportionate sense of loss.

After a small silence, he said, 'I should go.'

'You should.' She stepped out into the small hall and opened the back door.

'You'll ring if there are any problems?' He paused beside her.

'I will, yes.'

'I don't just mean with the pup.'

'That's kind of you. Doreen's made the same offer.'

'She's worried that you're staying at the clinic alone.' *So am I.* But he left the words unsaid.

'I know, yes. I'll be thoroughly spoiled by the time I leave.'

Matt felt his gut tighten. There she was again, bringing up the temporary nature of her stay. Was it to remind him or herself? Was she counting the days until she left Garrangay? He wasn't. Far from it. The more he saw of her the more he wanted her.

He stood there a moment longer, hands in his pockets. He

wanted to challenge her, point out the advantages of staying in Garrangay, of staying with him. But now was not the time. She had work to do and he needed to go home.

He leaned down, pressed his lips to her cheek. The delightful light perfume she wore filled his nostrils. Her sudden stillness, the startled look she flicked up as he drew back gave him some small satisfaction.

'Bye, Matt.' She stepped back, folding her arms. 'Give Doreen my best and tell her to take care of herself or I'll be around to growl. In fact, I'll be around to growl, anyway. Maybe tomorrow.'

'I'll pass on the message.' He smiled wryly. 'She might take more notice of you. She's adopted you into the family.'

An odd parade of expressions flitted across her mobile face. Joy, guilt. Despair?

'Caitlin?'

'I'd better get in and check on Spotty. Goodbye, Matt.'

She was right. They both had other priorities right now.

Gravel crunched beneath his feet as he crossed to his vehicle.

Like breaking the news to Nicky that his pup was fighting to survive?

And like Doreen. Her angina underlined the fragility of life.

A chill slithered down his spine. Change was coming and he couldn't stop it. He clenched his fingers around the steering wheel. He'd do everything he could to protect his little family but it might not be enough.

With one last look at the clinic, he pulled out of the driveway and headed for home.

CHAPTER FOURTEEN

'HELLO, SWEETIE.' Caitlin stifled a yawn as she peered at the drip chamber of the pup's intravenous line. Still running well and the bag didn't need changing yet.

She glanced at the clock on the wall. Not quite two in the morning. Nearly seven hours since Matt had brought him in.

Crouching to look in to the cage, her nose wrinkled.

'Phew, puppy. That's bad.'

Spotty's soft brown eyes blinked up at her glumly. He didn't make any effort to raise his head.

After snapping on a pair of gloves, she unlatched the cage and began changing the soiled paper on the floor.

By the time she'd resettled the dog and cleaned up, she was wide awake. She walked through the clinic towards the kitchen thinking she'd make a hot drink to take back to bed.

A strong beam of light shone through the window behind her, swinging brightly across the wall.

An emergency? No one had called. She changed direction, grabbing a white coat and thrusting her arms into the sleeves. Her fingers were still busy with the buttons as she turned to the door. Through the glass panel she could see a familiar figure.

Matt!

She pulled open the door.

The steady whirring pop of frog song resonated in the

distance as she stared at him. Her eyes roved his face, taking in his grave expression. The porch light glistened on his full bottom lip as though he'd just run his tongue across the surface.

And then her mind unfroze. Panic had her reaching out blindly to clutch the door frame. 'Oh, God! Doreen. Is she—?'

'She's fine.'

Caitlin's knees turned to jelly as the blood seemed to seep away from her brain.

'Caitlin! Doreen's fine.' Matt's voice was sharp, but she still couldn't seem to process the words.

She heard him swear softly and was vaguely aware of him stepping close, gathering her against his hard body, moving her back into the clinic.

'I'm okay.' Her voice sounded far away, almost dreamy. 'You gave me a fright. That's all. When I saw you…'

'You thought the worst.'

'Yes.' Something pressed into the back of her knees.

'I'm going to sit you down, sweetheart.' Her body was gently folded into a chair and her head pressed down between her knees.

'I'm okay. Really.' Her slippered feet came back into clear focus as blood rushed back to her head. Now that she understood she wasn't in imminent danger of losing her aunt, her system began to react to Matt's nearness.

'Of course you are.' Fingers stroked the sensitive nape of her neck in a soothing motion. Her skin quivered with delight under the tiny caress.

When he lifted her wrist, she realised he was going to take her pulse. No way did she want him feeling her heartbeat's frantic bumping and surging.

More insistent against his restraining hand now, she pushed herself upright in the chair. Since he was crouched beside her, his face was close. Green eyes searched hers with clinical thoroughness.

'So, if Doreen's all right, what are you doing here?' she croaked.

He looked faintly sheepish. The weight of his hand slipped from her shoulder. 'I'm on my way home from a callout. I saw your light on so I thought I'd check everything was okay.'

'It is, yes,' she said faintly.

'Good.' His eyes warmed, roaming her features, settling on her lips. Heat climbed into her cheeks.

She looked away and for the first time realised that he'd walked her through to Bob's office. The room seemed impossibly small with him in it. Panic cramped her chest. She had to get out.

'Why don't you come and see Spotty while you're here?' She got to her feet, relieved when there was no sign of residual weakness in her legs. 'I've just checked him. He's holding his own.'

She led the way back to the isolation area where she handed Matt an apron and overshoes. 'Here, you'll need these.'

Concentrating on her patient helped blunt the effect of his disturbing presence.

Spotty eyed them forlornly, his head resting awkwardly on the wide collar between his front paws, as Caitlin unlatched the cage.

Matt crouched beside her, reaching in to fondle the floppy ears.

She watched his hands so gentle on the pup's head. Spotty's eyes slowly closed on a sigh under the steady caress. Caitlin shifted her gaze to Matt's profile, unable to resist the opportunity to devour tiny details. The faint stubble on his cheek, his ear tucked so neatly against his head, the firm line of his jaw. The cables of his hand-knitted jumper stretched across broad shoulders, the way the blunt-cut edge of his hair curved into his neck. A couple of sections of the hair were slightly out of place, perhaps ruffled as he'd pulled on the apron. She stifled the urge to reach out and smooth them down.

'He looks miserable.' A muscle twitched along his jaw.

Dragging her wayward mind back to business, Caitlin focussed on the pup. 'He does.'

'How is he?'

'He's stable, Matt, and that's a good thing. I wish I could say more than that but I can't. Maybe later today.'

Keep thinking of the basics. He'll be on his way home in a few minutes. Last night, when he'd brought Spotty into the clinic, had been so easy. Matt had been a client with a patient. She'd had something to do, been able to take refuge behind her job.

'I know.' His eyes were sombre when they met hers. 'You said twenty-four hours. I'm sorry. I didn't mean to push. I wanted to be able to give Nicky and Doreen good news in the morning.'

His obvious concern for his mother and his son melted her heart, made her want to offer him comfort.

'I'm—I was about to make a hot chocolate. Only one of the packet varieties, but you'd be welcome to…' She trailed off. Damn. Was she insane? Hadn't she just been counting the minutes until he left? Now here she was inviting this disturbing man to stay longer. Before he could answer, she said, 'Though no doubt you want get home to your bed.'

Even worse. She bit her lip.

'Hot chocolate sounds good,' he said. 'Thanks.'

'We can wash up outside.' She stood up, aware that Matt was following her lead.

She dried her hands and watched Matt soaping his. He had strong and broad palms with long, well-shaped fingers. They were hands that promised strength and reliability, hands to hold and comfort. Hands to caress…

She shoved the towel back on to the rail. 'I'll put the kettle on. Come through when you're done.'

In the kitchen, she stood staring into the free-standing cabinet serving temporary duty as a pantry, her chilled palms cupping her cheeks. At this indecent hour of the night, her biorhythms must be incredibly low. That's why she was noticing things, feeling things she didn't want to. Hadn't she told him they couldn't be involved? She didn't belong here. But all her denials would count for nothing if she couldn't keep herself under control.

'Caitlin?'

'Matt.' Her hand shot out to grab the packet, fumbling then managing to catch it as it tipped off the shelf. 'Um, have a seat.'

Think of a nice safe subject, she commanded herself mentally as he hitched a hip onto one of the bar stools at the short length of usable bench. After flicking the switch on the jug, she collected two large mugs. 'Have you had any answers to your lost-dog notices, then?'

'Nothing yet.'

'It's early days but I suspect you might have a dog if you want one.' She spooned a generous serving of the drink powder into each mug. 'Perhaps even if you don't want one.'

His answering grin was wry. 'Nicky will be over the moon.'

'You won't be so pleased?'

He ran a hand around the back of his neck. 'I've been expecting someone to answer the advertisements.'

'The next logical step would be a home-wanted notice. You're welcome to put one up here.'

'Are you kidding?' He chuckled softly. 'Lost-dog notices are one thing, *home-wanted* signs and my life wouldn't be worth living. He's wormed his way into everyone's heart.' After a tiny beat, he added, 'Including mine.'

The jug clicked off and Caitlin picked it up. The rich aroma of chocolate wafted up as she poured hot water over the powder. She pushed a mug across to him before sliding onto a stool opposite.

'Thanks.' His eyes flicked around the room as he blew on the edge of the drink before taking a cautious sip. 'How are you coping with Bob's renovations?'

'I've been in worse.' Relaxed, with him safely on the other side of the bench, Caitlin looked around the room at the cobweb-covered wooden frame, the exposed wires and plumbing.

'At least I don't have to carry my own water here. I don't think I stood in a normal domestic kitchen until I went to boarding school.'

'Mum's worried you'll starve.'

'She's a darling.' She grinned at him. 'Though she shouldn't be fussing over me.'

'Try stopping her.'

'Her angina,' began Caitlin tentatively. 'How—how serious is it?' She really wanted to ask if a shock would be too much, if it could precipitate a heart attack. She wanted to be told that it wouldn't.

'It's been stable with medication. And she goes into Hamilton for regular check-ups.' He smiled wryly. 'It's point-less telling her to slow down. Though I've tried. Thankfully, she does pace herself a bit better these days.'

Not quite the definitive reassurance that she was after. 'You'd like her to slow down more?'

'Yes. And no. She puts me to shame.'

'In what way?'

'She seizes life and marches right along with it.'

Caitlin turned over his words as she swallowed the last of her chocolate drink. A thin layer of foam coated the base of the pottery. 'And you think you don't?'

'I march…cautiously.'

She laughed. 'Marching is marching, surely. And you have responsibilities.'

'Yes, I do. And I tell myself that. But I sometimes wonder if it's a handy excuse, too.' He propped his elbows on the bench and leaned forward. With his eyes heavy lidded and focussed on her mouth, the relaxed atmosphere changed abruptly. 'It'd be nice to do something incautious every now and then. Don't you think?' His voice was low and inviting.

'I'm not sure.' It was all she could do not to stutter.

'For instance, if I was less cautious I would offer to help you clean up that chocolate on your top lip.'

She put her hand up, shielding her mouth as she licked her lip.

'No,' he said softly when she took her hand away. 'Still there. Let me help.'

Suddenly he was a lot closer. Her heart stopped on a hard beat then jolted into a frantic gallop as Matt leaned over the bench, his intent obvious. She could have pulled back, out of reach. It would have been so simple. Instead, she watched him moving nearer, watched his gaze roam her face, resettle on her lips. She longed to moisten them, make them ready for his kiss, for that was surely what he was going to do. She could feel his breath on her skin, a soft caress, as he angled his head. Her eyelids wanted to flutter closed—she forced them open, met his eyes, saw the glitter of his hunger, his need.

His kiss was the barest touch, light, questioning. The warm, dry pressure of his mouth, the moist stroke of his tongue, the tug as he bit down gently on her bottom lip for a moment. She shut her eyes, giving her senses up to the moment. Only their lips were touching but she could feel the response through her entire body, a growing, glowing warmth.

'Caitlin?'

'Mmm?' she managed as she opened her eyes. The gravelly rasp of the sound was a surprise.

'Come out to dinner with me on Saturday night. Just the two of us.' He'd withdrawn a minute distance, only needing to tilt forward slightly for his mouth to cover hers again.

'Dinner?'

'Yeah. You know—the two of us with a knife and fork each and food. A date.'

Caitlin felt her mind clearing, her natural caution swinging back into place.

'Ah, one of those. I've heard of them.'

'I'm sensing a "but" here.'

She reached out to grasp her empty mug, circling the bottom on the bench as she considered her answer.

A grin lit up his face briefly. 'You don't find me attractive?

I'm polite, presentable, reasonably well behaved. Good sense of humour, non-smoker, social drinker.'

A snort of laughter escaped before she could suppress it. 'You sound like an advertisement for the "companion wanted" column.'

'Steady job, hard worker, low maintenance, low risk, house trained. Good teeth, strong bones, straight legs.' He grinned.

'Hmm. Or perhaps a breeding programme,' she said.

He sent her a wicked look. 'Proven fatherhood material.'

She swallowed. 'Tsk. I left myself wide open for that one, didn't I? Still, you could have resisted.'

'Sorry.' But he didn't look at all repentant. He removed the mug she fidgeted with, setting it aside so he could take her hands. 'There's a spark between us. You can't deny it, Caitlin. We've both fought it for our different reasons. But why shouldn't we explore where it takes us?'

Because she'd already had a taste of how powerfully he affected her. Any more and she could be a blithering, submissive mess. She didn't want to lose herself, become invisible. The way her father had disappeared in her parents' marriage.

'There are lots of reasons.' She watched his thumbs rub across her knuckles, soaking in the comforting sensation while she tried to remember what those reasons were. Thankfully her tired brain latched onto something that was safe to say. 'You've other people to consider. Your son, your mother.'

'Both of whom adore you.'

Her heart basked in happiness for a tiny moment before she forced herself to face reality. She was bringing them bad news, would cause them pain, especially Doreen. 'I'll leave in a few weeks. Why risk hurting each other?'

'We might not hurt each other. We might discover we're meant for each other and you won't be able to tear yourself away from me.'

'Perhaps that's what I'm really afraid of.' She blinked, mentally reeling from leaving herself so exposed, so open.

He groaned. 'You can't say something like that and not expect me to follow through on it.'

'Matt—'

'Hush, Caitlin.' He reached out to touch his fingers briefly to her lips, stopping her protest. His hand slipped around to the back of her neck, tilting her face back up to his. 'I think we communicate much better like this.'

'Far too well, I'd say,' she murmured breathlessly, when his lips released hers.

'All I'm asking for…' his mouth moved over hers again '…is one little dinner date.'

Could she? Did she dare? She couldn't think properly with his teeth gently sinking into her lower lip. 'Okay.'

'Good.' He ran a light finger over her mouth. 'Thanks for the chocolate. All of it.' His mouth curved into a smile as he stood. 'Go to bed. I'll lock the door on my way out. Sleep well, sweet Caitlin.'

When he was gone, she rested her chin in her hands and contemplated their empty mugs. Had she just made a huge mistake?

She didn't feel any closer to talking to Doreen. A couple of times she'd tried but there had always been an interruption or a concern for her aunt's health. And the truth was she'd welcomed the opportunity to put it off each time. Revealing the news about her father was going to be a shock. And she was a coward, afraid of hurting the people she wanted to be close to. Afraid that whatever wedge had driven Martin away would work to push her out, too. But if she didn't take a chance, she would never know.

She needed to be braver. And perhaps, if she was careful, if she could find the right time, the right words, she could be worthy of Doreen's love, a relationship with Matt. A future in Garrangay.

If she could do this right, maybe they would want her to stay, even after she'd told them the truth.

Matt padded along the hallway in his socks, pausing to push open Nicky's door. Soft light from the hall lamp spilled across the pillow and a thatch of tussled dark brown hair. The colour was part of his ex-wife's legacy to their son.

The rest of the bed was a jumbled mound. Spiderman was caught in mid-leap on the quilt cover and clung precariously to the edge of the bed.

He crossed the room and bent to straighten the bedding as much as possible without disturbing Nicky. He needn't have worried. His son slept with a soundness that implied absolute confidence in his world. Matt wondered if his sleep had been the same at that age.

He brushed the silky-fine fringe from his son's forehead. Caitlin was right. There were other people he needed to consider. But there was no reason why he couldn't begin paving the way. And he didn't anticipate any problems with either Doreen or Nicky.

With one last look at his sleeping child, he closed the door and continued down the hall to his own room.

His son's capacity for trust amazed Matt. He'd explained about Spotty's illness, doing his best to prepare his son for a bad outcome. But Nicky had been utterly convinced that Caitlin wouldn't let the pup die. That faith was at once touching and terrifying.

Even Doreen, who should know better, was confident that all would be well now the dog was in Caitlin's hands. Poor Caitlin. She had a lot to live up to with those two putting her on a pedestal.

Matt didn't want her on a pedestal. He wanted her as part of his life, part of his family. And he wanted her in his bed.

He stripped off and slid between cool sheets. Was Caitlin doing the same down the road? He tortured himself with the image for a long minute. Sleep suddenly seemed a long way off. Hands clasped behind his head, he lay staring at the ceiling, tracing the shadowed relief of the plaster rose.

Caitlin would never know what it had cost him to leave her tonight. Had it been just half an hour ago? Instinct had warned him not to push, regardless of how much he wanted to. Why did he have the feeling he worked against time? Urgency and caution, an impossible combination to balance. Did he deserve accolades for his sensitivity or ridicule for being a faint-hearted fool?

He rolled over to thump the pillow into a more comfortable shape. His kiss had put colour into her cheeks, a dreamy glow into her beautiful grey eyes.

Saturday night was too far away. Thirty-six hours. Perhaps he could drop by again to check Spotty's progress. He grimaced.

No doubt about it—he was a goner.

Now, if only Caitlin was as far gone, everything would be perfect.

CHAPTER FIFTEEN

'TIME we weren't here, Nicky,' said Matt, checking his watch. 'Clean your teeth and grab your gear.'

''Kay, Dad.' Nicky jammed the last of his toast in his mouth.

'Don't forget your lunch.' Doreen held out the box that she'd just packed.

Nicky pivoted at the door and raced back to the bench. 'Thanks, Nanna,' he mumbled around the mouthful of food.

Matt listened to his son's footsteps pounding down the hall, could picture the moment he hit the top of the staircase by the change in tempo.

Instead of making a move to follow, Matt watched Doreen come back to the table and begin tidying. He watched her hands as she closed the top of the cereal packet, screwed the lid back onto the strawberry-jam jar, wiped up a small pool of spilled milk. His fingers drummed lightly on the table. This was a good opportunity to speak to her. Alone. Now.

'I've got a date with Caitlin on Saturday night.' *Damn. That had come out so baldly.* Where was the carefully worded spiel he'd worked on in the shower fifteen minutes ago? 'Tomorrow.'

Doreen looked up from the plates she'd stacked, her eyes wide and her mouth dropping open in a stunned expression. 'Oh, my.'

He narrowed his eyes at the unexpected negative response. 'What? What's wrong?' he said warily.

'You're…just so…smitten.'

To Matt's sensitive ears it seemed like an accusation.

'I *like* her. A lot. Yes. What's wrong with that?'

Double damn. What was wrong with *him*? He sounded like a schoolboy defending his latest crush. In an effort to cover his agitation, he picked up the coffee-pot and tilted it over his mug. Black liquid splashed up over the edge and puddled on the table.

'There's nothing wrong with it. Nothing at all. Not a thing.' Doreen leaned forward and whisked the dishcloth under his mug before he could fix it himself.

Matt stifled a sigh and reached for his drink to take a deep fortifying swig. The fresh brew scalded the roof of his mouth. He swallowed quickly and felt the super-hot liquid travel down every inch.

'I thought you liked her,' he said, wondering why he'd imagined this might be simple.

'Oh, yes, I do. I do. Very much.' Doreen carried the dishes to the sink and busied her hands with gloves and sponges and detergent.

Matt had the distinct impression she was avoiding looking at him. 'So, what's the problem? Last week, you were match-making.'

'Yes, and I do want…. But that was before I was sure—' She stopped abruptly.

'Before you were sure about what?'

Clattering dishes and running water were the only sounds in the kitchen for a long moment. Finally, Doreen turned away from the bench, soapsuds dripping from her rubber gloves and a worried look on her face.

'Before she took the locum. She'll be leaving in a few weeks.'

'I'm taking her out for dinner, Mum, not proposing.' *Marvellous! Where had* that *little gem come from? Another Freudian slip?*

'Yes, dear, I know. It's…I—I don't want to see you get

hurt.' She turned back to the sink but Matt had the feeling she hadn't finished speaking yet. 'Caitlin's only going to be here for such a short time. Only until Gary's better. Then Bob will be back.'

Her comments tallied so completely with his own misgivings and with Caitlin's comments that he had to suppress a grimace.

'But she *might* stay longer, mightn't she? Why wouldn't she want to?' He sipped cautiously at his coffee. The liquid tasted bitter on his tongue. Crossing to the bench to tip it out, he continued, 'I've got so much to offer. Needy single father, country bumpkin, job with long hours so I'll hardly get underfoot.' He twisted his lips into a smile. 'Hell, Mum, I'm quite a catch.'

'Matthew!' Doreen looked up at him, her smoky blue-grey eyes full of reproach.

'I'm sorry, Mum.' He sighed and ran a hand around the back of his neck. 'I know you're concerned for me. When it comes to Caitlin, I'm concerned for me too. But I'll have to take my chances. And I've put the pieces back together before, haven't I?'

'Yes, you have.' She looked at him shrewdly. 'But I'm not sure it's the same. If it had been, I wonder whether you'd have left the city, come back to Garrangay.'

The piercing insight into his marriage left him momentarily speechless.

'I know there's chemistry between you and Caitlin. I've felt it myself,' said Doreen, sounding resigned. When he continued to stare at her, she smiled at him. 'And don't mock yourself, Matthew Gardiner. You are a *great* catch for some lucky woman. I should know—I brought you up to be one.'

'Perhaps you can put in a good word for me,' he said wryly.

'Perhaps.'

'Mum—'

'I know, dear. You're only joking. So am I. I wouldn't interfere.'

'Unless it suits you,' he said with a grin, as footsteps thundered back towards them.

Nicky exploded back into the kitchen, thrusting his arms into the straps of his bag. 'I'm ready.'

'Got everything? Lunch, homework?'

'Yep. Bye, Nanna.' Nicky crossed to his grandmother for his kiss goodbye.

'Let's go.' Matt dropped a kiss on Doreen's forehead. 'Don't worry, Mum, it'll work out. See you later.'

He followed his son out to the car, mentally girding himself to break the news about his date. Surely it couldn't be worse than the scene with Doreen…could it?

Saturday night and she had a date. She hadn't been this giddy about a date since…. Ever.

Caitlin smoothed a tiny amount of blusher over her cheekbones. Her reflection told her it was hardly necessary. Anticipation made her eyes sparkle, her skin glow.

Not even having to borrow clothes from Haley for the evening could dampen her spirits. Funny how things had a way of happening when a person was least prepared.

Getting invited out to dinner…

Learning about a long-lost aunt…

Finding a man who would be so easy to love.

Not that she was *in love*. With her hand pressed flat on her sternum, she could feel the wild skitter of her heart. Life was getting very complicated.

She picked up the slinky gold top she'd laid out on the bed earlier and slipped it over her head. The fabric felt cool and light and moved in a way that clung to her breasts and the curve of her waist. It made her feel…sexy, which was probably *not* a good thing at all. How could she keep Matt in line when she felt poised to leap off a precipice herself?

No amount of common sense stopped her bubbling excitement. Not even reminding herself that she had real reasons to be cautious.

Tomorrow she would do something about one of those reasons, she would try to talk to her aunt. But tonight…she wanted tonight for herself.

She slipped her feet into the strappy sandals that matched the top. More of Haley's generosity. She'd been *handled* by Bob's veterinary nurse, no two ways about it.

She was still astounded about their conversation over yesterday afternoon's surgery. All she'd done had been to ask a simple question as she'd closed up a feline abdomen. She grinned wryly as she remembered.

'Is there somewhere handy to buy a nice evening top, Haley? In Hamilton, perhaps? I don't want anything too fancy.'

Her assistant had looked up from the anaesthetic equipment, delight shining in her eyes above the green mask. 'Oh, wow! Matt's asked you out, hasn't he?'

'Wh-what makes you think that?' Just as well she hadn't been in the middle of a delicate surgical procedure. Her fingers had turned to thumbs.

'Gosh, Caitlin. Everyone knows he's got the—ah, that he's, um, sweet on you.'

So much for discretion. It sounded as though she and Matt were a hot topic in the town. Very hot. The thought was unnerving.

How would Matt feel about the gossip? Did he know? And had Doreen and Nicky heard it?

How did they feel about Matt taking her out? He would have given them some explanation about what he was doing this evening. Did Nicky mind? Or did he feel threatened by the idea of his father taking a woman out on a date?

It sounded like Sophie played a very small role in her son's life. But even in situations like that children often harboured secret hopes that their parents would get back together.

Or maybe the date had Nicky and Doreen's blessing. Caitlin

smoothed her hand over her stomach, wishing she could calm the nerves bouncing there. According to Matt, his mother and his son adored her. But, then, none of them knew her, *really* knew her. Would they feel the same way if they did? If they realised how closed in she felt sometimes, how desperately inadequate and lonely.

'You look gorgeous.'

Matt's wide, appreciative smile—now, *that* was gorgeous, thought Caitlin, her heart jittering. She didn't even try to suppress her answering grin.

'Thank you. So do you.' And he did. Smartly dressed in dark grey trousers with a burgundy shirt and a tie with interlinked patterns in shades of both colours. And he was here to take her out. 'Mine's borrowed plumage. Holiday packing doesn't extend to evening wear.'

'Haley?'

'It was, yes.' She debated for a moment whether to tell him that Haley had guessed why the clothes were needed.

Before she could make up her mind, he reached out and took her hand. 'Hey, thanks for ringing about Spotty this morning.' His voice was soft and mellow, filled with caring warmth, as though she'd done something really special.

'Oh, um, I knew you'd all want to know that our star patient had turned the corner.' She squeezed his fingers quickly before claiming her hand back to rummage for her keys.

'We appreciated it. I appreciated it.'

She swallowed and clasped the keys firmly in front of her. 'I—I wanted to say something last night when you rang but it was still too soon. I'm confident he'll make a full recovery now.'

'Thanks.'

She stepped outside, locking the door behind her. As soon as she began walking beside him, Matt put his hand in the small of her back to usher her towards the car. The divine fabric pressed hot and silky onto her skin where he touched.

'I'm afraid Haley guessed why I needed something to go out in,' she said, filling the small silence, hoping to take her mind off the exquisite sensations spreading out from her lumbar region. 'If you had any hopes of keeping things quiet…'

'No hopes at all. The residents of Garrangay knew I was interested in you almost before I did.'

'I guess it's one of the hazards of living in a small community?' she said slowly. He seemed very philosophical but she couldn't help feeling dismayed about being the topic of gossip. Was it guilt at her deception that made it seem so subtly threatening?

'Yes.' He removed his hand to open the car door.

'Thanks.' She lowered herself into the seat, still bemused by regret and relief in equal measure. The imprint of his fingers lingered on her skin. His touch was powerful beyond anything reasonable.

She watched him walk around the front of the car and slide in behind the steering-wheel. He started the engine then twisted to face her, laying his hand across the back of her seat as he looked over his shoulder, out the rear window.

His closeness was at once disconcerting and exciting. Thank goodness his attention was entirely on reversing out of the parking spot. His subtle musky aftershave enveloped her senses, making her want to lean forward and breathe deeply until the fragrance of him filled her completely. To burrow into the crook of his neck where the column of his throat met with the dark shirt collar.

Her eyes traced the line of his jaw—smooth shaven and slightly shiny. A neat ear, detached lobes—perfect to nibble on.

Heavens, she had to get a grip. She'd be throwing herself at him in a minute.

She swallowed, dragging her gaze away from his face along a nicely muscled arm tapering to a strong wrist. Her gaze settled on the hand manoeuvring the steering-wheel. He had great hands, long lean fingers. Practical and sensitive. She hadn't been a person to notice hands—but that had changed since meeting Matt. And when he touched her…

No, don't think about that now.

Find something to talk about. What had they been discussing? *Oh, yes, small towns.*

He braked and began to swivel back towards the front.

'Don't you mind everyone knowing your business?'

He paused, half turned, and focussed on her. 'Does it worry you?'

'Not worry exactly. But neither am I thrilled about it.'

He slotted the gear lever into drive and they moved smoothly out of the parking area.

'I grew up in the foster-system,' he said, after a long moment. 'All sorts of people knew my business. Social workers, police, teachers, doctors. Everyone in Garrangay.'

Guilt stabbed at her. Worrying about an evening out being common knowledge was so petty compared to Matt's life under the community's spotlight. 'I'm sorry, Matt, that was insensitive of me.'

'It was a long time ago, Caitlin.'

'Did you…did you want leave it behind sometimes? Be anonymous?'

'I did leave it behind while I was studying and first married. But the bottom line is I like the town and the people.'

Matt gathered his thoughts in silence. A lot hinged on Caitlin understanding his attachment to Garrangay, why he'd come back, why he stayed.

And why he wouldn't want to leave.

If they had a relationship, she'd need to stay. He couldn't move back to Melbourne. Not now. Maybe he wasn't being fair, but too many people relied on him.

He chose his words with care.

'My mother was born in Garrangay and lived most of her life here. This is where she came when she was pregnant.

People did what they could for her and for me. And I had Doreen and Pete.'

'Yes, of course.'

'The interest is well meant. Well, most of it.' He grinned as he glanced over at her. Solemn grey eyes met his and held for a moment. He stifled a small sigh. 'A bit overwhelming if you're not used to it.'

His tension level cranked a little higher as he waited for her reply.

'I suppose I *am* used to it, growing up around my mother's research projects,' she said slowly, as though making a discovery. 'Perhaps it's being in someone else's fishbowl that makes it unnerving.'

Her hands lay on top of her small evening bag in her lap. He reached over and gave her fingers a quick squeeze.

'Well, we've escaped from the bowl tonight. Let's make the most of it,' he said, hoping to lighten the mood.

'Deal.' She sent him a mischievous smile. 'As long as you remember I'll be throwing you back early if you misbehave.'

'Best behaviour. Absolutely. I won't do anything without your approval.'

'I'm not sure I'm greatly reassured,' she said dryly. 'And that would be a reflection on my character, not yours.'

Matt laughed, appreciating her quirky honesty. His system kicked with the confirmation that the attraction wasn't all on his side. It was tempting to throw caution aside, to let the heat burn between them as brightly as it could. But caution and patience had brought them this far. He could keep to his plan…which was not to say that he might not rupture something with all this self-control.

'This is grand,' said Caitlin, looking around after they'd been seated with menus. They were near a cosy bay-window recess.

'Yes. And unexpected after seeing the exterior.' Matt smiled ruefully. 'I wondered what we were in for.'

'It looked a bit dire, didn't it?'

The shabby exterior of the old two-storey hotel, clad in metal scaffolding, had given no hint of the wonderful atmosphere inside. A gleaming blackwood bar stretched along one wall, oiled wood dado panelling, cream walls. Subdued lighting from coach lamps and candles on the tables gave an aura of stepping back in time.

Flames leapt and flickered behind the glass panel of a wood heater at one end of the room, countering the chill of the night.

'Nicky never doubted you'd pull Spotty through,' said Matt, breaking the small silence after the waiter had taken their order. 'Neither did Doreen.'

'I'm glad Spotty and I didn't let them down.' Caitlin fidgeted with the end of her knife for a moment. 'It's a big responsibility, isn't it? When people believe in you like that?'

Matt's smile made her toes curl. 'I know. You don't want to let them down.'

'Yes. I hate disappointing people.' The memory of her ongoing deception tightened her throat. 'It—it's hard to avoid sometimes.'

'I believed in you, too.' He leaned forward, his eyes holding hers.

'Mmm.' An odd claustrophobic feeling swept over her and she glanced away, struggling to think of something to lighten the moment. 'But I imagine your belief came with a healthy dose of acceptance that bad things can happen no matter how hard a person might try to make it otherwise.'

'True.' Matt smiled.

She relaxed. 'Dalmatians need a lot of exercise. They were carriage dogs in England, you know. Perhaps even chariot dogs in ancient Egypt. Spotty comes from a long line of energetic ancestors.'

'But if he's a pedigree, doesn't it make it unlikely that he'd be dumped?'

'If he was show-dog or breeding material, it would. But he

has a lot of brown marking with the black. Tricolouration is considered a defect.'

'I don't think Nicky minds what colour his spots are as long as we keep him.' He looked so pleased about the idea that Caitlin hoped no one came forward to make a claim.

Spotty was part of Matt's family, a part of Doreen's family. Caitlin felt a small rush of envy. Animals didn't doubt their right to belong. If only it was that easy for people. But, then, animals didn't keep secrets from loved ones either.

A second waiter arrived with the wine and, after pouring some into their glasses, nestled the bottle into an ice bucket.

'A toast,' said Matt, his green gaze holding hers as he raised his glass. 'To itinerant veterinarians.'

Caitlin reached for her glass and chinked it lightly against the edge of his then sipped the chilled fruity wine.

'I'm glad you're here.' The dark warm glow deep in his eyes sent shivers through her system.

'Thank you. So am I.'

'I'm especially glad you're here tonight. With me.' His voice caressed sensitive nerve endings. Her heart thumped wildly, the force of it pulsing through her body. He made her feel so special and for tonight she wanted to bask in that warmth.

By the end of the meal Caitlin knew she'd fallen even deeper under Matt's spell.

There was a lull in their conversation after the waiter took away their plates but it wasn't uncomfortable. Caitlin reached out to toy with the base of her wineglass.

Matt's hand covered hers and she watched his fingers play with the plain gold band on her middle finger. The smooth pads ran lightly over her knuckles and every nerve in her body seemed to centre on the sensitive skin that he was touching.

'Did you wear a wedding ring when you were married?' Appalled at her gaffe, Caitlin stared at him. The question had burst out without conscious thought. 'Oh, dear. Don't answer that. I don't know what made me ask such a thing.'

'That's all right.' He smiled slightly. 'Yes, I did wear a ring.'

She glanced down at the fingers of his left hand where they rested over hers. 'You've no mark to show.'

'It's been a long time since I took it off.' His eyes were solemn, steady. 'Does it bother you that I've been married? That I'm divorced?'

'No. Why would it?'

He shrugged. 'Divorce means a marriage that failed.'

'Perhaps staying together when things are bad is a failure.' Though she couldn't imagine living with Matt would be a hardship. The people around him were so secure, confident of their place in his life. He was a man to rely on.

'Perhaps. Sophie and I had no idea of what to expect from marriage or from each other.'

'Don't you learn as you go along?'

'Sure. But better to start with some idea. To have kids, not to have kids. How it's going to work if you do.' His gaze dropped back to her hand. 'After Nicky was born, I expected us to work out times so we could share looking after him. Less time in day care, you know. But Sophie wouldn't slow down. I hated the thought of bringing him up in the city as a latch-key kid. We made a mistake with our marriage but I didn't want our son to be the one to pay for it.'

'It must have been difficult,' said Caitlin.

'Not for Sophie. She didn't want the responsibility of being a mother so she avoided it by working longer and longer hours.' He released her hand, reaching for his glass. Caitlin watched his throat move as he swallowed. He stared into the pale gold liquid for a long moment. 'And after a while she didn't want the responsibility of being a wife either.'

There was a small pause, his fingers whitened on the glass and then he said, 'She avoided that by having an affair.'

'Oh, Matt.' Caitlin's heart went out to him as she absorbed the shock of his revelation.

His eyes flicked back to hers, intense, sharply focussed. 'What do you expect from marriage, Caitlin?'

'I—I'm not sure.' He was so brave, so devastatingly honest that she felt compelled to try to be the same. As far as she could. 'I don't want what my parents had. An unequal marriage.'

'Because your father wasn't academic?'

'No, not because of that.' She pursed her lips for a moment. 'Perhaps one-sided is closer to what I mean. He was there for my mother but the commitment wasn't returned.'

She withdrew her hand from his and twisted the gold band on her finger. 'This is my father's wedding ring.'

There was a small silence.

'He wanted you to have it?'

'No. He—he wants my mother to have it. I haven't had a chance to give it to her because I haven't seen her yet. She hasn't been able to make a time for us to meet.' The tinge of bitterness in her voice surprised her. She'd thought she'd got over the hurt that had caused. 'It's been a year since he passed away.'

'She wasn't with you when he died?'

'No. She didn't come back at all.' She shrugged. 'In some ways I was glad. My father and I became very close. He had a marvellous way of looking at the world that I miss very much.'

Caitlin frowned. This compulsion to confide in Matt was perplexing…and fraught with pitfalls. But some part of her seemed to be determined to do it. Perhaps because anything less than truth would be shabby in the face of his willingness to share his past. And she could tell him this much. Doreen had the right to know the rest of Martin's story first. And soon. Tomorrow, she promised herself.

'You looked after him while he was ill?'

'Yes and no. He stayed with me and mostly looked after both of us.' She rubbed the ring lightly. 'He spoiled me.'

'You deserved it.'

'Maybe, maybe not.' She gave him a small smile and changed the subject. To her relief, the conversation moved easily onto less sensitive ground. As they got up to leave an hour later Caitlin was struck by an unsettling feeling that Matt had allowed her to make the change.

Back at the clinic, Matt walked her to the door.

'I've had a lovely evening, Matt. Thank you for asking me out.'

'Thank *you*. I've enjoyed it, too.'

Caitlin paused on the first step and turned to face him. 'I'd ask you in for coffee but…'

'It wouldn't be a good idea.' He reached up to tuck her hair behind her ear. The light brush of his fingers made her knees tremble. 'I'd probably try to stay longer than I should.'

'I'd probably want to let you and it's too…'

'Soon? Tempting?'

'All of that. And complicated.'

He stepped forward, touching his lips to hers. She sank into his kiss, the familiarity and delight. Her eyes closed as she revelled in the thrill of holding him close.

She felt the huge shuddering breath he drew in as the warm anchor of his mouth lifted from hers. The expansion and contraction of his chest against hers as though he'd been running hard.

'Very complicated.'

Her eyelids opened reluctantly. 'Yes.'

'I should say goodbye.'

'You should, yes.'

Caitlin wondered if her legs would hold her up if he let her go too quickly. Her hands lingered on his shoulders as she searched for the will to move away. She had to be sensible and let him go. It *was* complicated and for more reasons than Matt realised. He thought her reluctance stemmed from her temporary status in Garrangay, but that was almost beginning to feel like a minor problem to Caitlin. She loved the rural town, the countryside, the people.

'The boys are playing cricket in Hamilton tomorrow morning. Would you like to go?'

She hesitated. Tomorrow she'd promised herself she'd speak to Doreen. Her father's ghost loomed large in her mind. It was past time to reveal his part in her arrival in Garrangay.

'Nicky would love to show off his bowling skills.'

'Now I think you're playing dirty.' She laughed softly. How could she resist the man and his son? Maybe she could go to the game and find time to speak to Doreen later in the day. 'I'd love to see Nicky's prowess.'

'I'll pick you up around nine.'

She watched him drive out of the car park, a grin on her lips. Cricket. She was going to a cricket game. Voluntarily. Her father would never have believed it. But, then, watching the game wasn't the main attraction, was it?

CHAPTER SIXTEEN

'OH. OH.'

The small distressed gasps sent warning prickles down Matt's neck.

'Mum?' He dropped Nicky's cricket gear and dashed back to the kitchen.

His mother was slowly subsiding into a chair at the table, a fist clenched in the centre of her chest, her face pale and drawn.

'What's wrong?' He crossed to her side, aware of Nicky following in his wake. A fine sheen of perspiration dampened her skin.

'Oh, dear.' Her voice shook. 'Awful…heartburn.'

'Tell me where the pain is.' Was it an MI? God, he couldn't lose her. He ruthlessly suppressed his fear. Any sign of panic from him would be disastrous for his mother, for Nicky.

'In my chest and throat.' Her clenched hand rubbed along her sternum as though the pain could be erased through bone and flesh.

He laid a hand on her shoulder, feeling anxiety cramp his own chest. 'Just started?' A quick glance at his watch. Eight-thirty.

'I had a bit when I first got up. Nothing like this.'

'Did you take any angina medication then?' He breathed deeply, forcing his voice to stay calm.

'Yes. Antacids as well. It stopped straight away.' Her pain-filled eyes lifted to his in a silent plea.

'Good.' He gave her shoulder a quick squeeze of reassurance. 'Your tabs in the medicine cabinet?'

Her gaze went to the small cabinet at the end of the kitchen. 'Yes.'

'Stay there,' he said, when she started to get up. 'I'll get them.'

'They should be on the top shelf.'

'Are you okay, Nanna?' asked Nicky, as Matt released the childproof lock on the cupboard.

'Yes, darling. Just a little pain.'

Matt reached for the packets he needed, glancing over to see the strained smile his mother tried to give Nicky for reassurance. 'Any other symptoms, Mum? Dizziness? Nausea?'

His fingers fumbled briefly with the sealed end of the aspirin box. Another deep breath to steady himself.

'A—a bit of nausea. And I've got such a headache.'

'That'll probably be the angina meds you took earlier.' A car hooted as he crushed one of the tablets into water. 'Nicky, Davey's mum is here. Can you ask her to come in for a minute, please? Don't forget to take your sports bag.'

'Sure, Dad.' After another quick worried look at Doreen, Nicky set off at a run.

'Drink this.' Matt handed the glass to his mother who swallowed the contents with a small grimace. 'Okay. Now these, one to start with.' He handed her the nitroglycerin tablets.

Once a tablet was tucked under her tongue, he put his arm around her waist. He wanted to stop and hug her and tell her how much he loved her. But she needed him to be a doctor now, not her son. 'Let's get you over to the sofa. You'll be more comfortable.'

'Oh, dear.' Doreen got to her feet and shuffled the few steps. 'I'm sure it'll go away in a minute.'

'Sure to.' He settled her in a semi-reclining position.

Davey's mother appeared a moment later with the boys hovering anxiously behind her. Matt outlined the situation and arranged for Nicky to stay with them after the game. To Nicky, he said, 'I'm not going to be able to come to the game today, okay?'

'Oh, but…I think it's easing already,' said Doreen faintly.

'Of course, Dad.' Nicky gave him a man-to-man look. 'You need to look after Nanna. I understand.'

'Good boy.' He ruffled his son's hair.

After they'd gone, he took Doreen's blood pressure and pulse, recording the readings. 'How are you feeling?'

'A bit better. I'm sure it'll go completely in a few more minutes.' She smiled, obviously relieved. 'I'm sorry to cause such a fuss.'

'Hey, it's not a problem. I need something from the car so you rest here. I'll only be a moment.'

'Okay.'

Matt returned to the kitchen and unpacked the portable ECG unit, getting out a set of disposable electrodes and unravelling the leads. 'I'm going to hook you up for a few minutes.'

'This isn't really necessary, is it?' said Doreen.

'Humour me. I need the practice.' He peeled the backing off one of the electrodes as he explained where he needed to place them. Doreen obligingly pulled the top of her knitted shirt across so he could stick one high on each side of her chest.

With the third electrode stuck low on the ribs beneath her left arm, Matt attached the leads and switched on the unit. Narrow graph paper began smoothly feeding out, lines wriggling across the tiny squares.

'Well?' She craned her neck to look. 'What's the verdict? Will I live?'

'Highly likely. But we'll take a run into Hamilton to get this checked anyway.' The trace wasn't overtly that of a myocardial infarct but it was abnormal enough that he wanted a more experienced eye to look it over. And he'd be happier with a three-plane picture from the hospital's twelve-lead ECG.

'Oh, no. Matt! What about your plans for the day? Darling,

you have so little time for yourself. And aren't you taking Caitlin to watch the boys today?'

'She'll understand.'

'But I've got things to do for my birthday next weekend.' A distinctly mutinous gleam lit her eyes.

He allowed himself a small smile. If she was arguing with him, she must be feeling better. 'Hospital first. Everything else can wait.'

'Will you at least ring Caitlin?'

'When we've got you tucked up in hospital. Do you want your purse?'

'But—'

'Caitlin will understand,' he repeated. 'You know she will. She'd be the first person to tell me to look after you.'

He knew it was true. The more he knew of Caitlin the more sure he was they had something special. He was going to push their relationship harder once Doreen was back on her feet. Life was too short. Whatever was holding Caitlin back needed to be out in the open. Once he knew what it was he would deal with it.

'The hospital is far too busy for us to worry them with a little bit of indigestion.'

'That's what the hospital is there for and they'll be delighted if you turn out to be a false alarm. They've got more sensitive ECG equipment and they'll be able to take blood tests.' He dropped her bag on her lap and scooped her up, ignoring her indignant gasp. 'And that's where I want you to be.'

'Matthew Gardiner. Put me down this instant.'

'You've had a few angina attacks lately and I'd like them investigated.' He ignored her protests, elbowing his way through the screen door. 'This is only going to short-circuit your specialist appointment by a few weeks.'

'What about my things?' she demanded, as he crossed the verandah and negotiated the steps. 'You know I hate wearing hospital gowns.'

'You can make a list of what you want on the way there. For now, your medication's all you need and we have that here,' said Matt, recognising her complaints for the distractions that they were. He set her on her feet and opened the passenger door. 'In you get.'

'You're a bit of a bully, pushing your poor mother around like this.'

'Yeah, I know.' He helped her into the seat. 'I love you, too.'

Once he was on the road, Matt radioed ahead to the emergency department.

'Dr Matt Gardiner here. Could I speak to the cardiac registrar, please? I have a patient with chest pain. Over.'

A few minutes later a different voice sounded in his ear. 'Matt, Sarah Stewart here. How can I help?'

'Sarah, I'm on the road to Hamilton with my mother. She's having chest pains that have been going on for twenty minutes now. Some relief with nitroglycerin. I ran an ECG and there's some arrhythmia but no clear pattern. I'd feel a lot happier to have you look at her. Her angina's been less stable for the last few weeks.'

'What's your ETA?'

'Twenty minutes.'

'Copy that. We'll be expecting you.'

They had a smooth run through to the hospital. A nurse with a wheelchair took Doreen straight through to a cubicle. Matt followed and helped settle his mother on the gurney in one of the despised gowns. Sarah Stewart arrived moments later with a nurse pushing an ECG unit on a trolley.

He stood back, making a few pertinent comments while Sarah took a comprehensive history and explained to Doreen how they were going to treat her case. An ECG, blood tests for cardiac enzymes, an overnight stay at least.

'Matt, please go and ring Caitlin,' said Doreen as Sarah tightened the tourniquet around her arm. 'I feel awful about ruining your date for today.'

'Don't. Your health is much more important.'

'We'll look after Doreen, Matt.' Sarah grinned up at him then exchanged a conspiratorial look with his mother. 'You go and make your phone call so I can pump your mum for the juicy details.'

'Okay, okay.' He raised his hands in mock surrender. 'I won't be long.'

'Take your time, dear. Sarah and I will manage very well,' said Doreen, a cheeky grin creasing her pale face.

Matt walked slowly outside, feeling battered now that the emergency was safely in the hands of the cardiac team. His mother was such a precious part of his tiny family. He didn't want to lose her.

He took out his mobile phone and dialled Caitlin's number.

'Garrangay Veterinary Clinic.'

'Caitlin.' He took a deep breath and closed his eyes, realising for the first time how much he needed to talk to her.

'Matt? What's wrong? You sound awful.'

'We're going to have to cancel today. I'm at the hospital with Mum.'

'Doreen's in hospital? Oh, no.' Her concern was like instant balm. 'What's happened? Is it her heart?'

'Yes.'

'I'm coming in.'

'There's nothing you can do.' Even as he said the words he wondered at his perversity. He wanted her here. Fiercely. Yet he was trying to put her off. 'She won't be allowed visitors for a while.'

'I just want to be there, Matt. I'm leaving now.'

'Okay.' He swallowed around the hot lump in his throat. 'You're in the emergency department?'

'Yes.'

'See you soon.'

After she'd hung up he leaned back against the wall. Caitlin was on her way. The thought bolstered him. His heart swelled with emotion. She cared about his family. She cared about him. Enough to stay in Garrangay? He was beginning to hope so.

Thirty minutes later a nurse came through to Doreen's cubicle to let him know Caitlin had arrived. When he went out to the waiting room, she was sitting on the edge of a chair, her hands clenched on top of her handbag. As soon as she saw him she was on her feet, her arms opening to envelop him.

'Thank you for coming in.'

Holding her as tightly as she clutched him, Matt felt like he'd come home. He leaned into the embrace. This was the place he wanted to be. With his face buried in the crook of her neck, he breathed deeply, filling himself with her. With Caitlin beside him he could face the future. Whatever happened, he would be able to go on if she was there. Her hands began a soothing caress over the tense muscles of his back.

He lifted his head and saw the tears on her cheeks.

'She's going to be fine.' He cupped her face, wiping away the moisture with his thumbs. 'The cardiologist said it was a minor infarct. They're running some tests now to see if she needs a stent. We got treatment started quickly so there's every chance she'll make a full recovery.'

'Thank goodness.' She burrowed back into his shoulder.

Words of commitment trembled on his tongue, but he held them back. His emotions were so raw and needy. He wanted to pin Caitlin down, make her say she wanted to be with him, to be with them. But it wouldn't be fair to take advantage of her in a situation like this. She was too kind. He knew his desperation would make it hard for her to say no. They had things to talk about first and this wasn't the time.

Instead, he absorbed the comfort of holding her close, feeling the way she fitted into his arms, near his heart.

He'd wait a little longer.

But not too long.

CHAPTER SEVENTEEN

'YOU'RE not to treat me like an invalid,' said Doreen, sitting at the outdoor table a few evenings later. 'My cardiologist said it was important for me to keep active. I'll be sensible and rest when I need to.'

'Yes, but it won't do you any harm to be on light duties and we don't want to put your new stent under any more pressure than necessary.' Matt flipped the marinated chicken kebabs and rissoles that were sizzling on the hot plate. 'Besides, I'm enjoying teaching Caitlin the finer points of the great Australian barbecue.'

'Really. I would never have noticed.' The wealth of good-natured irony in his mother's voice was hard to miss. But, thankfully, whatever doubts she'd had about him and Caitlin seemed to have gone now.

He'd just finished arranging the cooked kebabs on a platter when the back door swung open. Salad bowl in hand, Caitlin held the screen for Nicky, who was carrying bread and serviettes.

'Good timing.' He arrived at the table at the same time, catching her eye as they arranged the food. The faint rosy glow that tinted her cheeks delighted him.

He could get used to having her around permanently. Who was he kidding? He was *desperate* to have her around permanently. All he had to do was get to the bottom of the resistance he felt from her and convince her to stay. He was sure they had something special, something that was worth taking a risk on.

He trusted her and that was a huge step forward to him. It proved he'd got past Sophie's infidelity.

He was ready to move on. Oh, how he was ready to move on. The dinner-table conversation flowed around him as he thought about when he'd kissed her. Blisteringly hot, intense kisses.

She'd been marvellous over the past few days, stepping in to help whenever she could. Today he'd been free to drive into Hamilton to collect Doreen because Caitlin had picked Nicky up from school.

'I saw Spotty at the clinic today.' Nicky's words interrupted Matt's thoughts. 'He's better, isn't he, Caitlin?'

'He is, yes.'

'Oh, wonderful news,' said Doreen. 'When do you think he can come home?'

'Whenever you're ready. But I can keep him at the clinic longer if you need me to.'

'Keep him at the clinic.'

Matt spoke at the same time as Doreen said, 'Bring him home.'

'It's grand to see you're in agreement, then.' Caitlin looked from one to the other with a grin.

'Bring him home,' Doreen said, her eyes turned to Matt in appeal.

'Yes!' Nicky grinned triumphantly.

Matt's smile was resigned. 'Are you sure he won't be too much for you, Mum?'

'No, he'll be fine. Besides, Nicky will look after him, won't you, dear?' Doreen switched her gaze to Caitlin and said casually, 'Does that mean you'll be able to move back, too, Caitlin?'

'Oh, um, no. It…it's easier for me to stay at the clinic. In case of an emergency. Or something.' She couldn't come back to living under the same roof as Matt now that things had changed between them. It'd be sheer torture to know that he was sleeping in the room above hers. So close, so tempting. Utterly impossible.

But the question made her wonder what she would do when Bob was ready to take over the practice. She'd be effectively homeless unless she came back to the bed and breakfast. She risked a glance at Matt and intercepted a lazy, knowing smile.

'Dad? Phone.' Nicky clattered his knife and fork onto his plate.

'I'd better get that.' Matt stood. 'Excuse me.'

Caitlin watched him walk into the house. Once Bob came back there was really no reason why she couldn't plan on going back to Melbourne. Once she'd told Doreen.... But how could she tell her aunt now while she was convalescing? With the stent in she should be strong enough...

'Can I be excused too, please?' said Nicky. 'I've finished all my salad.'

'Of course, dear,' said Doreen. There was a short companionable silence. 'It's nice to be back home. I haven't told Matt this but...when we first went to hospital I did wonder if I would be coming home.'

Caitlin's hands tightened on her arms. 'It must have been frightening for you.' *For all of us.*

'Yes. There are so many things I still want to do. One of them is my seventieth birthday on Saturday. You are coming, aren't you?'

'Of course. I wouldn't miss it for the world.'

Doreen nodded as though satisfied. 'Gary's come through the bone-marrow transplant with flying colours. Sally told me Bob's thinking of coming home on Monday.'

'Monday?' So soon. Bob had rung her a few times but hadn't put any time frame on his return. An odd panic gripped her. She hadn't even come close to achieving what she needed to do in Garrangay. And now time was running out.

'Will you stay on, do you think?'

Will you want me to once I've told you about your brother?

'I—I'm not sure what I'll do, Doreen.'

'What about you and Matt?'

Caitlin's heart skipped a beat, her mouth dry. For the life of her, she didn't know what to say.

'I'm sorry, dear. I shouldn't interfere…but with this latest episode I'd love to see Matt settled with someone who'll put him and Nicky first in the ways that count.'

Did her aunt see her as that person? It was such an honour and such a weight of responsibility. A huge ball of tearful guilt and longing and love clogged her throat, making it impossible to speak.

'Family's important to Matt, even more so because of where he's come from,' said Doreen, looking at her anxiously. 'I see the way you look at him. You love him, don't you?'

'I do…have feelings for him, yes.' Her voice was hoarse and tight on the wishy-washy words. But her heart was too vulnerable to let her answer more honestly.

Doreen reached out to grasp Caitlin's hand. The older woman's blue-grey eyes were dark. 'Don't leave things unsaid until it's too late, Caitlin.'

Caitlin hesitated. This seemed like such a good lead in to talking about her father, his apology. Almost as though Doreen knew, was giving her permission to break the sad news. But with her aunt still recovering from her heart attack…. Uncertainty held back the half-formed words still on her tongue.

'There are too many things I wish I'd said. We should tell the people we love how precious they are.' Sadness passed over Doreen's face like a bleak shadow. 'We don't always get a second chance.'

'Doreen, I—'

The screen door squeaked open and she swallowed the rest of her sentence.

'Another RSVP for Saturday night, Mum,' said Matt as he came back to the table. 'Remind me again just how many people you invited to this shindig.'

The moment for confiding was gone. A sharp stab of disappointment sliced at her. Would she regret missing this opportunity? Or find another time as good? Somehow she'd have to make one—and soon. Bob was coming back next week. Time was running out.

A job with a view to a partnership in the veterinary practice…. A chance to stay in Garrangay. Caitlin's mind whirled with possibilities after Bob's phone call. He'd rung again just after she'd finished the Saturday morning clinic.

Everything she wanted was within her reach. Security. Family. Maybe even the man she loved.

The people, the place, the way of life here in Garrangay had seeped into her, bringing an unfamiliar sense of belonging. *Needs that she'd never acknowledged had been soothed. Empty spaces in her heart and soul had been filled.*

Paradise…except for her secret. Now, with so much else at stake, her deception seemed huge, unforgivable. She'd lied, by omission, to the people she loved. Her reasons for keeping quiet had made perfect sense earlier. She'd been waiting for the right moment. Excuses to delay had been easy to find—not wanting to hurt her aunt, choking on her own unexpected emotion, seeing how things worked out with Matt, Doreen's heart attack.

Disturbed by her thoughts, Caitlin shoved open the car door and scrambled out to stand in the early afternoon sunshine. In front of her, the elaborate wrought-iron gates of the Garrangay cemetery stood open, rows of graves stretching across the small well-tended yard. She'd stopped to have a look but now she was here she felt oddly reluctant to satisfy her curiosity.

Instead, she looked around at the surrounding paddocks, at the lush green spring growth. The clinic would have its work cut out with overweight, under-exercised ponies in the next few months. She'd already handled several cases of acute laminitis.

To stay or not to stay. Everything depended on how she handled this crisis in her personal life.

Turning slowly to face the cemetery gates, Caitlin sighed. She was here…she had to look.

She found herself wandering the rows, reading the names. Young people and old. Doreen's stories lingered in her mind, fleshing out the names, the connections between families. Her unsuspecting aunt had been more than happy to talk about her research into the family history, to show off the wonderful collection of old, old photographs of her ancestors. Her own ancestors.

She stopped at a polished granite stone and read the words aloud. '"In loving memory of Albert and Frances Brown. Sixth of December. Together always."'

The anniversary was just under a month away. She realised anew how close to Christmas her grandparents' car accident had been. How much extra grief that must have added to the children they'd left behind. To Doreen, just married and suddenly responsible for her little brother. To Martin, who had been trapped in the vehicle until help had arrived. Too late for his parents. A terrifying experience for a twelve-year-old boy.

She stepped carefully to the head of the grave and crouched to splay her fingers over the smooth surface of the cool stone. There was room for more names. Her father's name belonged here. How would Doreen feel about having her brother added?

'Doreen's parents.'

Caitlin jolted at the sound of Matt's voice, snatching her hand away from the stone. Guilt sent heat surging into her cheeks then, just as fast, it receded, leaving her face cold, almost numb.

'Hey, sorry. You must have been miles away.' He frowned when she stared up at him mutely. 'Caitlin? Are you all right?'

'Yes.' Had that faint croak really come from her? She rose carefully. Her heart thumped in fast, hard beats making her feel sick and giddy.

'We were on our way home from cricket when Nicky spotted your car.'

'Did he?'

He looked back down at the headstone. 'They died in a car accident.'

'I—I know.'

He was standing at the end of the grave, his lips gently tilted at the corners. She should summon up an answering smile, make a disarming comment, move casually away from the grave. Instead, guilt and fear held her paralysed.

Matt's green eyes drifted back to the names on the stone. She watched him, noticing the way the sun caught the golden highlights in his hair, the way he stood, hands tucked into his pockets, relaxed. A sudden chill of inevitability swept over her, spinning her world out of control.

She didn't want to lose him.

Powerless to deflect the thoughts she could almost see coalescing in his mind, she waited. His lips parted and she watched them form the words she was dreading.

'Caitlin Butler-Brown,' he said slowly. 'I've just realised your father would have been a Brown.'

'Yes.'

'Wouldn't it be funny if you were related?'

The words hung between them for long silent moments. A shadow passed over the sun, robbing Caitlin of its precious radiant warmth, leaving her frozen.

'Would it?' She forced the question past the tight, gravelly lump in her throat.

He stared at her, his green eyes narrowing as he began to absorb the possibility.

'It's not a coincidence that you were travelling this way.' It was half statement, half question.

'No.'

He tilted his chin slightly towards the headstone, his eyes still fixed to hers. 'You're…related?'

'Yes.'

'How?'

She clasped her hands tightly. 'These are my grandparents.'

'Then you must be…Martin's daughter?'

She took a deep breath, hoping it would steady her for the developing crisis. 'I am, yes.'

The silence was terrible, a growing impenetrable wall, severing the weeks of happiness and connection between them. Sorrow congealed as a pain in her chest. Her heart a leaden thing beating from habit when she knew it should have been shrivelling and dying.

The sun popped back out, suddenly brightening colours, incongruously cheery. Its warmth on her skin merely exacerbated the bone-deep chill of her body.

'Why are you here? What do you want?' His face was hard, his eyes as flat and cold as his voice.

'I came because I want to know about my father's family.' She tilted her chin defiantly.

'You want to know—' He bit off the rest of the sentence and spun away from her as he thrust his fingers through his hair.

Caitlin looked at his rigid back, waited numbly for him to speak again. When he turned back, his face was drawn, his lips set in a straight uncompromising line. 'Why don't you ask him?'

'I-I can't. He passed away. He never talked about his family,' she said, struggling with a sudden need to cry. 'Until he was dying.'

A spasm of despair twisted his features. She was fiercely glad he uttered no words of condolence. Any indication of softness from him would have broken her fragile poise. But she couldn't help longing for a tiny sign that he would be able to forgive her. There was nothing except the coldness and anger that she deserved.

After a long moment he said, 'Doreen is going to be devastated by this. Martin chose not to let his sister be a part of his life. But now you're here to make her a part of his death.'

'I thought she should know, that she'd want to know.' Her mouth felt stiff and uncooperative.

'Why?'

'Da wanted to apologise to her. I promised him I'd come and see her, speak to her.'

'Did you?' His lip curled in disdain. 'And you're here to salve his conscience? Or your own?'

Caitlin was stricken by his unrelenting harshness. Nausea threatened with spasms that cramped her stomach. She swallowed the bile that rose in her throat and stared at him in silence. His reaction was even worse than she'd anticipated.

'Why haven't you said anything before now?'

'I haven't known how to. I thought, by getting to know Doreen, I'd find the right way to tell her.' She made a small gesture of defeat with her hands. 'I...I haven't.'

His eyes closed, Matt massaged his forehead with the fingers of one hand as though trying to rub away an overwhelming pain.

'Hi, Caitlin. Look what I found.'

She dragged her gaze down to Nicky's outstretched hand. A long green praying mantis sat motionless in his palm.

'He's beautiful.' She managed a small smile.

'Dad, can I take him home for show and tell on Monday?'

'Sure. Why don't you wait in the car, Nicky? I'll be right there.' When his son had gone, Matt turned back to her. 'We need to talk about this. *Before* you say anything to Mum. Do you understand me?'

She felt beaten, broken. 'Yes,' she managed.

He nodded once before spinning on his heel and striding down the grassy path.

She waited until he was gone, his car out of sight, before lowering herself slowly to sit on the edge of the concrete. It was a long time before she could find the strength to totter back to her car. Going through the motions of finding the keys, starting the vehicle, took every ounce of her energy.

Numb with a grief too deep for simple tears, she drove back to the clinic. Doreen had said to come early for the birthday party but Caitlin couldn't go to Mill House yet. How was she going to face Matt after what had been said? She'd thought she was so clever, coming to meet her aunt, to learn about her roots. Instead, she'd ended up falling for a man who now wanted nothing to do with her. She had an aunt whom she adored but would hurt dreadfully by revealing their connection. In short, she'd made a bloody mess of things.

Matt drove the car automatically, steering, changing gear, braking. Nicky's chatter filled the empty spaces. All he needed to do was murmur appropriate responses. His mind went over and over what had just taken place.

If only Nicky hadn't spotted Caitlin's car…

If only they hadn't stopped…

If only he hadn't had to learn his perfect woman was hiding a secret that could rip his mother's heart to shreds.

But Nicky *had* seen the car, they *had* stopped. And he'd learned his perfect woman, the woman he trusted, had feet of clay. All that time he'd thought they were building something worthwhile together and she'd been working her own agenda with his family. She'd betrayed him. Possibly even *used* him to gain more access to his foster-mother, her aunt.

She was like Sophie after all. Only this time he felt the perfidy even more sharply.

He loved her. He *loved* her. He'd wanted to make her a part of his family.

She hadn't just betrayed him as a man, she threatened all that was precious to him.

The best he could do was protect and defend what was left. And if that meant shutting Caitlin out, he'd do it. Regardless of how his heart bled at the thought.

CHAPTER EIGHTEEN

CAITLIN let her gaze drift to Matt for the hundredth time. The party had been well under way by the time she'd arrived and he stood behind the barbecue wielding a pair of tongs and laughing at something the woman beside him had said. He looked relaxed and comfortable. Not at all heartbroken.

But, then, she probably didn't either. Even though her spirit was shrivelling, her self-respect had demanded that she cobble the pieces of herself together. Present a reasonable façade. Strange how a person could be in so much pain and yet look perfectly normal.

Even with happy, chattering people surrounding her, she felt desperately isolated. As though she watched a puppet of herself perform socially. Her responses must have been appropriate because people kept smiling at her and she smiled back.

She filed across to the food with everyone else, picking up a plate and helping herself to salads. Everything looked delicious and she wondered how she was going to force any of it into her knotted stomach. A surreptitious glance at her watch confirmed it was still too early to make excuses to leave. The pager at her belt stayed wretchedly silent.

Plate in hand, she wandered through the crowd, exchanging a word here and there. Finally finding a secluded spot in the rustic pergola at the bottom of the garden, she sat her plate on a post and leaned on the rail. The evening sky was a spectacular wash of apricot and gold-etched clouds above the silhouette of the Grampians. When she left tomorrow she was going to miss this view.

Though not half as much as she'd miss the small family she'd come to love—Doreen, Nicky…Matt. Her heart twisted painfully as his name reverberated in her mind.

'Caitlin.'

She jolted at the sound of her name, her fingers digging into the wood reflexively. Taking a deep breath, she turned her head slightly. 'Matt.'

'I saw you walk down here.' He came to stand beside her. 'We need to talk.'

How could she bear it? She felt her chin quiver and hoped it was too dark for him to see her weakness. 'Do we?'

'I—' He turned away abruptly, spearing his fingers into his hair. 'Don't tell Mum why you're here.' The plea came out in a rush.

'Don't you think she has a right to know?' How composed she sounded. Unbelievable when she felt so close to shattering.

'Yes, she does.' He spun to face her. 'But I can't bear to have her hurt by this.'

The anguish in his voice pierced straight to her soul. She looked down at her hands clutching the rail. 'I wouldn't do anything to harm Doreen, you know that.'

'Then you won't tell her?'

Each word hammered his distrust home in a painful tattoo in Caitlin's vulnerable heart. Only the wood she held so tightly held her trembling frame upright.

She looked at him. The man she loved, the man she had to leave. Her hope for the future died. 'I won't, no.'

He shut his eyes, relief plain on his face. He hadn't been sure of her response—somehow knowing that made her feel even worse.

'Thank you, Caitlin. I understand how difficult this must be for you.'

'Do you, now?' she said, unable to keep the edge out of her voice. She felt an inappropriate urge to laugh but didn't dare. Tears were too close. He understood nothing. How could he when she struggled to understand it herself? 'How perceptive of you.'

'Doreen told me Bob's offered you a job, maybe even—'

'Don't worry,' she interrupted. He had what he wanted. Why couldn't he just leave her alone? 'I've turned it down.'

'Caitlin—'

'I think we've said all that needs saying, Matt.' Desperately scanning the gaily lit garden party beyond the perimeter of the pergola, she latched onto a familiar figure. 'If you'll excuse me, I can see that Joy Warren's arrived. I need to speak with her.'

Restless, Matt strode down the now deserted garden. Sweet perfume from the flowering pittosporum mingled with the scent of freshly mown grass in the still night air.

The evening had gone well. No surprise. Doreen had been in her element. His concerns about her overdoing things had been unfounded, though he'd packed her off to bed as soon as the last guest left. An army of willing helpers had already tidied up and the dishwasher was gurgling through the last of the crockery.

Caitlin had left early. She'd managed to slip away while he wasn't watching—an impressive feat since he'd hardly taken his eyes off her.

As he neared the pergola, moonlight glinted on a plate that had been left on the post. He looked at the untouched food, re-membering how Caitlin had fled after their brief discussion.

Had he made a colossal mistake? He'd begun to think so almost as soon as he'd spoken to her. Doreen *did* have a right to know about her estranged brother. His motives for keeping it from her didn't seem to stand up to scrutiny at this late hour.

He'd been furious when he'd found out Caitlin's purpose for being in Garrangay. He hated the thought of Doreen being hurt. Fear and anger had pushed him to demand Caitlin's silence and her defiance had folded. She cared about Doreen. About him. She was prepared to put her own needs aside rather than cause him pain.

He hadn't given her the same consideration.

After a lifetime of nomadic existence, she wanted stability. She'd found it in her work in Melbourne. But when she wanted to reach out, find her roots, find family, he'd stopped her.

He'd perceived her need as a threat to his security, his family's security, and he'd reacted to contain it. And he'd hurt her dreadfully in the process. Her pain had been clear in her eyes, her face, her demeanour.

He'd been angry with her. Seen her secret identity as a betrayal after making him love her.

But now he'd had a chance to calm down he realised he had to make it right, help her find a way to tell Doreen the truth. Even if he'd wrecked his chances of a future with Caitlin, he had to make sure she connected with her family.

Too late tonight, much as he was tempted to go right this minute. First thing in the morning, before he took Nicky to pony club.

'Haley? Is Caitlin there, please?'

Matt's voice on speakerphone sliced through Caitlin's concentration. She took a sharp breath in and then forced all of her attention back to the dog on the operating table. Years of training prevented the quiver in her mind from reaching the fingers performing the femoral-artery repair.

'Yes, she is, Matt,' said Haley. 'But she can't come to the phone right now. We're in theatre with an emergency case.'

There was a silence.

'Can you ask her to ring me when she's finished? It's important, Haley. I need to speak her as soon as possible. I'm not at home so she'll have to ring me on my mobile.'

'No worries, Matt.'

'Thanks. I'll let you get back to it.'

A moment later the veterinary nurse returned to the other side of the table.

'Could you retract that muscle, please, Haley?'

A gleaming tool moved into position, improving her view of the damage. The dog was lucky to be alive. If the owner hadn't been there when the bull had gored her pet, the animal wouldn't have survived. She tidied up the torn tissue.

'He's gorgeous, isn't he?'

'Who? Suction, please, Haley.' The nozzle moved into position, noisily removing the fluid pooled at the bottom of the wound.

'Matt, of course. It's so cool that you guys are going out together. He deserves to be happy.'

'Mmm. Let's unclamp.' She watched the clip being released, her hands poised to intervene if there was a problem. The artery swelled, turning dark red as the blood flowed back into the lumen. The suture line held, no sign of leakage.

'Good work, Dr Butler-Brown.'

Caitlin grinned. 'Thank you, Nurse Simpson. Let's check the intestines.'

It was another hour before they could close up. In the kidney dish beside the table lay a length of resected bowel that had been too damaged to repair.

She stripped off her bloodied gloves before gathering the groggy boxer in her arms. Haley collected the drip and opened the door into the cage area.

'Bless you for coming in to help with this, Haley,' she said as she settled the heavily bandaged animal on the bedding. 'I couldn't have operated without you.'

'I was glad to have an excuse to leave the house. Cam's repainting the lounge. That man adores renovating as much as I hate it.' Haley chuckled.

'Oh, dear. I *was* going to suggest I'd finish up if you wanted to go home.' Caitlin stood to adjust the drip and slanted a smile at her assistant.

'I've got a better idea,' said Haley. 'Why don't I finish up while you go and ring Matt?'

'Mmm. I'd appreciate it if you would.' Guilt pinched at Caitlin. She hadn't told Haley she was leaving today. The words wouldn't come. She promised herself she'd ring to apologise when she was safely back in Melbourne.

'You've got his number?'

'Oh, yes. I have his number.' But she wouldn't be using it. What could he want to speak to her about? Whatever it was, she didn't want to hear it. If that smacked of cowardice, it was too bad. The previous two encounters with him had left her wounded and fragile. She'd taken as much as she could.

Bob was back. Haley had gone home.

And Caitlin was on her way. Just a quick stop at Mill House. She had to say goodbye to Doreen.

Please, let Matt still be at pony club.

Her aunt was in the kitchen, setting scones out on a floured oven tray with quick, efficient movements.

'Doreen? I…I'm heading off today.'

'Where to, dear? Have you been over to see that new gallery yet?'

'No. Doreen…I'm leaving, going back to Melbourne.'

'You're leaving? But…' The sentence trailed off and Doreen's blue-grey eyes went wide with shock as she stood, a lump of scone dough suspended from floury fingers. 'But I thought… Sally told me Bob was going to offer you a position in the practice.'

'He did. But I'm a city girl.' Caitlin forced her wooden face into what she hoped would be a reassuring smile. 'Being here, working in a country practice, has been grand. But I need to get serious and find a job.'

'What about you and Matt?'

'We've spoken, said what needs to be said.' She fluttered her hands, seeking to distract Doreen from the quaver in her voice.

'But…Caitlin…there are some things that I…that I have to ask you.' She looked at the dough still hanging from her hand and slowly lowered it to the baking tray as she spoke. 'I've put it off because I thought there was plenty of time, but now… Let me make coffee.'

Caitlin glanced at her watch surreptitiously. She wanted, *needed*, to be gone before Matt came back to the house. 'I should really—'

'The jug's just boiled.' Doreen quickly rinsed her fingers and dried them on her apron before collecting a couple of mugs.

'There you are,' she said a few moments later as she placed two steaming mugs of coffee on the table.

'Thanks.' Caitlin sank onto a chair, frowning as she watched her aunt add spoonful after spoonful of sugar to her mug. The agitated clink of metal on pottery filled the silence.

'Doreen?'

'There's no easy way for me to say this so I might as well just come out and say it.' Her aunt fixed her with an intense scrutiny. 'There are times when I think I must be mad for thinking…. But then something…'

Caitlin interlaced her fingers and held them tightly in her lap. As fragile as she was feeling right now, she didn't think she could bear a well-meant heart-to-heart about Matt and their disastrous relationship.

'You're my brother's daughter, aren't you?'

Caitlin's mouth opened then closed. Finally she managed, 'I—I…. What makes you…?' She swallowed. What could she say? She'd made a promise. But she couldn't lie to her aunt. 'Oh, God. Doreen.'

'I've been waiting for you to say something.'

Hope vied with guilt in Caitlin's reeling mind. 'Have you? H-how did you…?'

'How did I work it out? I think I knew the first moment I saw you. You have his eyes and every now and then…your expression is pure Marty.' She shook her head slightly, a reminiscent smile playing around her mouth. After a long moment, she asked, 'How is my brother?'

'I'm so sorry, Doreen.' Quick, hot tears welled in Caitlin's eyes. She pressed her fingers briefly to her lips and took a deep breath. 'He—he…'

'He's gone, isn't he?'

'Y-yes. He passed away a year ago.' Her voice felt rusty and harsh in her throat. 'He had cancer.'

'Oh, Caitlin.'

She found herself enfolded in a warm embrace and Doreen's sobs joined her own. After a few minutes she pulled back, digging in a pocket for a handkerchief to blow her nose. Her aunt did the same.

'My baby brother was a father.' Wonder filled Doreen's voice. 'And look at you. You're gorgeous and clever. He must have been so proud of you.'

Fresh tears flooded her eyes. 'I think so. I hope so.'

'There's so much I want to know about you and Marty. So many questions I want to ask.'

'Da wanted to apologize to you for everything and especially for staying away.' She made a small mental apology to Matt. But it felt so good, so right, to finally be saying these things. 'I think if he'd been well enough, he'd have come to see you.'

'Poor Marty. Did he tell you why he ran away?'

Caitlin shook her head.

'We had terrible fights over his schooling after our parents were killed. I was so set on him completing his education.'

'He said he knew you'd only wanted the best for him but he was too bloody-minded.' Caitlin took her aunt's hand, wanting to soothe away the pain. 'He told me he'd done you terrible harm and he didn't know how to make amends.'

Doreen squeezed Caitlin's fingers. 'After he left, I lost my baby. It was late in the pregnancy and I started haemorrhaging. They had to operate to save me. Marty rang while I was in hospital and Pete told him what had happened.' She seemed to be gathering herself to finish. 'Marty never came home again. Never got in touch.'

Her smile was tremulous. 'Pete and I started fostering soon afterwards. I think I hoped that someone would take Marty under their wing.'

'Like you were doing for others with your fostering.'

'Yes, exactly. We had so many wonderful young lives in our home.'

Caitlin remembered the haunting picture of an intense, green-eyed youth that Doreen had showed her. 'And Matt was one of them?'

'Yes, he was a darling boy. We would have adopted him if his mother had let us. She was a drug addict, you know?'

'He told me.'

'Matt told you that?' Doreen sounded surprised. 'Drug addiction is a terrible thing, and not just for the addict. That poor little boy. All we could do was make sure he had somewhere to come when she went off the rails. She loved him enough not to take him away from Garrangay but not enough to stay away from drugs.'

'You gave him an anchor when he needed it. He loves you very much.'

'He's a man with a lot of love to give, my dear.'

Perhaps he was. But none of it would ever be for her, not now. Grief for what might have been crushed her heart all over again.

'I'm so glad you came, Caitlin. Oh, there are so many things I want to ask you and here you are going back to Melbourne. Are you sure you can't stay longer?'

Caitlin hesitated briefly. 'Not this time, Doreen. I'm so sorry. But we'll stay in touch and I promise I'll be back as soon as…as soon as I can.'

As soon as she knew she could face Matt without breaking down. As soon as her battered heart could cope. Too much to hope that it would mend, but a little time away from him might start the healing process. She wasn't going to let the thought of seeing him stop her from spending time with her aunt, not now that everything was out in the open.

'There's something I'd like you to have. It belonged to my mother, your grandmother.'

Caitlin watched Doreen hurry out of the room. She really needed to start her journey but it was beyond her to cut short these precious moments with her aunt.

Caitlin wasn't going to ring him, Matt was sure of it. He strode across the veterinary clinic car park and thumped on the back door.

'Bob!' The shock of seeing the vet took Matt a long second to assimilate. 'You're back?'

'Hello, Matt. Come in.'

'No, I…. Caitlin?' His mind felt sluggish and his feet stayed rooted to the steps. 'Where is she?'

'Gone.'

Panic punched him in the gut. 'Gone? Where?'

'Back to Melbourne. It was the strangest thing. She—'

'When?' Matt forced the question past numb lips.

'About half an hour ago. Didn't she—?'

'Thanks. Sorry, Bob. I have to go. We'll catch up later.' Matt ran to the car. She was going to leave without saying goodbye to him…without saying goodbye to Doreen and Nicky. Because of him. He'd run her off. He'd been such an idiot.

An *eejit*.

Just thinking of the way she pronounced the insult made him want to groan. God, he had to find her. She could call him all the names under the sun as long as she stayed.

He yanked open the car door. How was he going to find her? Would she take the direct route back to Melbourne?

'She said something about calling at Mill House to see Doreen,' yelled Bob, from the back doorstep.

'Thanks.' Matt stabbed the key into the ignition.

As he drove home, he rehearsed the words he wanted to say to Caitlin. Tried to imagine her response.

The more he'd thought about it, the worse his interference seemed. Was she going to be able to forgive him for the things he'd said?

Caitlin had a right to share her grief about her father with someone who'd care. He'd denied two of the most important people in his life the opportunity to comfort each other.

Matt had suffered loss in his life but Doreen and Pete had always been there. A solid foundation, a place to lay his sorrows, to seek consolation. People, family, who accepted him no matter what.

Caitlin had no one. Her mother sounded distant in more ways than one. And now, in his selfishness, in his concern that his life didn't change, he'd denied her access to her aunt.

Matt smiled grimly. Once Doreen heard about the way he'd treated her niece, he was going to get a thorough ticking off.

Doreen was getting older. He had to acknowledge that he was going to lose her one day. Perhaps that was another reason why he wanted to hold onto things as they were for as long as possible. But change was inevitable.

Relief shuddered through him when he saw Caitlin's little MG parked at the side of Mill House. He wasn't too late to speak to her. Would he be too late to salvage their relationship? He didn't know but he was going to give it a damned good try.

His mother and Caitlin were hugging each other in the hallway as he came through the front door. He knew the moment she realised he was there. A shudder of shock ran through her body and the colour drained from her face.

'Oh, Matt. You're home. Thank heavens,' said Doreen, relief plain on her face. 'I didn't want Caitlin to leave without seeing you.'

'No. I don't want that either,' he said softly, placing his keys on the stand as he walked towards them. 'We have things to discuss. Caitlin has some things to tell you.'

'I know. She's my niece, Matt.'

His footsteps faltered for a moment as the words sank in.

'She told you.' A tiny dart of disappointment needled him. Caitlin had broken her promise after all. But what did it matter? He wanted the truth to come out.

Out of the corner of his eye he saw Caitlin stiffen.

'She didn't have to.' His mother was radiant with happiness. 'I've suspected from the very first day.'

'You knew? All this time?' He stared at Doreen. 'Why didn't you say something?'

'I nearly did. It seems stupid now that I didn't.' She turned back to Caitlin. 'But I was afraid in case I scared you away by prying. I thought you'd say something if I gave you enough time.'

Matt cleared his throat. 'She would have, Mum. I told her not to.'

'You told her not to?' Doreen looked up at him in obvious confusion. 'Why would you do that?'

'I was trying to protect you.' He ran a hand around the back of his neck, feeling the tension in the muscles. What an arrogant fool he'd been to think he knew best.

'But, darling, of course I'd want to know about Marty. His leaving has always been like a hole in my heart.' Doreen's face creased in a look of mingled reproach and affection.

'I know.' His gaze moved back to Caitlin. *A hole in the heart.* That was exactly what he was going to have if he couldn't convince the woman he loved to stay.

After a short pause, his mother said, 'Yes. I can see that you do.'

'I need to talk to Caitlin, Mum.'

'Yes, and mind you do a good job of it.' She took Caitlin's hands and held them. 'Let him grovel, Caitlin, dear. Something tells me he's earned it.'

The silence, after Doreen walked away, seemed to take on a life of its own. Caitlin cautiously drew in a deep breath,

needing the oxygen in her lungs but loath to disturb their
tableau. She'd thought earlier she couldn't feel any worse.

She was wrong.

'Caitlin?' Matt's voice was low and charged with emotion.
When his hand reached towards her, she pulled back, wrapping
her arms around her waist, holding herself tight. If he touched
her now she'd surely shatter. After a moment he lowered his
arm to his side. 'Come through to the study.'

She stood her ground. 'I kept my promise to you.'

'I know.'

'I'm not sorry Doreen knows the truth.' She had to hold onto
that. She had a family. Falling in love with Matt had been an
unfortunate detour.

'Neither am I.'

'I— You're not?' She struggled to grasp the meaning of his
words. 'Then what else is there to say? I've got a long drive to
make, Matt.' She was proud of the way she sounded. Firm, determined. Not like she was falling apart inside.

He moved closer and she stepped back.

'I'd like to get back to Melbourne before it gets too late.'

'Yes, I understand.' He reached past her shoulder. She retreated another step. Two.

'I'll need to do some shopping since I've been away so
long. Milk and…' Now she was babbling. That wasn't so good.
'Milk and stuff. Bread. You know.'

'Yes, I know.' His voice was soothing, as though he was
trying to calm a skittish animal.

She turned away, took several paces then stopped short as
she realised she was standing in the study. There was a small
click as the door shut behind her. The tiny sound sent a tremor
through her body.

She was alone with him. It took every ounce of self-discipline
to quell the urge to bolt. She tightened her arms across her
stomach. Whatever he had to say, she would survive and move on.

She *would*. She was strong.

Tilting her chin, she turned to face him. He was standing so close, his expression too gentle, almost…loving. *No, that couldn't be right.* All she knew was if he didn't stop looking at her that way, her bracing internal lecture would be worthless.

'What's so important, then?' she managed through stiff lips.

'I was wrong to stop you talking to Mum about her brother. About your father.' His voice was rough with emotion.

She'd been ready for a fight. His admission knocked the starch out of her. 'Oh.'

'She had a right to know.'

'Oh. Th-thank you.' Caitlin felt she should say more but her mind refused to function.

'I'm sorry.'

'You—you wanted to protect your mother.'

'You're making excuses for me.' He smiled crookedly and reached out slowly, giving her time to move away if she chose. Her breath froze in her chest as he skimmed her ear, tucking away a strand of hair. Taking his time. The expression on his face was so beautiful it brought a lump to her throat. 'It wasn't Mum I was protecting, my darling. It was me. I was afraid.'

'I was afraid, too,' she murmured. His hand rested on her shoulder, the warmth seeping through her. He'd called her his darling. What did it mean? A wayward spark of hope blossomed in her heart. 'I nearly told you why I was here. I didn't know what to do. I was so afraid of hurting Doreen, of hurting all of you.'

'I know. You humbled me when you said you'd walk away rather than cause her pain.' His hand moved to the nape of her neck, the thumb rubbing sensitive skin at her throat. Could he feel the crazy beating of her pulse? She should move away but her brain refused to send the signals to her feet.

'I love you.' His voice was a soft caress.

She gulped in a breath as the meaning of the miraculous words slowly sank in. 'You—you love me?'

'Yes. And I'll tell you every day for the rest of my life if you'll stay here and let me. You belong with me. I want us to be a family,' he murmured, his hands coming up to cup her face.

She stared into the warm green of his eyes. 'I don't know if I'm any good at family. What if I mess up? What if I—?'

'Shh.' His thumbs came up to press against her lips, stopping her words with soft insistence. 'Caitlin, you're already *great* at family. Trust me, darling.'

He placed his lips on hers, spinning her thoughts wildly out of control. She slid her hands around his waist, needing to anchor herself.

'We belong together.'

'Oh, Matt.' She bit her lip. 'I want that so much.'

'Then that's all that matters.' His mouth slanted across hers. 'Marry me.' But he didn't give her a chance to answer, instead leaving her breathless with another kiss. 'We can live in Garrangay.'

'Yes,' she gasped, as his lips pressed to hers again.

'Or wherever you want to.'

'No, nowhere else. Why would I want to leave Garrangay?' She drew back to meet his eyes. 'Everything I need is right here.'

Hope and happiness flared in the deep green. 'You'll stay? You'll marry me?'

'Yes and yes. I love you, Matt Gardiner.'

His arms wrapped around her, scooping her up on his chest so she looked down on his broad grin. 'You won't regret it. I'll make you happy. We'll make you happy.'

She could hardly breathe but she didn't care. She wanted him to hold her like this. Tight to his body, tight in his life. The way she was going to hold him and never let go.

EPILOGUE

SHE was getting *married*. Today. *Now.*

A shiver of delicious terror shuddered along Caitlin's nerves. Marrying Matt was what she wanted more than anything in the world.

So why was she loitering in her room, putting off the moment of facing everyone?

Putting off the moment of facing Matt?

She loved him. She loved his family…her family.

But just because she wanted family, a place to belong, it didn't mean she'd be good at it, good for them. She'd had no practice, no experience at stability. It wasn't just her life that would be affected if she messed up.

She needed to see Matt, talk to him. Draw strength from him. But Doreen had been adamant. Grooms did not see their brides before the wedding—it was bad luck. So he'd been dispatched to stay at Bob and Sally's last night, to be delivered back here in time for the ceremony.

He would be standing out there right now, waiting, wondering what was keeping her. If she didn't unglue her feet, she was in danger of being an unfashionably late bride.

She jumped at a small tap on the door. Doreen must be back to see what the problem was.

'Yes? Come in.' She pinned a smile on her lips.

Nicky's face popped around the edge of the door. 'Hi, Caitlin.'

'Hi, yourself.'

Spotty's head appeared a second later and the dog bounced into the room.

'Sit, Spotty,' Nicky said sternly. The spotted rump immediately plopped to the floor, the tail still wagging frantically, sending vibrations through the lean frame.

'Wow, you've been working hard on those obedience lessons.'

'Spotty learns quick. He's real smart.' Nicky came to stand beside the excited pup.

'And so are you for teaching him.' She looked at him. He was a miniature version of Matt, dressed in a smart dark grey suit and red tie. 'Don't you look grand in your finery, then?'

'Nanna said that, too.' He smiled. 'Dad sent us. He said you might have cold feet.'

Her lips quivered, just a little. 'Did he, now?'

'That means you're scared, doesn't it?'

'That is what it means, yes.'

'But that's silly, isn't it? Why would you be scared 'cos you're marrying Dad? It means you get to live with us for ever and ever.'

Love for her stepson-to-be overflowed from her heart. 'So it does.'

Nicky's face screwed up with concentration. 'And Dad said to say we'd do it one day at a time.'

'When you put it like that, it's quite simple, then, isn't it?' And it was, she realised. 'Your dad's pretty smart, isn't he?'

'Yep. He said you'd understand. So are you coming now? Dad's waiting.'

'Then let's not keep him waiting any longer.' She held her hand out. Nicky's small fingers closed over hers. Spotty seemed to sense they were ready to go and bounded out ahead of them.

She walked through the garden with her escort, peripherally aware of everyone. Matt stood under the rose arch. Her heart squeezed with love as his mouth curved into a secret smile. How could she not love this wonderful, perceptive man? He'd understood, sent his emissaries to help her.

'We got her, Dad. You can get married now.'

'Thank you, Nicky,' Matt said softly, as he exchanged a man-to-man look with his son.

Caitlin watched Nicky and Spotty go to stand by her aunt. When she raised her eyes to her groom she found him watching her, his green eyes filled with love and concern.

'All right, darling?'

'I am, now, yes.'

Warmth and confidence flooded her. She was going to love and be loved by her new family, each and every day for the rest of her life.

GROOMED
FOR LOVE

HELEN R. MYERS

Chapter One

"Rylie, sweetheart, you are the best thing to happen to Sweet Springs since they started putting in drive-through windows at pharmacies."

Rylie Quinn, the new groomer at Sweet Springs Animal Clinic, grinned at Pete Ogilvie, the eldest of the four war veterans who conducted a daily coffee klatch in the corner of the building's reception area. It was she who'd dubbed them the four musketeers after characters in the famous Alexandre Dumas novel, and Pete himself Athos, after the eldest of the adventurers, because the former marine was the boldest yet most complicated of the group. He also had somehow taken Jerry Platt under his wing. At sixty-six, Jerry, whom she called D'Artagnan, was the youngest and had become the fourth member of the veteran group, as D'Artagnan had become the fourth musketeer in the story.

"Why, thank you, kind sir." Holding out the hem of her maroon smock, as though it was a skirt, she offered a quick curtsy, bemused, even though the comparison was confusing. She suspected he hadn't meant to imply that she was appreciated because she was a convenience. "All because I asked Mr. Stan if he wanted sweetener in his coffee?"

"That's right! None of us can tell him that he's being an old grouch the way you can and still bring a smile to his face."

Stanley Walsh—aka Porthos, as far as Rylie was concerned—was sixty-nine, the second youngest, and an ex-navy man, as well as a retired master sheet-metal fabricator. Sometimes—like today—his hangovers caused him to grouse a little more than usual, which was saying quite a bit, since Stanley had a dry sense of humor to begin with.

"That, along with being as bright and as pretty as a black-eyed Susan, which is about the only damned flower that can survive the summer like we had with any grace. Whew, can you believe it officially became autumn yesterday?" Pete asked around the room. "If you hold that front door open for too long, I swear those bags of dog food stacked on the shelves over there are gonna pop like popcorn in a microwave."

As others grunted their agreement, Rylie said, "I'm sorry for the strain it is on animals, but I sure don't mind it being warm. I was born and raised in the desert country of California. That said, I'm getting seriously partial to your trees here, especially the pines." She had arrived in this Central East Texas community early in July, in time to attend Dr. Gage Sullivan's marriage to Brooke Bellamy last month, the niece of the lady who used to be

Gage's neighbor. That neighborhood, as well as several parts of town, was enhanced by pockets of the pines and hardwood trees that had once earned the region its other name—The Piney Woods. She told the men, who had also attended the wedding, "If I had Doc and Brooke's yard, I'd sleep with the windows open every night to listen to the breeze whispering through the trees."

"Well, don't try it here, even if your fancy RV's windows are high off the ground," Roy Quinn said from inside the reception station in the center of the room.

As usual, her uncle pretended to have as gruff a personality as any of the old-timers, but Rylie knew the middle-aged bachelor saw her as the daughter he'd never had. "I wouldn't do that. Besides," she reminded her only relative in the area, "as far back as those trees are beyond the pasture, it's easier to hear the highway traffic out front." The clinic was on the service road of a state highway that ran north to south on the east side of town. The overpass that led to downtown was only a few dozen yards beyond the clinic's parking lot.

"Good. Keep those miniblinds shut at night, too. What we lack in woods, we probably make up for in Peeping Toms and lechers, and word's getting around about you and that RV being parked in back."

As he spoke, he glanced over her shoulder to fork his fingers from his eyes to Jerry, who tended to think of himself as quite the ladies' man. Recently, Jerry Platt had the bad judgment to get involved with a certain widow in town, who had really been angling to get closer to Doc. It had caused quite a stir among the old-timers, who feared losing the congenial atmosphere at the clinic, and they were keeping Jerry on notice, too.

Rylie shook her head, thinking Uncle Roy was being

silly. Jerry was more than a decade older than him! Besides, he'd been nothing but a gentleman to her. Noticing Jerry's embarrassment, she leaned over the counter to whisper, "I'm twenty-five, not fifteen."

Roy grunted. "You'd have to dye your hair gray to convince anyone. I'll bet you still get carded when you go out for a beer."

"My last beer was a week ago with you guys at the VFW hall, and you know they would serve me anything because I was with you." However, he was right; she did look ridiculously young, but what could you do when you had red hair and a squeaky-clean face that made you perfect for the front of a cereal box but was never going to trigger wolf whistles as a cover girl's would? Something else she didn't have going for her was height—she hadn't grown an inch above her five foot three since the seventh grade. To redirect Roy's focus, she reached across the counter to straighten his wrinkled shirt collar lying awkwardly over his maroon clinic jacket. "If you don't like to iron, at least take your clothes out of the dryer before they dry all mangled. Better yet, let me do your ironing for you."

"Don't change the subject." Roy playfully swatted away her hand away. "Just remember that I have to answer to your parents if anything happens to you here."

She thought about her parents, who were considering becoming foster parents since she, too, had "abandoned the nest," as her parents put it. Her older, adopted brother had struck out on his own four years earlier, finding his career restoring old homes on the East Coast. "Nothing is going to happen to me, Uncle Roy. I was born under a lucky star, remember?"

It was her longtime joke, ever since learning that she

had been born one night on the side of the road after the family car had suffered a flat on the way to the hospital. When asked as a child, "Which star?" she would spread her arms wide and declare, "All of them!" The truth was that Roy had been a lifesaver in helping her get a job here, and Rylie intended to quickly make him see that she was fine on her own before he found out the full truth about why she had made the move.

"Well, Ms. Lucky," he said, nodding toward the front, "your first appointment is arriving—along with her sourpuss courier."

Noting his grimace, a confused Rylie glanced over her shoulder to see a sleek black BMW sedan pull up to the front door. She couldn't stop a little sigh as she recognized that once again Ramon Bustillo wasn't here in Mrs. Prescott's Cadillac.

"I wonder how Mrs. P talked His Highness into delivering her pooch again."

"Behave." Rylie looked from her uncle to the four musketeers, to see if they were listening, then back to the expensive car. She knew why Uncle Roy called Noah Prescott that—Noah wasn't only the son of Mrs. Audra Prescott, one of the state's most admired ladies in society, he was also District Attorney Vance Ellis Underwood's assistant and expected successor—and he acted the part. As a result, her uncle didn't care for him, calling him a "stuffed shirt," and, after two meetings with the man, Rylie had to admit Roy had some cause for his opinion. However, Noah was maddeningly sexy, too, with his intense brown eyes, serious five-o'clock shadow that tended to keep her from having a clear view of the slight cleft in his chin, and gorgeous, wavy brown hair with enviable gold highlights. The first time she met him, she'd concluded that he must shave three times a day to keep the elegant image his tailored suits and expensive shoes exuded. He undoubtedly went for a weekly manicure, too. His long-fingered, pianist's hands had made her want to shove her banged-up, laborer's hands into her jeans' back pockets.

"Ramon must have experienced some kind of problem again," she replied. Ramon Bustillo wasn't only Mrs. Prescott's driver; he was the caretaker at Haven Land, the family estate. Last time, Ramon had needed to get Mrs. Prescott to an early doctor's appointment, so Noah had brought her dog, and it was evident to anyone with eyes that Noah couldn't wait to be rid of the adorable bichon frise, registered as Baroness Baja Bacardi. It had been equally clear that the little dog couldn't wait to get into friendlier hands, as well.

"I suspect having an audience won't improve his mood any, so I'm going to take MG and Humphrey out back. C'mon, Humph," he called to Doc's basset hound. "MG, pretty girl," he added to the large, black retriever-mix dog. "Let's go out."

"Thanks, Uncle Roy." Seeing Noah struggle with closing the car door, she started toward the front door to help, only to stumble. "Oh!"

She knew immediately what had happened—instead of following her uncle's directive, MG had come to stand beside her as though waiting for permission. Luckily, Rylie had good reflexes and grabbed the edge of the counter before falling face-first to the tile floor.

"Rylie—good Lord! Are you okay?"

Seventy-year-old Warren Atwood, the "Aramis" in the group, rose from his chair. Retired from the army and a former D.A. of Cherokee County himself, his dear wife was in a local nursing home suffering from the last stages of Alzheimer's. Rylie had learned that he was so devastated by it all that he could barely stand to be there without becoming emotional.

"Not to worry," she assured him and the others, who also looked concerned. "I should have known she would come to me first. She's still getting used to Uncle Roy." Rylie covered her embarrassment by quickly hugging the sweet-natured, long-legged dog. She thought she'd been doing so well; she hadn't bumped into a wall or tripped over anything in days. "Let's go, Mommy's Girl. Go out with Uncle Roy. You know it's your job to watch over Humphrey." She walked the black, silky-haired animal to the swinging doors, where her uncle and Doc and Brooke's basset hound waited.

"I don't get it," Roy muttered. "Dogs like me."

"She likes you."

"So much that she runs to you at the sound of my voice. She's going to give me a complex." After the mock complaint, her uncle gave her a concerned look. "Are you sure you're okay? You aren't getting all flustered over Golden Boy, are you?"

"You're sounding more and more like a jealous school-girl." Shaking her head, she started for the front door again.

By the time she had her hand on the handle bar, Noah Prescott had championed the outer door. Barely. She couldn't help but laugh at the awkward way he was holding the little cutie. Was he afraid that the adorable white bichon frise was going to try to take a bite of his earlobe or that the young dog would ruin his very attractive silvery-gray suit?

"Thanks for the prompt assistance," Noah muttered when he finally made it inside.

"You're very welcome, A.D.A. Prescott," she replied cheerfully, purposely misunderstanding his sarcasm. "I would never have guessed a little eight-pound dog with such an amiable nature would scare a man with the entire police department at his service."

"I. Am. Not. Scared." Checking his edgy tone, Noah added stiffly, "I'm simply trying not to get dog hair on my suit. I happen to be due in court within the hour."

"Well, you're wearing the best color to hide a strand or two," Rylie assured him, all smiles and pleasantness. "Hello, Bubbles, you cutie." She relieved Noah of the tiny bundle, who had been nothing but obliging during her two previous visits. "I hope nothing has happened to Ramon," she added to Noah. "Your mother's driver?" she added, after his odd look.

"I *know* his name. I just thought it unusual that you did."

Maybe Uncle Roy was right—Noah Prescott could be the snob Roy claimed. Unable to resist, Rylie said with several more degrees of sweet demeanor, "Why wouldn't I? Because he's *only* a driver? I'm only a dog groomer. Who am I to put on airs about the hired help?"

After staring at her as though he would like to put her behind bars, or at least walk out without another word, Noah replied with painstaking civility, "Ramon is at the dealership. The car had a flat before getting out the driveway. Mother didn't want him driving way down here on the spare, then all the way back to Rusk."

"That sounds just like her. She's such a thoughtful woman." Audra Prescott was also turning into her best customer so far, thanks to her preference for having her dog groomed more often than the average person. With a few more clients like her, Rylie knew Gage and Uncle Roy would be convinced that there was definitely a market for another dog groomer in the area. "You're a good son, too," she assured Noah, with impish humor, "for helping out in a crunch."

"I can't tell you how that reassures me." Checking his watch, he added quickly, "I take it that Mother gave you instructions on what she wants done?"

"Bathing, trimming…the cut still a little shorter since the days are still quite warm, even though it's shorter than the AKC prefers—" Turning to reach for her reservations book that she'd left on the lower level of the reception counter, Rylie misjudged the distance and bumped her elbow. She hit hard enough to gasp and jerk back, and she had to do a neat little jig to keep her balance. "Oops. Sorry, Bubbles. That's the last misstep for this visit, I promise."

From behind her came Noah's droll observation. "I take it that it wasn't runway modeling that you gave up for this line of work?"

"As a matter of fact, it was," she replied, her wicked humor kicking in. "Call me crazy, since there's only so much demand for five-foot-three glamour girls. But I just love animals too much." She kept her smile bright, determined not to let her disappointment in him show. But who was he to add a jab at her height into his cutting remark? Mr. Glass-Half-Empty Prescott might reach six feet *if* someone gave him an inch of credit for his ability to look down his nose at her. While he had the face for it, no modeling agency would hound him to sign a contract, either. "As I was saying, aside from the usual care, Bubbles will get—"

Noah silenced her with a dismissive wave. "Don't bother. That Mother relayed instructions is all I care about. Good grief, primping is primping. Any of the shops between here and Rusk would do the same thing."

Sexy, but grouchy, Rylie thought with renewed disappointment. All because he had to drive a few extra miles for his mother's dog? She couldn't resist rubbing it in a bit. "Yes, I am fortunate to have her, Mrs. Collins's and Mrs. Nixon's support, as well. They've all been very kind about spreading the word. As it happens, I'm a little different from some in the business because I've been doing this kind of work since I was old enough to know the difference between the front and back end of animals. And for the record? The term *primping* is condescending. There are a good number of health issues related to good grooming for animals, just as there are for humans."

In a moment that couldn't have been better choreographed if she'd tried, Bubbles started licking Rylie's hand as though apologizing on Noah's behalf. Rylie nuzzled the little dog.

"Aw...thank you, precious." She returned her focus to Noah. "I also don't believe in sedating animals, whatever their temperament. How safe or wise would it have been for your mother, or nanny, to sedate you when giving you a manicure or trim?"

From the corner of the room the four musketeers chuckled and snickered.

Noah Prescott stared at her as though she'd just burst into "The Sun Will Come Out Tomorrow" and took a cautious step back toward the exit. "Just call my mother when it's ready. Ramon should be home by then."

Almost before the doors drifted shut behind Noah, Stan Walsh launched the inevitable commentary. "What-

cha trying to do to the poor guy, Rylie? You had him acting like he'd OD'd on sticky buns."

As the others laughed, Rylie stroked the adorable animal in her arms and gave them her most innocent look.
"Now, Stan, are you accusing me of being an instigator?"

"Never met a honeybee who wasn't."

"It's been my experience," Pete Ogilvie offered, "that
the harder a guy tries to convince a gal that he doesn't
approve of her, the more he's really trying to deny he's
attracted."

"That sounds like forced logic to me," Jerry Platt
scoffed.

"That's because you have the libido of a rabbit," Pete
countered, "and the mind of one. You think that any female who happens to cross your path is a gift from the
gods."

As the men burst into laughter, Rylie pretended the
need to cover Bubbles's ears. "This conversation is getting way too frisky for our tender ears, baby girl. Let's
go."

Damn her perkiness.

She was the most annoying female he'd met in some
time, and what was driving Noah crazy was that it was
for all the reasons that usually attracted him. What the
heck was going on? Rylie Quinn was friendly, good-
natured, a born optimist. How could he fault someone
who tried to see the bright side of things? Yet for some
bizarre, quirky reason, he was discovering that he had
no problem where she was concerned.

She was an irritating mix of sweetness and provocation, deceptively packaged in a Peter Pan–size body that
her maroon medical smock would mostly hide, except

when it wasn't fastened today any more than on his other visit to the clinic. That gamin-short hair didn't help make her look fully grown, either. The short, punkish style left her looking more like a nine-year-old boy than a woman in her early or mid-twenties, an ironic observation, since he liked his women slender and sleek. But then she did little to enhance her femininity—maybe just mascara and some lip gloss, and yet every receptor in his molecular being went on full alert the instant she was within sight.

It was those gray-green eyes that got him on edge, he decided. Sure they were incredibly framed by lashes that would make a sable proud; however, their color was that unnerving shade of storm clouds before a tornado dropped from them and turned your life inside out. *That's it!* he thought, feeling as though he'd locked in on some important detail. She looked at him as though she had a secret, and she wasn't telling. Well, he wasn't big on secrets. It was one of the chief things that made his work so difficult and, often, ugly: secrets and lies.

As Noah sped north to Rusk, and the courthouse, he considered phoning his mother again to ask if she really knew what she was getting herself into trusting Rylie Quinn. Just because her equally dog-crazy friends approved of the young woman, Rylie's claim that she didn't use drugs to keep animals calm during grooming didn't mean she hadn't, or wouldn't, in a crunch. He also didn't believe for a moment her self-laudatory proclamation that she got along with any and all critters. Maybe it was working to sell herself as the female rendition of the *Dog Whisperer;* however, she'd been at the clinic for only about a month. The jury was still out, as far as he was concerned.

On the other hand, Dr. Gage Sullivan's reputation was

impeccable. He just hoped the guy hadn't been suckered in by a red-haired con artist the way his mother and others may have been.

At the thought of his mother, he sighed heavily. He accepted that he was struggling to understand her and had been since the accident that put her in a wheelchair. She had always been a pragmatic, no-nonsense person, but no more. *Who registers their lap dog as Baroness Baja Bacardi?* he thought with a new wave of dismay and embarrassment. What a title for a creature that could almost fit in a restaurant take-out box. Granted, his mother had little pleasure in her life anymore—a dog, the pool therapy, her painting and the visits from a small handful of trusted and dedicated friends, as well as her minister, lawyer and accountant. Otherwise, her society was "Livie," Olivia Danner, her live-in nurse, and Aubergine Scott, the resident housekeeper-cook. Considering the whirlwind life of a socialite that she'd juggled before, his mother's life was as shockingly different as if Hillary Clinton suddenly chose to exit the political world forever and cloistered herself in a nunnery! Under those circumstances, Noah didn't have the heart to deny her this bit of frivolity even as he groused to others over being inconvenienced. Audra Rains Prescott had earned a certain amount of indulgences, regardless of how silly this one seemed to him.

Three years ago, his parents were involved in a head-on collision with another vehicle, one whose driver passed out due to side effects of her prescription drugs. The crash had killed his father and the other driver instantly. It was a miracle that his mother hadn't died, too. She had, however, lost most of the use of the lower half of her body. Nevertheless, there was enough nerve connectivity to trigger chronic pain and insomnia, which in turn added to bouts of depression. If it wasn't for their dedicated people on the estate, he would need prescriptions, or at least a therapist himself.

For example, Ramon wasn't just dealing with a flat tire; there was a recall notice on his mother's Cadillac that he hadn't let her know about, due to her fragile perspective when it came to all things motorized these days. It had come only two days ago, so the tire issue had been fortuitous in a way. Ramon knew to keep the more serious issue between the two of them. He just hoped the repair wouldn't take all day.

"Hell," he muttered, "if you can't trust America's classy tank, what can you trust?"

It was a relief to reach Rusk and the courthouse. He'd become the assistant D.A. for Cherokee County soon after his return to East Texas to supervise things at home. Until then, he'd been the hottest "gunslinger" at one of Houston's top law firms. Had he been able to stay there, he had no doubt there would already be talk about him becoming a partner by now, even though he was only thirty.

Coming home, it had never occurred to him to just manage the family estate and enjoy a gentleman's lifestyle, which had been an option. True, he could also have opened his own private practice; however, that didn't appeal to him, either. Divorces, will probates and small lawsuits needed good counsel to be sure, but not from him. He needed something with more intellectual challenge, and so when Vance Ellis Underwood, the current D.A., discreetly asked him if being the assistant D.A.— with the understanding that he would be seen as Underwood's heir apparent when Underwood retired—would be something he would be interested in, Noah saw that as his best option.

If only he was handling his return to a more rural lifestyle as well. While there was no denying the countryside's beauty, he missed Houston and the nightlife, the buzz and being in the inner circle of what was happening in the city and state. But someone had to oversee the family's estate—the mansion, the near-thousand-acre ranch and tree farm, along with oil and gas leases. His mother had left all of that to his father, although she had a good basic knowledge of what was what. Unfortunately, she was no longer mobile enough to keep on top of things.

At the town square, Noah parked in back of the courthouse building, where their offices were on the first floor. Grabbing his briefcase, he hurried inside. While driving, he'd already answered two calls from the D.A.'s secretary, the last time assuring her that he was as good as in the building. Court commenced in minutes, and today they were choosing a jury for a case related to the largest drug bust in the county's history. The fact that the accused was the son of a prominent family in the area was garnering a lot of media attention, and it would be the worst day to be late.

Noah rushed into the office just as Judy Millsap exited the D.A.'s office, a bulging file and her steno pad in her arms.

"Oh, thank goodness." The silver-haired, usually calm woman exhaled with relief as she set her load on her desk. "This is all for you. He's coming down with a full-fledged case of some bug or other. He thought he could get things started and then let you do the most of the jury interviewing, but he just admitted that even sitting in court might be more than he can manage."

At sixty-six, Vance Underwood had suffered a few health problems in the past year and had confided that he wanted to retire as soon as his term was over in two years. Catching something as common as a virus could turn things serious quickly.

"Do you think you should get him an ambulance?" Noah asked in concern.

"I asked. He vetoed the idea, but I insisted he let a deputy drive him home. I'll take his car and hitch a ride back with the officer."

"It sounds as though his heart doctor should be notified, as well."

The plump woman with the wedge hairdo nodded her agreement. "So do I, but it's not up to me. I will call his wife and warn her we're coming while I wait for the deputy. Perhaps I can convince her that she needs to make that call."

"Good luck with that." As much as Noah didn't want to seem too eager to take control, he was also discreet about making any comments about Mrs. Underwood. It was well-known in the office and elsewhere around town that Elise had never been given a prescription drug she didn't develop a loving relationship with. Chances were that she wasn't even out of bed yet, let alone coherent enough to be of any assistance to her husband.

Reaching for the stack, Noah said, "Let me know if there's anything else you need."

"Pick an excellent jury."

Three hours later, Noah was back at his desk. As luck would have it, the judge had come down with the same virus that the D.A. seemed to be suffering from and the entire day's docket was rescheduled. Minutes ago, Noah had encouraged Judy to take an early lunch, assuring her that he would stay and watch things at the office. She was grateful, having missed breakfast due to the morning's hectic situation.

Alone in the office—since their clerk, Ann, was finishing a task and directly heading off to lunch, too— Noah called home to check on his mother. "Has Ramon made it back from the dealership?" he asked.

"I'm glad you called. No, he hasn't. They just started on my car and told him it would be about two hours. How can a simple matter like a flat take so long?"

Noah wasn't about to tell her, and replied instead, "They could be shorthanded. We have a lot of illness going around here, too. Or else they saw that the car's mileage was close to the next scheduled oil change and servicing and convinced Ramon to go ahead and do that."

"Oh. Well, then, will you be a dear and pick up Bubbles during your lunch hour? Rylie called and Bubbles is not liking being locked in a kennel at all."

Noah closed his eyes and pinched the bridge of his nose. "Why can't she bring her to you?" She must take a lunch break herself, and since she was eager to build up a clientele base, this would be a great way to make points with a valued customer.

"Shame on you!" his mother replied. "That's not her responsibility." After a slight pause, she said more calmly, "If you have other commitments, darling, just say so. I only feel badly for everyone having to listen to my baby acting up. I'm sure she's upsetting the other animals, too."

It was on the tip of his tongue to claim that he was due back in court too soon to do that for her, but his conscience wouldn't let him. The whole purpose of returning here was to make his mother's life as stress-free as possible.

"Judy's taking her lunch at the moment," he said. "But she'll be back in about thirty minutes. I can go then."

"Bless you, darling. You're the best child a mother could hope for."

"Give me a compliment that bears repeating," he replied drolly. "Everyone here knows I'm an only child and that you have nothing to compare me with."

At least when he hung up, she was laughing.

When Noah pulled up to the clinic, it wasn't yet one o'clock and the closed-for-lunch sign was still on the door, although Noah could see the old-timers sitting around their table. He wondered if they ever went home. Or was there anyone at home to go to? He had noticed pockets of seniors around Rusk, too, who collected wherever they weren't in the way yet could get out of the heat or cold, depending on the season. Loneliness and old age weren't necessarily synonymous—he knew plenty of senior citizens living full, active lives—but apparently something was going on. It was good of Gage Sullivan to allow the guys to hang out here.

One of the seniors spotted him and pointed around the building toward the back.

Hoping he understood correctly, Noah drove that way, only to utter a soft, "Whoa."

He'd heard that Rylie Quinn was living in a camper in the back of the clinic, but what was parked ahead of him wasn't just an RV. It was one of those monster coach things that well-to-do traveling retirees and touring rock stars used. Didn't those things come with a hefty price tag? It seemed a lot of vehicle for a woman only in her mid-twenties. Grooming dogs was apparently more lucrative than he'd first thought.

As he exited his BMW, he gave the two-tone bronze machine a once-over from behind his sunglasses. This was a model where both sides could extend out from the main structure for extra sleeping and dining space, converting it into a virtual house on wheels. The size of the thing also had him wondering who else might be in there. A boyfriend? Husband? Rylie didn't wear a ring. Come to think of it, she didn't seem to wear any jewelry at all. Interesting bit of trivia for such a lively, even flamboyant, person.

Before he could knock, the door opened, and he looked up into Rylie's smiling face. A determined smile, he noted.

"Hey there. Twice in one day—my cup runneth over. I guess your mom managed to twist your arm? When I called her and learned that Ramon was being held hostage at the dealership, I offered to bring Bubbles to her, but she said you would be happy to do it." Upon seeing Noah narrow his eyes, she threw back her head and laughed with delight. "Oh, how funny! She conned you."

"So it would seem," he muttered. The *why* bothered him, too. His mother hadn't met Rylie, so she had better not be getting any ideas about matchmaking.

"Come on in, you poor oppressed soul. I was having lunch here to let Bubbles have more space, and so the old-timers could hear each other talk. For a little thing, she does have powerful lungs."

After a slight hesitation, Noah did step up into the vehicle. He couldn't deny that he was curious as to what things looked like inside. "That's what Mother claims to have been worried about. At home Bubbles has about ten thousand square feet to roam around, all in a safe environment." As soon as he said that, Noah inwardly kicked himself. Not only did it sound as though he was bragging, but he knew better than to offer details to strangers, particularly about the family's wealth. Granted, one had only to drive by the property to know they were well-off, but to him this was just another sign of how easily Rylie Quinn could undermine his discipline.

"Lucky girl. At least we don't have to worry about her getting enough exercise, regardless of the weather." Rylie stepped back to make room for him. "I wondered how Mrs. Prescott could be feeding her all of those treats she admits to, yet this munchkin stays at a healthy weight." She leaned over to pick up the little dog that—upon Noah's entry—had gone straight to her and planted one tiny foot on Rylie's sneaker.

Noah didn't miss the move, which struck him as possessive. That left Noah with the uncomfortable feeling that the dog could sense his conflicted feelings about Rylie. Or was the animal sticking close to her because she hated the idea of having to ride home with him? At this rate the spoiled fur ball was going to have Rylie thinking he was abusive.

"She also likes to chase around the pool," he continued, "while my mother has her therapy."

With a sympathetic sound, Rylie said, "I heard about what happened to Mrs. Prescott—and the terrible loss you both suffered. I'm so sorry."

Although he nodded his thanks, he had to look away after feeling an unexpected pulling in his midsection, as though someone was tethering them together via invisible strings connected to each of their ribs. In self-defense, he changed the subject. "This is quite a setup you have here. When I heard you had been working out of an RV, I pictured something less...comfortable."

Rylie glanced around, her expression reflecting her own sense of good fortune. "A business contact of my parents helped me get a great price and terms. It's a repo," she told him. "I didn't really need anything so big, let alone lavish, but the extra space would have come in handy if Doc hadn't been so generous in letting me use the clinic's facilities. But you never know. The clinic business keeps growing, and if things get too crowded for him—especially if he adds staff—then I'll have to work in here again."

Taking that in to mull over later, Noah's gaze zeroed in on the master bedroom at the far end of the RV. He saw the king-size bed with the blue-and-purple bedspread and small berg of matching pillows piled against the sapphire-blue, cushioned headboard. It was too easy to imagine Rylie lying there, and when his wayward thoughts started to edit what she might—or might not—wear to bed, his body stirred with hunger.

"Do you have our bill ready?" he asked, abruptly.

"Oh...of course," Rylie said, immediately contrite. "Sorry for wandering on. I know you have to get back. Actually, I have another appointment in a few minutes myself." She went to the dinette table and picked up the invoice lying there beside a half-eaten salad. "I gave your mother a discount because this is Bubbles's third visit in just over a month, meaning there's less matting than I usually have to deal with. Also please let her know that Bubbles's nails didn't need trimming this time. You're such a good girl," Rylie cooed to the dog.

After eyeing the fresh coat of purple nail polish on the dog's toes, Noah saw Bubbles lick Rylie's chin, then give him a look as though telepathically saying, *See? This is how I like to be treated.*

Accepting the bill, Noah reached for his billfold. As he handed Rylie the correct amount, he asked, "Would you mind bringing her to my car? I can really do without the ladies in the courthouse snickering at me when I return smelling like I've been hanging around a perfume counter."

Choking, Rylie insisted, "You're exaggerating. I can't handle excessive scents myself, nor can Bubbles. I use a very light touch on my animals."

Some inexplicable something egged him on, and Noah intentionally rubbed the tip of his nose. "If that's restrained to you, we'll have to agree to disagree."

"Don't listen, cutie." Rylie cuddled Bubbles again. "He's determined to try to make us think the problem is with us. I think you smell as delicious as your name, and your mommy will, too." As the dog reached up and touched a paw to her cheek, Rylie laughed in pleasure. "You are a heart stealer, yes, you are. Let me just stamp your bill as paid," she told Noah, "and—"

"That's not necessary."

"But I always make sure your mother has a detailed—"

"I'm handling this for her."

Rylie's face lit with pleasure. "How nice of you." Leading the way, she opened the door and took care going down the steps. "Gotta be careful with our precious cargo, huh, sweetie?" she crooned to the little dog. "Isn't it a beautiful day?" she added to Noah.

"It's hot for autumn."

"But the evenings are so nice. Doc has a couple of kenneled dogs this week and he's letting me walk them. Then they get to spend the night with us. As you saw, there's plenty of room, and they enjoy it so much more than being locked up in pens."

Noah lost the battle with his curiosity. "Us?"

"MG and me. My dog."

"And MG stands for...?"

"Mommy's Girl. They told me when I got her from the shelter that they'd named her Marnie, but it was soon apparent that we were going to be very close, and she's seriously maternal. She instinctively steps in to help whenever she decides I need her assistance with an animal."

Noah was sorry he'd asked. Sure, he believed there were special relationships between some pets and their owners, but *Mommy's Girl?* That was laying it on a bit thick.

Unlocking the BMW with his remote, he opened the passenger door for Rylie. Looking over the hood of the car, he considered the grassy area and the woods beyond it where she said she walked. It was more a wild pasture than a park. "Aren't you concerned about snakes, or getting eaten up by chiggers and mosquitoes?" Texas also had more than its share of wild hogs, coyotes and an increasing number of abandoned dogs, too, he thought.

"We haven't been bothered yet," she said, shrugging. "Maybe there's safety in numbers. In any case, I tend to take a live-and-let-live approach. It's more important that the dogs get some attention and exercise. They're missing their homes, and some are overweight, so being constricted in pens for days is just unhealthy." She began to put the dog on the BMW's black leather seat only to rear back. "Oh! Please put on the air conditioner and give us a moment for things to cool down. She'll get burned."

"Try putting her on the floorboard." When he saw her stubbornly resist, Noah did get into the car and start the engine. Sure, it had gotten warmer in the short time that he'd been in her RV, but it was nowhere near as bad as it had been in July or August. As the vents quickly blew cold air through the inside of the vehicle, he reiterated, "The floorboard, please. I don't want claw runs in the leather."

"But she won't be able to see, and it's a rougher ride down there."

The Mother Teresa of furry creatures really was beginning to push his buttons. "For crying out loud, this car's shock absorbers are the embodiment of foreign skill in cushion and spring. She has no idea what *rough* is."

With a sigh of exasperation, Rylie said to the dog, "Your big brother is determined to be disagreeable, isn't he, precious?"

Big brother? "Okay, that's enough," Noah said, having had his fill of this nonsense. "Put the damned dog in now. Please." He had to get out of there before she fried what brain cells he had left.

With a mournful glance, Rylie did as ordered. Carefully shutting the door, she backed away.

As Noah cut a sharp U-turn, he decided he was going to tell his mother that her pet's groomer—cute as she was—was a nut job who needed a reality check. There were kids, even in this area, who needed help with essentials—food, clothing—not to mention finding a safe family environment. Spending any more time on inanity like this was ridiculous. How could a woman be so adorable, yet irritating at the same time?

As he circled around the clinic and cut a sharp turn

onto the service road, Bubbles barked at him as the force of the turn tipped her over.

"Oh, put a lid on it," he muttered.

Chapter Two

As Noah expected, his mother was parked in her wheelchair within sight of the front door and applauded with excitement as he entered Haven Land with Bubbles. Adding to his soured mood, she immediately started complimenting Rylie's work the instant her precious four-legged princess leaped into her arms. Even if he wanted to pass on Rylie's comments and messages, he couldn't get a word in due to her effusiveness.

"Isn't that shade of purple ribbon adorable, Aubergine?" she said to her housekeeper, who was standing with the glass of tea and the small cup of medications Audra needed to take. "Livie—look at her nails! A perfect match. And she's so happy to be home."

Aubergine Scott had been with the family since before Noah had graduated from high school. She was a single mother of two children, now grown, gratefully educated by his parents. Daughter Rachel was a lawyer in Washington, D.C., and son Randolph was a teacher in Houston. Each had tried to make the sixty-year-old retire, to pay her back for all she'd done for them, but Aubergine liked her independence and was devoted to his mother.

Olivia "Livie" Danner quit her RN job when Noah's mother had been discharged from the hospital in Dallas, and joined their makeshift family. Quiet, bookish and athletic, at fifty-seven, she was as reserved as Aubergine was outspoken, but both possessed a dry sense of humor that Noah appreciated, even though quite a bit of it was directed at him. What he cared about most, though, was that his mother liked and trusted her.

"She's as pretty as a valentine," plump and short Aubergine declared.

"Charming," tall and toned Livie added, with a tolerant nod. "Please take your medication, Audra."

"In a minute. Oh, she smells good enough to eat," Audra gushed, all but burying her face in the dog's fur. "Did you properly thank Rylie for me, dear?"

Ignoring Aubergine's barely repressed grin, he shoved his hands into his pants pockets to keep everyone from seeing him curl his fingers into fists. "Mother, trust me, she knows how supportive you are of her. She all but rubs it in my face. If anyone should be appreciative, it's her for having your business."

His mother gave him a distressed look. "I swear, you are sounding more like an old grouch every day. And you were raised to have better manners. Do I have to call her and apologize on your behalf?"

"No, ma'am, you do not," he said, with only a modicum of guilt. Also not happy to be scolded in front of the other two women, he continued, "Do you mind if I get

back to work now? Vance went home sick, so I'm holding the fort today."

"What? Then why are you standing there breathing
on your mother?" Livie immediately started pulling the
chair toward the living room.

"I'll get the disinfectant spray," Aubergine assured
her partner-in-protection. To Noah she said, "You heard
her, get going. You know her lungs don't need any more
work than they already get."

Noah held up his hands in surrender and quickly
backed out of their presence. He knew he'd blundered,
and the sooner he made his exit the better.

"Oh, Noah, they're only being protective," his mother
called after him.

"And they're very good at it," he said with a courtly
bow. "Don't worry about dinner. I'll eat out. Have to
work late." He didn't really, but it wouldn't be a bad idea
to work ahead.

Judy was on the phone when Noah returned to the
office and Ann, the junior clerk, was either still on her
lunch break or in some storage room hunting files. Ann
was more Judy's assistant than any help to Vance or himself, and Noah often forgot she was even employed there.
From the looks of the poor woman, whom someone had
nicknamed "the beige person" for the way she dressed
and behaved, she might have easily just emerged from
the bland walls one morning and retreated into them at
night. She rarely spoke that he could hear.

Back in his corner, where he was framed by a window, a wall and on the third side file cabinets—the closest thing he could develop into an office—Noah took
the extra time to check his email account and then on a

whim typed Rylie's name into the search engine box. He wasn't proud of it, but he had just enough annoyance left in him to want to see what would happen.

As expected, there were no clear results. There was a link to *Riley's* Car Wash, another *Riley* who could read your psychic vibes for twenty bucks and a masseuse. For a second he wondered if Rylie changed the spelling of her name to moonlight in an even more lucrative field. Hindsight being what it was, he regretted not having written down the RV's license plate number. That would be easy enough to check, even if they were still California plates.

About to start a different search, he saw Judy put her call on hold. "Noah—it's the sheriff," she called back to him. "With the D.A. out, he was wondering if you two could meet regarding upcoming cases he thinks are ready for us."

"Of course." With reluctance, Noah shut down his web browser. "Where does he want to meet, here or at his office?"

"Well, if you come now, we'll see you right away,"

Roy put his hand over the phone's mouthpiece and gestured for Rylie not to leave as she'd been preparing to. Curious more than disappointed at not getting to call it a day yet, she backtracked to wait beside him.

Putting his hand over the mouthpiece, he said, "Noah Prescott. Emergency." After that he said into the phone, "Come to the side door. If people see vehicles in front, they'll think we're open for regular business. We'll be watching for you."

As soon as he hung up, Rylie commiserated on her uncle's bad luck, while worrying about Bubbles. Uncle Roy had planned to meet the old-timers at the VFW hall to watch a Texas Rangers baseball game this evening. What could possibly have happened to the little dog? "Bubbles is hurt?"

"Audra Prescott dropped a glass. You can picture the rest. Noah is running the pup over here."

"Poor little thing. How badly is she cut?"

"Bad enough that neither he nor Ramon could get the piece out. The dog snaps at them when they try to get a good look."

Rylie wasn't surprised about her reaction to at least one of the men. "That's a surprise about her snapping at Ramon." The caretaker, who was closer to her uncle's age than Noah's, appeared to get as much of a kick out of the little dog as his employer did.

"If you ask me, Bubbles is just partial to women," Roy said. He nodded to MG. "Like someone else I know."

Nudging him affectionately due to his lingering fretting over why MG wasn't warming to him as much as he expected, Rylie said, "Either way, I know Mrs. Prescott is stressed. You go on, Uncle Roy. I'll manage this."

Although he looked tempted, he hung back. "You haven't even started your certification as a technician yet. What happens if the dog needs stitches or something else that requires she be put under sedation?"

"Then I'll notify Doc and I'll keep Bubbles as calm as possible until he's back from his emergency call. Go enjoy your game with the guys, and if something changes that I can't handle, I'll holler." The VFW was only a half mile down the service road.

Roy seemed tempted, but the pull on his conscience was clearly stronger. "You don't have a key to lock up in case Gage isn't needed."

"So lock that side door and leave the back one open.

I'll keep an eye on things until you can make it back here to close up."

Roy rubbed at his whiskered jaw. Like Rylie's father, he took after the Black Irish side of the family, while Rylie favored her red-haired mother, whose ancestors were from England as much as Ireland. "I would give you my key and you could give it back in the morning," he ventured.

Rylie loved him for the gesture but shook her head adamantly. "Hey, I will get a key when Doc is ready to give me one."

"Which will be soon," Roy assured her. He gave her a quick hug. "Have I told you lately what a great job you're doing? I'm really proud of you."

Afraid that he was going to ask questions again about why she'd quit veterinary school when she'd been in her last year, she assured him, "That means more to me than I can tell you. Now, go. Enjoy! And I'd like to hear that you actually talked to a woman while you were over there." She didn't understand why he was still single after all these years. He didn't even have someone special he was seeing. On first glance he did appear severe with his stark coloring and serious manner, but he was attractive and fairly fit, although probably a bit too shy with the opposite sex for his own good.

Relenting, Roy dug his keys out of his jeans pocket. "I'll see you right after the game is over—unless it's a total blowout from the beginning. Then I'll head over here sooner. We can play a couple hands of poker over a beer. It's time we find out if you can finally keep up with your old uncle."

"Be careful for what you wish for," Rylie countered with a cheeky grin.

Waving goodbye, she rounded the building to wait on Noah. She knew if she didn't, he would be confused, then annoyed that things weren't the way Roy had said he would find them. Also, knowing Bubbles would be stressed, she wanted to make things go as quickly and easily as possible for her, too.

She couldn't deny that she was feeling an odd mixture of apprehension and excitement at the idea of seeing Noah again. Maybe she was being a glutton for punishment, but she wanted to make him see what others had no problem noticing—that she was good at what she did and fun to be around.

She didn't have to wait long for him. Noah must have really kept his foot on the accelerator to arrive only a minute or two later.

"What's going on?" he asked her, upon parking in back and emerging from the black BMW.

He looked much more approachable dressed in a pale blue denim shirt and designer jeans, but his lack of a tan and his Italian loafers made it obvious that he was no outdoorsman, let alone a cowboy. Nevertheless, Rylie's heartbeat kicked up a notch and she almost forgave him for his curtness earlier.

"Doc had an emergency and Roy had a previous commitment. He'll be back later. We agreed that he would just keep this door unlocked instead."

"They don't trust you with a key?" he asked, rounding to the passenger side of the vehicle.

So much for wishing that he'd come with a better attitude, Rylie thought. "I've only been here for a short while. Uncle Roy didn't get a key when he first started, either." She couldn't, however, resist adding, "Have you always acted so condescending and superior with people, or is this a side that only I bring out in you?"

Noah looked taken aback. "Me? Condescending? Serious maybe. Mine is that kind of profession. The price for putting criminals where they belong means having to fixate on the unpleasant, often brutal side of life. Not everyone has the luxury of seeing the world as glass half-full every waking moment as you do."

Oddly enough, Rylie was almost consoled by his answer. If that's how he saw her, she thought, opening the door herself, then she was a better actress than she'd hoped. "Well, all of that fixating is doing bad things for whatever charm you inherited from your wonderful mother. Maybe you should consider a job change before it starts to affect your health." Before Noah could reply, she reached for Bubbles and cooed, "Poor darling. Easy does it. We're going to get you feeling better. I promise."

The pink towel the young dog was lying in was significantly stained, warning Rylie to lift her with extra care. Once the dog was in her arms, she turned for the back door.

"Can you get that for me?" she asked Noah.

Without comment, he slammed the car door shut and pressed the remote lock on the key. Then he jogged the few steps to open the steel-and-glass clinic door.

Inside, Rylie led the way to the nearest stainless-steel operating table. The fluorescent lights remained on, and it made the room as bright as midday. Whispering soothingly to the little dog that was trying to burrow her head into Rylie's armpit, she eased Bubbles onto the table.

"Poor friend. What happened here, huh? Gonna let me see so I can make it better?"

"You're authorized to do this?" Noah asked, coming up beside her.

Without taking her eyes off the wound, Rylie said, "I'm at least capable of seeing how badly she's hurt. Did you manage that much?"

Noah admitted, "No, and neither did Ramon."

"Were you present when the accident happened?"

"I was pretty much the cause of it." At Rylie's startled glance, he continued. "Mother was annoyed with me. I was supposed to be working later than she expected. After changing, I came downstairs and caught her trying to have more wine than is safe for her. With her nurse upstairs preparing her bath, and our housekeeper outside in the garden, she thought she was alone."

"You startled her."

"I did," he said, regret deepening his voice. "She doesn't have the strength she thinks she has despite the therapy she gets, and the bottle and glass slipped from her grasp. A moment later, upset at the commotion that followed, Bubbles got into the mess, and the rest you can see."

It was apparent by the way Noah looked everywhere but at her that he was either embarrassed, or ashamed, or both. Rylie had heard enough to understand that it didn't matter how much money you had, a condition like Mrs. Prescott's was difficult for more than the patient.

"I'm very sorry," she said with the utmost sincerity. "I promise that won't go any further, and I hope she wasn't cut, too?"

"Externally, no. However, you can imagine what it did to her emotionally to see the hurt she'd caused her *baby*."

"I suspect *you* will always be her baby," Rylie assured him. "The thing is that Bubbles is who she's allowed to coddle. If you can learn to look at it that way, it might not annoy you so much. Besides, you don't strike me as a man who would enjoy being stroked and petted relentlessly."

"It depends on who's doing it."

The throaty reply made Rylie grateful to have the dog to focus on. It would seem that the county's assistant D.A. wasn't quite the cold fish he pretended to be. That was information her imagination didn't need.

"It's okay, sweetheart," she assured Bubbles. "I'm just going to... Yeah, there it is. There's a shard about the width of a large sewing needle between her toes. It did some slicing before getting lodged where it is now."

"Will she have to be sedated?"

"No, which is also good news because we can do this without waiting on Doc."

"Are you authorized to take care of this?"

"I have more schooling and skills than most certified technicians, plus the common sense to know it would be good to get this over with quickly. However, if you want to leave this little girl in pain, it's your call. Or you can help me keep her still while I use tweezers and take out the glass." All the while that she spoke, she kept her tone soft and soothing, and her expression pleasant to reassure the whimpering dog watching her with trepidation. While it seemed to have a positive effect on Bubbles, Noah remained a hard sell.

"Fine. I guess. As long as Dr. Sullivan is told about what you've done."

"I wouldn't have it any other way."

Aware that any frustration or annoyance with him would transmit itself to Bubbles, Rylie started humming a lullaby her mother had often sung to her as a child, as she carried the dog with her to the cabinets to get what supplies she needed. Once she had the tweezers, cotton balls and antiseptic, she returned to the table. Finally, she set down the dog, still keeping her arm around her.

"Casually move over to the other side of the table to face me, and with your hands, brace her hips to keep her still," she told Noah. "She'll squirm and kick, so be prepared, but only be firm, not rigid. I'll be as quick as I can."

As soon as he complied, she deftly plucked out the splinter.

Bubbles made a slight yelp and then barked at her.

"Yeah, fooled you, didn't I?" Rylie quipped. "But guess what? You're going to be feeling better and better by the second." She soothingly stroked Bubble's tummy, only to connect with Noah's fingers. Surprised that he hadn't already released his hold, she looked up at him, only to find that he was staring at her. That close scrutiny and the physical contact created a circuit that sent a strong wave of something hot and heavy through her body. "You...can let go now."

He glanced down and appeared surprised himself, but recovered quickly. Taking a step away from the table, he allowed, "You are fast."

His raspy admission had her smiling as she carried Bubbles to the sink, where she got a stainless-steel bowl and filled it with warm water. Then she set the dog carefully on the counter and coaxed her to put her foot into the warm water.

"Let me get the blood off," she told Bubbles, her tone all reassurance. "We can't send you home all messy."

As soon as she was through, she wrapped the dog in a clinic towel and collected more items. Then she returned to the surgery table to treat the wound.

"Does she need to take antibiotics?" Noah asked.

"Not unless she comes down with an infection. She's a healthy girl, so I'm not looking for that to happen. I'll put Betadine on her—"

"What's that?"

"A great antiseptic. Part iodine. It's widely used in hospitals. If the wound happens to reopen, you could use Neosporin, too, and save yourself a trip back here."

"Ramon thought of hydrogen peroxide."

"In a pinch, okay, but that can be harsh on skin."

"What else?"

"That's it. Tell your mother to try to keep her quiet for a day or two. If she shows signs of prolonged limping, or licks the wound too much, bring her back. Go ahead and give her a low-dose aspirin when you get home. It should help keep down any fever and might help her sleep."

"Sounds easy enough. One more question."

"Sure."

"Why do you have more education than a certified technician?"

Oops. One thing she would say for Noah Prescott, he listened well. "As I said," she replied with a shrug, "I've been doing this for years." She all but held her breath, hoping that rather evasive answer satisfied him.

Although he looked as if he was going to continue probing, he just frowned and asked, "What do I owe you this time?"

Rylie shook her head. "Forget about it. I was already here, and we didn't do anything major. Just give your mom my best." From Noah's unsatisfied expression, she concluded that it made him uncomfortable to be beholden to her, and that made her grin wickedly at him. "What's the matter, A.D.A. Prescott—worried that you might have to be nicer to me now? Don't strain yourself, or *you're* the one who might end up needing stitches."

He grunted his opinion of that, and yet a hint of amusement lit his brown eyes. "I just knew there was a touch of smart-ass in you."

"Shocking," she replied, her tone playful.

For the next minute, she worked on gingerly drying off Bubbles's paw and then applying the Betadine. As expected, Bubbles didn't think much of that, but the slight stinging eased quickly. "Sorry about the bit of yellow staining, but this way you know it's keeping her safe from infection."

When she was through with that, she got a fresh towel to wrap Bubbles in, explaining to Noah, "Tell your mother that I'll soak hers and return it the next visit. Don't worry about this one." With a nod to indicate her intent, she started for the door.

As they exited the building and walked to his car, Noah sped up to look her in the face. "I should have said it sooner, but I do appreciate this, especially since it's after hours."

Sweet, Rylie thought. If only that frown didn't continue to mar an otherwise handsome face. "You're most welcome."

Once Noah opened the BMW's passenger door for her, she just stood there looking at him. He caught on immediately.

"Right." He rounded the sedan and climbed in, not only starting the engine, but also turning the air conditioner on high to cool off the car quickly. "Happy now?"

"Practically speechless with it." Rylie eased Bubbles onto the floorboard. Stroking her reassuringly, she said,

"You're going home now. Be a good girl and no more owies."

Although she thought she hid it well, she was sorry to see Noah drive away. She knew that intimate moment by the surgery table was the cause...second only to seeing that she'd made him smile. At the same time, it saddened her to hear there were some serious issues going on at Haven Land. The accident was three years past, but life wasn't running smoothly for Noah, any more than for his mother.

He sensed you understand that.

"Oh, stop the mental contortions," she muttered to herself as she returned to the clinic. "He's still way out of your league."

And probably always would be. At twenty-five, she had lived a busy, full life so far, but had yet to fall in love. Heaven knows, she had opened her heart in invitation. She had plenty of friends and acquaintances, and up to the moment when she put California in her rearview mirror, her social life was as active as anyone her age who enjoyed people and school. However, although she'd had only a handful of relationships, two that she wrongly thought could be the real thing, neither of those men—boys, really—had managed to make her feel what seconds in Noah's presence did. The encounter this evening proved that, after a mere graze of flesh. How unbelievable was that?

As she pondered that, she wiped down and disinfected everything with even more gusto. By the time she got MG out of the RV and went to put the kenneled dogs on leashes, she was ready to dismiss the experience as an anomaly.

"I'm being ridiculous, MG," she said to her dog. "If

I start breaking into song like I'm in a Broadway musical, bite me."

The long-legged retriever-mix pranced beside her, happy to be with her again and about to get some exercise. Having full awareness of what the word *bite* meant, she barked, ending her commentary with a throaty growl.

Rylie laughed. "I knew I could count on you."

He would have said something. Even as he went to work on Tuesday, Noah continued to dwell on how yesterday had ended at the clinic. He'd been left…unsatisfied.

Rylie slammed the car door in your face!

Okay, he amended, so she'd shut it without giving him a chance. The point was that he would have at least thanked her again, to further prove that he wasn't the curmudgeon she seemed to believe he was. Why were they rubbing each other the wrong way? Such…friction was new to him. Usually, he had no problem getting along with people. Granted, he tended to be measured, cautious, but then he had his family name to respect and protect, and now his position with the D.A.'s office. But he wasn't inaccessible, let alone mean-spirited or cruel. He was someone who kept up with fraternity brothers from college and classmates from law school, for pity's sake!

Entering the courthouse, he already knew that Vance would be out of the office again. His boss had called while Noah had been driving to town to confirm that he was still feeling poorly, even though he'd been to see his doctor. That meant Noah would be fielding calls and handling several matters on behalf of the D.A.'s office, including having lunch with a civic group that had been scheduled months ago. That would be no problem, since he had made similar presentations before. This was a great opportunity to make more residents of the area aware of who he was.

Even with all that on his plate, Rylie's face appeared in his mind. Noah all but groaned in frustration.

It's because you touched her.

The contact had been clinical, inevitable due to the need to keep the dog still. There was no reason for him to read something sensual into the experience, but tell that to his body. It had responded as though he'd walked face-first into a furnace, and he'd remained thrown off balance long into the night, until he'd indulged in a second shower for relief. Thank goodness his mother's car was back in good shape, and Ramon would take over these clinic trips again. Clearly, he needed to protect himself from his own imagination.

After starting the coffee machine, Noah went to his desk with his collection of newspapers that were stacked daily on the hallway bench outside the office door. But as he sat down, the computer's dark monitor screen was what captured and kept his attention. It stared back at him in bold daring, a portal to…what?

Your best opportunity to find answers. Go ahead. You know you want to.

He checked his watch. The empty office would stay quiet like this for another half hour at most. Temptation won.

Noah booted up the machine. *Just one more search,* he told himself. He didn't want to dream about her again tonight. Yes, she was cute, yes, she was a new experience to him, but was it sane to become obsessed with a woman who lived in an *RV!*

As soon as that censorious thought formed in his mind, he felt shame, only to get defensive. Experience

had taught him that few people had the Teflon skins at-
tributed to some Washington, D.C., politicians that they
could survive scandal or the weight of relentless gossip.
If he was going to run for office, the shortest distance to
that goal was to choose your society with circumspec-
tion. He needed some information, any excuse to get
Rylie Quinn out of his head.

Try the social networks.

Although he grimaced at the thought of venturing
there, Noah knew as friendly as Rylie was, she probably lived every free moment on Facebook and Twitter.
It didn't take but seconds before he logged in to his own
account—a tedious requirement for him per office policy
to make the public feel connected—and typed her name
in the search box. Her page came up within seconds.

There was no ignoring the jump in his pulse as he
clicked through her photo album, seeing that at her high-
school graduation, she'd had waist-length hair. His next
thought was that she had a ton of friends, including guys
still carrying a crush, and a very proud family, he thought
after seeing her parents gaze at her in each photo with
love and adoration. Noah would never do the profiles or
answer the idiotic questions they asked, but Rylie didn't
seem to have a problem with them. Some, anyway. Actually, she had a contagious sense of humor, he thought,
as he caught himself smiling, and then chuckling a few
times. At other times, he was left transfixed.

She'd thought about joining Cirque du Soleil before
heading for college to become a veterinarian. Being an
athlete and cheerleader in high school explained why.
In college, she'd continued with the cheerleading and
had been the highflier. Noah suspected that's also what
came with being the smallest in the group. Having wit-

nessed her questionable balance, though, he wondered if she'd spent more time on crutches and in slings than on the practice floor.

She loved potatoes and gravy, wildflowers, pears in rum sauce, and confessed to craving steak too much to become a vegetarian. Nevertheless, she vowed she would jump at any chance to be on someone's fishing boat, and found lightning both terrifying and hypnotic.

Her dislikes were questions about dislikes. She didn't want to focus on the negative; every day was a new opportunity to her.

Just as you thought, the original optimist—or an eternal kid.

Then why were there secrets in her eyes?

"Good morning!"

Judy Millsap entered, bringing with her the scent of lavender and doughnuts. Since many sheriff's deputies, bailiffs and clerks passed their open door numerous times a day, Judy liked to bring a box of doughnuts to place by the coffee machine on the counter. Goodwill to all who passed. In her own way, Judy was the older rendition of Rylie—without the impishness—the ambassador of their office. At least Judy was a realist and mostly did it because—as she put it—"You get more flies with honey than vinegar."

"Morning," he called back to her. If his heart wasn't entirely in the greeting, it was because he knew he would now have to get focused on his day job. "Everything okay on your end?"

"It will be after another big mug of caffeine. I was up half the night ridiculously transfixed on listening to coyotes. Say something nice to me before I take off these sunglasses and offend you with the feed bags under my bloodshot eyes."

"You run the best office in East Texas," Noah replied, truthfully.

After a moment's hesitation, Judy slid off the glasses and gave him a pained look. "For an attractive and intelligent man, you are truly clueless, Noah Prescott."

Startled, Noah sat back in his chair. "What?"

"You don't have a clue, do you?"

"I just complimented you."

With the smile of a patient mother, Judy replied, "You complimented what I do. That's not who I am."

He groaned inwardly. Women. Surely, Judy didn't believe the two were separate. Not at this juncture of her life. She had been with the office for over twenty years, and there had been few eight-hour days, even in a small department like theirs.

"Have you been watching old Errol Flynn movies or that Don Juan something or other with Brando and Depp?" he asked, suspicious.

"*Don Juan Demarco*—as a matter of fact, I did. Last night because that horrible howling does bad things to my imagination. And even though I watched in the living room, would you believe Dwayne said the flickering lights coming down the hall and the audio—though set low—ruined his sleep, too?" From a singsong voice, she went almost feral. "Why couldn't he just say that he missed having me beside him? You men never say what you mean."

He thought he had. Noah suggested with more care, "You could always move. Away from the coyote problem, I mean."

Judy rolled her eyes in disbelief. "You of all people have no business saying anything like that, Noah Prescott. Could you leave Haven Land?"

His first impulse was to remind her that he had done so. Before the accident that left him with responsibility too great to delegate to others. But Judy had lived in Cherokee County her entire life, and had never wanted to go anywhere else. She'd earned her business degree through a combination of the community college, on-line and via UT Tyler. Nothing wrong with that if it was what you wanted. He, on the other hand, hadn't felt as though Haven Land soil was somehow intrinsic to his heart and liver function. Fate, though, seemed to be insisting otherwise.

Instead, he said, "I'll catch the phones while you have your coffee." With regret, he shut down the Facebook page. He would have gone on to the next idea/source, since he'd learned Rylie was from some small town around Palm Springs, California. Palm Springs gave him the hunch that there was a good reason why she could afford that RV. No wonder she hadn't been star-blinded by his family name, or his mother's friends. She had to be used to wealthy clients. That raised the question, what else was she used to?

"I'm used to a lot, and I'm game to try more."

Rylie had been armpit-deep into a pregnant cow's womb often enough not to hesitate trying to help Gage with a pygmy goat having a difficult labor due to tangled kids inside her. It was six hours after closing. She'd been in bed, asleep, for an hour when Doc had called her asking if she was up to helping with the emergency he was coming in to tend to. Now they were in the brightly lit clinic, and Gage had failed to get his big hand in far enough to remedy the problem.

"I know you're borderline on time," she added, "and need to do a cesarean soon or risk losing all of them."

"That's right," Gage replied, "and you have the smallest hands, so you're likely to be the least intrusive for the poor doe. Now we'll see if you have the dexterity and strength. I'll give you one try, and then I'm going to be forced to call this."

"Yes, sir."

Giving the animal's owner—Vicky Turner, a long-time customer—a reassuring smile, she went to work, reaching in to feel what Gage had already discovered for himself. "Ah...I see what you mean," she told him, keeping her eyes closed to rely on the most important sense right now—touch.

"Three, right?"

"Give me a second." Hoping she was right in separating the twist of legs, Rylie suddenly felt a yielding, and slipped out the first baby, slick and slippery. From the protesting movements, it was apparent this one was alive.

"Great," Gage said, immediately using a little suction bulb to make sure the mouth and nostrils were clear. "We have one pretty strong boy," he said, laying the firstborn by the mother's head.

She immediately set to licking him clean, and Vicky moved to that end of the table to make sure the infant didn't inadvertently fall or get knocked off the table.

"He's probably the biggest, so maybe the others will be easier." Rylie reached in again. Sure enough, while the puzzle of body parts continued, she was able to pull out a second baby in half the time. "Hurry, take this one," she said to Gage. "The next one is acting like this is a sprint to the finish line."

Gage scooped up that baby and proceeded to give it the same treatment. "Hopefully, that's it," he said. "Mama's wide, but not a big girl herself. Isn't three her standard, Vicky?"

"No, this is Wink's third litter, Doc. While she had three her first time, she had four last time," the anxious woman reminded him.

Sighing, Gage stroked Wink. "Don't you know you're supposed to stick with two?"

"Well, Mrs. Turner, I have a feeling that's what's going on this time, too," Rylie said, delving into the womb again. "Why else did a pretty girl like this try to emulate a small aircraft carrier?"

Just as the wife of the grocery-store manager laughed, the third baby emerged. Trying to catch the wet thing was like trying to grab a fish. Thankfully, she managed. This one was about the same size as the second baby. "Looks like we have two girls and a boy," she announced.

"Excellent. Girls tend to be easier to sell," the woman replied.

"Better check a last time," Gage told Rylie. "You're starting to make a believer out of me."

Once again, Rylie eased her hand into the mother and gasped. "Oh! There is one more. Poor little thing was pushed way in back." Rylie grinned as she learned through touch what was happening. "I guess with finally having some room, she's content to stretch out and enjoy herself for a while."

"Do you really feel movement?" Mrs. Turner moved

the third cleaned baby to the mother's teats. "It's not just a birth reflex? I've lost a few of the ones that have to struggle for space."

Gage nodded to Rylie. "Get it out. The sooner we get them all a good dose of colostrum, the better."

Rylie knew the "first milk" from the mother needed to occur within the first hour of birth to help build immunity. Searching again, she finally got a safe hold and drew it out. As soon as the tiny creature emerged, it started wailing lustily.

"Ha!" Rylie chuckled. "Nothing wrong with her lungs."

Vicky's eyes welled and Gage grinned.

"Good job," he said, automatically making sure the infant's mouth and nostrils were free of mucus. Then he gave the baby to the mother. "Here you go, Mama. Three girls and a big boy. Wish they gave awards for that."

Vicky told Rylie, "Thank you for saving me a surgery bill, too. I really appreciate that."

"You're very welcome. I was thrilled to assist." And she was. However, she was also feeling bittersweet, aware that this still wasn't the same as being the doctor-in-charge making that life-or-death decision whether to do the cesarean or not.

Giving herself a mental shake, she continued to help, until they had all four kids in a carrier kennel in the SUV. Then they put the mother in the second one. Dawn was still hours away as they waved to their happy client while she drove off.

Side by side at the deep stainless-steel double sinks, they soaped up and started scrubbing. Standing on his right, Rylie could feel Gage's scrutiny.

"I'll bet you're ready to crash," she said. There had

been so much overtime lately—and Gage's schedule had already been virtually nonstop when she'd first arrived in Sweet Springs. "I hope you unwind enough to get a few hours' sleep. Feel free to add an extra hour. When Roy arrives later this morning, we can split the usual chores between us."

"What?" Gage protested. "You want me to give up this sleep-deprived look? It's getting me plenty of sympathy from my bride."

"I can imagine, but you can't keep up this pace, so please, please, please, feel free to let me help whenever you want."

After a short silence, the tall, gentle-mannered man said, "I just can't keep silent any longer, Rylie. You're a natural at this. What happened that you couldn't get through a few more months of school?"

Rylie worried her lower lip, trying to think of another evasive answer to buy herself more time; however, she was growing more and more fond of him—as she was everyone here. That was making it difficult not to be completely forthcoming. In the end she could only offer, "I promise to tell you one day soon, Doc. I'm not hiding anything that will embarrass or upset you. I'm just not ready to talk yet."

Although he looked disappointed, Gage replied, "Okay. Ask my wife if I have patience. It took a lot of mental fortitude to outlast Brooke's determination to get back to Dallas and resume her career, not to mention to make her see me as the guy she was going to fall in love with."

Appreciating the playful note in his voice, Rylie chuckled. "I'm glad she saw the error of her ways."

"Me, too, since she's carrying my baby!" Then he grew serious again. "If it helps, all you need to know is that you're an asset that I don't want to lose. I'm all the more convinced we need to get you your technician's certification as soon as possible. How do you feel about that?"

"Wow. I knew you were suggesting that we'd be working toward that, but I thought I needed to prove myself over a sixty- or ninety-day trial period. Thank you, sir!"

"For heaven's sake, will you please call me Gage?" He glanced over his shoulder. "Unless someone with a badge is present and I need to look like a serious authority figure."

Rylie nodded, grinning. "That's not a problem you'll have to worry about with me."

"I'm so relieved that you were here," Gage continued. "As great a helper as Roy had been, his hands aren't much smaller than mine. Sleep loss aside, I'm also glad this didn't happen during regular hours when you had a grooming appointment. That's not to take away from what you're achieving with your business. I'm aware of the clientele you're taking from Rusk as a result of word getting out about you."

"Mrs. Prescott alone saved me plenty on advertising costs."

"Well, keep it up. I'm working on getting us more help."

Although she was doing better dealing with the abrupt turn in her career path, Rylie couldn't ignore a sinking feeling. "Have you settled on anyone yet?" She was aware that he'd talked to a few people, but no one had come in for a tour and meeting yet.

"I'm afraid not. Does that make me seem too particular?"

"Not at all. I can't imagine having to try to fit personalities and abilities to their best effect."

"Thanks. You don't by chance have a twin with your talents? We could use another technician, too."

Rylie knew her uncle was happy in the reception area and managing the stock and storerooms, but she couldn't help but wish more for him. "You can't change Uncle Roy's mind about working toward his certification?"

Gage shrugged. "He's willing to help in an emergency, but he said he thought it was time to get some younger help to handle the more physical stuff. I can't completely regret that—he's excellent and honest to a fault when it comes to the paperwork side of things."

"That's a wonderful compliment, but I can't help wishing more for him."

"Well, I'm sure I'm not sharing any secret," he drawled, "but he feels the same about you."

Once again she saw how Gage was perfect for this work, and why he was so well liked in the community. He had an ability to at least appear laid-back and able to go with the flow. However, she had seen enough to know he missed nothing and was on top of everything at all times. No wonder he'd had the patience and savvy to outwait and outmaneuver Brooke.

Rylie couldn't help but eye him with growing affection. "You sure seem happy despite the workload, Doc. *Gage*. How's Brooke doing? Any more morning sickness?" He had shared the news about them expecting their first child, and that the baby was due in the late spring.

"No, thank goodness, she's about done with that, I hope. But she's starting to look like she might cry every

time she goes to the doctor and has to step on the scale.
To keep her from obsessing, I've locked up the one at
home."

Rylie chuckled. "Now that is being a *gentle*man."

"Yeah, well, if she's carrying a boy, he's likely to take
after me. The sooner she forgives herself for every few
ounces she gains, the better for everyone within hearing distance."

Rylie thought how wonderful it would be to have
someone whose every thought was about *you*. "Have you
started thinking of names?" she asked, as they headed
toward the back door, where he would lock up.

"A little bit. I got 'the look' for suggesting Gager,
which I thought was a clever avoidance of Gage Jr. I
think we're narrowing things down to Mitch, short for
Mitchell after my grandfather, and she gets to choose if
it's a girl. Her Aunt Marsha never cared for her name and
warned her not to do anything nostalgic on her behalf."

"I visited a few minutes with Mrs. Newman at the
assisted-living center yesterday," Rylie told him as he
held the door open for her to pass into the quiet night.
"She's doing so well."

"I'm glad you think so. Brooke still has moments of
guilt for moving her in there, despite it being on the doctor's directives. Marsha seems to be having fun, though.
She's among friends, she still gets to see Brooke as much
as she wants, and she's no longer burdened with business
and property concerns. Old age should be a time when
you enjoy the fruit of your labors, or do other things
you've been thinking about with the experience and skill
you've worked a lifetime to achieve."

"She does seem to be blooming. While I was making the rounds with MG, she was in the atrium with the

dominoes players, and the way they were carrying on, you'd think it was New Year's in Times Square."

"I'll be sure to pass that on to Brooke." Gage slid his key into the dead bolt. "So MG is liking her therapy work?"

"Mostly." Rylie felt a wave of sadness momentarily block her voice. "There's a patient—Mr. Wagner—he's in bad shape after cancer surgery and isn't dealing with his radiation well. MG crawled up on the bed with him— with the nurse's permission—and just lay there quietly until he had no more strength to stroke her." She had to clear her voice to continue. "She's so patient and compassionate with people, Gage. I love that, but it also breaks my heart, too. She had a bad dream later."

Testing the door, Gage turned to her, frowning. "You think there was a connection?"

With a one-shouldered shrug, Rylie said, "I can only say that it's not like her. She's only had a couple of troubled dreams since I've had her, nothing this disturbing or prolonged. And when I woke her, she snuggled closer against me as though relieved that I understood, or that she wasn't alone."

"She's an intelligent, sensitive dog," Gage replied. "But if you think she's taking on too much, I wouldn't blame you if you wanted to rethink using her as a therapy dog."

"I would hate that for the patients' sakes—and as social as she is, I think she would be disappointed, too."

"You know it could be that her first owner was an elderly person and that's brought back sad memories."

"I hadn't considered that."

"Let me know if the dreams continue." Rocking his head to get the kinks out of his neck, he nodded to her

RV. "Get yourself inside and lock up, so I can head for the house for some shut-eye."

"Yes, sir!"

Chapter Three

After that abbreviated night, Rylie thought she would be dragging by lunchtime—after Gage generously bought breakfast, she sure wasn't hungry—but she found that she was too wired to even put up her feet for a ten-minute power nap, so she borrowed her uncle's truck to "run an errand," as she explained it to him.

It was time, she decided. If Gage was going to use her more, she would have fewer free moments than ever to take care of getting herself permanently settled in as a resident of Sweet Springs, Texas. A trip to the county DMV in Rusk was needed to transfer her driver's license. The only reason she refrained from explaining that was her fear that something could go wrong, so with Roy agreeing to watch MG and Humphrey, she took off.

Autumn was finally arriving in Central East Texas, and the skies were growing cloudier by the hour, the

winds stronger. Strong thunderstorms were in the forecast for the evening, when a front would bring plum-
meting temperatures. She took great care driving to the
county seat, and had no problem finding the courthouse.
Having ascertained by her laptop that the Department of
Motor Vehicles would be within walking distance, she
pulled into the first parking spot she could find in the
busy heart of town.

Locking up her uncle's truck, she crossed the road
and then started down the street, only to hear, "What
are you doing here?"

For a fraction of a second, she almost believed she'd
conjured him; after all, this was *his* territory, and she had
been thinking of him more and more as she approached
the city. Even so, her heart pumped harder once she spun
around to see Noah Prescott slamming the door of his
BMW and taking loping strides to reach her. With only
a wallet to clutch, since she rarely bothered with purses,
she hugged herself despite the eighty-degree temperature.

As usual, he looked suave and confident in another
tailored suit—this one navy blue. No athletic hunk, which
was fine with her, he had this smooth-drink-of-water look
that would make him perfect to play a highly educated,
prodigal son of some organized-crime figure, most dangerous when he smiled, as he did now. In comparison,
she felt like a member of the janitorial service at Guan-
tanamo in her Day-Glo lime T-shirt and jeans.

"Hello, you," she managed, hoping she sounded wryly
amused. "How's Bubbles?"

"Almost as good as new. Mother was most relieved—
and grateful," he added with a hint of a bow.

He was on his best behavior, which just made her feel
all the more nervous. She offered a weak, "Small world."

He shook his head, all confidence. "My territory this time. What's your excuse?"

"Oh…I'm… I need to transfer my license." After that confidence stumble, she shrugged to suggest the chore was no big deal. Unfortunately, the truth was that there were going to be complications. "You all—excuse me, *y'all* are more tolerant than in California, but I figured the sooner I did this the better."

"They're closed for lunch."

Rylie told herself that this would be a good moment to check her watch if only to stop staring at him, but she didn't wear jewelry. Working around upset and injured animals and every type of farm and clinical equipment was dangerous enough without inviting injury. That left her with only the option to grimace. At least he couldn't know that her disappointment was more about their ill-timed meeting than his news. "I guess I'll go grab something to eat and try to be first in line when they reopen."

"You don't have to rush back for an appointment?"

"My next one is at two o'clock, but I'll definitely call and let them know what happened, in case Doc needed me sooner."

Noah studied her for another few seconds and suddenly said, "Come with me. I know the lady who operates that facility, and she usually brings her lunch from home. I'll ask her to make an exception for you and give her an IOU for lunch."

The latter part of his solution had her feeling almost sick. She could just picture an Angelina Jolie–type being offered lunch with Noah Prescott, an image that helped her uncharacteristically floundering ego nosedive to Dismalville. As it was, anyone looking at Noah, then her, would not see much reason for him going out of his way to gain her favor. In the vast international range of beauty, she thought herself as cute on a good day when life wasn't coming at her at a hundred miles per hour. This was not one of those days. At least she wasn't wearing her maroon clinic smock that hid any sign that she had breasts and hips, such as they were.

With an adamant shake of her head, she replied, "No, really, I appreciate the thought, but I don't want any special treatment."

Behind his sharklike smile and brown-eyed gaze was a speculative glint. "It's the least I can do for Mother's favorite dog groomer."

I must be projecting. Stop projecting.

She knew from her years of work with animals that words were often unnecessary to communicate and that he was sensing her discomfort, and it was making him all the more intrigued. What was going on with the man? Usually he couldn't wait to get away from her.

"You know what?" she said, glancing toward her uncle's truck with longing. "I'll just come back another day."

As she started her escape, Noah followed her up the sidewalk. "After coming all this distance? That's a wasted trip, not to mention gas."

"Well, with the weather about to change, I'm glad to have been outside for a bit. Thanks for the offer, though. Tell your mother that I said—" As she pivoted on her right heel, she clipped her shoulder hard on the stop sign's post. "Ow!"

"Are you all right?"

Idiotic question. Gritting her teeth and gripping her shoulder, Rylie rode out the worst wave of pain. She knew never to turn right without more care, but being right-handed, it was still her instinctive choice.

"You know, they tend to put these signs at every cross section of roads."

If he hadn't had the decency to look at least a tad concerned, she would have gladly replied with something totally unladylike. At the least, he deserved a dry-cleaning bill for that insult-upon-injury remark. Instead, she reached for her usual self-deprecating humor. After all, this area was not just her new home, it was Uncle Roy's and Gage's, and she needed to set a good example for them, as well.

"Glutton for punishment that I am," she quipped, "I was trying to add to my collection of scar tissue."

"Take my arm," he said, all Southern charm. "Before you forget there's traffic, too."

Being thought of as an amusing klutz hurt worse than being disliked, she realized, even if she'd more or less invited the perspective. Feeling her eyes begin to burn from tears, she muttered, "Hilarious. Now would you please go away and—and *persecute* someone who deserves it!"

What the hell...?

Rylie's words startled Noah, and as he watched her drive away in the red pickup truck, they began to gnaw at him like a haunting wound. Nothing was as it seemed with her. The embarrassment he understood well enough; she really was an awkward little thing, but why on earth the tears and accusation that he was persecuting her?

She must have hurt herself worse than he thought, or maybe it was a second blow to an old injury? He thought again about the cheerleading. That could be it.

No, she was upset from the moment she saw you, and it got worse when you offered to get her into the DMV office.

As he returned to the office, Noah saw that Judy was busy on the phone, so when he settled at his desk, it was all but inevitable that the first thing he did was start typing California Department of Motor Vehicles into the search box. But just after the site came up and he began to type in Rylie's name, he caught a motion across the room.

Judy was waving at him. "It's Vance. He wants to talk to you about the Condon case. I'm off to get these affidavits logged with the county clerk and then help Ann in the file room."

Resigned that his detective work would have to wait yet again, Noah exited the page he'd been on and picked up his phone. "Yes, sir? How are you feeling today?"

"As the saying goes, 'Better than the other guy.'"

Gage's words replayed in Rylie's mind as she jumped out of bed. Friday was also starting too early, although not as much as Thursday had. At minutes before five o'clock, her cell phone started playing the theme from *The Lion King,* and she automatically knew it was Gage. Grabbing for it, her response had been, "Are you okay?"

It turned out that he was asking her to be ready when he arrived within the next ten minutes. There was a dog that had been hit by a car at the southern perimeter of the county. Dairy farm she suspected, considering the hour.

She grabbed for clothes. Fortunately, she was learning to keep a clean set handy for this kind of situation. As for her usual morning shower, that would have to wait. She knew Gage lived close and would move fast, giving her enough time only to brush her teeth and throw water at her face to finish waking up.

When she emerged from the RV, she was greeted with fog. Perfect autumn conditions for stagnant air masses.

The front hadn't pushed through all the way. If there had been storms, she'd slept through them. No wonder there had been an accident. As thick as this stuff was, the driver probably had never seen the dog until he—or she—was right upon it.

Restricting MG to only a quick potty break for now, she locked her back in the RV. "I'll come get you as soon as the emergency is over," she assured the good-natured dog.

Just as she came around to the side door, Gage turned into the parking lot. Even though they'd come from different directions, not far behind him was a white pickup truck. As they drew nearer, Rylie saw a young teenage boy in the bed of the truck. When the driver stopped behind Gage's vehicle, she went to look at the dog lying between the boy's legs on a blanket. There was no blood, thank goodness, but the canine was alternately licking its leg and the owner's hand, then whimpering, clearly in pain and trying to communicate the injury and desire for help.

"Hey," Rylie murmured to the sleepy-eyed, anxious boy. "How's he holding up?"

"Not too good. I think the leg is broken." Nodding to the blond-haired youth, who looked no more than thirteen, she thought if that was the case, and there were no major organ problems, there was no place better equipped to help the poor animal—if the father okayed the expense. "I'm Rylie. Who are you?"

"Bryce. This is Jackson."

"Jackson is one of the most beautiful chocolate Labs I've ever seen. He looks...maybe two?"

"Next month. Hopefully."

Hearing the worry in the boy's voice, Rylie knew it

was time to get him to thinking more positively. "Celebrating his birthday early, huh? Is that why he was in the road at this hour?"

Bryce almost smiled. "We were working our dairy cows and usually Jackson listens to me, but he spotted a red fox. He'd never seen one before and he just couldn't resist going after it. The newspaper-delivery guy tried to miss him but didn't quite make it." He gave her a sheepish look. "He did annihilate our mailbox, though."

"Ah." Rylie nodded with sympathy. She glanced up to see Gage had the clinic door unlocked. "Just a second while we get the lights on and we'll be out to help get Jackson inside."

She nodded to the father as she went to help Gage get things set up. "Morning," she said to her boss.

"Sorry again for another early call," he said.

Since he sounded as if he was barely awake himself, she decided to help him with a little humor. "You should be. You ruined my best dream in months. Brad Pitt had just walked away from Angelina Jolie to ask me to dinner."

Gage snorted. "Only dinner? Woman, the guy can afford to buy you your own restaurant. We need to have a talk about wasting good sleep."

After grinning, she offered what she'd gauged so far. "The Lab's name is Jackson. Beautiful chocolate Lab. On first, minimal glance, it looks like a clean fracture. He was lured away from the boy by a red fox."

Gage's gaze shifted briefly to her own red hair. "It's the only color that will grab attention in fog like this."

"Jackson's a good-size two-year-old. Maybe we should put him on a cart?" Rylie asked.

"Nah, that'll only stress the poor guy even more. I

know big babies like that. I'll go carry him in. Just get the X-ray machine ready—and if you get a second after that, putting the coffee machine to work would be great, too," Gage said.

"Consider it done."

Less than an hour later, Rylie helped Gage put the dog into an enclosure with a half wall and cushioned bed to finish sleeping off the anesthesia. Jackson's leg was wrapped securely and protected by a splint that would ease the pressure on the limb when he was ready to stand.

Bryce looked unsure about this so-called "help" for his dog. "How's he going to get around?"

"At first, he's not supposed to, but he'll learn to hobble on three legs," Gage told him. "That's seventy-five percent of his usual power compared with your fifty percent if you were the one hurt."

Bryce grunted. "I guess so."

"We'll keep him in this enclosure instead of the kennel as he wears off the sedation, so he'll stay calm," Rylie added. She knew that was the next question coming from the boy. "If we put him in the kennel, the other dogs' barking would be a bit much for a guy with a hangover."

"Can I stay with him, Dad?" Bryce asked his father. "There's nothing going on at school today."

Daniel Black glanced at Gage and Rylie with a wry expression. "It's only the first full month of school and there's nothing happening." To his son, he added, "You're going to classes, and maybe by the time you get home, Jackson will be ready for us to visit for a minute."

"Not to worry," Rylie assured the crestfallen boy. "We take good care of our friends in recovery. And my dog,

MG, will happily lay in there with him to keep him company if he's feeling lonely. She's a therapy dog."

The boy brightened. "She is? Wow! I heard about them. Can I meet her?"

"When you come see Jackson."

Daniel Black nudged his son toward the door. "Thanks, Doc. Rylie. I appreciate all that you did—especially considering the hour."

Once they left, Rylie breathed a sigh of relief. "I was afraid Mr. Black wouldn't okay the expense of treating Jackson."

"I should have told you that they have three other pets that are older," Gage replied. "But there wasn't the discreet opportunity. Their long-term commitment to their animals is a given."

Pleased, Rylie said, "Well, I don't know about you, but I'm ready for another dose of caffeine. What a week it's been."

They were still on daylight saving time, and daybreak was more than a promise. There was no chance for either of them to return to bed, although Gage would have to go get Humphrey.

"I'm ready," Gage said. "You'll find me logging this procedure into the computer."

"As soon as I get you yours, I'll go take MG out. Would you like me to get you something to eat from my freezer? I can offer you a nuked sausage and biscuit or a day-old bran muffin."

Gage shook his head. "So it's true, you and Brooke are the two least useful women in a kitchen?" he teased.

"If I could look as elegant as she always does, I'd call that a compliment." Rylie gestured helplessly. "I can give

Uncle Roy a call and have him pick up something more than the usual doughnuts on his way in."

Gage shook his head. "I'll take care of breakfast for us when I collect Humphrey. It's the least I can do when you're not getting much more sleep than I am."

By the time they regrouped, the old-timers were camped out at their corner table and a third pot of coffee was being brewed. MG kept nudging Rylie's leg, wanting to repeatedly check on Jackson.

"What a good girl you are, MG," Gage said, following them to the enclosure to check on Jackson's progress himself. "Yeah, we have a different kind of patient, don't we?"

MG sniffed, then licked Jackson's bandage once and then quietly lay down beside him. Except for the "patient" being canine, it was typical behavior for MG, but Gage was impressed.

"If she wants to stay in here with him," he told Rylie, "I wouldn't mind. Let me know if her attitude changes to where you think she's troubled or concerned for him."

"Are you worried something isn't right?"

"Not at all. I'm just wanting her to use her obvious talents." His stomach growled and he rubbed it sympathetically. "There's something that doesn't need interpretation. I'm off to get Humph and breakfast."

By the afternoon, everyone was doubly grateful that it was Friday, although they would be open half of the day tomorrow. There was no chance to bother trying to run to Rusk in the hope of getting her license transferred; besides, she'd learned through some online research that she could go to any of the other DMV offices in the area, and she had about convinced herself that was what she should do to avoid another run-in with Noah. It was also a good thing that they'd had an opportunity for a big breakfast because there was barely time to take a bite of their sandwiches at lunchtime.

Rylie was chewing fast when Roy passed her with boxes the UPS man had delivered. He pressed his lips together trying not to laugh.

"Go ahead," Rylie said, holding her hand in front of her mouth. "Call me Chipmunk Cheeks."

"If you promise not to throw the rest of that sandwich at me, I was wondering if MG and Humphrey tripped you and tried to lick you to death, or is that hairstyle an homage to the punk look?"

Although Rylie often styled her hair into a spikier look, she knew what he was referring to—earlier, she'd had to wrestle one of the kenneled dogs into his pen after his outside time, and the goofy Great Dane—every bit as tall as she was—had shown his affection by licking her head repeatedly. Because they'd been nonstop busy, she'd forgotten about the incident, until now.

With a sigh, Rylie put down her sandwich and crossed to the bathroom, where she opened the door to look in the mirror. "Oh, jeez." She combed her fingers through her short, stiff hair with no results. Nothing short of sticking her head under the sink was going to help the situation, which she didn't have time to do. To resolve the situation and keep from being teased by the old-timers when they spotted her, she grabbed one of the white-and-maroon baseball caps that Gage kept for staff by the coat rack at the back door and slipped it on, tugging it low over her forehead.

"Thanks," she told her uncle. "I swear, this has been a day for the books."

"Can I do anything so you can finish your lunch?" Roy nodded toward the front of the clinic. "We're quiet up front for the moment."

"I so appreciate the offer, but I don't think you're up to putting metallic-pink nail polish on Annabelle Leigh." The toy poodle belonged to the Leigh family, who owned a car dealership in Rusk and Tyler, and she was sitting patiently in her kennel in the first examination room, acting very satisfied with her wash and trim. All that remained was the polish and matching bow, and she could go home with Mrs. Leigh, who was picking her up within an hour.

Roy made a face. "You're right. I'll end up with more polish on me than on the dog, and then never mind those guys out there teasing *you*. They'll laugh me out of Texas."

"What you could do is take out Humphrey. That would be a big help, since the little fire hydrant just gulped down half a bowl of water. MG is okay. She's still with Jackson."

"Poor Humph. Dumped for a big, strapping Lab," Roy teased, going to collect the basset hound.

Minutes later, just as Rylie finished Annabelle and returned her to her kennel, Gage came from the opposite side of the clinic. "I hate to bother you, but if you could give me five minutes, I could use your help with a Manx needing inoculations in Room Four. While I have no problem with most cats, that one acts like she wants to rearrange my face."

How odd, Rylie thought. "I always believed that breed was considered the sweetheart of the feline world. Do you think you have too much canine scent on you?"

"No more than you, but—" he glanced over his shoulder to make sure the examination room door remained closed "—frankly, her owner is a pretty tough customer, too, and I think the cat picks up her negative vibes toward me."

Rylie was doubly surprised and intrigued. Gage was a 24K darling, and if you couldn't get along with him, you probably needed psychiatric care. "Lead on. I have your back, boss."

Although prepared for anything, Rylie hesitated one step into room—not due to any concern for her or Gage's safety, but rather for the unusual pair waiting for them. The Manx and owner were both attired in a smoldering gray, the cat endowed with luscious long fur, the woman, maybe in her late thirties, wearing a leather vest over a matching T-shirt and jeans. Of average height and build, the cat's owner sported red hair, too, except it was a shade that could be achieved only via the help of chemistry. It also appeared that she cut her own hair, and not necessarily while looking into a mirror. However, considering her recent bad luck in the hair department, Rylie just adjusted her cap and continued inside.

"This is Rylie. She's going to assist me and hopefully reassure your pet."

With a smile, Rylie approached the table while calmly analyzing the situation. It was impossible to ignore the array of tattoos and body piercings adorning the woman. While they weren't excessive, there were more than she could ever perceive of wanting. She couldn't help but wonder where the hidden ones were located.

Closing the door behind them, Gage finished the introductions before busying himself with getting the inoculations ready. "Rylie, this is Jane Ayer."

Rylie was sure she'd heard incorrectly. "Excuse me. Did you say—"

"Yeah, yeah," Jane said with equal parts weariness and sarcasm. "Spare me the jokes. Not *that* Jane Eyre. Spelled with an A. What's more, the last time I was in a petticoat was in the seventh grade when I wore it with boots and a bustier to the junior-high dance that I was ejected from."

"Okay, point taken." Usually when she met people with all of the body art that Jane sported, they tended to be fairly comfortable in their own skin. But Jane seemed on the defensive side, or at least sensitive. Hoping to ease that, Rylie focused on the tattoo on her forearm. "Love the panther. My brother has one coming over his shoulder like that. Your artist did a good job."

The woman had been staring hard at her, but Rylie's observation seemed to at least trigger some curiosity. "Thanks. What does he do?"

"Restores old houses. Up in New England."

Nodding thoughtfully, Jane stroked her cat on the examination table. "This is Rodeo."

Rylie tilted her head as she considered the gorgeous cat with her short torso and strong hindquarters. Of all the names she would have guessed for such an exotic breed, it wasn't that. "Rodeo, huh? She's a fair-size female, but she still looks a little delicate to be a bull rider."

At first, Jane looked as though she was going to rebuff her attempt at humor, but she finally said, "I named her that because of how she plays with the mice she catches."

"An alpha girl. I'm all for women handling their own vermin extermination." Aware that Gage was taking an inordinate amount of time to make notations on the cat's record sheet, which Roy would put into the computer, she added, "My favorite fable about how the Manx ended up with no tail is that they were on the slow end of getting to Noah's ark and the door closed on them."

"Ha—not this one," Jane replied. "She can smell when it's going to rain for two days out. She's not too fond of water, but then I rescued her from the rain barrel her previous owner had thrown her into. No telling how long she'd been paddling around in there trying to get a good grip in order to climb out."

Rylie looked sympathetically at Jane and then the cat. "How awful. But what a relief that you happened to be there to rescue her." She was used to seeing welcome and good humor in this breed's big eyes, but Rodeo was all caution, like her mistress. No doubt Gage was right about Jane giving the cat some unwanted signals—it happened with dogs all the time. But she'd believed cats were far too independent to be easily influenced—until now. "How does she prefer to be approached?"

"Not at all. But she looks like she's starting to be interested in you. Maybe it's the hair."

Not a lot of it was showing. Rylie removed her hat, hoping her hair had been flattened enough by now not to look too ridiculous. If the cat thought redheads were okay, then that's what she would use to gain her acceptance.

Sure enough, the cat made a guttural sound not unlike a human saying, "Huh," as in "Go figure."

"I think," Rylie said to Jane, "if you wouldn't mind shaking hands with me, I'll be able to reassure her by having some of your scent on me. Unfortunately, I've just come from a poodle, and that can't be welcoming news to her refined senses."

After a slight hesitation, the woman nodded and extended her hand. "Why didn't you think of that, Doc?" Jane asked Gage.

Ever the unflappable one, he finally glanced their way. "Because this is only your second visit and I didn't know whom to be more afraid of, you or Rodeo."

Jane finally managed a real smile, though a reluctant one. "If I didn't approve of you, I wouldn't have come back."

Gage said to Rylie, "Jane brought in Rodeo a short time before you joined us, but Alpha Girl, as you call her, was having nothing of this place and Jane had to leave. I'll admit that we had more dogs in the building that day. I recommended that she give Rodeo a few days to recover and try again. Baby steps and all that."

An almost palpable easing of tension spread throughout the room. Grateful, Rylie shook hands with the woman and then let Rodeo smell her before stroking the cat's dense coat. The Manx gave what could have been a warning sound, only to flop onto her back and starting to play with Rylie's fingers as though taunting a mouse before the kill.

"Is this really play or am I about to become dinner?" Rylie mused.

Jane snorted. "She's not going to bite you. She's just making sure you're worthy of her grooming you. In other words, you're okay. Like I said, she belonged to some jerk before I got her. He ran a gas station up north. To get her out of harm's way, I lit up the paper towel dispenser in the ladies' bathroom to get his attention. We've been together ever since."

"Jane drives a Harley," Gage offered as though he was reporting the weather. "Rodeo rides in a kennel on the backseat secured by a bungee cord."

Rylie whistled softly. "A Harley, huh? I would have to bench press this examination table for weeks before I could manage one of those. I'm very impressed," Rylie told the no-nonsense woman.

Rodeo started licking her fingers, drawing her attention back to the cat. "Well, you are one of a kind, aren't you? Thanks for the affection." She noticed that Gage was ready. "I'm sorry that we're about to make you doubt your goodwill, but as the saying goes, it's for your own good."

As Gage approached them with the first needle, he gave Jane a tentative look. "Go for it. It'll be fine now," Jane assured him. "If I'm okay with you, she will be."

That turned out to be exactly right. Rylie easily got a comfortable hold on the cat. Then Gage did his usual, admirable job in giving the shots quickly and with such minimal pain, Rodeo barely reacted.

"It's been real," Gage said to the cat, as he retreated toward the door. "Rylie will get Roy up front to log this information and get you your tags," he told Jane.

"That wasn't too bad, was it?" Rylie asked, ruffling the cat's fur, while being careful to avoid the tender spots. "You just like to call the shots, don't you?"

"We both do," Jane told her, all but sighing. "It sure would be nice not to have to."

Sensing a lonely soul, who was probably also hurt badly at some time, Rylie offered, "Stop by for a cup of coffee sometime when you have the time. You'll find everyone here is pretty laid-back and accepting. People come and go all the time to shoot the breeze with the guys," she added with a nod toward the reception area, "or to ask one of us if we know someone when they're looking to find a pet or they're hoping to locate a new home for one that they have to give up."

Jane didn't look sold on the idea. "I'll think about it. I stay pretty busy as it is."

"What do you do—if you don't mind my asking?"

"I'm helping out at the dairy farm on the east side of town. Rodeo likes that I get free milk whenever she wants it."

"Lucky kitty. Hard work for you, though." Gesturing to the door that led back into the reception area, Rylie said, "Let's get you finished up. Have you actually met my Uncle Roy? He's been here for several years. I'm relatively new. He handles all of the front-desk stuff."

"I guess he's the one who put us in this examination room and told us to wait on Doc. He's kind of gruff."

"Oh, he has a deep voice, all right, but otherwise what you noticed was shyness. Except when he has to keep the guys in the corner straight. Then you'll see how protective he is of ladies—not that they'll say anything. They're a sweet bunch, just ornery between themselves."

"I wondered what that was all about," Jane said. "I guess it was so busy that I didn't see them the last time I was here."

Leading the way to the counter, she waited as Roy handed another customer his receipt then came over to reach for the patient chart before Rylie could even say a word. Rodeo hissed and swatted at him, causing her uncle to recoil quickly.

"Hey, pretty girl," he protested. "I'm not the one who gave you those vaccinations."

As Rylie stroked the cat's head, she quietly explained to her uncle, "Rodeo's previous owner was abusive."

"Aw. Thanks for telling me. There should be a special hell for people like that—right next door to those who hurt kids." Roy sighed. "She's a real pretty specimen," Roy said to Jane, only to give the chart a quizzical look.

"You've been here before? Sorry. I must have been tied up with a delivery, Mrs. Ayer."

"Ms." Jane glanced at him from under her short, un-painted lashes. "Rodeo here is the only family I have."

Roy nodded outside at her bike. "That's a grand bit of machinery."

"Do you ride?"

"Not in years."

Rylie tried not to gasp as his words jarred memories. "I'd almost forgotten, Uncle Roy." When he all but ig-nored her, she looked from him to Jane and thought she saw something happening. *Go figure,* she thought. How often had she tried through the years to find out why there was no one special in his life, and here he was sending out signals. What's more, Jane was sending her own back at him!

"Now that I think about it," Jane ventured, "I've seen you at the car wash from time to time scrubbing on your truck's hubcaps."

"You probably did. I'm guilty of liking my vehicle looking like it did when I first drove it off the lot." He started typing data into the computer. "I don't guess I saw a bike like that while I was there, though."

"No, I take care of it at home. But I take my 1957 Chevy Impala to the car wash."

Roy's gaze lifted from the screen in record speed. "The red one? Man, that's a gorgeous machine. Did you happen to restore it yourself?"

Jane acted as though she'd just been told she was the most beautiful woman on two continents. "I did, thank you. Everything on it is original."

Roy's stare reflected his astonishment—and admira-tion. "Well, I am proud to meet you." Cautious of Rodeo, he extended his hand, which Jane accepted. "So you like restorations?"

"I like things well put together."

"Okay," Rylie drawled, catching Jane give her uncle a slow once-over. "So I have a poodle going home in a minute, and I have to go prepare a ticket. Good meeting you, Jane."

"Oh, you, too, Rylie. And thanks!"

Rylie decided she was the one who should be thanking Jane. She'd never seen her uncle show this much interest in a woman. Fascinating, since Jane's style was a bit "out there," and not the kind of look she would think her uncle responded to, but so much for her hunches. She sure wouldn't mind if someone looked at *her* the way Roy was looking at Jane.

Correction...not "someone." Noah.

No, she thought sadly. She'd pretty much ruined any possibility of that fantasy coming true after the way she'd run from him the other day. And slamming into that post had cinched things. Now more than ever, Noah undoubtedly thought she was too easy to resist.

It was minutes before closing time, and Rylie stood up front with Gage and Roy double-checking that today's patients' files had been thoroughly updated on the computer. In between they were joking with the guys in the corner, who'd just finished a game of dominoes and were packing up to leave. Gage was in a hopeful mood, thanks to the phones remaining quiet. With no emergency calls, he was going to make it home before dark for a change. As for Rylie, she was debating how to spend her evening.

"Come to the VFW hall with us," Roy told her. "It's fish and chips night."

Before she could answer, Pete Ogilvie called, "Incoming," and everyone's attention was drawn to the parking lot.

The sheriff's SUV was pulling in. Occasionally a deputy came by to ask to put a dog in quarantine for having bitten someone, or to ask for help in getting a dead animal checked for rabies, but never Sheriff Marv Nelson himself.

"What's he doing here?" Roy asked. "He doesn't have to campaign for another two years."

That won him a few chuckles, but they all kept their eyes on the vehicle as it parked up front. There were clearly two men inside, and when Noah Prescott emerged from the passenger's side, Rylie felt a tightening in her chest. She also self-consciously ran her hand over her hair. She'd had a chance to quickly wash her short hair, but not much more. At least it wasn't acting as if she'd gone headfirst into a tub of wall plaster.

"Did you have a break-in that you didn't tell us about, Doc?" Warren chided from the corner. "Get some drugs stolen?"

"Not lately," Gage replied, his eyes narrowing as the men entered.

Sheriff Nelson nodded to Gage and barely glanced at the others before his gaze settled on Rylie. "Miss Quinn?"

"Yes, sir," she said cautiously. Although he was an impressive man in height and girth, it was impossible not to look from him to Noah, who followed him inside. The look on Noah's face was one of anger and distaste. "What's going on?"

"I have a warrant for your arrest."

Chapter Four

Sheriff Nelson's incredible announcement had Rylie reduced to staring at Noah. Now she understood his excessive interest in her the other day, and it had nothing to do with attraction. "What have you done?" she whispered.

He would have to have been totally blind not to see her utter shock and despair, and he momentarily had the grace to look somewhat unsure of himself. But he rallied well enough. "Are you going to deny that you know what this is about?" he asked stiffly.

"I suppose I can make a ballpark guess."

"Rylie!" Roy sounded as astonished as she was resigned. "What on earth…?"

Reminded of the many eyes on her, she aimed her reassurance at her uncle and Gage. "It's nothing like what you might be thinking. It had been my hope to get all of this taken care of before I explained. In fact I just sent the money for two of the tickets last week. There's probably some delay in the processing," Rylie added to Sheriff Nelson. "I can get you a copy of the checks. And I'm certain that I'll have the other paid for by next month."

At that news, Gage frowned and crossed his arms over his broad chest as he eyed Marv and Noah. "Seriously, gentlemen? You want to let them haul her back to California for a couple of traffic violations?"

"Technically, one was a parking violation."

"I'm still learning how to drive the monster," Rylie told her uncle and Gage. "Parking is a whole different story."

"The last one was an accident," Noah intoned.

"A fender bender!" Rylie was determined to protect at least a modicum of her unraveling reputation before it was distorted into something unrecognizable. "And the reason I'm late with paying the tickets is because I paid for the other driver's paint repair out of my pocket. I didn't want my insurance company to drop me."

"I can say that there was no evidence of intoxication or drug use," the sheriff pointed out, as if trying to be of help to her—or at least be fair. "But apparently she also got stopped in Arizona for having an expired license."

"The officer never wrote me a ticket," Rylie countered. "I'd explained that I was moving to Texas and was trying to avoid duplicating the procedure. In the midst of that, the officer had another emergency come over the radio and, when I assured him that I would stop at the RV park just ahead and call a friend to finish the drive for me, he let me go with that warning. That's exactly what I did—you saw yourself that Cliff got me parked here," she reminded her uncle. "And he told you that he was going to see family in Austin before heading home.

That's the other reason I'm late with paying my fines. I had to buy him a plane ticket back to California."

Roy nodded his confirmation to the sheriff. "I saw the young man with my own eyes. Very polite. His sister picked him up the next morning."

Although Sheriff Nelson nodded, his expression remained regretful. "It does appear that you're trying to get your problems resolved, Ms. Quinn, but the authorities in California don't seem satisfied, what with you operating a vehicle that seems above your abilities to handle."

Rylie slid Noah a bitter look. "No doubt confirmed by Assistant District Attorney Prescott, who believes that I'm incapable of walking and breathing at the same time."

"Are we supposed to wait until something serious happens here?" Noah asked.

"But she hasn't driven anywhere in the RV." Roy stepped forward to put his arm around her shoulders. "Look, there has to be a good explanation. My niece has always been a conscientious and safe driver." He gave Rylie's shoulders a squeeze. "Tell them, honey. You hadn't had any tickets until this. Lots of kids get two or three before they graduate from a permit to a full license. Not Rylie."

"Uncle Roy, it's okay." Realizing that she'd run out of time, she turned to him and Gage. "I should have told you both everything from the beginning, but it was important to make you see me as normal first."

"Of course you're normal!" Roy declared, reaching for her again. "What a thing to say."

"Well, not exactly," Rylie admitted, gently resisting his hug. Taking a deep breath, she took hold of his hands and gripped them, relaying her need for him to let her say what she needed. "This is about why I couldn't continue with vet school, too. It turned out that I discovered I had a tumor behind my right eye, just as I was starting my final year of veterinary school. Long story short, I'm fine now, but…I've lost my sight in that eye."

Murmurs of shock from the old-timers buzzed behind her, and she saw the sheriff and Gage hang their heads, while Noah suddenly looked positively ill. Rylie stood tall seeing her uncle's eyes fill with tears. "Hey," she whispered. "None of that."

"But sweetheart…" Roy had to clear his throat to regain his composure. "I can't believe this. You look—I mean it looks—"

"Like I can see. It's okay to say it, Uncle Roy." Rylie totally understood. Heaven knows she'd spent her share of time—too much time—looking into mirrors wondering if anyone saw the subtle changes that she saw, which she thought belied the doctors' assurances. Fortunately, or unfortunately—depending on one's perspective of human nature these days—most people were too preoccupied with their own lives to have noticed.

"That's the good news. I've retained muscle movement. You probably remember when Sandy Duncan had this happen to her. She's successfully continued her career in show business. I think all of her high-flying as Peter Pan onstage has been after the fact."

Of all people, Sheriff Nelson murmured, "I remember that. My wife took the kids to see the show."

"'After the fact'?" was all Uncle Roy said.

Giving Gage a "help me here" glance, she continued. "Yes, and that relates to me because you need your peripheral vision when working around larger animals. You can slap all of the extra bubble mirrors on a vehicle to make sure you can see the traffic around you, but you

can't safely manage a horse or cow—any large animal—
without two working eyes, any more than you can with
a missing limb. Besides, it wouldn't be right to endan-
ger whoever else is around you, either, or the animals."

"It's a matter of safety, yes," Gage admitted. He
gave her a soul-searching look, and then reached out to
squeeze her shoulder. "I'm so sorry. That was a lousy
turn of luck." Hearing her uncle choke, Rylie grimaced
and rubbed his back. "He's remembering how I got the
nickname Lucky. Hey, I still am fortunate, Uncle Roy. As
I said, cosmetically, nothing's really changed."

"But you've wanted to be a veterinarian since you
could speak. I was there the day you came home from
kindergarten with your first drawing of a dog with half
his body bandaged and a big red heart painted on it."

Touched by his recollection, Rylie offered a philosophical shrug. "So I couldn't fulfill that ambition. But
I wasn't going to waste all of that schooling and time.
You know that not being around animals isn't an option
for me, so I knew what I had to do."

Roy wiped his eyes only to interject, "Wait a minute.
Your parents never told me a thing about this."

Hoping he would understand, Rylie said, "I had the
procedure done near school and recuperated at a friend's
apartment. My folks still don't know, Uncle Roy."

He shook his head, rejecting the possibility. "They
were shattered when you dropped out…and disappointed."

Remembering too well, Rylie repressed her own mis-
ery to explain. "Letting them think I'd let them down was
preferable to them convincing themselves that I needed
to be nursed and hovered over 24/7 like some invalid."

"Are you telling me they believed that you had your

heart suddenly set on being a dog groomer?" Roy demanded, incredulous.

Her uncle was nobody's fool, and her answering look admitted to him that things didn't go smoothly between her and her parents for a while. "At least I proved quickly enough that it's a lucrative market when I sold my truck and bought the RV."

For once Roy wasn't buying her glass-half-full perspective. "This is me, sweetheart. I know you, and I know this business. You had to have about killed yourself after serious surgery to manage the pace that you did to come as far as you have."

"The family had high expectations, Uncle Roy. *You* had high expectations…and I had dreams."

"You don't have to give them up," Gage said. "You could have discussed the matter with your instructors and professors. You could still specialize in small animals and do routine surgeries."

Rylie smiled. "My ego stumbled. That didn't seem like enough. Then, hearing that I'd have to learn to adapt my balance and everything, I thought a definitive time-out was necessary. Look, I don't know if I'll ever be so resolved or stubborn again, but in this case, determination and stubbornness worked for me. I'm *fine*."

Roy, on the other hand, was still having a hard time taking this in. "You should have called me. My God… there was no reason for you to handle this all alone."

Hating that this conversation was taking place in front of Noah and Sheriff Nelson, Rylie was starting to feel the months of hard work take their toll. The news of the warrant still had her shaking, which showed her how emotionally tired she was.

"You are helping me," she reminded him. "You have

helped, more than I can tell you. As for my parents, who would have gone back into debt for me...Uncle Roy, you know they've made a comfortable living for themselves with their antique-and-salvage business, but they're not wealthy. Even so, with me grown and Dustin off creating his own life, they're thinking about adopting again or trying foster care."

"Adopting—at their age? Why am I the last to hear of any of this?"

Rylie kissed his cheek. "That's Dad. Why linger on important details when you can laugh with your big brother on the phone? Uncle Roy, you know he worships you—his veteran-hero brother. The thing is that I didn't want them to sacrifice something as wonderful—and helpful—as adoption by taking on my financial minefield. Really, it was almost under control until...this."

Gage turned to the sheriff. "This is so clearly a case of simple misunderstanding. Can't we work this out without the flashing lights and handcuffs?"

Sheriff Nelson looked torn. "Forget the flashing lights nonsense, but, Doc, a warrant is a warrant. I'll admit that from what she's said, Ms. Quinn has been an admirable member of society—a little naive about the handling of such a big vehicle, but I admire her independence and conscientiousness. However, I can only act on behalf of the State of California's edict. I'll have to take her in, until we can see how California wants to handle this."

"That's nuts," Roy declared. "I'll cut you a check for whatever you need right here and now." He pointed with his thumb over his shoulder. "I always keep a spare check in my wallet. It's in the safe in the storeroom."

"If he can't cover all of it, I will," Gage added.

From the corner of the room, Warren Atwood declared, "You can count on us for whatever you need, sweetheart!"

Rylie pressed her hand against her chest. "Guys… everybody, stop. You're going to make me cry." She struggled to steady her breathing. "I don't know what to say."

"Well, I know what I have to say," Roy told the sheriff. "This is all a joke. You don't have to take her. It's not like she's a flight risk."

Sheriff Nelson said, "I agree. But considering how politics are being played on virtually every front page of newspapers these days, I'm not taking any chances. This job is enough challenge without politicians and newspaper editors making it worse. Ms. Quinn, you are going to have to come back to the office with me, but I swear, we'll get on the phone with California straight away to clear this up. For my part, I'd take your check or whomever's gladly, but I don't even know what the total is. So what do you say that we get this resolved?"

"That would be a relief," Rylie said, although not at all confident that luck would ever be on her side again.

"Well, then I'm coming, too!" Roy declared, scowling at Noah. "Why are you in on this? Your mother relies on Rylie's work. Do you even have a clue as to what will happen if my niece is formally arrested? Gossips don't care if they have facts straight. It's all about the adrenaline rush that comes with *maybe, could be, possibly.* What's the matter, you can't stand for her to even have half a dream?"

Trying to make eye contact with Rylie, but failing, Noah replied, "I had no idea it would come to this. All I did was do some checking online."

"What?" she gasped. "You investigated me? On what grounds? Because I *annoyed* you?"

Noah's bowed head told her that she was close enough to the truth not to need an answer. With a sound of disgust, she asked Gage, "Please, watch MG for me in case I don't get back tonight?" She dug her keys out of her jeans pocket and handed them over to him. "You'll need these."

"You're coming home," Roy declared, staring hard at Noah. "I'm following you to Rusk and we'll get this resolved in no time."

"In that case, you'll be needing my services," Warren said, rising.

Both the sheriff and Noah looked uneasy as the former D.A. of Cherokee County joined the group. As the other veterans applauded their friend, Marv Nelson pinched the bridge of his nose. "Folks, we don't need to make this any harder than it already is."

"Yeah, well, you're the one taking her away from us, Marv. We all served so everyone could have a fair shake at justice," Stan Walsh, Rylie's Porthos, declared. "This doesn't smell like justice to me."

"No, it reeks," Jerry Platt muttered.

Still anxious, but heartened by this show of support, Rylie extended her hands to the sheriff. "Do you need to cuff me?"

Sheriff Marv Nelson grimaced and waved away her offer. "Quit that. But you do have to give me your word that you won't attempt bodily harm to our assistant D.A. here as we drive back to Rusk—not that I would blame you if you tried."

"As tempting as the idea is," Rylie assured him, without sparing Noah so much as a glance, "I have no desire

to waste any energy on him." Rising on tiptoe to give
her uncle a last kiss, she led the way out.

"Don't worry, baby, we're right behind you!" Roy
called after her.

In the privacy of her own mind, Rylie hoped so! Because inside she was shaking like a gelatin salad in an
earthquake and couldn't believe she was still able to stand
on her own two feet. Discipline had always been her "go
to" remedy in times of challenge, but this situation might
be too much. Betrayed by the man she'd wanted to—

To what?

It didn't matter now, she decided. Hoping that Noah
took note, she went straight to the sheriff's car, but to the
passenger door on the driver's side, making good her as-
surance that she wanted no other contact with him. Sheriff Nelson opened the door for her and waited for her to
fasten her seat belt before shutting it.

Once Noah got in on the front passenger side, he
turned to speak. Unlike the other department vehicles,
this one had no metal grid separating them, which disappointed Rylie. From here on, she wanted all of the distance and barriers from him that she could get.

"I thought you were acting suspiciously," he began,
sounding more than a little regretful. "The other day
when you were in a hurry to get away—I thought you
were hiding something. It never crossed my mind that it
could be a medical problem."

"Please shut up," she muttered, turning to look out
the passenger window. "You've caused enough trouble
and humiliation to last me a lifetime. To never have to
speak to you again would be a gift." Tears of humiliation
blinded her, and all but garbled her words.

"Rylie, once the authorities in California understood

where you were, I had to at least follow through and bring in Sheriff Nelson before this blew up into something we couldn't keep out of the news."

"Why couldn't you have thought about that before-hand?" She covered her face with her hands. "Oh, my God, there may be reporters? Do you realize you're going to hurt Doc's practice, too? He'll have to fire me just to protect his business!"

Settling into his seat, the sheriff raised a calming hand to Rylie, but he spoke to Noah. "Call ahead to your people. I already warned mine that no one better notify the press."

"They just knew I was out on a call with you, not the reason," Noah assured him.

That proved to be the first good news for Rylie. More followed, but it was over three hours before she could leave the sheriff's office a free woman with a clear record. When she did, she was framed by Uncle Roy and Warren. She had never been so relieved in her life!

The authorities in California had, indeed, been willing to accept payment—with a penalty for their time invested on the case and legal expenses. Before Roy could reach for his check, Noah had his checkbook in hand, scrawled the amount, signed his name and handed it to the sheriff.

Although startled at first, Rylie quickly snatched it and ripped it to shreds. "How dare you," she whispered. "This may clear your conscience, but it doesn't undo what you did as far as I'm concerned."

"Believe me, I understand. But it's the least I can do."

"I think you need to leave," Roy said, handing his own check over to the sheriff.

"You might take that under advisement," Sheriff Nelson told Noah, looking none too pleased with him, either.

Noah did leave and Roy muttered as he glared after him, "I'm going to get Gage's permission to make sure that so-and-so never comes to the clinic again."

Rylie grabbed his arm. "Uncle Roy, think. Mrs. Prescott is a lovely woman. She probably doesn't know anything about this."

"I hope not. You deserve her business more than ever—and that of her friends."

"Well, you're free to go, Ms. Quinn," the sheriff told her. He smiled, although he looked almost as tired as she felt. "I guess I don't have to tell you that I'm as relieved as you are. You're a brave young woman, and I admire your determination not to inflict expense or worry on your loved ones. You shouldn't have trouble getting your license, but if there's anything I can do to help you in the matter, let me know. Just promise me that you won't be driving that monster RV of yours too much."

"No, sir, I know I have plenty of help around if that's necessary. Uncle Roy has also let me borrow his truck if I need to go somewhere, until I can afford my own, and I always put on extra side-view mirrors."

"How come I never saw any?" Roy asked, scratching the back of his head.

She gave him an impish smile. "Probably because I removed them just before I got back to the clinic."

Roy scowled. "Well, just leave them on the thing now so when you need to borrow the truck, it's ready for you. Wait—you know what's a better idea? The truck is yours. I'm going to treat myself to a new one."

Stunned, Rylie cried, "Uncle Roy, it's barely two years old."

"Yeah, but I sure like the new models they had at the county fair."

"You didn't get to go to the fair this year. You told me that you were too busy at the clinic and missed it." Rylie gripped his arm. "Uncle Roy, I love you for this, but I can't let you do it."

"Why not? You're my only niece. Why shouldn't I spoil you if I want to?"

"Because you love that truck. You were just saying as much to Jane."

Her uncle shrugged and gave her a sheepish smile. "So I'll love the new one even more. It's not like I have anything else to spend my money on."

Rylie hugged him fiercely. "What would I do without you? You're the dearest uncle ever!"

"What does that make me, a grapefruit?" Warren complained, feigning a scowl.

Rylie quickly hugged him, as well. "No, sir! You are a darling, too."

They were laughing as they exited the building and went to the truck. On the drive back to Sweet Springs, Warren couldn't contain himself.

"So that seemingly clumsy trait every now and then is you still learning to adjust, huh?"

"Shucks, you did notice." Rylie sighed, disappointed that apparently she hadn't successfully fooled anyone. They'd all thought she was less than graceful, not the unfortunate victim of situations beyond her control. "Yes, sir. That was another reason I stayed with friends while I was getting through this. I didn't want my parents panicking every time I misjudged spacing and bumped myself, or have them trying to do things for me that I needed to relearn how to do for myself. It's been hard enough to get through the emotional and psychological aspect of this."

"I can imagine," Roy mused.

"Do you think Gage is going to let me stay?" Rylie asked, as some of her doubt returned.

"Why on earth wouldn't he? You not only have helped business, but you make our jobs easier."

All but confirming his words, as they pulled into the clinic's parking lot, Rylie was astonished to see not only Warren's vehicle still there, but everyone else's, too, including Gage's pickup truck. "Oh, my gosh," Rylie whispered. "They stayed?"

"You are loved, sweetheart," Warren told her. Once they entered, he was the one to announce amid the applause, "Everything is resolved and fine." As cheers erupted, he added with glee, "I thought the sheriff was going to throw Prescott out of his office."

At the mention of Noah, Rylie felt a deep pang. Granted, she was foolish to feel anything but loathing, but that was the human condition—sometimes illogical, especially where matters of the heart were involved. How much sweeter it would have been if he'd liked her, admired her or at least approved of her.

"Congratulations, honey!" the men said in near unison, drawing her out of her introspection.

Gage held out his arms and gave her a hug. "That's from Brooke as well as me. I hope you don't mind that I called her. I needed to explain why I was expecting to be ultralate getting home."

"Of course not—and thank you." Rylie looked at him with chagrin. "I know I should have been straight with you from the beginning—"

"I understand, believe me. And now that we know

what's going on, I'm doubly impressed with you. I wish we could clone you. Your dedication and determination are second to none."

He made her feel as though this horrible experience had almost been worth it. "That's so much nicer to hear than, 'You're fired.'"

"You say something as crazy as that again and I'll let the air out of your RV's tires."

Everyone around her laughed.

"Now we're definitely going to get your certification on the front burner," he added. "And Monday, you take off and get that license business done. I don't care if we have a clinic full of Manx cats snarling at me. Well, check that," he said, as though having second thoughts.

This time Rylie joined in on the laughter.

"I'll drive her so Roy can keep his truck here in case of an emergency," Jerry said.

Warren snorted. "You'll keep your lecherous self away from her. You're still on probation after your last so-called helpfulness with you-know-who. Besides, Roy here is buying himself a new vehicle over the weekend, so she won't have a problem in that department—and if she does, I'll take her."

"Jeez, guys," Rylie said, once again pressing her hand to her heart, "my cup runneth over."

Noah dreaded the drive home, knowing what awaited him. He would have to explain everything to his mother. She was going to be seriously upset with him, considering how she'd reacted to his fussing over having to take Bubbles to Sweet Springs. This was a dozen times worse; he'd almost been responsible for putting Rylie behind bars.

It's not like you wanted it to go that far.

No? Then what?

To find something wrong with her so that you could stop thinking about her. To make her go away.

"Congratulations," he told himself with disgust. "You almost succeeded."

In the process, he'd also made himself the laughing-stock of the county. It would be a miracle if the sheriff ever took him seriously again. But it was his mother he was most worried about. If she didn't have a stroke—after she verbally disowned him—it would be a miracle.

After parking at the house, each step up the walkway left him feeling as though he was the one about to get ill. Thankfully, no one was around when he first walked into the old plantation-style dwelling. Most of the lights were off, and considering the hour, that was no surprise. His mother should already be in her bed, although if she was asleep, it was only to doze. She wouldn't turn off her lights until he poked his head in to tell her that he was home. That was a habit she'd begun since the accident, now that he was all she had left in the world.

Setting his briefcase at the foot of the stairs, he went to the living room, where he intended to pour himself a stiff drink. He had the lead glass in his hand and the stopper off the crystal bourbon decanter, when he heard a scurrying, and then Bubbles ran into the room and barked at him.

"Same to you, dust mop," he muttered. "Why aren't you upstairs?"

"Why are you so late?"

Closing his eyes, Noah said, "Evening, Aubergine."

"Phones not working at the office? Your mother's been fretting herself sick."

"I apologize. I'll go up in a second."

"Did you eat? If you did, you look like it isn't agreeing with you."

"It's not that, and I don't think I could keep anything down, but thank you for asking."

Aubergine scowled. "You getting sick? Then you stay out of your mama's room, hear?"

"I'm not sick, just—" He shook his head, unable to continue, and concentrated on putting several ice cubes into his glass. "Is Livie in her room?"

"That's right. Waiting on you, so she can tuck your mother in for the night."

Nodding, Noah poured the bourbon. "Good night, then." As Aubergine left, he took a fortifying sip, and then another. The stoutness should have made him shudder, but it didn't. Another bad sign. He was so numb with the bruising he'd taken that near-straight alcohol had almost no effect on his usually discerning taste buds.

"Let's get this over with," he told the little dog that stood by staring at him.

With a low growl, Bubbles hurled herself up the stairs ahead of him. Noah suspected that if the dog could talk, she would be ratting on him well before he reached his mother's room.

"If it wasn't for your high-maintenance self, I would never have met her, and this mess would never have happened," he said, picking up his briefcase and following the animal.

At the top of the stairs, he set down the briefcase again, since his rooms were on the west end of the house, while his mother's were to the far end of the east wing. They were not his childhood rooms, but they provided the privacy and independence he'd insisted on to make this move back.

The moment he entered his mother's bedroom, she asked, "Are you being ugly to my baby girl again, dear?"

As usual, too short-legged to jump onto the high bed without help, Bubbles had used the tiered method, leaping up onto the chaise longue at the foot of the bed, and then using pillows on it to make it the rest of the way. She now lay tucked comfortably at her mistress's side and gave him a "What are you going to do about it?" look.

"She started it," Noah said, before taking another sip of the potent drink.

The mauve, ivory and gold room smelled like gardenias— his mother's favorite scent—and at sixty-seven, she still looked like the blonde actress in that old TV series about dynasties, with her ash-blond hair—a lovely gift from nature yielding to silver, but still styled in a perfect pageboy. As always, she was cocooned in silk, satin and enough pillows to stock a boutique. Not all of that was aesthetics; his mother's body needed the support so her lungs could continue to work adequately.

Bending over to kiss her cheek, he marveled, as always, that she had almost no wrinkles; her skin was as smooth and soft as a child's. She remained a beautiful woman, thanks to great bones in her triangular face and warm, cognac-colored eyes.

"When are you going to stop waiting up for me when I'm running late at the office?"

"When it's a woman. Better yet, a woman you love making you late." Audra frowned as she studied his face, and she touched the back of her hand to his forehead. "You look ghastly."

"I feel worse, but then I deserve to."

"Bad day at the office?"

"That's the understatement of the year. Maybe since I passed the bar."

Eyeing his drink, she said, "It sounds like I'm going to need a drink, too. If you were a good boy, you'd pour half of that in my water glass."

"You're on medication," he reminded her, as he often had to, "and I'm not up for the joint retaliation by Olivia and Aubergine."

"A half glass of white wine with lunch and dinner isn't my idea of being fair. It's practically European austerity."

While taking another drink, Noah yanked his navy-blue-and-silver tie, then opened the top two buttons on his pastel-blue shirt.

Looking increasingly concerned, Audra closed the book she'd been reading on a white leather bookmark. "All right, you have my full attention."

Instead, Noah frowned at the book. His mother read everything from romances to suspense, to sagas and history, with plenty of nonfiction in between. He thought her one of the best-read women he'd ever met and would claim so even if they weren't related. "Why aren't you using the tablet I gave you at Christmas?"

"Because this is a borrowed book, and because I still prefer a binding and paper to a screen. I'm on the computer enough. I can't see how all of these screens can be healthy for one's eyes."

"Probably not." Noah thought that he deserved to go blind for all of the problems and hurt that he'd caused via an electronic screen.

"Good grief, darling, you're turning green. Sit down and talk to me."

"Maybe I should get out your old riding whip first. You're going to be tempted to use it on me in a minute."

As expected, his mother's eyebrows lifted as she grew intrigued—and worried. "That bad?"

"Mother—" unable to look at her as he said the awful words, he yielded to the need to pace "—I hurt and humiliated Rylie Quinn today. If there was any way to take back the last several hours, I would. I would do anything not to keep seeing her shock and pain in my mind, but I know it's nothing less than what I deserve."

"What have you done?" Audra whispered.

"That's exactly what she said, how she sounded, when I brought the sheriff to the clinic to arrest her."

"You *what?*"

Noah watched her cover her mouth with her right hand. Her diamond wedding and engagement rings twinkled in the lamplight. It had taken her an entire year before she'd had the heart to move her rings from her left hand to the symbolic widow designation on her right. Tonight it was just another reminder to Noah of how all she had known these last years had been grief and pain, and it devastated him to add to that.

"Noah, what on earth?"

"If I'd known it would trigger so much curiosity in California, I would have been more careful about how I probed into her background."

"What right did you have to do that?"

That was the question that would yield the most condemning answer. "Because I wanted her out of my mind. Because she seemed too good to be true." As soon as he spoke those words, he took another drink.

"That's the most ridiculous thing I've ever heard."

"Yes."

"Ramon says she's cheerful and like—what did he

say?—a Fourth of July sparkler. What in heaven's name is wrong with that?"

"I thought she was playing everyone, including me. I thought it was all pretense." Of course, now he knew some of it had been, but for a totally noble reason.

"She's a businesswoman," Audra reminded him. "It's important to remember to be polite to people, even people who may not be deserving of it, or whom we feel have wronged us."

"I *know,* Mother." Noah regretted his edgy tone, but what she was telling him wasn't anything he didn't already know. "I know," he whispered again, his pained look beseeching her not to torment him more than he was already doing to himself.

"Tell me the rest," she demanded, her expression already tightening with disappointment and disapproval.

Unable to bear that, he returned to his pacing. He was going to be blunt, but that would reflect only on him, not Rylie, as it should. "Long story short, the reason she'd gotten all the tickets that precipitated in an arrest warrant being put out on her was that she had a tumor and lost the vision in one eye. That was also why she dropped out of veterinary school."

"Oh, Noah! That poor dear!"

"Yes."

"To want something so challenging and admirable, only to have it snatched away. Her heart must be broken. Is there no way she could fulfill that dream?"

"Would you have let a one-handed surgeon operate on you?" he challenged, only to wish he could take back those words. Damn his survivalist legal training.

His mother gave him a reproving look. "If you remember correctly, I'd have been perfectly content not to have been operated on at all."

Noah's grip on the glass was so tight it should have shattered, but the damned thing was just too thick. "I was supposed to let you lie in E.R. screaming?" For days afterward, he'd wakened sweating, feverish as he remembered those sounds.

With a calming motion of her hand, Audra said, "I shouldn't have said that. Go on."

Noah explained the peripheral vision challenge, and how Gage had agreed with Rylie as she'd explained it to her uncle and the rest of them. "It's my understanding that women are already professionally challenged by large animals anyway—it's the whole size-and-weight thing factoring in with a woman's inferior strength to that of a male vet. Add a high-strung horse or an ornery or downright mean cow or bull, or whatever creature they have to deal with, and you're facing the threat of injury or even death. Gage did say that she could still be a vet, but with primarily smaller animals. She acted like that was a Miss Congeniality award to her."

"Yes, I see," Audra said, nodding slowly. "What an awful situation for her. I suspect she was also left with medical bills on top of her college expenses, so even the hope of the lesser license wasn't of much reassurance. Could her family not help?"

"She didn't tell her parents in order to keep them from using their savings."

"Oh, Rylie," Audra whispered. "What a big, generous heart you have." She looked at Noah, her expression incredulous, but also admiring. "So to stay near the animals she loves and honor her debts, she's become a groomer. What an incredible but inspiring story. I'm so glad to have been told about her. Now more than ever I want her to keep caring for Bubbles."

"Dr. Sullivan is assisting in getting her certification as a technician, as well. She'll be able to do quite a bit—give shots and do some care, as long as the vet is on the premises." Having heard some reference to that between Warren and Roy, he'd looked up the job description online.

"I haven't met Gage Sullivan, but I already know I like a man who would try so hard to help an employee."

What she'd left unsaid, Noah thought, enduring a new wave of shame, was that in comparison, he had acted in the exact opposite way.

"Now, about these tickets. You've covered them for her, I hope?"

"I tried to, but she ripped up the check." However, Noah felt compelled to defend himself on at least one point. "Doesn't it bother you that she could have caused a more serious accident being behind the wheel? You of all people have paid a high enough price for someone's bad judgment. Good grief, she even tried to drive that big RV of hers from California to here."

Rather than agree with him, Audra asked, "Why did she need to leave California? Did she know there was a warrant out for her?"

"I don't know that there was one at the time. She just didn't want her parents smothering her with good intentions and trying to make her dependent on them."

"Well, I for one think we were blessed when she made her decision to come here, but Noah...I'm deeply ashamed of you."

"I'm pretty sick of me, too."

"What has happened to the brave and compassionate boy and man I used to know?"

What indeed? It was one thing to get chewed out by a boss, or a mentor, but his mother was the person he respected and loved most on earth. For her to find him morally and ethically wanting was another blow that had him downing most of what was left in his glass to where he thought about excusing himself to get a refill.

"Don't you go sneaking off on me."

Suspecting that she was picking up on his body language, Noah countered with, "If I'd wanted to avoid you, I would have stayed away until I was certain that your door was closed and your lights off." But when he sat down on the foot of the bed, he did sigh wearily. He would listen for as long as she wanted to berate him, but he didn't have to enjoy it. He did, however, feel it was his duty, since he was also hoping for a woman's perspective.

"I don't think I've ever seen you quite this way before. The accident—that changed you."

"It changed both of us."

"Of course. I think we're both still dealing with anger issues on top of our huge sense of loss." Audra nodded slightly. "Maybe that's why your first reactions to Rylie seemed so strange. Everyone else thinks she's a doll, and she just made you more bristly. And now you look…hunted."

Maybe he wasn't up to advice yet.

"Why don't we give voice to what the truth seems to be?" Audra prodded when he didn't respond. "You're attracted to her…. Maybe it's already become more than that?"

"But I don't want to be." There was no reason to try to pretend or try to keep anything from her. She knew him too well. And clearly, he wasn't as good an actor as Rylie was an actress.

"Because animals are her life and you have no use for them?"

"I don't really have a problem with that—as long as people remember they have four legs, not two," Noah added drily.

"If that's supposed to be another hint that I spoil Bubbles," his mother countered with equal dryness, "maybe that's partly your fault. I fear any possibility of grandchildren will come after I'm too far gone to enjoy them."

Noah wasn't ready to visualize her condition degenerating any more than it already had, so he took on the next-hardest hurdle. "It's not her work. It's just *her* that's the problem."

"No, she's not your usual type, is she? My friends tell me she's very pretty, energetic and charmingly unpretentious. Let me see…she has no piercings, not even in her ears? That's almost delightfully old-fashioned in this day and age."

Noah gave her a mild look, completely aware of what she was doing. She wanted *his* description of Rylie. It was too easy to do, and it would give away too much. However, to refuse would be even more obvious.

"She's built like a dancer—petite and slim. Long legs and arms, rather than a gymnast's sturdiness. Indoors, her hair appears the color of cinnamon. No, what's that spice that Aubergine puts on my favorite dishes that I've asked about before?"

Audra smiled. "Paprika."

Noah snapped his fingers. "That's it. But when outside the color is…well, it defies real description."

As she lifted her artfully tinted eyebrows, Audra asked, "And her eyes?"

That was more difficult yet. "A frustrating gray-green."

"You might mean *beguiling*," Audra mused, "if you have to try so hard that the simple question leaves you annoyed."

"They're green, okay? But in certain light the shade of green takes on a smoky tint."

"How interesting, and expansive for someone you've only met twice."

"It's been five—no—six times, counting yesterday." When his mother didn't reply, he glanced up from his preoccupation with the increasingly naked ice cubes in his glass and saw amusement. "Go ahead and say it."

"I was only going to correct myself. You aren't falling for her—you've fallen."

"Well…that's not a good idea."

"As though what's wise or preferred has anything to do with whom our hearts and souls link themselves with."

Noah managed not to groan. Barely. "Feel free to stop at any time."

"What I don't understand is why can't you let yourself feel what you're feeling?"

"Because she's never going to forgive me, let alone trust me again, and even if she could, she's all wrong for the life we live, what I expect for my future."

That wiped every sign of pleasure from his mother's face. "You can't be serious! Why? Because she's not a society princess? You tried one of those, remember? And from such a fine family that her father is in federal prison, and she's contracted an agent to scout for a spot on a re-ality show, while her mother is trying for a book deal to share more of the family scandal. Such humility, such principles," Audra scoffed. "Rylie could only dream of living up to such high expectations."

The reminder of his close call with tainting the family name wasn't necessary for Noah, but he did wince at the memory of his brief but colorful time with the Houston debutante. True, she'd been a fun girl, yet he'd hit the elevator down button fast after his first and only dinner with her family and "man-to-man" chat with what was meant to be his future father-in-law.

"It's not as though we were ever engaged," he reminded his mother.

"No, however, she didn't take 'goodbye' gracefully, did she?" Audra shuddered delicately. "I would never have been able to show my face in public again if we'd needed a blood test to prove a child's paternity." She fussed with Bubble's bow. "You did get yourself medically checked afterward, I hope?"

"Mother...yes."

"Thank you." As he rolled his eyes, she continued. "Your father and I came from decent, hardworking stock. That is what you benefited from, and that continues to provide our privileged lives now—not to take away from your success before coming back here. All I'm saying is that from what little I've talked with Rylie on the phone, I've found her to be professional and articulate. Heaven knows she would be a huge asset with the livestock."

"It takes a little more than that to hold your own against the movers and shakers in this or any community, and you know it. Vance's wife and the mayor's went to SMU together—I've watched them turn a perfectly nice person into sushi before the poor soul knew what had happened."

"Those two self-starving, surgery-loving mental patients are exactly what we don't need around here, and it's about time they were replaced with people with common sense and wholesomeness. And by the way, I hold the men just as accountable as their women. If you saw or overheard something any of them said that wasn't right, and didn't immediately stop it, then you're as bad as they are."

"Vance is my boss, Mother."

"He's a servant of the people, too." But as quickly as her indignation flared, Audra grew forgiving. "At least you've given me something to get excited about. You've been acting like a monk rather than a child from your parents' loins for too long."

"Mother." His parents had been a romantic couple, and he didn't need the reminder. Even though he'd arrived late in their marriage, he'd witnessed plenty of displays of affection while growing up to know they'd shared a healthy sexual life.

"Oh, excuse me. I'm not supposed to mention s-e-x." Audra tried to lean forward to reach for his glass. "Give me that. I want a sip."

"Impossible. I know what time it is, and Livie is about to come give you your last meds for the night." He rose to go knock on the nurse's door. He knew it was the only way his mother wouldn't try to wear down his defenses.

"Judas," Audra whispered.

"I love you, too." As the door opened, he met Olivia Danner's ghostly, makeup-free face, framed by equally washed-out hair. One glance at her shrewd gray gaze and Noah knew that she'd heard every word of his conversation with his mother. Belatedly, he remembered that by this hour, Livie had the intercom on that sat on his mother's bed stand. Its partner was on Livie's nightstand. "Tuck her in, General," he muttered.

As he crossed the room and began pulling the door shut behind him, his mother called, "I better not learn that Bubbles is no longer welcome at the clinic."

Noah leaned back into the room. As Livie—dressed in flannel pj's and robe—drew her stethoscope from around her neck and put the plugs in her ears, he said, "You know that's out of my hands."

"No, it's not. And penance *is* necessary."

What could possibly be enough? Noah wondered. "Flowers?"

"At the very least. Dr. Sullivan's wife has a shop in town. Go talk to her."

Noah thought he'd endured enough glares from residents in Sweet Springs. He suspected there were plenty more "friends of Rylie" whom he hadn't met yet. "Why can't I just call?"

"Because you could use an advocate. She's undoubtedly fond of Rylie and will be the best bet to know her tastes. Find out what you can."

"Married to Doc, she also probably knows about what's happened. What if she doesn't want my business?"

Audra gave him a "spare me" look. "You are my son. You're named after a man who managed to get two of everything on a ship for a flood that everyone insisted wasn't going to happen."

"I thought I was named after your father?"

"Smart-ass. Are you going to tell me that you've become suddenly tongue-tied and socially incompetent?"

"Merely humbled by the depth and breadth of my stupidity."

"Use that." Audra smiled. "It has its own charm. A woman loves to see a man squirm with regret as much as with unrequited love."

Seeing Livie glance up from logging pulse and blood pressure figures to look over her shoulder at him, Noah felt about sixteen and replied to his mother, "You're embellishing."

"And you're going to make me give Olivia upsetting numbers." She waved Noah away. "You have all of the information you need. Now off with you."

Chapter Five

By nine o'clock on Saturday morning, Noah was in downtown Sweet Springs. He had been here only once before since returning home, and that was for a civic function on behalf of his boss. Otherwise, he hadn't been in this area since his high-school days. Things had changed quite a bit. There were many more and new businesses, and most of the old structures had undergone serious face-lifts, including Newman's Floral and Gifts. The whitewashed brick with the artsy copper-and-brass sign along with the green awning was classy. He hoped that what awaited him inside was as inviting.

Chimes rang a cheery welcome as he entered, and a perky blonde restocking a shelf from her perch on a short ladder looked down to greet him.

"Hi! Happy Saturday!"

The greeting was so like something Rylie might say

that he had to chuckle. The young woman did look close to her age. He wondered if she knew her, too.

"Good morning." He glanced around. "There's a lot to look at in here."

"We do our best. I didn't think I'd seen you before. I'm Kiki. Can I help you find something?"

"Actually, I was looking for Brooke. Mrs. Sullivan."

The young woman nodded over her shoulder toward the back, where the two woman stood conferring. "She's with Hoshi going over some orders. We have a wedding tomorrow."

Noah nodded, having attended enough of them to have a clue as to what an undertaking that was—at least for the brides. Then his gaze fell on a crystal cross on a stand and he paused. The etching was fabulous, and the way the light played off the piece made him think of his mother and how she liked to sit in the sunroom for hours at a time watching the sun change the shadings on all of the plants inside and out. The cross would look beautiful in there between her many plants.

"Thank you," he said, his gaze lingering, as he headed down the long main aisle.

He realized that Brooke Sullivan was a blonde, too. She was a few years older than Kiki, and petite. Maybe even an inch or two shorter than Rylie. She moved with a natural grace yet confidence, which was evident in her initial smile.

"Hello," she said as he approached. "Did I hear my name?"

"Yes, I was hoping you could help me. I'm Noah Prescott."

Brooke's welcoming countenance froze. "Oh. I see."

Noah knew if he ever needed that charm his mother

spoke of, it was now. He exhaled heavily and hung his head. "So Dr. Sullivan told you."

"I'm afraid he did."

"Mrs. Sullivan, the last twenty-four hours have been some of the worst in memory—and I've been through a few, as you can imagine if you know anything about my family."

Some of the ice melted in Brooke's demeanor. "I admit I did ask Gage more questions after he told me about what you did to Rylie. I'm very sorry for your family tragedy."

He nodded his thanks. "Then perhaps you'll have the generosity to understand how badly I feel about the humiliation and pain that I caused Rylie, and you'll agree to help me. I need to make a gesture worthy of my regret to her."

"You want to send her flowers?"

"I was thinking that would be a good start."

"Do you want to deliver them yourself?"

He gave her a doubtful look. "I'm a thick-headed man, not suicidal."

That won a slight smile from her. "When would you like to have them delivered?"

"As soon as possible—although I understand that you have a big event pending."

Although she nodded, Brooke said, "We have that under control. Besides, if it involves our Rylie, I'm not about to send you to my competition. What were you thinking of?"

"I don't exactly know. Roses seem appropriate gesture-wise, but they don't exactly seem like *her,* do they?"

"I like the way you're thinking already. No, she wouldn't be moved by the long-stemmed variety, and it would be a rather blunt display of affluence. On the other hand, pink baby roses in a pink round vase—" she pointed to the selection of roses in the cooler to his left and then to the vase on the second shelf of a display beside the cooler "—that shows thought, and we could add a little humor…or romance… with a bow or balloon, or teddy bear."

It struck Noah the instant he saw the two items that Brooke understood what he was trying to do. The arrangement would be charming, even endearing, considering the size of the cute flowers—petite like the person receiving them. He also wondered if Brooke had added the word *romance* because of something she knew, or was she simply fishing?

"I think I like the baby roses, definitely."

Brooke reached for an order pad. "To do this right, we should use two dozen due to the size of the vase. We'll put baby's breath in between to create a fuller, dreamy effect."

Noah reached into his camel-colored sports jacket for his billfold. The jacket, worn with khaki Dockers and a white silk shirt, minus a tie, was as casual as he got when away from the privacy of home. "Whatever you think serves the situation best." He glanced over his shoulder again. "There is one more thing. The crystal cross…it caught my eye as I entered."

Brooke's demeanor went all soft and tender. "Isn't that lovely? We only got that in yesterday, and I haven't been able to stop looking at it."

"Then will I upset you if I take it, as well? I mean take it with me. For my mother," he added at her confused look. He could tell her first reaction was that it was also for Rylie. "She's confined to a wheelchair—"

"I've met Audra. We keep the foyer flowers fresh at Haven Land."

Tapping his left temple, Noah sighed. "I actually know that, since I oversee all of the bookkeeper's reports for the estate. Pardon my memory glitch." He decided that he was going to have a few words with his mother, as well. The sneak had made the suggestion to come here as though it had simply been a hunch. That would teach him to check only the totals in the bookkeeper's monthly statements. If he'd inspected actual receipts, he would have saved himself yet more embarrassment. "Well, then you know the sunroom she loves to spend time in. I thought the cross would look wonderful on one of the tables."

"It would, and how thoughtful of you. Let me get it safely boxed and wrapped. Is this a special occasion?"

"Another apology...or thank-you."

Brooke looked pleased. "We have some stunning autumn wrapping paper that I'll use. It's almost as gorgeous as the gift itself."

"That sounds perfect. As you probably know, Mother takes art classes, so everything down to the wrapping does mean a great deal to her. She's all about texture, color and visual sensation."

"She's very talented. I've always admired creative people. I'm afraid I tend to be too left-brained to be more than a mimic." As she set to work, she asked, "So have you adjusted to being back in East Texas?"

"Sometimes more graciously than at other times," Noah admitted, and then remembered what his mother knew of her situation. "You were used to the faster-paced corporate world, too, weren't you?"

Brooke nodded, humor deepening her dimples and bringing a new sparkle to her warm, brown eyes. "But you can't pout for too long around Gage. Now I can barely imagine living to work sixteen-plus hours a day. Besides, we have an addition to the family to focus on, as well."

Noah glanced down as she laid a protective hand over her almost flat tummy. Only then did he realize she was wearing a rather loose poet shirt. "You and Dr. Sullivan are expecting? I didn't realize. My warmest congratulations."

"They are warmly accepted."

Once Brooke had the cross packed and wrapped, and the order for the flowers written up, she ran through his credit card and handed him the receipt to sign.

"What about a card?"

"Ah." There was another clue that this whole experience was throwing him completely off his axis. At Brooke's suggestion, he chose one of little note cards, only to stare at the blank space. In the end, he said, "I'd better let the flowers do the talking," and put back the card.

"Do you want me to call you when the delivery is made?" Brooke asked gently.

"Only if there's a problem."

"I understand. Usually, we have Charles—our deliveryman—handle things, but in this case, I think I'll do it myself. I haven't seen Rylie yet this week, and we need to catch up."

Feeling as though he'd passed some test, Noah was grateful. "I do appreciate that." He reached for his billfold again for one of his business cards. "This is my office number." He scrawled his cell number on the back. "And my private number."

"I'll be in touch. In the meantime, thank you, again. On behalf of Gage and myself, good thoughts to your mother. She's a very brave woman."

"She is, and will appreciate your kindness, as well. She said some very nice things about you, too."

Despite the compliments she'd been receiving all morning—from customers as well as from her uncle and Gage alike—Rylie struggled to maintain her usual cheerful demeanor. She was almost grateful that this was one Saturday when the old-timers weren't gathered at their table for their usual coffee klatch. It was difficult enough to see and feel Uncle Roy's and Gage's concerned gazes as they all took care of clients and daily chores; however, a buddy of the musketeers' was in the hospital, and they were keeping vigil with him.

"I think we should go do something different after we close up," Roy said to her moments after she sent off a cocker spaniel that she'd groomed. He knew that Toby was her last appointment for the day, so any other work she had was whatever Gage needed her to do. "You like fishing. You want to go to the town lake with me after we close up? I hear there's been some good catfish caught on the north side of the lake."

Although she gave him a grateful look, Rylie said, "I'd have to get a license, and it's almost year-end," she told him. "That's sort of a waste of money, and taking a risk fishing without one isn't something I want to gamble on, given my luck lately. The last thing I need is to be ticketed again, even for something as innocent as having a line with a hook in the water."

"Well, then let's find someplace new to have dinner. I haven't been up to Longview in a long time. Want to see what's happening there? We might even take in a movie."

Rylie couldn't help but give her uncle a disbelieving

glance. "What was it that you'd recently said to Pete? The last movie you went to see was *Jaws,* or was it *Rocky?*"

"Which proves that I need a change of pace, too."

"In that case, why don't you mosey over Jane Ayers's way and see if she's available? Maybe she'll take you for a spin on her Harley."

Roy's coloring wasn't conducive to blushing, but what he lacked in that department, he made up for in getting tongue-tied. "I don't want to—I mean, I can't—aw, I just wanted to spend some time with you. Shoot the breeze a little. I have a hunch there's a lot more going on with you that I don't know about."

Rylie momentarily paused at sweeping up the dog hair in the reception area left by the morning's shedding clients. "I appreciate your intentions, but I'm fine. Stop worrying about me."

"You say. If what happened to you happened to me, I would want to box that Prescott jerk's ears until they were as big as the space in between."

"Nice," she drawled. "Violence resolving vindictiveness. But aside from letting you vent, I don't think we'll venture down that road. I've scared Doc enough, not to mention almost caused him serious trouble. Oh, look…"

Roy looked up at the car entering the property. "Say, that's Brooke. She's going to be disappointed when she learns that Doc's out on a farm call."

True enough, Rylie thought. Brooke didn't come to the clinic often, what with her own business interests expanding even faster than the clinic was. Plus, there were doctor appointments and a nursery to plan for. When Rylie usually saw her, it was apt to be at the assisted-living center, or when Brooke and Gage invited her and Roy to dinner, so when she saw her boss's wife circle her Mercedes and pick up something out of the passenger floorboard, she instantly knew it wasn't going to be a dog emerging. After all, Humphrey was too heavy for her—besides, he was here napping with MG in back.

"Uh-oh," Roy said.

Brooke was carrying a gorgeous arrangement of pink baby roses in a pink glass orb that looked like a princess's crystal ball. It took both hands to manage it, forcing her to close the car's door with her hip.

"Think that's for you?" she asked her uncle.

"Ha! If it is, I'm going to stop worrying about you and start worrying about me. Could be a nice gesture from Doc and Brooke," Roy mused, going to get the door for Brooke.

"He's already given me too much by letting me hook up out back, not to mention fast-tracking me to get my certification," she replied, setting aside the mop. "Hi," she said, as Brooke entered. "Lost?"

"Not at all. This is yours."

As quickly as Rylie came to greet her new friend, she backed away, clasping her hands behind her. "Noah?"

"How many other sexy-but-conflicted lawyers almost turned your world upside down?" Brooke held up the arrangement in the fluorescent light to admire it. "He came to the store this morning. You have to admit, the man does have good taste."

It was the first part of that comment that left her open-mouthed. "He drove to Sweet Springs?" Her gaze was drawn to the windows as though she half expected him to be parked up the service road to watch the reception his gift would receive in order to gauge his next move.

"He did. He was quite humble, too. Extremely concerned for you and totally a gentleman." Once again Brooke tried to hand over the arrangement.

"Oh, Brooke, they're lovely, but I don't want them."

"Will it help to know that my heart sank when I realized who he was? I didn't want to take his order, but I have to confess he grows on you. Fast."

"Wait until Gage hears that."

Smiling at the obvious, though weak, tease, Brooke continued. "You don't think he's sincere?"

"Of course, but I still can't take them." Rylie stuck her hands into her back pockets to keep Brooke from trying to force the gift on her.

"You mean you won't." Brooke's demeanor grew sympathetic. "I feel awful for what happened, too, Rylie, and I let Noah know he wasn't well thought of for doing what he did, but he didn't need my input. He looks pretty miserable, and ashamed."

"He should," Roy snapped.

Letting that pass, Rylie said to Brooke, "He's made it clear that he's disliked me from the moment we met."

"I think quite opposite is the case. He picked this himself. A person just going through motions because of guilt that someone told him he should feel would have sent a dozen roses via the phone or online. Noah was painstaking. While in the store, he also found a lovely gift for his mother that seemed to affect him, as well. The man's not all cold strategy with feet of clay."

"That's reassuring to hear, but the person I remember wasn't so commendable. He enjoyed making me feel... inadequate."

From behind them, Roy puffed up. "He did *what?* Well, I guess I still have a few things to say to that stuck-up—"

"No, you won't. I said all there is to say. Now it's over."

Rylie returned her attention to Brooke. "I just want to move on. Please, give those to the assisted-living center. They'll look wonderful in the main living-room area."

Although she looked regretful, Brooke didn't argue. She did, however, shift the arrangement in order to give Rylie a hug. "I hope you don't mind that Gage told me about your vision."

"Of course not. It's actually a relief to not have to pretend anymore. I'm not usually a secret keeper—about myself, I mean. I like life simple and honest."

"Well, you're doing beautifully, if that's any reassurance."

"It is, thanks. And I think I am getting better at balancing and adapting by the day." But eager to get off the subject, Rylie pointed to her new friend's tummy, hidden by the gauzy material of her blouse. "How's my future babysitting assignment?"

Brooke grinned. "Growing fast. If this isn't a boy, my poor daughter is going to have to deal with the confusion of looking down at her mother by the time she's ten, yet still having to obey me." She eyed the flowers again and gave Rylie a final wistful look. "Please reconsider and accept these? I think I'm a good judge of character, and while I admit Noah made some huge mistakes with you, in hindsight, I could see that as a monumental compliment. You've quite gotten to him, and he's at a loss as to how to deal with his feelings."

If she had heard that shortly after their first or second meeting, Rylie could have found the generosity to overlook a great deal and be patient, as Gage had been patient in winning Brooke's love; however, Noah's dogged determination to be right about her being flawed was crushing.

"I'm sorry, but I don't know if I could really trust him again," Rylie admitted.

Nodding, Brooke winced. "That's not something I ever had to worry about with Gage. Well, then...I'll just tell them at the center that this is your donation. Expect to be hugged a lot when you and MG next visit." At the door, she paused and glanced around. "Speaking of...where's Humphrey and MG?"

"Oh, in a kennel outside while I mop up in here. If I let them have their usual run of the place, they would see this as a game and I'd never finish."

Nodding, Brooke said, "That I understand. I can't believe the difference in Humph since you and MG arrived in his life. He's a totally different dog at home now, and when we open the gate, all he wants to do is get into the truck to get here." With a wave, she headed back to her car.

No sooner did she exit than Roy stood his ground. "I think you should have taken the flowers. Not because I want you to forgive Prescott, but because you deserved them."

Rylie shook her head, unable to tell him that the thought of looking at them day in and day out would be almost painful. "No, I don't. There are people dealing with a lot worse injustices than I did. Now, if it turns out that the rest of my vision gets compromised, we can talk pity party, but my doctors said that this was just a fluke and I should be safe from worry. So I'm ready to move on."

"Well, put up that mop and figure out what we're going to do this afternoon."

Voicing an impulse, Rylie said, "What would you say

if I called Jane and the three of us went to the barbecue place in town this evening for music and good food?"

Roy's chest shook with his restrained laughter. "You not only want to fix me up with a date, you want to chaperone? Let me handle things in the Jane department, okay?"

"I just wish you would—handle it." Rylie took a deep breath. "Okay, then…we'll go truck shopping for you. Don't think I didn't see you checking the newspaper ads earlier."

"Now you're talking!"

"That's not what I expected to hear," Noah said. "Correction, what I'd hoped to hear." When Brooke Sullivan called him shortly after noon, he grabbed for his cell phone like a man waiting for an organ-donor call. But Brooke had little good news to share, and when she told him where she'd ended up placing his gift, he'd been deflated. "I suppose I should have anticipated this outcome," he told her, "but I'm disappointed nonetheless."

"I understand," Brooke told him. "But you're not giving up, are you?"

Noah stopped in midstep as he paced along the outside of the pool at Haven Land. The afternoon was gorgeous, with just enough autumn coolness, but none of that helped his melancholy mood. "I…don't want to. At the same time, I don't want to continue upsetting her."

"Without betraying a new friendship, I can tell you that she was torn over what she was doing. She thought the flowers were glorious and the gesture good of you. She just wasn't ready to embrace your generosity."

"Because?"

"In the end it's always about trust, isn't it?"

"I guess that's a subtle improvement over all-out loath-ing."

"I would say *subtle* is significant."

Noah took heart from that. "So we'll try again. But… what? Flowers again?"

"Gage and Rylie use a lot of repetition with animals to build trust, but does she need that in her personal life? I don't think so. She hears what you're saying. It's your job to convince her that you really mean it."

Noah figured at some point, he would owe Brooke a huge gift of her own for getting him through what he re-alized was totally foreign territory for him. He'd never had to pursue a woman in his life! "What do you have in mind? I'm guessing no arrangement at all?"

"We handle chocolates now. Locally made fudge, to be exact. Maybe we'd put a nosegay on the package? It would have to be Monday, though."

"Sure. A nosegay? They still do those things?"

Brooke laughed softly. "You're right—it's almost an archaic word and there's no real call for them except as a bit of whimsy, or for smaller, informal weddings. I did read that they're usually made of the most fragrant flow-ers, which, duh, explains the name. So much more ap-pealing than a bow on top of the box, and she could then put it in a small vase, which I could provide, giving her what amounts to three gifts in one."

Noah wasn't certain. "Rylie didn't strike me as the kind of woman to be so…"

"Feminine?"

"She's very feminine." He frowned at the mere idea of anyone not seeing that. "Just not…fussy."

"I promise, it won't be remotely fussy," Brooke re-plied, a smile in her voice.

Relieved to sense Gage's wife continued to approve of him, he added, "Be generous with the chocolates. It's obvious calories slide right off her."

On Monday during his lunch break, Noah returned Brooke's call that he'd missed due to being in court. His trepidation turned out to be warranted. "She didn't accept that, either, did she?" He could tell by the tone of Brooke's voice message, although she'd said only, *"Please call me at your convenience."*

"No. And she was embarrassed that all of the guys at the clinic saw it. But I was discreet and drew her to the back to actually try to convince her to change her mind."

"I appreciate your efforts. You're my sole ally, except for my mother." How to gauge if there really was hope after all? he wondered. "So she's still opposed to giving me at least the benefit of the doubt?"

Brooke made a soft musing sound. "We're looking at a bit of stubbornness now. But part of that could have been a reflex for having the audience at first. I should have known better, so I owe you this next try, because given her expressions when we were alone, I do think she appreciates that you're still trying, and some of her resistance is crumbling."

"I don't want surrender or resignation," Noah said, turning his back to the room, afraid that Judy or Vance, who was feeling better and was in deep conference with his secretary, saw his own emotional turmoil. "I just want to be able to talk to her again. Where does she want you to take this gift?"

"A young girl in Sweet Springs who'd survived a cancer scare. You probably read about her in the local newspaper. She's barely eleven, Noah. It's a dear gesture."

"Yes. Of course, and I did see that." Noah ran his free hand over his hair, at once admiring Rylie for her thoughtfulness, and on the other hand trying to figure what it would take to make her want to keep something from him. "What do you suggest next?"

"We have some great fragrances that Kiki developed herself. They're becoming quite popular in the area."

"But I don't know what Rylie would prefer—or that she even wears a fragrance." He wasn't going to admit he thought he'd caught the hint of something tropical and flirty once when standing near her. Peach? He'd figured it was a result of a shower gel, not an actual fragrance she'd sprayed on.

"I don't suspect she does too often, considering that she wants the dogs to get used to her natural scent, but it's always nice to have something for special occasions. I'm thinking forward," Brooke told him, her tone conspiratorial.

"Thinking forward would be nice, but I'm not the optimist I used to be. What else could you recommend?"

"We have some cute stuffed animals."

He remembered seeing a nice display in one corner of her store. "I think I would rather go with that. I saw a kangaroo..."

"I sold it shortly after you were here."

Disappointed, Noah tried to think of what else had caught his eye. "The giraffe?"

"Um...the giraffe that's almost her height?"

"I know it's probably the most expensive thing in the store, so I insist you put it on my bill. You can tie a note in the shape of a heart on ribbon around the neck that reads, 'I'm stretching my imagination to convince you that I have one.'"

"Noah, I'm impressed," Brooke replied, laughing softly. "And I can do better than snipping at construction paper. We have pretty lace doilies that will work beautifully."

"Good, very good, because that about used up the one creative gene in my DNA."

"But, Noah, about the giraffe…it's cute and would probably make her laugh—"

Noah could hear her moving around the store.

"—here it is. I have a sweet mini schnauzer. It's white and I could make an equally dainty basket of flowers to stand beside it. That seems more her size, and the heart would work even better, if you ask me. It is my favorite of the stuffed animals, and I think she might like to use it in her clinic display advertising her grooming services."

"That sounds like the winner to me. Okay, thanks, Brooke." Since their initial conversation, she had insisted he call her by her first name.

For the next few hours, Noah waited, barely able to concentrate on his work. When he returned from court and Judy blocked his way to his desk, saying, "A Brooke Sullivan is on your line," he all but lifted her to move her out of his way and get to the phone.

"Yes, Brooke," he said, unable to keep the anxiety and hope out of his voice.

"Well, she didn't send it back with me."

"You mean she accepted it?"

"I'm hoping that's what she's doing."

"Well, what did she *say?*" His voice sounded so tight and foreign to him that he had to check himself. He couldn't remember when he was more eager to hear something positive.

"She stared at it a good while and finally said it looked

very lifelike. Then she asked if she sent this back, would you keep ordering things? I told her that was probable."

"How did she react to that?"

"She was quiet for a moment and then she thanked me for bringing it."

Noah didn't try to hide his relief. "Thank you, Brooke. I sincerely appreciate all that you did."

"I just hope something good comes from this. My opinion of you has changed—if that makes any difference."

"It means a great deal."

But now what? Noah thought after he hung up.

She just didn't know what to do.

On Tuesday afternoon that dilemma preyed on Rylie's mind. Her first impulse yesterday had been to return Noah's gift to Brooke again, but she knew Gage's wife was right—he would only send something else, and she didn't want him wasting his money on her. Okay, so she was somewhat flattered that he had done everything he had so far, but there was no future in it. They were apples and oranges—more accurately Dom Pérignon and diet soda. By closing time, she asked her uncle for a favor.

"Do you suppose they were wrong about your new truck not being in until later this week?" On Saturday, they'd had fun shopping the dealerships in the area and then having dinner to celebrate Roy's deciding on one. But the silver extended-cab Chevy wouldn't be delivered from its current location at the Port of Houston until tomorrow or even Friday.

"I've dealt with them before. The interior package that I wanted was hard to find without special ordering, so, yeah. I'm not expecting a call until then. Why?"

Knowing he was too sharp not to read into what she was going to say, she said, gently, "May I drive you home and borrow the truck for an hour?"

Roy—and everyone else—had already picked up on Noah's latest gift, and that she'd kept it. Therefore, his narrow-eyed stare was less intimidating than it might have been.

"What are you going to do?" he demanded.

"Go talk to him."

"I don't like that idea."

"Well, it needs to be done."

"I'll drive you."

"No, you won't. I'm twenty-five, not fifteen. Either you'll lend me the truck or I'll figure out something else." She hadn't yet gotten her license changed, as planned. Regardless of everyone's good intentions to get her there, Monday had been crazy and Tuesday's scheduling turned out to be not much better. At least now she wasn't worried about being bothered by the police.

"Staying put is the idea I like best," Roy grumbled.

Rylie tried gentle persuasion. "I just want to make sure he understands that I only accepted his gesture because I wanted him to stop."

"That can't be said over the phone?"

"Important things should be done in person, Uncle Roy."

In the end, her uncle relented, only to insist on waiting in the RV for her to return. He would be comfortable watching MG as he kept up with the latest baseball play-off game on TV. Rylie had reminded him that there was beer and the rest of the pizza from lunch in the fridge, and had driven off.

Now, what if Noah was out for the evening? she wondered while en route to Haven Land.

When she pulled into the estate with the grand stone entrance where the electronic gates were open, she almost lost her courage. She'd passed the place a few times now on her way to Rusk, and the acreage was every bit as stunning as the stately white-pillared mansion. *A modernized Tara,* she thought, eyeing the sunroom on the left side overlooking a pool every bit as large as the one in the city park.

Her confidence turned into full-fledged nerves when she spotted Noah in front talking to a shorter and darker man whom she quickly recognized as Ramon. As she drew closer, she saw a series of mounds near the driveway, which was probably what had Noah concerned.

As she came around the circular drive, Ramon's eyes widened with surprise. Then, with a wave of his Western hat—he was clearly on yard duty at the moment— he hurried off toward the barn with the spray canister he had been toting.

As Rylie parked and approached Noah, she tucked her hands into the back of her slim jeans and asked as though they'd just talked minutes ago, "Showing Ramon what a fire-ant mound looks like?"

The mild sarcasm was a subtle reminder of his tone with her during their first meetings. Noah's self-deprecating smile indicated that he remembered only too well.

"As usual, he's four or five steps ahead of me. I was only worried that Mother would come out in her chair to admire her roses and accidentally roll into the ant nests before she realized they were there. I should have known that he'd already been mixing the poison. Thankfully, he's patient with me." Noah's tone then grew far more tender and husky. "It's so good to see you. Words are inadequate."

Rylie studied him in the late-afternoon light. He looked less browbeaten than Brooke had suggested, but there were undeniable shadows under his eyes and he was a bit paler than the last time she saw him—undoubtedly losing himself in his work more than ever. She wished she could take some satisfaction out of that, but she'd never been that kind of person. It was time to just say what she meant and get this behind them.

"I didn't come here looking for compliments. I came to thank you for the gestures, but to ask you to quit. That's why I accepted your last gift. You need to know that I've put what happened behind me, so you can, too. Stop, I mean."

Still wearing the white dress shirt and gray pants from the suit he'd obviously been wearing at work today, Noah looked as underdressed as was probably possible for someone like him. Nevertheless, he retained the power to make her pulse do crazy things. In comparison, she was in a turquoise T-shirt and jeans, but at least she'd ditched the maroon lab jacket, and the four-legged critters had been easy on her clothes today. Given the compliments she'd received now and again, the turquoise seemed to do nice things with her hair and eyes.

Noah looked stymied by her directive. "Stop…? I don't know that I can."

Was he kidding? He was the assistant D.A. of Cherokee County, probably the next D.A. He'd been groomed to convince, coerce, chide, mock, herald and warn off in nuances a mockingbird would envy. Where was the difficulty for an orator in canceling an ongoing flower-shop order?

With curiosity getting the best of her, she asked, "Why not?"

"I'm on a mission. What's more, just because you're generously putting this—what I did—behind you, that doesn't mean you've really forgiven me. That's what I need to be convinced of."

"You're forgiven, okay? It's done."

Shifting his hands on his hips, he shook his head. "No, it's not."

His stance might look bold, but his words weren't arrogant. They were simply, quietly spoken. "What difference does it make to you anyway?" she replied, feeling a little desperate now. Her resistance was crumbling under the power of this somber, intense Noah.

As soon as she uttered those words, she wished she could take them back, because he started to walk toward her. The expression in his gorgeous-but-compelling brown eyes had Rylie backing away, completely forgetting the truck behind her, until she bumped into sunset-warmed metal. From bra line to hips, she felt the heat; however, that was tepid compared with what his look stirred inside her.

When Noah was toe-to-toe with her, he framed her face with his hands. "Only this," he whispered against her mouth.

For a man with so much brooding going on within those intelligent eyes, his hands and lips were incredibly tentative and gentle, inviting and appealing. His touch seduced, as well, as he caressed her skin, exploring her cheekbones, her jawline. He treated her as though she was made of the fibers of a sweet dream, and all the while his lips moved over hers with the ardor of a man who was willing her to hear the words trapped in his mind.

At first, Rylie gripped his wrists, only to freeze on the impulse to push him away. But, his kisses were already too potent. She could no more resist what he was offering, and asking of her, than she could remember why she should remember the need to protect her emotional welfare. She could only absorb.

His tender appeal almost brought tears to her eyes. By the time he paused to catch his breath, or steady some wave of emotion within him, she felt as though she'd been through a tumultuous, but brief summer storm, as well. So when he simply rested his forehead against hers, and closed his eyes, she swallowed against the ache in her throat.

"It's a relief to discover you can be reasoned with," she said between shallow breaths.

His attempt at laughter brought a soft caress of air against her lips. "I can't believe you let me touch you, let alone kiss you. This goes way beyond my fantasy."

"If fantasizing is what you're doing, you could have dressed me better."

"You're delectable. But what I'm really trying to see is what's in your heart."

Rylie remained bewildered—in an amazing way. "I don't understand you," she admitted.

"You will." His voice held the velvet vibrato of promise. "The way I behaved, have been behaving—I was lost in anger, and emotionally AWOL. This is me, Rylie. This is me."

He kissed her again, a deeper kiss this time, which had her releasing her hold on his wrists, only to slide her hands up his chest and wrap her arms around his neck. Here…on his family's driveway, under God's sky. She couldn't write poetry, she rarely read it, except when she downloaded lyrics for a song she loved and wanted to learn. She knew it existed all around her in nature—at birth, and death—but this was the first time she'd tasted it and ached to imbibe it.

For a precious space of time, life's pain and unfairness lost its hold on them. Rylie's entire being basked in the aura of being totally present and in tune with the universe. She realized that she'd just been blessed—she was not going through this life without knowing something like this existed.

When Noah finally ended the kiss to gently, quietly wrap her in his arms and hold her against his pounding heart, Rylie could only whisper, "Noah...this is surreal."

"Yes."

"And pretty crazy."

"Crazy was fighting this. Denying what I was feeling."

"I have just enough sense not to share what I'm feeling right now. As it is, I'm not sure I remember how to get home."

That confession earned her a pleased look from Noah as he tightened his embrace in a quick, urgent hug. "That's probably the best thing anyone has ever said to me. And you can't go home yet. Come inside and say hello to Mother."

His invitation yanked her back to reality faster than a sudden downpour could have, and she abruptly slid sideways to escape his embrace. Go inside? After practically begging him to make love to her? "Oh, no! I'd be too embarrassed."

Before she could take another step backward, Noah took hold of her hand. "Listen—that's Bubbles barking. She's spotted you—probably from the sunroom window." He gestured to the left side of the house that was width and length floor-to-ceiling windows. "Mother's in there painting, so it won't be long before she drives her chair to see what the fuss is all about. Actually, I'll bet she's already watching us." He caressed the soft inside skin of her wrist with his thumb. "Rylie, there's nothing to be embarrassed about. She's on your side."

If true, that was a relief. Rylie had enjoyed the few times they'd conversed on the phone.

"You'll see," Noah said when she looked at him for verification. "She's been thoroughly disgusted with my behavior." His gaze searched her face and lingered on her right eye. "I'm so sorry for what happened to you," he added, his voice husky. "Does it help at all if I swear that it doesn't show?"

"The doctors said that, and some nurses. Most of the time, I figure people are just being nice."

"You can believe me—and in what's between us, as well. This isn't going to only be about sex."

Her humor stirred back to life. "There's going to be sex?"

He burst into laughter. "After kissing me back the way you did, there damned well better be." As quickly as the moment grew lighthearted, he got serious again. "I've never reacted to anyone the way I have to you. You've knocked me a galaxy away from my constellation of pre-conceptions, never mind my comfort zone."

As he started to draw her up the sidewalk, Rylie wasn't sure all of what she'd heard was a compliment. "So handsome, brilliant you feels something for little, insignificant me, huh?"

Halfway up the sidewalk, Noah paused, visibly startled. "That can't be how you see yourself. Little, maybe, but you have the heart of a giant. Life threw you a hell of a curveball—that happens to plenty of people—but what did you do? Instead of embracing the support you know would be there from your family, you exuded a superhuman effort not to worry or burden them. In the meantime, you've built a new career and paid off a small mountain of debt.... You call yourself insignificant? There are CEOs of Fortune 500 companies who would like to tap into your perseverance and discipline." Noah shook his head. "My God, woman, you're amazing."

Before she could respond, he resumed his eager escort toward the house. Rylie was still basking in the delight of his words when they passed the threshold into the mansion, only to have to deal with a new assault on her senses.

"Mercy. I didn't think that it could be even more stunning inside."

The foyer was a rectangular space of light, which was interesting since there were no visible windows except for the two that framed the front door. But the buttercup-yellow walls and the ivory chairs and tables set around the room created an atmosphere of merriment and welcome. In the center of all that was a round white marble table on which sat a flower arrangement that Rylie suspected was every bit as tall as she was, concocted of seasonal flowers, branches and dried seed pods from plants she didn't believe grew on this continent.

"Where's the light coming from?" She hadn't meant to whisper, but the stateliness of the place seemed to demand the respect.

"A skylight we put in at the top of the stairs. Mother didn't like the big chandelier over the arrangement competing with the flowers."

"That explains it," Rylie said with a nod as she continued taking it all in. "My parents would writhe in envy if they knew I was in a place like this. They would know with one glance what the stairs are made of and what era the chairs are from."

Noah cast her an apologetic look. "You said something about their work—no, your brother's. I'm sorry that I don't remember who does what."

"Dustin renovates seriously old and historic homes on the East Coast. In California, my parents are the people whom people like you call when something breaks and you need to either repair or replace it—or you're looking for something that's one of a kind. They reclaim old things and store them for when a decorator, contractor, renowned builder or even an independent rehab aficionado needs them, which is what I would be if I ever bought myself a place."

"I would think that takes a good eye—and tons of patience. It would drive me crazy to see a doorknob sitting on a store shelf for two years just collecting dust."

"Frankly, me, too. In that case, you also have craftsmen working for you, as my folks do. You can turn something like that doorknob into a birdhouse foot grip. Or if you need impromptu storage or hanging space in an apartment, you fasten the knob to a rustic board or shutter, and it becomes a hanger for a jacket, or robe...maybe the house and car keys."

"Mother is going to love pulling stories out of you." Placing a hand at the small of her back, he directed her to the left, where they entered an equally lovely room about four times larger than the large entryway, resplendent with darker woods, tall majestic hutches, perhaps a mile of bookcases, a piano and a very large flat-screen TV built into one of the cases. The upholstered furnishings in here were a mix of leather and velvet, pewter and burgundy.

Rylie didn't get a chance to comment on any of it because Bubbles came charging out of the sunroom yapping happily. As Rylie scooped up the canine version of a greeting card, Noah sighed.

"Hello, you cutie," Rylie said, cuddling the young dog. "Good to see you, too. I see that foot isn't giving you any more trouble."

As the dog licked at her chin, Noah led Rylie into the sunroom, where Audra Prescott was sitting at her easel, paintbrush in hand. Her excited expression told Rylie that Noah had been right. She'd looked to see why Bubbles was acting up and had realized it was her.

"Rylie—my dear!"

Although they'd never been face-to-face, apparently Noah, or even Ramon, had described her enough to take an educated guess. "Yes, ma'am. I'm sorry to intrude."

"Nonsense. I'm overjoyed that you could bring it upon yourself to speak to this rascal again." After giving Noah a wry look, she reached out her arms to Rylie. "Come give a lonely old lady a hug. It's so wonderful to finally meet you."

Warmed by the welcome, Rylie did lean over to do that, but she couldn't help teasing her, as well. "At least I know where Noah gets his gift of blarney. 'Old lady' is seriously stretching the truth. The compliments I've heard don't do you justice."

"Oh, my friends are kind because they know I'm never going to compete with them for their cosmetic surgeon's time. But I did want to thank you for taking such good care of my Bubbles, especially after that wound she suffered. Noah said you were so calm and good with her."

As Audra grasped her hands, Rylie realized where Noah had inherited the shape of his from. She, too, had the long, elegant fingers and the pianist's reach. It hadn't been surprising to glimpse the grand piano in the far end of the living room by the fireplace. And Audra's nails were impeccably cared for. In comparison, Rylie had hands the size of a child's, only the skin was a bit tougher from wrestling with animals and machinery and having to wash so much. That didn't make her self-conscious, though. Audra was too accepting and warm to make her feel uncomfortable.

"Bubbles is a delight," Rylie assured her. "One of my best-behaved clients."

"Wait until I brag to my friends."

"Most of them have darling pets, too."

"Which doesn't? Oh, I know you won't tell me," Audra said, with a wicked smile and wink. "But I had to ask."

She was fun and it left Rylie with a bittersweet feeling to know she was a shadow of the woman she'd been when her husband was alive. She couldn't imagine losing the person who made your life whole. Without needing confirmation from Noah or anyone, she believed that was the kind of relationship Audra had shared with her husband.

Rylie turned her attention to the work on the easel and was enchanted at the watercolor in progress. "That's what you see when you look out these windows? I definitely need to go see my ophthalmologist. How lovely!"

As Audra chuckled, Rylie admired the autumnal scene— still weeks away by the East Texas weather schedule— where amber and russet-colored trees framed a quiet pond where a family of wood ducks swam in absolute contentment.

"That's actually the pond where I grew up. Noah's

father proposed to me there. It's easy to paint it from memory."

Noah must have heard the emotional hitch in her voice as Rylie did, and he stepped forward to ask, "Can I get you a glass of wine, Rylie? Mother, here's your one chance."

"You know you don't have to ask me twice," Audra replied. "I'd love a chance to celebrate and get to know Rylie better."

"I shouldn't." Rylie saw Noah's mother deflate and reassured her. "This was meant as a quick trip. I do need to get home, since my uncle is watching my dog and waiting for his truck back. Besides, it will be getting dark soon and I'm not yet familiar enough with the roads to risk driving with only half of my vision."

Audra nodded, her look sympathetic. "But Noah can lead the way, can't you, dear?"

"It would be my pleasure," he assured Rylie.

Chapter Six

"So what did you say?"

It was the following Friday and the week had passed in a busy, but happy blur. Certain that Roy would be talking to her parents soon, Rylie had called her folks during the lunch break to tell them the truth about everything. She'd meant to do it sooner, but either they were tied up with clients, or she was helping Gage on an evening emergency call.

Naturally, her parents were shocked and upset. Her mother had even begun to cry over the fact that her daughter had carried the weight of everything on her own. Their one reassurance was that Roy was there to represent them.

As for the matter of Noah and the warrant scare, they were indignant on her behalf, until she explained that she and Noah had made peace, and were "officially" seeing each other. There was a little commentary on that, but Rylie assured them that they needed to give Noah a chance, as she had. It helped to brag about Haven Land and Audra Prescott's warmth and hospitality.

"Yes," she said now. "I stayed for a drink and Mrs. Prescott, Audra, was lovely." Afterward, Noah had followed her home like a true gentleman, but she'd stopped out front to make sure he left at that point. "Uncle Roy is back there," she'd explained to him. "He's still having issues with all of this."

"If you kiss me good-night, I'll go without protest," Noah had said.

Thinking about the kiss, she barely heard her mother now say, "It sounds like he's sincere—and his mother clearly likes you."

Rylie could only smile to herself and touch her lips that had held the tingling sensation of Noah's hungry kiss until she'd fallen asleep. "I think so. My only concern, Mom, is that they're as well-to-do as some of your Hollywood clients. They might not be of the oldest Texas aristocracy, but they mingle in circles that I don't."

"Who's going to turn up their nose on a young woman who knows almost as much about animals as a licensed vet does? You're a professional even if you didn't achieve your ultimate goal. Clearly Dr. Sullivan is seeing your worth. Wait a second, your father is adding his two cents…. Oh, he says it's not like you to turn chicken."

Rylie had to smile. Leave it to her father to try to get her back up. "Okay, okay, don't use reverse psychology on me. I promise to be open-minded about this."

"And call your brother to tell him what's happened," Denise Quinn instructed. "You know he was crushed when you dropped out of school, too."

So much so that he'd kept his distance for months. That had hurt Rylie, but she couldn't forget they'd been as close as "blood kin," as Uncle Roy would call it, until then. "I will," she assured her mother. "He's next on the list, but as I said, we've been swamped here. Speaking of…it's time to prepare for my next client. Talk soon. Love you, bye."

As she pocketed her phone and returned inside with MG and Humphrey, who'd been enjoying the respite out back, she saw Roy coming through the breezeway from the front. "I just spoke with Mom and Dad as you urged, and they send their love."

With a satisfied nod, he asked, "How did they take the news?"

"About as you would expect, but with you here, they're not as upset as they might have been."

"You think Dustin is going to take it as well?"

Her adopted brother was only five years older, but he could act three times that. "Nope. So I warned them not to say anything until I have the time to call him myself."

At the busy inference, Roy said, "That's why I came looking for you. Gage needs you in Room Two. I'll receive your next appointment and get things ready for grooming."

And so went the afternoon. Fortunately for her, she got to breathe a little easier when they locked the doors at five o'clock. But while she could finish up some things, Gage was already out on calls.

When her cell phone rang, she was relieved and delighted to see it was Noah. "I thought you'd still be in court."

"I'm about to be. We've been waiting on a jury to come in with a verdict and just got word that they've reached one. On that good news, I wanted to see if I can talk you into dinner."

Rylie would pretty much drop anything for him—short of helping Gage if he'd asked for her assistance. "But you know you have at least another hour before you're free," she reminded him, "and I'll be cleaning up in here that long, too, and then need a shower." Their schedule had been that way since they'd last parted. But they had talked every day and often just before bedtime, and their conversations were growing more and more flirtatious and intimate.

"Imagine me washing your back. Then your front. All of you."

Feeling her body heat in response, Rylie whispered, "Noah! I hope you're not where someone can hear you."

"Barely." He cleared his throat. "I meant dinner tomorrow. If memory serves, you're only open a half day on Saturdays."

"Oh." She really was dead on her feet, but the idea of having to spend one more day without seeing him was a disappointment. "Yes, that's true."

"I thought I would come get you at three and bring you to the house for that tour Mother wanted you to experience last week. Then we could have a leisurely early dinner with her, and finally have some time alone."

"That sounds wonderful," she said. Particularly the alone part.

But only seconds after she hung up, her nerves kicked in. "Okay…" she said to herself. "So what do you wear for an occasion like that?"

Noah's heart was pounding with excitement on Saturday afternoon, and he kept catching himself going over the speed limit on his way to Sweet Springs. Thankfully, he reached the animal clinic without seeing a police vehicle, and he drove around to park beside the RV. For the past twenty-four hours, he had been thinking of little else besides the pleasure of Rylie agreeing to see him again. He felt like a high-school kid going out on his first date. True, he hadn't exactly dated much since returning here, but he knew that had nothing to do with what he was feeling. This was all about the *whom,* not the what.

He'd barely shut off the car's engine when the RV door opened and Rylie descended. Noah's throat went dry. She was dressed in an emerald-green sheath with a silk shawl in shades of blue, purple and green draped casually around her for the coming coolness of the early October evening. But as she began to close the door, MG squeezed her way outside, too.

"No, MG. You know you have to stay here this time. Get back in."

Instead, MG planted herself at Rylie's feet and gazed up at her with adoration. When that didn't get her the response she wanted, she raised her paw and offered a soft, "Woof."

"Looks like she wants to go, too," Noah observed as he emerged from his vehicle.

"I know. Sorry. That's what comes from letting her go almost everywhere with me," Rylie replied. "Give me a second. She's usually very good about obeying. MG—"

"Bring her along." The words were out before Noah realized he'd said them; however, he felt rather proud of himself that they came so naturally.

For her part, Rylie could only stare. "Have the pod people replaced you with an alien? Open the trunk! I know my curmudgeon is in there probably stunned by a ray gun."

Accepting her teasing, he explained, "Mother loves animals, not just Bubbles. She was an excellent horse-woman, and being restricted as she is has denied her the company of other creatures, as well. She used to ride the pastures to enjoy seeing the new calves. Anyway, I've seen enough of MG to know she's a well-behaved dog. She's certainly been good around Bubbles." He leaned over and asked MG, "You don't even care that Bubbles has a title and you don't, do you?"

MG uttered something throaty that sounded agreeable and with impressive civility offered her paw.

Noah smiled up at Rylie. "See? We're in agreement."

Crossing her arms, Rylie replied, "Cute. What about your expensive leather seats?"

He had already noted that she kept MG's nails trimmed. "I overreacted with Bubbles, you know that. If you have a blanket or towel we could set down for her in back, that should take care of things."

"I do. Just a second."

When she reemerged with a thick flannel blanket, he was at the door to take hold of her waist and help her down. Any excuse to get near her now. But her high heels gave him pause. "I guess you forgot that we were going to take a tour?" he asked, although he liked the taupe slingbacks on her. Her feet were as slender and small as the rest of her.

"I don't expect you to take notice of the purse," she said, nodding to the taupe shoulder bag on her shoul-der. "To know me is to know I have to be crossing state lines to carry one—or going farther yet. My sneakers are in there."

Satisfied, Noah took the blanket from her and escorted her and a prancing MG to the car. If he'd been wondering how to win over Rylie's four-legged companion, he received his "pass" quickly. She was delighted to climb into the backseat, and even seemed to realize the gesture by the way she daintily sat down on the blanket, a big smile on her face, followed by a soft growling sound, clearly meant to hurry them up.

Once he and Rylie were seated and fastening their belts, she said, "You'll get comments when the people who detail your car notice the nose prints and saliva spots on the back windows."

Although that gave him a moment's pause, Noah mentally shrugged it off, as well. "This will be a good test to see if they're doing everything I pay them for."

"You know I'm only teasing you about being fussy, don't you? Brooke told me she was the same way about having Humphrey in her BMW. That's how Gage arranged to see more of her—he insisted on bringing Humph to the clinic every day in his truck, so she could focus on the shop and her aunt."

"They seem to have built something special between them."

Rylie looked at him with new respect. "I like that— built, not found. It's true that relationships take work. That's part of what makes the results all the more precious."

Nodding again in agreement, Noah shifted into reverse. "I'm late in saying it, but you look beautiful."

"I don't know that I'd go that far."

He found her near shyness endearing. "You want to argue? Already?" Noah kept his tone teasing, but he was curious, too. "You always look fresh and appealing. Tonight you're a Rylie I've never met, and she's even more intriguing."

She dropped her gaze to the hands clasped in her lap. "Thank you."

"Surely you've been told you're beautiful before?"

"It's my brother's favorite word to me. But he's clinically prejudiced."

"Sounds to me like he knows what he's talking about. How much older is he?"

"Five years. My parents had tried to get pregnant for the first ten years of their marriage and nothing was happening. Only weeks after adopting Dustin, my mother discovered she was pregnant with me. We've been as close as blood relatives—in some cases more so, considering what some friends and classmates told me about squabbles with their natural siblings."

"My mother kept miscarrying," Noah replied. "She was almost thirty-seven when she became pregnant with me. Her doctor point-blank ordered her to bed. He said if she wanted to carry me to term, she needed to stay there, and that's exactly what she did."

"I'm sure she didn't regret one day of that."

He glanced at her profile to note her serene expression and saw that she was wearing more makeup beyond the touch of sable-brown mascara and lip gloss that she usually restricted herself to. The smoky eye shadow and liner made her eyes more mysterious, and the slightly darker-toned lipstick enhanced the tempting bow of her mouth. That she had great bone structure, he already knew. That she had the cutest nose, he'd only just realized.

"Do you want to pull over and let me drive?" Rylie asked, although she didn't take her eyes off the road.

Noah grinned. "Okay, I'll be patient. Just don't complain once we get to the house and I don't want to take my eyes off of you."

"Please don't embarrass me in front of your mother."

Dear God, she made him want to pull over and haul her onto his lap this second to kiss her until she said yes to anything and everything. "I suspect that's impossible," he drawled, "unless you disrobe at the table and dash in your birthday suit for the pool."

"Considering that I know you have staff, I wouldn't do that even if I thought we were alone."

"What I'm saying is that she's utterly delighted that you're coming," Noah continued, unable to stop smiling himself. "She could barely settle down enough to take her nap, what with all the excitement, and believe me that's heartening, because while she puts on a good show when someone other than myself or staff is in the house, she struggles to show any genuine enthusiasm for anything."

"Can you confide what her prognosis is?" Rylie asked. "I'd like to be as supportive as I can, but at the same time not stick my foot in my mouth."

"She broke her back in two places and almost her neck. By rights, she should have died in the accident, too. She'll never walk again, and although we try to buy her time with the pool therapy and massages, there's chronic pain, and there's no expectations that she'll reach the normal life span for a woman. She has days when she wishes it was all over. That's when Livie and I—Olivia Danner is Mother's live-in nurse—have to be extra watchful of her alcohol intake." After a pause, he added, "And we never, ever keep her medication where she could get at it herself."

Rylie sucked in a sharp breath. "Oh, Noah, I'm sorry. That's a challenge for all of you, not just her. Now I'm doubly glad that your mother has Bubbles, and tries to stay interested in her painting."

Noah couldn't resist the impulse to reach over and cover her hands with his. "You'll be good for her. You're an optimist as much as a nurturer."

"I suppose I am, given my preference to work with animals. I haven't really thought about it. I just know that I don't like contention for silly or immature reasons. That happens easily enough without manufacturing it."

"I wasn't being exactly mature in my reactions to you at first."

"Or with Bubbles," Rylie added, with an impish smile.

His answering groan was only half-affected. "My four-legged baby sister."

When she laughed spontaneously, he felt as if something burst open in him and bloomed. She had a lovely, musical lilt that pleased the ear and heart. If she broke into a helpless, full-fledged, tears-down-the-cheeks laugh, he supposed that would be it for him. He would have to fall head over heels in love.

At the house, when Noah escorted Rylie up the sidewalk, he noted how MG walked serenely beside her. "She's really an amazing animal."

"Oh, she quite agrees with you," Rylie drawled. "Her reaction to everyone's surprise at how well she behaves is, 'What's not to love?'"

Noah was still chuckling as they entered the house. "We're here!" he called as they passed through the threshold.

"We got eyes. You don't have to show off for your little lady," Aubergine huffed from the kitchen, her intimidating alto voice surprising on someone not much taller than Rylie. But the plump sixty-year-old had a torso that a century-old oak would admire. Her skin was a flawless rich caramel, and her eyes were as black as the cotton tunic and pants that she wore as a uniform, along with her sensible black orthopedic shoes. Usually as stern as the tight bun pinned to her nape, she did possess a wicked and dry sense of humor, something Noah tried to excavate as often as possible.

"Aubergine Scott is our housekeeper," Noah explained, "but the truth is she's the majordomo of Haven Land. Aubergine, the 'little lady' is Rylie Quinn, who deserves any and all credit for keeping the dust mop looking halfway decent."

"I know who she is. Hello, child." The woman stopped before her and sized her up with unapologetic interest. "You better be hungry because I got a glimpse of you a few days ago, and I intend to feed you. There won't be any pushing food around the plate, either. We don't use forks as hockey sticks in this house."

Rylie put her left hand in the air and her right over her heart as though taking an oath. "Miss Aubergine, I eat like a Clydesdale. And having heard so many enviable stories about Southern cooking, all I can say is bring it on."

That had the woman looking at Noah with haughty approval. "Thank the Lord, you ain't brought home a food pecker." Before Noah could reply, Aubergine looked down upon MG. "And what do we have here?"

MG was sitting obediently beside her mistress and Rylie said, "Say hello to Aubergine, MG."

The dog lifted her right paw.

Aubergine looked long into the retriever-mix's eyes before bending to accept her paw, and said softly, "Well, you are an old soul, aren't you? Welcome, darlin'," she cooed. "I'll bet you'd like your own dish in the kitchen, wouldn't you?"

"You'd guess right," Rylie assured her. "You won't have any trouble with either of us when it comes to cleaning our plates."

Suddenly there was a yap and then Bubbles came scampering from the direction of the living room. At the sight of MG, she threw herself at the bigger dog's feet and rolled onto her back in welcome.

MG gently nuzzled the little dog for a moment before Rylie scooped up the merry bundle of white fur.

"Hello, happy girl," Rylie said. "Are you ready for MG to give you your exercise for the evening?"

Aubergine considered the difference in the sizes between the two dogs. "This should be interesting. Y'all go in and say hello to Miz Audra. Noah, are you going to take care of drinks?"

"I will, thank you. Can't let you prove straight off what a superwoman you are and put me to shame."

"I reckon she'll find out soon enough."

Winking at Rylie, he led her into the living room, with the dogs following. When he noted her continued awe at the size and splendor of the room, he leaned closer to her ear and whispered, "It's just home."

"You say. They could play an NBA game in here."

As they entered the sunroom, Audra was sitting in eager anticipation. She was wearing a favorite ice-blue caftan that zipped in the front, with matching blue ballet slippers. Rylie started to extend her hand, only to have Audra draw her closer for a hug.

"No more of that. Remember I told you that I'm a hugger, and I'm so happy to see you again. Oh, and how lovely you look."

"Thank you for the invitation, as well. This is my dog, MG, which is short for Mommy's Girl. I hope you don't mind her tagging along. Noah seemed to think it would be okay. MG, say hello to Mrs. Prescott."

The graceful dog sat down before the wheelchair and politely raised her paw. Naturally, Audra was delighted.

"What a beautiful girl. I heard Aubergine say she was an old soul. I see that in her eyes, too. How did she come into your life?"

"Pretty much the usual way for strays. She was someone's throwaway. My prize of a lifetime." Rylie quietly directed her dog, "Hug, MG."

The dog put her head on Audra's knee.

"Oh, what a heart stealer," Audra told her, stroking her silky head tenderly.

"Did Noah tell you that she's a therapy dog?" Rylie asked. When Audra shook her head, she explained, "We visit the local assisted-living center and nursing home regularly."

"How marvelous for the inmates. I've heard of such patient and giving creatures, but never met one. What a treasure you are, MG."

MG gave her two soft woofs as though thanking her.

As Audra petted her for that, Rylie said, "You'll get exhausted doing that before she gets tired of compliments, Mrs. Prescott."

"Again, it's Audra, please."

With a nod of thanks, Rylie looked around in wonder even though she'd been here briefly only days ago. "It's simply breathtaking in here. I would sit here, too, especially if the weather kept me indoors." Her gaze happened to settle on the cross. "Oh, that's lovely."

"It was a recent gift from my son," Audra said with a twinkle in her eye.

Rylie glanced over at Noah. "So this is what I heard you also found at Brooke's? You have good taste."

"And it's improving by the minute," he replied, his look intimate.

"You will let Noah show you around this time, won't you?" Audra asked.

"That would be wonderful. As long as you don't let me intrude on your schedule," Rylie told her.

"I get entirely too much rest as it is," Audra replied. "Noah, we should have drinks now. What would you like, Rylie?"

Rylie gave Noah a questioning look.

"Wine? White? Red? Sweet? Dry?"

"White and dry would be perfect, thank you."

"Talk away," he told them, slipping off his navy blue, light wool sports jacket. "I can defend myself from the bar."

It was good to hear laughter in the house…and conversation that wasn't about dosages, pleading for cooperation or assurances that things would get better. Rylie clearly had as good an effect on humans as she did on animals.

After he set the jacket over the back of a chair by the chess table, he rolled up the sleeves of his white silk shirt. He wanted Rylie to feel as comfortable as possible; that's why he'd worn dress jeans instead of a suit. As he poured the wine—red for himself and his mother—he listened as Rylie moved around the room taking in the minijungle of plants, water fountains and pieces of sculpture, some of which were his mother's own work. He heard his mother give a name and explanation of whatever Rylie apparently pointed to that she especially liked.

"You'll have to tell me when I talk your ears off, but I do love to share my plants, my books, *my* interests. I'm totally selfish in that way," Audra said.

"Go right ahead," Rylie encouraged. "Part of the fun of doing what I do is also learning what people's passions are. I don't read as much as I should these days, but I love plants. I hope to sell the RV and buy a little piece of land one of these days so MG and I can have a garden and flowers, too. We would spend most of our time outside if we could."

"Noah tells me that you're from California. You still have family there?"

Rylie briefly explained what she'd told him earlier about her parents and her adopted brother. "Unfortunately they're on opposite sides of the country. I'm grateful for today's technology. Otherwise I'd miss them far more than I already do. Would you like to see a sample of my brother's work?"

Noah was returning with their glasses as Rylie showed his mother pictures on her iPhone. "This is Dustin's restored project in Massachusetts. It had belonged to the son of one of the signers of the Declaration of Independence and now it's owned by a former soap-opera star. This one is in Vermont—he helped convert it into a successful B and B. This is the one he's currently working on in Maine that belongs to one of the state's top chefs."

"Well, we know who to call if we're in need of assistance," Audra said, all admiration. "He does painstaking work…and he's quite handsome in a darkly romantic way."

It was true, Noah thought, catching a glance of the guy over Rylie's shoulder. He'd been picturing a bulky lumberjack, but the guy in the photo was tall, lean and

looked as if he drank cognac and read Byron instead of
King or Conrad. As Rylie closed the app, Noah distrib-
uted the glasses, and then raised his in a toast. "Here's to
more opportunities to learn via eavesdropping."

It was a scrumptious dinner. Aubergine wasn't merely
a fine cook, but she was also forever aware of Audra's
health, and after a fresh garden salad, her stuffed salmon
with Haven Land's own vegetables steamed over broth
with wild rice was mouthwatering. The whole-grain rolls
were also homemade, as was the cheesecake with the
warm cherry sauce. Rylie couldn't have eaten one more
thing and was grateful when Noah offered her the tour.
She was ready to walk off some calories.

Noah suggested they start upstairs first because, he'd
explained, his mother would be turning in soon. Once
Rylie ordered MG to stay at the base of the stairs, they
headed up. She got a better idea of how large the house
was when they reached the second floor and she realized
there were two full wings of bedrooms. Noah led her to
the right first, taking her all the way down the hall.

"This is Mother's suite," he said, beckoning her
through the opened door.

The room faced the back with a great view of the
grounds. Rylie loved the romantic balcony and the bay
window that also allowed for sitting indoors and enjoying the view. There was a huge bathroom that had been
adapted for a handicapped person's needs, and the king-
size bed had an ethereal canopy. The main color scheme
of mauve, gold and cream seemed regal yet soothing to
her.

A side door opened and a tall, toned woman entered
with prim confidence. Somewhere in her fifties, her

short, straight brown hair swung with each energetic step belying her age. She was dressed in a white nurse's pantsuit and nodded at them with a tight-lipped smile. "Excuse me. Good evening."

"Rylie, this is mother's other real-life angel—Nurse Olivia Danner. Livie, this is Rylie Quinn, Bubble's groomer."

"Ah." Livie's thin lips became less pinched. "How do you do?"

Her formality had Rylie starting to retreat from the room. "We're in your way…"

"Not at all. I'm just going to turn down the bed before I go down to bring up Audra. By the time she has her bath, she'll need to get under the covers to avoid catching a chill."

"We missed you at dinner, Livie," Noah said.

That earned him a double take from the all-business nurse, and she melted a bit more, almost allowing a crooked smile. "Audra needed some time with you two, and I wanted to take advantage of this weather and have a brisk walk, before the next front blows in tonight. But thank you. Next time, perhaps."

After they were down the hall a few steps, Rylie asked, "What was that all about?"

"Livie and Aubergine dine with us. I wanted her to know that there's no reason for that to change."

Rylie touched his shoulder, but then kept walking.

"What?"

"You surprised me…in the nicest way," she said softly, aware voices carried easy in this tunnel-long hallway. She didn't think he could have said anything else that would have made her trust in him more.

Noah caught up with her and entwined his fingers with hers.

They looked at two of the four bedrooms on this wing. Each was luxurious without being fussy and included queen-size beds, ready for guests at a moment's notice, and separate bathrooms. Aware that Noah was an only child, she wondered how much company they had.

"Does Aubergine have help keeping up with all of this?" Rylie asked. "This is an insanely big house, even if most of the rooms are rarely occupied."

"She does bring in Ramon's wife and daughters on Mondays for a cleaning of our rooms and most of downstairs, then twice a month they do the rest of the rooms."

He led her down the opposite hallway to the very end, where a shut door led to a room that obviously faced the front of the house. As he opened it, he murmured near her ear, "Enter if you dare."

The shiver that ran down her spine had nothing to do with concern; rather it was the warm hand that was at the small of her back, and the fact that he'd barely taken his eyes off her since she'd stepped out of the RV. Every touch and look was a communication that he wanted to do more, and so did she.

"Does that line work with the others?" she asked softly as she stepped into the room.

"You know there haven't been any others up here."

"I believe you." She saw his chest expand as he drew in a deep breath and knew it was the best thing she could have said to him. This was like a first dance. They were both tentative, but they had the same goal.

As she felt her pulse dance like raindrops on fragile petals, she tried to focus on the decor. It was a handsome room. They both seemed to be drawn to blues, his preferences mostly indigo and peacock with brown and bronze accents. It was masculine, but quietly elegant.

She stroked the bedspread, a design like waves in a deep sea, and breathed in his scent. It was more defined here and made her mouth water, even though she had only just eaten. Initially, there were the woodsy, deep male layers, but then came the surprises of chocolate and coffee bean.

"I believe you," she said again, "because if anyone inhaled this yummy scent, it would take a crowbar to get them out of here."

He came up behind her and slowly caressed her bare arms. "You think I'm yummy?"

Hearing the smile in his voice, she turned to face him, and he immediately enfolded her against his body. This was the first time they'd been this close since Tuesday, and she was instantly under his spell. "Much too soon to tell you. You'll get a swollen head."

"Not with you. I'm too grateful for any crumb of kindness from you." As he spoke, he ran his lips down her neck, his warm breath as much a caress as his words. "God, I want to lay you down and make love to you here. Right now. I know it's supposed to be too soon, but it's what I feel, so to hell with reason."

"It's the same for me, but I have too much respect for your mother to behave in a way that would offend her on her own property."

"We'd shut the door."

She had time only for a brief laugh before he kissed her, a kiss that almost made a liar out of her. She could lie down with him here and make love. Ached to. He was allowing her to see more of his hunger, and also that his control wasn't what it had been. As he deepened the kiss in search of the tongue-tangling dance and probing exploration that made her ache to take his hands and bring

them to her breasts, or her hips, she couldn't stop a soft
sound of yearning.

"Me, too, darling. Me, too."

Rylie looked up into his eyes. "I'm glad you're not
who I thought you were."

"I'm glad you gave me another chance." His gaze lowered to her mouth. "Now help me get you downstairs before I lose the battle with my good intentions."

"How does your mother get upstairs?" she asked, striv-
ing to regain her composure as they descended the stairs.

"Right there." As they reached the foyer again, he
pointed to the gated door to her left. The elevator was
partially hidden by a tall palm plant.

"How clever—and a relief for her." She leaned over
to accept MG's happy greeting. Bubbles stood by eager
to get her share of attention, too.

"I had it installed while she was still in the hospital.
Let's take the dogs outside, so they can burn off more
energy. I'll show you some of the grounds. If you thought
the sunroom was something, wait until you see the vegetable and cutting gardens."

As stately as the front of the property appeared, the
back was breathtaking. Roses, gladiolas, peonies, zin-
nias, sunflowers...there was an abundance of offerings
in the full acre of blooming beauty. "You didn't need to
go to a florist," Rylie said. "You could have brought me
a bouquet from here. It would have been equally special."

"Then next time I will," he assured her.

He was right about the beauty of the rest of the
grounds, as well. It was resplendent with fountains, a
stocked pond, stables and hundreds of acres of pasture
where cattle grazed leisurely. "Who manages the animals?" she asked.

"Ramon's brothers. Impressive *caballeros.* Every once in a while, we'll have a bull here, or one of the neighbors' animals take down a fence and the boys will load their horses, jump into their trucks and race off. Before you know it, the renegade animal is back where it belongs, and they have the fences repaired. Ramon runs a strict operation here, and I appreciate that. I'd be lost without him."

"Do you ride?"

"I can—you can't be a Prescott without being able to sit on a horse—but my father was more hands-on. I think I'm better at managing the financial side of things."

"You didn't want to come back here, did you?"

Noah's expression exposed his struggle. "It's home. It always will be, but this was my parents' passion. I thought I would create my success in a different direction."

No wonder he'd seemed bitter and like a caged animal when she first met him—edgy, restless and resentful, despite his love for his mother. And here she thought she'd just set off something negative inside him. Rylie touched his arm. "Can't you do both?"

He took her hand and raised it to his lips. "I'm beginning to feel that I want to."

Reassured, they walked on. The dogs enjoyed themselves, playing well together, until it was clear that Bubbles had exerted herself trying to keep up with MG. "We'd better head back," Rylie told Noah. "I have to be heading home anyway. There are still chores to do and tomorrow will come soon enough."

"But it'll be Sunday."

"Your people here work on Sunday to some degree or other—feeding, cleaning stables or whatever. Besides, Gage presented me with my own key today. I'm defi-

nitely going to buy him a sleep-in morning and tend to
the chores in the kennel and stables myself. Barring an
emergency call, it'll get him most of the day off. It's the
least I can do after all of his support, as well as his and
Brooke's kindness to me."

"Want some company?"

Rylie couldn't believe he'd actually offered. "Seriously?"

Once again, he reached for her hand and laced his fingers through hers. "At some point you're going to believe
me when I tell you that I want to spend time with you.
We both have demanding jobs and hectic schedules. Is
an hour for dinner here and there enough for you?" His
gaze grew intent. "It isn't for me."

"Not me, either." Despite the admission, she continued to look dubious. "You're sure? Vet work is physical
and messy."

"I grew up on the estate, remember? Dad made sure I
spent evenings and summers working side by side with
the hands. What's more, I understand that animals are a
part of your life and always will be, so warning me off
is a waste of energy."

Finally convinced, Rylie teased, "Okay...only please
don't come dressed in designer jeans and Italian loafers,
or I'll think you forgot everything you ever learned."

"Come here and apologize," he growled, drawing her
into his arms.

She did, repeatedly, and it was several minutes before
they caught up with the dogs, who by then were napping
at the patio's French doors.

The next morning when Rylie unlocked the back door
of the clinic at minutes after seven o'clock, she felt as

though she'd had one mug of caffeine too many, she felt so jittery with excitement. It wasn't only that Noah was coming back this morning, but before he'd left her last night, he'd kissed her again.

"To get me through the long, lonely night," he'd told her.

He'd taught her that there was a world of difference between kissing a boy or a man with a one-track mind, and a man who saw it as important to please as to be pleasured. It amazed her that she'd been able to sleep at all; her body had been left humming with awareness and need.

She'd barely started working on the animals inside when she heard him pull up in back and park by her RV. There was no repressing her smile of joy as she went outside to greet him. Then it widened as she took in the well-worn jeans and boots he wore with a jeans jacket over a simple white T-shirt for the cooler weather.

"What did you have to pay Ramon for the clothes?" she asked, her tone wicked, as he leaned over to pet MG, who ran to him in welcome. Her own jeans were stuffed into knee-high rubber boots for hosing down the kennels and mucking stalls, and her black T-shirt bore the UC Davis emblem for the veterinary school out of San Diego, which she wore under a navy blue windbreaker.

"In rare form, I see." His own narrow-eyed gaze roamed over her with a mixture of pleasure and possessiveness. "How can you be all bright-eyed and bushy-tailed when I didn't sleep after I left you last night?"

"I'm younger, more resilient." After his bark of laughter, she nodded inside. "There's coffee."

"You're an angel." But when she led the way, he stopped

her a step beyond the door and drew her against him. "That's it? That's my welcome?"

"You're right," she said, wrapping her arms around his neck. "Good morning. I'm so happy you came."

His arms became tight bands around her, and his bold kiss told her that his appetite wasn't just for coffee. "Better," he said against her lips. "If I could look forward to this every morning, I wouldn't need as much caffeine."

"My, you are turning leaf over leaf," Rylie purred. But needing to slow things down before she lost her head, she asked, "How's everyone at the house? Did you leave before your mother was up?"

"No, she was already downstairs having coffee with Aubergine and Livie at the kitchen table."

"Aubergine…now there's a romantic and dramatic name."

With an affirmative murmur, Noah pressed a kiss on her forehead, and went to get the coffee. "She has a sister named Sapphire pronounced the French way, *Sa-feer*. She lives in New Orleans."

"I'll bet those two have some stories between them."

"They must well have. Aubergine recently mentioned her only once and fleetingly, after she'd finished a tiny glass of absinthe on what was her sixtieth birthday. The bottle and dainty glass had come from New Orleans the day before. I haven't seen either since. Knowing Aubergine as I do, she's likely buried everything in the vegetable garden somewhere in the hopes of gaining points with God or seducing the garden fairies."

"Ah…*absinthe*…" His droll humor triggered some memory about the liqueur. No, she amended, remembering sugar wasn't added, meaning that technically it was a spirit. A very strong spirit. "I've heard of it. It experienced some resurgence a few years ago, and some of the kids in school were talking about trying it. Wasn't it once banned in France and said to be a hallucinogen?"

With a slight shrug, Noah replied, "As potent as it smells and tastes, it could well have been. Fortunately, I tend to be a boring stick-in-the-mud when it comes to my alcohol preferences. No testimony on truth in advertising."

"Was the family surprised when you told them where you were going this morning?"

His expression turned wry. "I now have a keen understand of the expression 'deafening silence.' I'm sure hilarious laughter followed as soon as they heard the front door close behind me."

"I'll bet you're wrong."

After giving her one of his intimate looks, Noah gestured with his mug. "What can I do?"

"I'll be easy on you to start, but finish your coffee first. Then get a leash—" she pointed to the dozen or so hanging by the door next to the coat rack "—and take Dumpling for a walk in the pasture out back. He's one of our two larger boarded dogs, in the other building between here and the stables. I'll deal with Pacino as soon as I'm done tending to the smaller animals in here."

Noah frowned. "Start me off easy? You don't think I can handle both of them?"

Rylie gave him a sympathetic look. "Pacino is blind, like the character Al Pacino plays in *Scent of a Woman*. His owner is a police-dog handler who rescued him from being put down after he was injured in the line of duty, and she's at a seminar out of state until tomorrow. It's taken me since day one to earn his trust. I don't want you to suddenly find yourself on your back with a hundred pounds of German shepherd standing on your chest just because you said the wrong thing."

"Dumpling it is," Noah replied, holding up his free hand in surrender. Then he asked, "What breed is he?"

"A sheepdog. He's a big sweetie."

"Thank goodness Ramon isn't here to witness me cooing, 'C'mon, Dumpling,'" Noah muttered.

"Oh, believe me," Rylie replied, "that's the least embarrassing thing that's apt to happen to you when working at an animal clinic."

Chapter Seven

"Take that picture and I won't be responsible for my actions."

Although Rylie couldn't help but laugh at Noah's expression as he sat in the middle of the spilled contents of the wheelbarrow, she was only teasing about recording the moment for posterity on her iPhone, and tucked it back into her jacket pocket. Then she shut the stable door before the chestnut mare decided to add injury to insult.

"I was only kidding, but I did warn you to watch Lady B's head. Now you know what the *B* really stands for besides Barbra from Bentwood Farms. Be glad she's a head butter and isn't inclined to kick." Of course, Rylie would never have sent Noah in there if the horse had been mean rather than mischievous.

The mare with the attitude had been there a week, and was another animal going home tomorrow when her owners returned from a trip to a family wedding out of state. While Rylie had cleaned the messier pens in the cow barn, Noah had done Lady B's and had just put her back into her stall, only to be knocked back out the moment he let down his guard.

"Are you okay?" Rylie asked, with sincere sympathy.

"The body is intact, but I think my pride is terminal. Thanks for talking me into putting my keys and wallet in your RV. I'd hate to have to dig them out of this stuff."

Extending her gloved hand, Rylie said, "Let's get you out of that."

"Sweetheart, you don't need to join me down here."

"I'm stronger than you'd think," she replied. "It's a job requirement to be able to wrestle with all sizes of animals. Come on." She did succeed in helping him to his feet, only to shake her head in regret. "I really am sorry. You almost made it through the morning in good shape."

"Do you have about ten plastic garbage sacks that I can spread over my car seat? I sure can't get into it like this."

She had no intention of letting him do that. "Aubergine will take one look at you and bolt the doors. We'll hose off your things and you can shower in my RV while I throw your clothes in the clinic's heavy-duty washer and dryer. You'll be as good as new in a couple of hours."

He leaned over to right the wheelbarrow and Rylie stopped him. "I'll get that. Go on and get those boots off by the RV door, then strip down to your shorts and leave everything on the concrete."

"My fantasy was that I talk you out of *your* clothes." He cast her a wry look. "You're sure? I can call Ramon to bring me something."

"No doubt the poor man has plenty enough to do before he gets to enjoy Sunday with his family." She gave him a challenging look. "What's the matter, Prescott, afraid I'll come in for a free peek?"

"If you don't, I'll be seriously disappointed."

His look sent Rylie's pulse skipping as much as his invitation. As he headed for the RV, she drew a deep breath. *So it's come to this.*

She couldn't have been more touched or grateful as he'd worked with her these past few hours. Never could she imagine the Noah Prescott she thought she knew several weeks ago doing all they'd done getting the pens and stables in shape and the animals fed. He'd not only been a good sport, but he'd teased her as much as she had him—and flirted twice as much. As she heard a whistle, she glanced over her shoulder and saw that he was still at it.

He had his boots and socks off and his jacket and T-shirt. Smiling in invitation, he began a slow, provocative striptease as he unzipped his jeans.

For a man who claimed he preferred a courtroom to ranch labor, he had an impressive body, broad shoulders and narrow waist and hips with enough muscle tone to make her fingers itch to explore every inch of him, as well as the soft nest of hair tapering down his chest and into his briefs. Then she saw that her staring was having a powerful an effect on him.

"Get inside before you cause a wreck on the interstate," she called to him.

As he did that, Rylie finished cleaning up, and then went to deal with his boots and her own. She could actually feel her pulse growing stronger. She knew she was going to him in a few minutes, but in the meantime, she welcomed the anticipation. Once she had his clothes taken care of and in the washer, she turned to MG.

"I'm going to get you a treat for being a good girl, and

you can nap while the washer runs," she told her beloved pet. MG would be fine while the machine was running, and if she woke before Rylie came back, there were dogs in the inside kennel to check on and keep her entertained.

Done, she locked the back door and sat on the RV stairs to remove her boots and set them beside Noah's clean ones. Stepping inside, she heard the shower water still running.

Removing her windbreaker, she set it on the hook by the door and slipped off her socks on her way to the back. By the time she reached the bathroom, she had her T-shirt over her head and was working on her jeans.

"Are you going to leave me any hot water?" she called to him.

"Not unless you hurry."

Grinning, she barely got her jeans off before the door opened and he snatched her around the waist and lifted her inside.

"You're crazy!" She still had on her underwear, which became plastered to her skin within seconds.

"No, starving," he replied, as he claimed her mouth for a kiss that proved it.

Rylie wrapped her arms around his neck and gave herself up to the moment. It was perfect. *He* was. Among the longing, the hot water pummeling them, her sensitized body and his hard and aroused one, she was instantly elevated to a new experience in pleasure.

As Noah drank in her throaty moan, he rasped, "That's sexy, and you take my breath away."

He'd begun caressing and exploring her only seconds into their first kiss, and before she knew it, he'd removed the last bits of her clothing, and what had been covered in silk was now being caressed by his lips and tongue.

Rylie let her head fall back and lifted her face to the water as warm liquid transported her from above, and sensual man from below.

Those hands she'd admired before deserved a new designation—lethal, she thought as he threatened to be her undoing. Wherever he caressed her, she kept being thrust to what she thought was her climax, only to be drawn back, and then flung close again. He discovered the same thing, as his fingers probed the ultrasensitive, sleek place between her legs.

Unable to help moving against his hand, she groaned, "Oh, damn."

"Go ahead. Do you know what it does to me to know I can make you feel this way so quickly?"

When he replaced his fingers with his mouth, she didn't have a choice. His gifted touch shot her straight over the edge, dragging a sharp cry from her. Pleasure vibrated through her body in wave after wave, until she thought her legs would no longer hold her up. Seeming to sense that, Noah rose to clutch her tightly against him.

His body hard with tension and desire, and his heart pounding like a runner's, he rasped, "I have to get my billfold."

Remembering that it was way back on the dining table, she said, "Try the right-hand drawer of the vanity. There's an unopened box."

"Unopened, huh?"

There was no missing the satisfaction in his voice, or the adoration in his gaze, before he stepped out to get them.

Once he was back, and quickly ripping the cellophane, she said, "Thank my brother. It was in his care package when he heard I was moving. Otherwise I wouldn't have even thought about getting some. 'To be kept within reach whenever around smooth-talking cowboys,' is what his note said."

"Fooled him, didn't I?" Noah drawled.

"Oh, I don't know," she replied, loving the chance to finally explore his body as he had hers. "Haven Land is half ranch, and with this body, you can't tell me you sit at a desk all day and night researching and prepping for your next trial."

Instead of denying or confessing, he grew serious as he framed her face with his hands. "Angel, I want you to know, I've never had unprotected sex."

"Neither have I," she said, a bit sad that such things had to be discussed these days when every fiber in her being told her that she could trust him. "And I'm on the pill, in case you were worried about that side of things."

"My only concern is that I'm not going to get in that sleek, little body soon enough. God, Rylie," he groaned, lifting her into his arms. "Come here."

Even as she wrapped her legs around his waist, he began the careful probing. He watched her face for any sign of discomfort.

"Are you going to be my lover or my gynecologist?" she teased, bemused at his intent study of her every facial nuance.

"Both this first time," he said, his voice showing the strain his patience was costing him. "You're tighter than this latex, but damn, you feel like heaven. Kiss me."

She did, and he continued to claim a place for himself inside her. She'd never felt safer, more cherished—or more feminine. Noah was introducing her to what adoration felt like, and she blossomed under his tutelage.

"I think we're running out of hot water," she gasped, every breath laborious now.

"It's okay. I'm running out of endurance." His voice was all strain, and his vise-tight embrace told her even more about how close he was to climaxing. "It's your fault for feeling too damned good."

If she could have found her voice, she could have said the same about him. Human nature was strange that way. Anatomy was just that—bone, musculature, skin, nerve endings…but how incredible that when two certain people came together, the results could create such magic. Rylie was glad that it was happening with this man.

They were so in tune that no more words were necessary. He increased the momentum of his thrusts and she tightened her embrace outside and in, until their kisses took on a near wild abandon.

In the last moment, Noah pressed her against the fiberglass wall and gave her every bit of himself that he could, a harsh cry breaking from his lips. At the same time, Rylie sobbed helplessly, as a climax more powerful than the first shook her entire being.

The water sluicing off them was now only tepid, yet Rylie could feel Noah continuing to pulsate within her. "You're lasting a long time."

"That's all you, darling. What you do to me." He kissed her shoulder and said, "I want to do this again in bed—where I can use both hands."

"Oh, yes, *please.*"

He chuckled softly and shut off the water, then reached for the bath sheet on the rack to dry them both. Rylie didn't think he stopped touching her once, and by the time he lowered her onto the bed, she was aching to have him inside her again.

He already had another condom packet between his teeth and quickly put it on. "I wasn't even in such a hurry when I was sixteen," he admitted, wryly.

"Poor girl. I hope she wasn't a virgin."

"Believe me, she wasn't, and hadn't been for several years."

Taking hold of her wrists with one hand, he drew her arms over her head and with his other hand, he stroked her slender length from arm to knee and all of the sensitive places in between. "Believe me," he rasped, sliding between her thighs to seek a home in her again, "I've never wanted anything more than I want you."

"It's the same for me," she whispered.

"Since it's been some time, you might be sore."

"Uh-uh."

"I have a serious appetite."

"So there's no need to list today's specials?"

"Heck, no. I'll take the whole menu."

And as he claimed her mouth for a deep, thirsty kiss, Rylie abandoned herself totally to the experience.

Long afterward, they lay replete in each other's arms, absorbing the subtle sensations that trickled through their bodies. This time their skin was slick from exertion and determination to get every ounce of pleasure they could from each other, and Rylie felt a pleasant ache in muscles rarely used even in her physical job.

"You don't want to nap?" Noah asked, his tone musing as he traced circles over and around her puckered nipples.

"Not possible with you doing that. Besides, your clothes aren't going to dry if someone doesn't get them into the dryer. I can also hear MG telling me that she's been locked inside long enough. I could close the bedroom door so you can sleep, though."

As she got up to get new panties out of a drawer, she felt Noah's possessive gaze follow her every move. She'd been around nature and had been studying anatomy for too long to be self-conscious about her body or anyone else's, but that didn't mean she was desensitized. On the contrary, she reveled in the knowledge that even momentarily sated, he didn't want to take his eyes off her.

"Get back in this bed and I'll show you who's tired," he drawled.

Rylie chuckled but slipped on her panties and clean jeans, and then a T-shirt, leaving off the bra. The lack of lingerie was going to be obvious the way he was staring at her, but she figured she wouldn't be wearing it all that long anyway. "Thirsty?"

"Dry as an old tree stump. I could handle a beer."

"I'm going to have wine. This was too special for beer."

"Special, huh? Make it wine for me, too. I want to taste like you do, so you'll want to keep kissing me."

"I don't think you'll have a problem there."

"And you don't mind if I'm in no hurry to leave? You're not tired of me yet, are you?"

That was so incredibly opposite of what she was feeling that Rylie laughed all the way into the clinic.

By Thursday, Noah knew he was in trouble. He was glad he and Rylie had spent all of Sunday together because he hadn't seen her since, and they'd barely had a chance to talk, except in the evening when they were both pretty worn out from the demands of their work. It was lunchtime and he was buzzing her cell, hoping she wasn't having to work through lunch. Considering that more and more her assisting Gage was overlapping with her grooming appointments, that was entirely possible.

"Hottie Central," came her lilting voice after the second ring.

Sitting back in his chair, Noah grinned. "Yeah, you are. I take it that you're alone?"

"In the RV with MG and Humph, trying to have a calm few minutes before we return to the circus inside. How's your day going?"

"It's less physically demanding than yours, but also high theater. Hung jury on the Slattery case."

Rylie offered a sigh of commiseration. "I'm sorry. People can't see that lowlife for what he is? They need to throw the book at that slick con man, who found it easier to rip off old people and widows than actually work for a living."

Noah knew that she'd followed the trial in the news enough to grasp the essentials of the case. "I told Vance it was a mistake to put those younger people on the jury panel. They think it compromises their religious beliefs to stick him in prison with such a hefty sentence when the victims are old anyway, and it's only money."

Rylie yelped in indignation. "That's their reasoning? Obviously, they haven't had to work to make car payments or pay rent or tuition. I don't know how you're keeping your cool. How do you reason with ignorance like that?"

"I remind myself that they're Vance's choices. He'll have to live with the results." Then Noah said, "Let's not waste another precious second on that. Say something soft and sexy. I miss you."

"I miss you, too. It's starting to feel as though Sunday was a figment of my imagination."

Noah frowned, not liking the inference of what he'd heard. He knew their relationship was in its fragile, early stages when outside influences could still steal her away. "We have to do something about that. Is there a chance we can have dinner tonight?"

She uttered a regretful sound. "I'm staying late to do two dogs. There was no way to fit them in otherwise. And Gage had asked me to do a dairy-farm call to do inoculations, so it would go faster, but Uncle Roy is filling in for me instead."

"What about after your appointments? I could be coerced to spend the night...bring a change of clothes and head for work from your place in the morning."

"Determined to send tongues wagging, are you?"

Noah was heartened by the smile he heard in her voice. "Frankly, my dear, I'd be proud to," he said, hoping he sounded at least remotely similar to suave, who-gives-a-damn Rhett Butler. "I'm all for doing whatever it takes to make it clear that you're taken."

"Then I'll see you later," she said softly, only to utter an apologetic groan in the next instant. "But if you're hungry, you'll have to pick up something on your way down. My fridge is empty except for beer, wine and pickles. I haven't even had time to think about the grocery store. If Gage didn't carry dog food, MG would be begging for pizza and hot-link dinners from the musketeers."

"I'll handle the food," Noah assured her. "Call you when I'm on my way."

"Don't call, just come. No cell phones while driving."

"So I'll text you before I head out there. This way you can start thinking of me kissing you—all over."

* * *

By eight o'clock that evening, a cold front was pushing through. Strong winds with driving rain were battering East Texas, and temperatures were expected to drop thirty degrees. It was the first real precursor of things to come, a signal to wildlife that hunting season had arrived, and that geese would be seen and/or heard for the next week or so as they headed south for the winter.

The dropping temperatures had Rylie's teeth chattering by the time she locked up the clinic and waited on MG to do her business a last time. As soon as she got into the RV and towel-dried the dog, she ran for a hot shower.

She'd just changed into clean jeans and an oversize sweatshirt that she used as a sleep shirt and thick socks, when she saw lights play around the edges of the mini-blinds. Not lightning, she realized, as Noah parked his BMW as close to her stairs as possible.

Quickly opening the door for him, he shoved a huge bag of takeout and a bottle of wine at her.

"Take that and I'll get my suit bag," he yelled above the howling wind and driving rain.

Worried that she would lose her hold of everything, she gave up trying to keep the wind from slamming the door against the RV's outer skin and ran to dump her armload on the dinette table. By the time she returned to the door, a thoroughly soaked Noah scrambled up the stairs and yanked the door shut behind him. MG barked her approval of that move.

As he hung the clothes bag on the door frame so water would only drip on the rubber mat, Rylie ran to get him a towel. "You shouldn't have been driving in such weather," she called back to him. "The roads must have been treacherous."

"There are some trees down," he admitted, shrugging out of his soaked suit jacket. He hung it over the back of an iron barstool. By the time Rylie handed him the towel, he had his tie off, too. As he mopped his face and hair, he added, "I heard on the radio that sections of the county are without power."

"At least the tornado warnings are about to expire," Rylie replied, "otherwise, I'd insist we ride this out in the clinic. Did you check on your mother?"

"She and her two attack-dog guardian angels were ready to get into the storm room." Noah had shown it to her, behind the pantry, when he'd given her the tour. "And if they lose power, Ramon knows how to get the generator system operating." He gave her a tender look. "She was equally concerned for you."

"How sweet." She accepted the towel back and hung it in the bathroom. "Can I have my hug now?"

"I'm still drenched," he warned, working on the top few shirt buttons and the ones on the cuffs.

"That's how I like you best."

With a deep-throated sound of pleasure, he enveloped her in his arms and kissed her eagerly. "God, what a relief," he said between eager kisses. "I've missed you."

"Me, too, you."

"This is nuts. The weather…our schedules…"

"At least we don't have to be concerned that we'll get bored with each other anytime soon."

That earned her a one-word expletive from him, and his next kiss was meant to prove that there wasn't going to be any talk about boredom as long as she was in his arms. Even when MG nudged his thigh, wanting some recognition for herself, Noah wouldn't break the kiss; he only reached down blindly to pat her.

When he finally took a moment to catch his breath, Rylie planted a kiss in the V of his opened shirt, only to discover his skin hot to the touch. "You aren't coming down with something, are you? You're practically feverish."

"I should be. I was in foreplay mode driving here, aching to touch you and feel your hands and mouth on me." His gaze was as intent as his touch was urgent. "Are you absolutely starving, or can you wait fifteen minutes before we eat?"

With a graceful leap, she wrapped her legs around his waist. "How's that for an answer?"

With a husky, "Bless you," he took the few strides necessary to reach the bedroom, and kicked the door on MG. From the other side came the dog's indignant "woof."

"She'll pay you back," Rylie said, as Noah laid her amid the pillows. "We may emerge from here to find whatever you brought already devoured—or splattered around the room like a Pollock painting."

"A small enough price to pay for this." As he peeled off his clothes in record time, he clearly enjoyed watching her watch him. "You're adorable in that getup."

"Pinocchio. At best I look shower fresh. You got here before I could at least put on some mascara."

"With lashes like that you don't need it...but you are still wearing too many clothes." Naked himself, he went to work on getting her out of her things. In the process, he kissed and tasted every inch of satin-smooth skin that he exposed, until she kicked off her panties to speed up things.

"God, I'm crazy about you." He pinned her against the bed with the lower half of his body. "Kiss me again before I explode."

She did, eagerly giving herself up to this spontaneous reunion. As long and hard as the day had been, she felt renewed in his company. She also liked that she could reduce Mr. Cool and Confident to a state that was anything but. Having such power over a partner had never mattered to her before, but if you were going to turn to mush whenever you were anywhere near the man whom you couldn't put out of your mind or heart, it was a huge relief to know that he felt the same way about you!

As he ran his hands over her, she arched into the caresses, and when he duplicated the journey with his lips traveling down her throat and over her breasts, then her stomach, she raked her short nails over his back, his tight buttocks and hard thighs. It was she who reached for the condom and slipped it on him. Outside, the massive front continued to push through, but inside she and Noah created their own force to be reckoned with.

When he entered her, Noah moaned near her ear. "Baby, you're going to hate me for how fast this is going to be over. But I want you so badly. I can't—"

"It's all right," Rylie whispered, bending her knees and digging her heels into the bedding to aid him. "As long as it's you, it's good."

He uttered an indecipherable something, and then his thrusts grew harder and faster. "I promise to make it up to you," he uttered between gasps.

"I promise to remind you," she whispered, tightening inner muscles around him.

With a raspy oath, he lost control and found his release.

* * *

It was almost ten before they ate. By then they were beyond ravenous. Sweetly forgiving MG had behaved, and her good manners and calm demeanor earned her a few slivers of Noah's steak. Rylie watched, looking amused and pleased that her beloved pet wasn't seen as a nuisance to him.

"I think you're a fraud," Rylie chided, when he gave MG his last bite of meat. "You like dogs. You probably had one when you were a boy."

Taking a sip of his wine, Noah thought back to those days. "There were a few cow dogs on the place—still are—but they've always lived with the hands. Ramon's uncle had the job back then. My father wasn't big on animals in the house." Seeing her disappointment, Noah reached across the table and took hold of her hand, stroking the soft back with his thumb. "I had a great childhood, a privileged life. No regrets. Traveled through two continents, and Japan. There isn't much that I couldn't afford if I wanted it."

"But if your father hadn't died, you wouldn't be here. We would never have met."

Noah hated that her usually optimistic attitude had stumbled on that thought. Sitting forward so he could bring her hand to his lips, he kissed each finger before saying, "I have a feeling that on one of my visits home, I would have come upon you with a flat tire in front of the house, and I would have noticed that irresistible little tush as you stubbornly tried to put on the spare yourself. No, no, too mundane. You'd be driving this monster and accidentally cut me off as you tried to pull over to recheck your directions to the clinic. I'd be so beguiled by your sexy self, that I would borrow one of Ramon's dogs as an excuse to come see you."

"You wouldn't need an excuse," she said quietly. "Not if you came smiling the way you are now."

Noah shook his head. He couldn't get over how quickly her sweetness and honesty went straight to his heart, and groin. Pushing aside his glass, he rose and drew her to her feet as well, then lifted her into his arms. "Say good-night to MG."

"Night, pretty girl."

It was midnight when they made love the last time. Using his shoulder as a pillow, Rylie had slipped off into a deep, contented sleep, but Noah was still reveling in what they'd shared—and listening to the wind continue to blow in cold air.

Hearing another sound, he saw the door ease open and MG quietly approach Rylie's side of the bed. After observing the situation for a moment, she hopped up and curled in the V created by her mistress's bent knees.

As he felt himself drifting off to sleep, Noah reached over to fondle the dog behind her ears.

"If no one needs me, there's something I need to do on my lunch hour." Friday morning was proving to be as busy as Thursday had been, but Rylie made her announcement just before noon, determined to take care of an important matter. "Uncle Roy, you're okay with monitoring MG and Humphrey, right?"

"Sure, sweetheart. But is it anything that I can do for you, instead? You're looking a little tired. Did the storm keep you from getting much sleep?"

He wasn't fooling her for a second. Uncle Roy had arrived this morning just as Noah was leaving, and he had acted disappointed in her ever since. She knew he felt she should hold a grudge against Noah, just as she knew he understood that any fatigue she exposed had little to do with last night's storm. At least Rylie could take comfort in the fact that they were in the back of the clinic and the old-timers weren't hearing any of this.

"Shame on you," she replied, albeit gently. "If I'm not allowed to ask about Jane Ayer, you're not allowed to needle me about Noah." Rylie had been itching to bring up the redhead's name ever since Brooke happened to mention observing Roy and Jane entering the grill across the street from the flower shop last Saturday. During the quiet hours between lunch and dinner, when it was least likely that that they'd run into anyone they knew, Rylie suspected. She was dying to know how their date went and when her uncle would ask Jane out again. He deserved to be happy.

"Okay, okay," he groused. "Just be careful."

"Driving?" she asked, her expression all innocence. "You know I will be. Now that you have your truck, the bubble mirrors are permanently fastened on mine."

"Wise guy," he muttered.

"You know I appreciate your generosity very much," she added, dropping her teasing tone. She had gotten her driver's license transferred and the truck title changed into her name on Tuesday afternoon. "And your concern about everything else."

"Anything for you," he said with a sigh. "You know that. All I'm saying is that you've been through enough disappointment for someone of your tender years."

"I love you, too," Rylie said, kissing his whiskered chin. "I won't be long. It's just that Noah's phone fell out of his pocket and he's stuck at court."

"Mr. Big Shot needs it so much that he can't send an underling to collect it for him?" Roy sniffed. "He sure is romantic—not to mention concerned about your welfare."

"Since he helped me clean the kennels and barns on Sunday," she announced, "I thought this was the least I could do to reciprocate."

Roy all but gaped. "He was here Sunday, too?"

"Oh, Uncle Roy, he's a good man."

"And considering how preoccupied he was that he almost clipped me leaving this morning, I'm guessing that he's been rewarded plenty for that," Roy muttered.

With a gasp that he'd actually been so frank, she swatted his arm. Then, exchanging her clinic smock for her windbreaker, she left.

Her uncle's worries aside, Rylie was delighted with the chance to see Noah for even a minute. She grinned all the way up to Rusk, as she remembered how he sounded on the phone when he realized what had happened as a result of his drawn-out love play before he'd forced himself to head for the office.

"See what you do to me?" he'd moaned, when she'd confirmed that she found it had slid farther under the couch than they'd checked.

She did have to deal with one worry, though. The incident about the warrant could still be fresh on some peoples' minds. It would be embarrassing if she crossed paths with someone from the sheriff's office, or the courthouse, who looked at her with continued suspicion or censure. As much as she wanted to put the matter behind her, the memory of what a close call she'd had couldn't quite be forgotten. As a result, when she pulled into the courthouse square and didn't see Noah outside waiting for her as they'd agreed he would do, she drove around and around the building, thinking she'd mistaken which door he would be at. Finally, she pulled into an empty slot and hurried inside. Like it or not, she had to get back to the clinic.

Thinking that he may have been called back to court, she decided she could only hand off the phone to whoever was at front desk in the department. To her amazement, she found the room empty—except for Noah speedily collecting papers on his desk, and then turning around to glance through the miniblinds.

Relieved to see that he hadn't forgotten about her, she playfully scoffed. "Too late, Mr. Assistant District Attorney!"

He wheeled around, and his expression was a priceless mixture of worry-turned-surprise-turned-pleasure. In the next instant, he was rushing across the room. Momentarily ignoring the iPhone that she offered him—he hugged her, rocking her in his arms. "I'm sorry that I wasn't outside. I was waylaid by the defense attorney on this case."

Perfectly willing to forgive him the small inconvenience, she handed over the phone. "I'll bet you felt lost without this. I sure missed your text messages."

He chuckled. "I missed sending them. The rest of the time, I felt naked without it."

"Interesting," she mused, and slowly ran a finger down his red tie. "I haven't noticed you being shy about nudity around me."

With a glance over his shoulder to check the doorway, he took hold of her upper arms and started walking her backward.

"Noah...?"

He didn't stop until they were in a small, secluded

space made up of file cabinets and supply shelves. "I can't let you go without at least one taste of you."

He locked his lips to hers and drove his tongue deep. Almost instantly, Rylie felt his body harden against hers. She moaned softly, helplessly leaning into the kiss.

Then, like that dreaded and cruel bucket of cold water, someone cleared his throat.

They jerked apart like kids caught necking in a parked car. "I'm so sorry," Rylie whispered to Noah. Before he could respond, she rushed for the exit, keeping her head ducked as she passed District Attorney Vance Underwood.

Just as she reached the hallway, she heard, "Noah? Wasn't that the trailer-park girl? The one Marv Nelson had trouble with a week or so ago?"

"No trouble, sir. A misunderstanding easily enough resolved. And there's no trailer park. Her RV is quite a machine."

"What was her name?" Vance went on, clearly ignoring him. "Quince?"

"Quinn. Vance, you're wrong—"

"Now you listen to me, Noah," Vance continued, an edge entering his voice. "I didn't imagine that an out-of-state warrant existed, did I? And from anyone on the outside looking in, she got special treatment and never spent so much as an hour in jail."

Frozen in place, Rylie couldn't have left if she wanted to. Not only did she find his censorious tone offensive, but he was acting as though the sheriff had done the wrong thing in letting her pay her fine and go home.

Noah remained civil, but firm. "There was no such thing as special treatment. The matter was discussed with all parties involved and—considering the mitigating circumstances—we saw no reason to make a huge production out of something that would cost taxpayers needless expense. Ms. Quinn has satisfied her debt to the State of California and has otherwise been a model resident in our county. I should confirm, this had the sheriff's blessing."

"Maybe," Vance replied, in his subtly droning, nasal voice, "but the whole thing has the unpleasant aftertaste of favoritism, Noah. I appreciate your youth and virility. You work hard and deserve your playtime, even if I question where you're shopping for it."

"That will be enough. Sir."

"No, this is enough," Vance whispered, his *s*'s sounding like a serpent's hiss. "You don't embarrass *my* office. I don't care who you do what with in your free time. You remember that you want and need my endorsement to become my successor. That's not happening if she's part of the package."

Stunned and sickened by what she was hearing, Rylie couldn't stand to hear any more. All but running from the building, she barely dodged an elderly couple coming up the sidewalk and overcompensated, slamming her forearm into a U.S. Mail drop-off box on her right side.

"Sorry, sorry," she cried, blinded by pain.

It was a relief to reach her uncle's truck and get away from there. The tears that flooded her eyes were as much from emotional pain as the physical kind.

The D.A. had all but called her a slut! Trash! She knew that her pedigree was nothing like that of a Prescott— she honestly didn't know anything about Vance Underwood's family tree, but it didn't matter considering his position. However, he'd had no right to besmirch her family's good name. They were humble and hardwork-

ing people who'd built their own success one customer
at a time! And what was the D.A. threatening to do to
Noah's future? Her heart ached. He'd already given up so
much of his dreams by leaving his position in Houston.
Now he was in danger of even losing a post that Rylie
knew was beneath his abilities.

She couldn't let that happen.

How she made it back to the clinic, she didn't know.
Wishing she could run into the RV and bury herself in the
pillows where she and Noah had made love last night, she
forced herself to enter the clinic. Her forearm was throbbing and she thought some cold tap water would help.

She was holding her arm under the faucet when
Gage came out of his office with a stunningly beautiful,
Amazon-tall woman. Naturally, ever sharp-eyed Gage
took in her situation and frowned.

"What happened?"

"You know me. Miss Clumsy."

"Uh-huh." Gage turned to the raven-haired goddess.
"This is Rylie, who I was telling you about."

Hearing undercurrents she wished she didn't, Rylie
shut off the water and quickly patted her arm dry before
grabbing up her clinic jacket. The last thing she needed
was a guest looking at her with pity.

"Rylie, I want you to meet Dr. Laurel Lancer, a recent
graduate of Texas A&M's veterinary school. She's finishing up an internship south of here for extra certification and wants to do another here. I'm hoping after that
we can bring her in as a partner."

Having given herself a pep talk that things couldn't
get worse, Rylie realized she'd been a fool. "How—how
wonderful for you, Dr. Lancer. Welcome." As she sum-

moned a bright smile, she felt a new pain—as if someone was taking out her appendix using only fingernails.

"I've heard great things about your talents with animals, and your rapport with the locals," the young woman
replied. Her onyx gaze dropped to Rylie's injury. "That's
going to be some bruise, and it's already swollen. Are
you sure you didn't break it?"

"Fortunately, I don't have the weight to combine with
speed to create enough velocity to do anything thoroughly," she quipped. "It's just another bump to add to
the collection."

Rylie didn't know if it was the woman's superior
height, her stop-you-in-your-tracks beauty that appeared
to be partly credited to some Native American heritage,
her enviable degree and future, or that she was simply so
close to Rylie's age that she represented everything Rylie
would never be…but it didn't matter. Dr. Laurel Lancer
was here on the tailwind that had already kicked Rylie
off of her dreamy trajectory. Enough was enough. She
was cashing out on everything. The Amazon was going
to be a partner, and Rylie had to leave.

As though from another dimension, she heard Gage
say, "Most of her family is up in Montana."

"Oh," Rylie replied, suddenly frowning. "Um…isn't
yours…?"

"That's right, it turns out our families know each other
slightly."

Great, Rylie thought.

"Laurel's father and some brothers are ranchers, and
another brother is in oil."

So what was she doing in Texas? Rylie thought. They
didn't have veterinarian schools in Montana? Belatedly,

she forced herself to extend her hand. "Mine is mostly in California. They're in building, dust and rust."

Laurel just studied her as though she was a lab project, while Gage choked back a laugh. Feeling like a bigger fool than before, Rylie said, "You'll have to excuse me. I...I have a Pekingese waiting for me up front, who, like Mick Jagger, has a face that only a mother can love. It'll take every second I can spare him to get him in shape."

Could things get any worse? she wondered.

At least Dr. Stunning was gone by the time Rylie was done with the Pekingese, Wokie, as his mistress called him. But at soon as they were gone, Rylie's uncle appeared, acting like a mosquito buzzing around her head.

"You look terrible. What's happened? Did Wokie bite you?"

"Of course not." Rylie showed him her hands to prove as much, but it was a mistake. Her bruise was now a lump the size of a kiwi, and about the color of the fruit's seeds. Not something that Uncle Roy could miss.

"How the hell did you do that?"

"It's Senior Citizens Day. You see one, you automatically throw yourself at the nearest mailbox in celebration."

"Oh, baby." He sighed. "The right eye again?"

She gestured, signaling that talking about it wasn't worth his energy or hers. "I guess you met Dr. Lancer?"

"Yeah. Wow. I knew Doc was talking to someone, but I didn't expect...that."

Keeping her back to the old-timers and her voice low, Rylie said, "It's okay, Uncle Roy. You can say 'gorgeous.' Great pedigree to go with the capital investment. Add an actual license qualifying her to make independent ranch and dairy calls. What did I leave out?"

"Your feelings are hurt."

Rylie didn't hear him come up to the front. But in her current frame of mind, which was anything but reliable, she chose to be less than honest and shook her head stubbornly as she turned to face Gage. "I'm good. And God knows, you need someone to have your back, Doc. But I've been thinking…with another doctor, things are going to get a little crowded in here. If you need me to clear out, I'll totally understand."

Gage looked flabbergasted. "Are you kidding? I'm trying to build up the clinic, not whittle it down to the smallest common denominator. And there's plenty of room yet in this building. When there isn't, we can expand." He tilted his head, trying to get a better look at her face. "I thought you were happy here."

Feeling as though her heart was taking a torturously slow turn through a shredder, Rylie whispered, "Oh, Doc…I am. I was. I just…" She swallowed, determined to put the best face on the situation. She loved everyone here and wanted them to understand that.

"I've been a fool," she said with a self-deprecating shrug. "It's not just about what you're doing. I understand it. I may not be head-over-heels thrilled, but I'm a big girl, I get it. It's just that it's been one of those revelation days, you know? It's made me see that maybe it's best for everyone if you go with a whole change of scenery."

To his credit, Gage kept his usual calm demeanor and waited for her to say what she really meant.

"I'm not a good fit here," she told him. "And I'm not right for someone like Noah Prescott, either." She laughed mirthlessly. "The irony is, he needs someone like…like… Dr. Lancer."

Chapter Eight

Wondering if closing time would ever come, Rylie was relieved when she could finally retreat to her RV. While it was evident that Gage had wanted badly to continue their discussion, considering her out-of-right-field outburst, life—in their case, business—intruded. The reception room started filling up as if there was an epidemic. Then came news of an overturned cattle truck several miles up the interstate, which had forced Gage to apologize to those with pets still waiting to be seen and hurry to that emergency.

Rylie's uncle Roy had gone, too. She was relieved. She didn't want to answer questions, and she desperately needed time alone to think. Then, of course, there was Noah.

He started sending her text messages shortly after she'd left the courthouse. For the first time since they'd

started to indulge in that method of communication, she
didn't respond. Later the calls started, and she ignored
them, too. It was no surprise, then, when, only minutes
after she retreated to the RV for the night, she saw car
lights coming around to the back of the clinic.

With her heart working like a Triple Crown contender,
she forced herself to open the door to him. He looked
the same—handsome, concerned, polished. The "can
do" guy. And he would succeed if she had any say in
the matter.

"Thank God," he said, jogging up the stairs. "Did your
phone go out on you? When you didn't answer my calls,
never mind my texts, I got really worried." He paused
only long enough to take in first impressions of her standing there, her arms wrapped around her middle. "You're
sick?"

He wasn't totally wrong. She'd showered and brushed
her teeth twice, hoping she would stop feeling as though
she'd spent the afternoon losing what wasn't in her stomach, only none of that had worked very well. However,
going with the affirmative would still be lying by eva-
sion. "It's just been a long day."

"They all are for you these days."

"A particularly long one." For him, too. Was he going
to tell her? He didn't look much better than she did, but
he had a better grip on his self-control than she did. That
gave her an ugly thought: maybe what she was going to
do would end up being a relief for him.

"I heard about the accident on the interstate," he said
slowly. "I'd hoped Doc wouldn't take you out there."

"No, my uncle went."

"Because of that? Sweetheart, did you get it x-rayed?"
He'd noticed the bruise. "No need. But I'm sure it had

something to do with that." Rylie watched MG try to get Noah's attention, and when he failed to realize that, Rylie made things easier for him. "MG, down. Not your time."

Her tone was one she rarely used. It brooked no nonsense and, looking crestfallen, MG went to the couch and curled up in the corner of it and hid her face in the cushions.

Perfect, Rylie thought, hating herself for hurting her sweet friend. With a sigh, she gestured to Noah. "I was going to have wine in the hope that it would make me sleep. Would you like a glass?"

She prayed that he would decline. She was losing her nerve to go through with this, and hoped in his worry about her needing rest, he would leave. But that wasn't happening. Watching her as though he was still analyzing what was going on, he nodded at her offer.

"But I'll get it. Sit down."

As he took off his jacket and poured the wine, she chose to sit in the recliner by the door. He was less apt to try to draw her into his arms there. Tucking her bare legs under the sleep shirt, she hugged herself again and tried to make sensible small talk. Maybe the more normal she sounded, the sooner he would be willing to leave.

"How did the rest of your day go?" she asked, hoping her smile didn't look as false as her voice sounded to her own ears.

"I have to admit, long, too."

The grim note in his voice told her that he was thinking about Vance's nasty remarks again. Now he would tell her, she thought.

"It's better now that I see for my own eyes that you're safe, if not one hundred percent." He brought her glass and waited for her to sip a little.

Noah leaned over her to kiss her gently. "You're aw-fully preoccupied."

His observation gave her a branch, something to grip on to. Maybe it could still make things easier than the truth. "Doc interviewed for a partner today."

"A partner?" Noah's dark eyebrows drew together then lifted as he took stock of that idea. "I thought he was just looking for help, not someone to share in the business with him."

"That surprised me, too. Worse yet, she only gradu-ated a while ago."

"Ouch." Scowling, Noah reasoned, "That has to be a painful reminder. What was Gage thinking? He couldn't find someone with a little more experience?"

Rylie shrugged and took a sip of her wine, although her stomach warned her that she would pay for it. "It isn't in his makeup to intentionally cause anyone embarrass-ment or hurt. Dr. Lancer is undoubtedly as special as she is qualified."

Rylie thought that the woman may have squeezed him into her itinerary at the last minute. Maybe she'd been disappointed wherever she'd interviewed previously. Maybe that's why Gage hadn't given them more warn-ing. The list of possibilities kept growing. Whatever the case, Gage couldn't be faulted. Things just happened the way they did.

"You know what you need?" Noah said, taking her glass and putting it down on the side table along with his own. "You need to stop thinking so much." With that he lifted her into his arms, only to sit down himself, set-ting her onto his lap. Then he began kissing her, gently, repeatedly, first only on her mouth, then over her eyes, her chin, between her eyebrows and the hollow at the base of her throat.

This was something they could agree on, Rylie thought with bittersweet emotions, making each caress feel all the more poignant. One last time...

Her decision made, she wrapped her arms around his neck and kissed him back with everything in her heart. Noah immediately responded with a welcoming murmur and tightened his arms. He slid his hand into her short hair to keep her close and feasted on her lips and urged her on with his tongue.

Beneath her hips, she felt his quick arousal. She rocked against him and brushed her breasts against his chest.

"Are you sure, sweet? Because my self-control isn't at its best tonight," he told her, his breath starting to grow shallow.

"That's what I want. Make love to me, Noah."

Without another word, he carried her to the bed.

The room was lit only by the light coming from the other side of the RV, which was a relief to Rylie. She didn't want Noah to study her with his usual intensity for fear of what he would see. For her part, she closed her eyes and just gave herself up to the moment.

"You know what keeps taking my breath away?" he whispered against the side of her neck as he worked on unfastening his clothes. "It's how fast you've become a necessity to me." He began spreading kisses down her chest, at the same time drawing up her shirt, until he reached bare skin. Then he slipped the fabric over her head. Next he slid his palm down over her silk-clad mound, directing his fingers between her thighs, and planted a kiss on the bare skin just above it. "I think about this all the time—how perfect you are. How you respond to my touch."

Rylie knew what he intended, but she couldn't bear it—not tonight. This was going to be hard enough without that intimate gift. Writhing free, she urged him onto his back, slipped off her panties and finished releasing him from his clothes. "I just want you inside me."

Her urgency released, and then fed Noah's, and he shucked his pants while she spread his shirt wide to where she could kiss him all over. Only when she began taking him inside her, he hesitated. "Protection…?"

"I told you, I'm on the pill." And she wanted to feel all of him, just once.

Noah wanted it, too. She knew from the way his hands trembled slightly as he took hold of her hips and urged her closer, and deeper.

Tears burned behind her closed lids as she rocked against him, urging him on in the eager dance that was quickly going out of control between them. As delicate muscles contracted around him, she felt him spasm, then pour into her. It brought her own ecstasy, and she collapsed against him, letting the pillows absorb her tears.

As the silence between them grew, Noah remained almost motionless except for stroking Rylie's hair. He had the strangest feeling—as if he was waiting for something that he knew wasn't coming.

Finally, he eased her onto her back, so he could see her face in the dim light. He knew she was awake by her breathing, but she kept her eyes closed. Even so, he could swear there was moisture under her lashes. He stroked the delicate skin beneath her right eye and it came away wet.

The worry that had been growing all day was now a

tight band around his chest. "What's wrong?" he asked, wiping the moisture from beneath her other eye.

"Nothing," she whispered. "It was perfect."

Every time was perfect with her. "I'd be the happiest man on earth if I knew those were tears of joy."

Rather than voice that lie, she covered her eyes with the back of her hand. "Noah, don't ruin this."

The band tightened to where he could barely drag in another breath. "What's that supposed to mean?"

"I can't do this anymore."

Do what? he wondered, each beat of his heart a worsening pain. Make love with him? But she'd asked him to. Or was that only her parting gift to him?

"That sounds like…goodbye."

"It is."

"Why?"

Her lips moved, but no sound came out.

"You're leaving," he said, voicing the only thought that came into his head. "Gage didn't fire you. He wouldn't."

"I'm making it easier for him."

"Where are you going?"

"I don't know yet. Just somewhere better suited to me. Somewhere where I'm better needed."

"You're needed here. *I* need you here."

She finally opened her eyes. They shimmered with new tears. "Noah, I heard what the D.A. said to you today. I'm sorry—I never meant to eavesdrop, but the moment he began criticizing you, I froze."

He groaned and leaned over to kiss her forehead. "Baby, I'm sorry. He was being an ass—and a hypocrite. His wife may be a former congressman's daughter, but she's on so many prescription drugs, most of the time he has to hide her car keys to keep her from hurt-

ing herself or someone else. He has no business lectur-
ing anyone about anything."

"He knows the voters. I'm not right for where you're
going. You deserve someone who will complement your
life."

"I'm looking at her."

With a sound of frustration or desperation, she sat up,
reached for her shirt and tugged it over her head. "You're
not listening to me. We grew up in a two-bedroom house
with one tiny bathroom. When I was too old to sleep in
my parents' room, I was moved to the couch. It wasn't
until I was thirteen when they turned half of the garage
into a bedroom for Dustin that I had my own room. Sure,
by the time I was fifteen, we moved into a bigger house,
and my parents have a comfortable life now, but I still
remember those days when Dustin outgrew his T-shirts,
they became my pj's and play clothes because there was
no money for buying us both new things. I've worked
since I could give change for a dollar, five dollars, a ten
and a twenty. And I never even went to the prom, Noah,
because I was working two jobs, scared to death that I
wouldn't have enough saved for college tuition."

Noah had already learned enough to know that their
pasts were polar opposites, but that didn't matter. What
mattered was what you did with what you had.

"The fact that you got through college despite all of
that is beyond admirable," he declared. "Then most of
vet school. I know I acted like a jerk when we first met,
but you forgave me for that."

"Of course. I told you."

"And no one will ever be able to accuse my mother
of being a snob."

"Noah!" Rylie cried. "You can't win the D.A. seat without Vance Underwood's endorsement."

"Who says?" He framed her face with his hands. "Rylie, I'm in love with you. The rest doesn't matter... unless you don't feel the same way?"

He never expected the words to come out—not that way. She deserved better. He'd intended to do this right, to create a moment, a moment she would never forget. Instead, he watched everything disintegrate in front of his eyes as she bowed her head.

"I'm sorry," she whispered. "But I don't."

"Have you lost your mind?"

Rylie didn't know how much more that she could take. Of all people, she thought that Uncle Roy would be relieved that she'd sent Noah away and wouldn't be seeing him again. Noah's reaction last night—the stunned silence as he'd dressed, and the way he'd walked to the door, paused and then uttered a hoarse "Goodbye," without looking at her—had almost been her undoing. Now her uncle was clearly going to finish breaking her heart because of the rest she'd told him—that she was going to leave Sweet Springs.

Wearily, she shifted the three-quarters-full coffee-pot to the extra burner and started the second pot. "You heard me. Please don't yell. I'll explain."

"What's to explain? I have ears. You're walking away. From this." He swept his hands to encompass the clinic.

Rylie pressed her hand against her stomach. Aside from not getting any sleep last night from all of the upheaval, she felt sick. There was proof that upbeat people didn't handle the downfalls of life better than anyone else.

"I think it's in the best interest of everyone," she began. "Gage has a great opportunity with Dr. Lancer."

"But why does that mean you need to leave?"

"Because now I'll have two bosses, and I'm not sure one of them will be thrilled to have me around. It's also better if she has input on the staff here."

"She will," Roy replied. "For those coming next. But I know during that closed-door meeting that Gage showed her what's in the computer. He would have to for someone taking in a partner. So she already knows what an asset you are. And Doc confirmed it several times over as he gave her a tour of the place. I heard your name mentioned repeatedly in reference to ideas you'd suggested, and improvements in operations." Taking a stabilizing breath, Roy shook his head and poured himself a mug of coffee. "I knew something was wrong yesterday when you got back from Rusk. You looked like—" He stopped the mug halfway to his lips. "Well, crap. This isn't about Dr. Lancer at all."

"Oh, really, Uncle Roy," she replied with a shaky laugh, "she's part of it."

"Bull. This is all about Prescott."

"What's all the hollering about?" Stan Walsh complained as he shuffled down the side entrance to join them.

Roy hooked a thumb at Rylie, his expression disgusted. "She says she's leaving."

Stan squinted at her as though he couldn't see her, let alone grasp the idea. "Seriously?"

She gestured helplessly, having no energy to start from the beginning again.

"Aw. That's not right," Stan said.

"What's not right?" Pete Ogilvie demanded as he entered the room.

"Rylie here says she wants to leave."

"She doesn't *want* to leave," Roy all but snarled. "She's got issues." He cast Rylie a speaking glance as if to suggest that was as far as he was going to defend her—or buy her time before she had to say more.

"Is one of them the life-size doll who was here yesterday?" Jerry Platt asked as he arrived. He paused at the box of doughnuts Roy had brought, eyeing them, even though he patted his still-trim belly. "I love you bunches, Rylie, but I'd consider adopting a pet if it would get me an appointment with her."

"Oh, put a muzzle on it," Stan snapped. "The only animal you should be allowed to adopt is a porcupine." He squeezed Rylie's shoulder, his expression growing tender. "She seems like a nice lady," he told her, "but you'll always be our number one. Besides, you accepted us right away. I got the feeling that she didn't cater to us being here."

"Aw, Stan, that's sweet," Rylie told him, rising on tiptoe to kiss his weathered cheek.

"Where's Warren? Isn't Warren here yet?" Jerry asked, glancing around. "If anyone can talk you into staying, he will."

"Warren won't be coming this morning," Gage said as he entered through the back door. "His wife died during the night."

As Rylie gasped and the others murmured words of regret and concern for Warren Atwood, Gage shared what he knew. Apparently, the chief of police had called him first thing this morning to say he'd just come from the nursing home himself, and that Warren was at the funeral home with the body.

Bernadette Atwood, "Bernie," as Warren and everyone else who knew and loved her had referred to her, had spent the past few years in the Sweet Springs facility as Alzheimer's took control. They all knew that he visited her every morning, before coming to join his *compadres* at the clinic, and ended his day sitting with her. But it had been rough on him, as Bernie had spent a few months now between this world and the next. Now that devoted watch was over.

As everyone grew silent, Rylie pressed her hand to her mouth, thinking of how awful this had to be for poor Warren. He was a strong man, and a tough man, but the disease had been his Achilles' heel, the way Bernie had been his heart.

She felt a hand on her shoulder. Turning, she saw Gage tilt his head toward his office.

"Let's talk."

As conversation resumed, Gage poured himself a mug of coffee, then led the way down the hall to the paneled room. He waited for her to pass, and then shut the door behind them.

"I won't beat around the bush," he told her as he motioned for her to sit down. "When I first walked in I heard someone talking about you leaving and something about Laurel not wanting you around. Let me just confirm that nothing could be further from the truth. I wouldn't consider her if she couldn't blend in with everyone here, and I do mean everyone."

"I appreciate that," Rylie replied, grateful for the chair.

She hadn't even bothered getting any coffee yet, unsure that it would stay down. "The guys…don't really understand. Neither does Uncle Roy."

"Neither do I," Gage said drily as he settled in his seat behind the cluttered desk. He took a sip of the steaming black coffee, then set it on a clear spot on the blotter and rested his forearms around it as he leaned toward her and studied her with tenderness and concern. "Why don't you explain it to me? The fact is, we can't afford to lose you, Rylie. This whole idea was to enhance, not to detract from your presence here. Good grief, you've increased our revenue by twelve percent just in the short while you've been here. That's not counting that you've relieved me to do more that I needed to do. And don't tell me that you couldn't work with Laurel. You could charm the tusks off a wild boar. Now, I appreciate that she represents a painful reminder of what you've given up. My heart aches for you, and Brooke's does, too. We consider you like a little sister already. That said, I believe that you're just too fine a person not to be able to work through whatever feelings you might have against her."

"Please stop," Rylie said, rubbing at the tension headache threatening to split her skull wide open. "You're being way too kind and generous. I admit, I wanted to dislike her on sight, and when you said 'partner,' a part of me was crushed."

Although he nodded in understanding, he said, "But you won't let it because you're not a quitter."

She rolled her eyes, but a hint of a smile twitched up one corner of her mouth at his high opinion of her. It meant the world. "I don't want to be a quitter…only sometimes things happen that make you realize it would be better for the other person if you weren't around."

Gage narrowed his eyes, his gaze speculating. "We're not just talking about Laurel, are we?"

"I guess not." she admitted softly.

"Is there anything I could do to help?"

She knew he and Brooke had discussed that, too. "I think I've done enough. At least, I know I've hurt Noah too deeply for him to ever want to speak to me again."

Gage looked skeptical. "He practically got you thrown in jail and you somehow worked through that."

"Let's just say, I couldn't let him sacrifice what he would have to for me."

Taking that in, Gage nodded slowly. "You have to love someone a whole lot to be that sacrificing."

This time she was able to smile, but it was a smile of sadness. "I'm glad you understand. Only, this conversation is just between us, okay?"

"Provided you give me a full two weeks' notice?" he countered. "Heck, it'll take Laurel a month before she has her business settled, gets back to Montana for a quick visit and gets back here."

"Of course. I owe you more."

"Don't tempt me," he replied with a determined look. "And don't think I won't use every single day of that time to reason you out of this decision."

The next two days were all about Warren, and the mood around the clinic was solemn and sad. For the first time in almost a year, Uncle Roy told Rylie, the round table had a missing member for more than one day.

Gage closed the clinic for the morning of the funeral, and an evergreen wreath with a black ribbon was put on the door below the note explaining the reason for the temporary inconvenience to customers. Having lost a

son in Iraq several years ago—the highest-ranking officer to be killed there—Warren had no immediate family
left and he asked Rylie to sit beside him at the service. It
was both a proud and painful experience, as he held her
hand between his throughout the service.

The rest of the day passed in a blur, the shortened
business hours creating a packed waiting room for over
an hour after closing time. When Rylie finally made it
to the RV, she was so emotionally and psychologically
spent, she collapsed on the bed and fell into the deepest
sleep of her life.

She woke up the following morning feeling as if she
was rising out of a coma, and it took her several moments
to realize where she was and to remember all that happened yesterday. Coming quickly on the heels of that was
Noah, and her heart wrenched anew. Somehow she had
to not think about him. There was too much to do, and
she needed to be able to function.

"Oh, jeez," she groaned, as her gaze landed on the
clock on the nightstand. It confirmed what the daylight
around the miniblinds also did. She was going to be the
last person at the clinic, not the first—and MG had to
be in total discomfort.

Thankfully, she'd passed out still dressed in her black
T-shirt and jeans. She ran into the bathroom, telling MG,
"Give me one minute more. Thank you for having an iron
bladder the size of a watermelon."

She brushed her teeth and didn't even run a comb
through her hair. While MG did her business, she would
poke her head into the clinic and explain and apologize,
then get a quick shower.

Wondering why no one had knocked on the door or

buzzed her cell phone to wake her, she yanked on her windbreaker and opened the door to let MG out—only to shriek in surprise, before clapping her hand over her mouth.

Oh my—

Laughter and cheers erupted through the crowd. Someone yelled, "Surprise!"

Surprise nothing, she thought. She was in the process of having a heart attack. Everyone she knew was out there—Gage, Brooke, Uncle Roy, Jane, the musketeers...

"Jane?"

As MG barked and trotted down the steps, her tail wagging as though she thought all of this company was for her, Rylie tried to make sense of what was happening. Then her heart skipped a beat as her gaze locked with Noah's.

If the brisk morning air didn't cause her to shiver and clutch the windbreaker tight around herself, she would have been convinced that she was dreaming. But, no, there was Audra in her wheelchair with Ramon gripping the handles, and Aubergine and Livie framing her like human bookends.

As her gaze returned to Noah, Uncle Roy stepped forward to offer his hand to help her down the stairs. "It's an intervention, Sunshine."

"It's something, all right," she muttered, belatedly realizing that she hadn't showered or washed her hair and the makeup she'd put on yesterday must be long gone.

"Come on down out of there so we can all watch this. I can't see."

Who was that? Rylie wondered, finally taking her uncle's hand and descending the stairs. Then she saw more people—their mailman and the chief of police, Bob

Burnett—whom she'd barely spoken to beyond saying "hello"—and about a dozen more. But once again her gaze was drawn to Noah. She couldn't help herself, or keep from letting him see how wonderful it was to see him again, regardless of what she'd told him.

"I don't think she gets it yet," Audra said, beaming.

"It's shock," Livie said matter-of-factly.

Audra squeezed Noah's hand, only to push him forward. "Get to work, son. Make me proud."

He made his way to Rylie. Dressed in a navy sports coat and jeans, he looked his usual charismatic self. But his hand was shaking as he took her cold left hand in his, and he lowered himself to one knee.

"Oh, my God," Rylie whispered. Suddenly, her hand started shaking as much as his.

"Sweetheart, you already know how I feel about you. You burst into my life and through my defenses like nothing I'd ever experienced before," he began. "You lit a fever in my heart that was numb from neglect and bad choices. I wake needing to see you, and go to sleep aching to hold you. No one and nothing can come before that. Marry me, Rylie. You're as precious and necessary to me as my next breath."

Unable to deny what she was feeling, or the yearning burning in his eyes, Rylie could manage only to nod. However, that was enough for Noah to draw a ring out of his pocket and slip it onto her finger. Then he stood and crushed her against him to the sound of cheers and applause. The ruckus got even louder when he kissed her.

"You don't have to say it so loud that everyone hears," he whispered near her ear. "But you'd damned better say it to me. I can see the truth shimmering in every inch of your face, and feel it in the arms hugging me back."

She threw her head back and laughed with joy. "I love you!" she declared. "You, you, you. From the first, it was you!"

Epilogue

"It's time to cut the cake and go, my love."

Rylie leaned back against Noah's firm body and covered the hands tenderly holding her at the waist with her own. "I'm ready."

She had been Mrs. Noah Jamison Prescott for almost two hours, and she had yet to be alone with her husband for one minute. She only had to turn and look into his glowing brown eyes to see passion waiting to be unleashed.

They had been married in the Prescott family's church—Sweet Springs Methodist—and the reception was at Haven Land. Even though over one hundred were in attendance, it was generally easy to make their way to the dining room, where the cake was set up.

Rylie loved the bouquet Brooke had made for her, a happy autumnal collection of chrysanthemums, some of which almost matched the warm glow of her hair. She also loved how her gown whispered with every step. It had a lace bodice with a straight cut, Audrey Hepburn neckline, V-back and full satin skirt. Noah had remembered her sadness over never having worn a gown and convinced her that she have a one-of-a-kind dress for the wedding. He'd also insisted on flying in her parents and Dustin, and they had been staying upstairs in the guest rooms for two days now.

As they passed Dustin, Rylie stopped to give him another hug. They would be leaving on their honeymoon for a week in Ireland right after they changed clothes, and she didn't know how long it would be before she saw him again. She cupped his darkly handsome face in her hands and kissed him on both cheeks.

"My, munchkin, you clean up fine," he said, his dark gray eyes saying much more.

He'd been as upset as her parents had been with the news about her partial blindness, and when he'd first gotten off the plane, he'd swept her into his arms and hugged her so fiercely, she'd thought she was going to end up with a cracked rib.

"I'm so glad you approve—and that you came."

"I had to see for myself that you were really happy." Dustin released her to shake Noah's hand. "See that she stays that way," he added, with a mock narrow-eyed glare.

The two of them had hit it off almost immediately and, laughing, Noah hugged him easily. "Count on it. And don't be a stranger. There's always a room for you here."

Next they stopped to say a few words to her parents

and Uncle Roy, who were still catching up on news. Rylie had told her uncle to bring Jane, but he'd confessed that there would be so much family talk going on that she would be bored. Rylie hoped that was all, and that the budding "couple" hadn't actually hit a road bump.

"I'm so excited for you," her mother whispered to her as they embraced.

"And proud," her father added, kissing her forehead.

It was good to see the musketeers, especially Warren, who was looking better in the past weeks since Bernie's passing. Rylie kissed each one, and Gage and Brooke, who stood nearest to the cake.

Brooke looked radiant in her royal-blue matron-of-honor dress with her baby bump now unmistakable. Best man Gage kept his arm around her waist, his fingertips never far from the gentle swell of her abdomen. They were going to keep MG at their place while the newlyweds honeymooned, since MG and Humphrey were solid pals.

Although they had been invited, Vance and his wife sent their regrets. When Noah announced he felt he should resign, Vance quickly apologized for his remarks, and had been decent if not warm and fuzzy ever since. It was clear that he knew who the best candidate for the office was, and smart enough not to cost the county Noah's service.

Laurel had been invited, too, but she was still in Montana one last week to spend Thanksgiving with her family before starting at the clinic.

Rylie and Noah posed for several pictures of the cake cutting for the photographer, and then stopped to kiss Audra on their way upstairs.

"Don't party so much that you tire yourself out," Noah warned her.

Rylie echoed his concern. In the weeks since she'd sold her bus to Jerry Platt—who planned to treat his buddies to a trip to Vegas, while the newlyweds were on their honeymoon—she'd been staying in the spare bedroom across from Audra's, and they'd enjoyed getting to know each other better.

"I won't, darlings. I know if I'm not on top of my game, you'll deprive me of all the stories about your trip when you return."

Once up in Noah's bedroom and the door was shut, Noah reached for Rylie. "Oh, God, I need this," he said, claiming her lips for a long, deep kiss. "Whose idea was it to spend so many hours in a plane?" Being circumspect, he had done without her company for nearly a month, and the strain of being in opposite wings in the mansion had taken its toll.

"Yours. Be glad my ancestors don't come from Australia," she teased, turning in his arms so he could unzip her gown. "And at least we have tonight in the airport hotel before our flight in the morning."

"I'm not sure I'll even last through that drive," he said as he exposed bare skin, and the daintiest lingerie. He groaned as he cupped her lace-covered breasts. "Sweet heaven," he said, pressing a kiss to her bare shoulder. "You're sure Aubergine is going to have your things moved in here by the time we get back?"

"The moment the furniture store delivers the extra armoire. Why you thought we needed another, I don't know. My clothes will fit perfectly in the closet."

"It's for all the sexy undies I plan to buy you," he said, caressing her until her nipples were taut nubs. Then he grew serious. "Love, I know we've talked and already made tentative plans about school, and all, but I was wondering…"

Rylie turned to face him. He'd made her cry when he'd insisted on paying off her college debt and suggested—with Gage's encouragement—that she return to school to finish her veterinarian training. She might not be able to handle every case, but she could specialize in small-animal care—and Gage said he would welcome her as a partner, as well.

"Ask away. Anything," she said, meaning that. She loved him so much, if he asked her to wait a year before returning to school, she would.

"I just wanted Mother to have the strength to hold a grandchild in her arms. It would break her heart if she grew too weak."

"No, you're right," Rylie said, moved that he was being so considerate. "So…I'll leave my birth control pills behind?"

Exhaling shakily, Noah touched his head to her forehead. "You know Aubergine will tell Mother when she finds them."

With a wicked grin, Rylie said, "Maybe even before my parents head back to California. That'll be our going-away gift to them all—and more incentive to your mother to stay strong."

"Thank you, my heart. It's been ages since this house has had the sound of children's laughter flowing through it." After a reverent kiss, he added lightly, "What a relief and blessing to have married a woman whom I see eye-to-eye with on the important things."

"Correction, many…many things," Rylie whispered,

drawing him closer until they shared the same breath and she could tease him by brushing her lips against his.

"Oh, yes," he murmured, and kissed her with hunger and promise.

*   *   *   *   *

MILLS & BOON

THE HEART OF ROMANCE

A ROMANCE FOR EVERY KIND OF READER

MODERN

Prepare to be swept off your feet by sophisticated, sexy and seductive heroes, in some of the world's most glamorous and romantic locations, where power and passion collide.
8 stories per month.

HISTORICAL

Escape with historical heroes from time gone by. Whether your passion is for wicked Regency Rakes, muscled Vikings or rugged Highlanders, awaken the romance of the past.
6 stories per month.

MEDICAL

Set your pulse racing with dedicated, delectable doctors in the high-pressure world of medicine, where emotions run high and passion, comfort and love are the best medicine.
6 stories per month.

True Love

Celebrate true love with tender stories of heartfelt romance, from the rush of falling in love to the joy a new baby can bring, and a focus on the emotional heart of a relationship.
8 stories per month.

Desire

Indulge in secrets and scandal, intense drama and plenty of sizzling hot action with powerful and passionate heroes who have it all: wealth, status, good looks...everything but the right woman.
6 stories per month.

HEROES

Experience all the excitement of a gripping thriller, with an intense romance at its heart. Resourceful, true-to-life women and strong, fearless men face danger and desire - a killer combination!
8 stories per month.

DARE

Sensual love stories featuring smart, sassy heroines you'd want as a best friend, and compelling intense heroes who are worthy of them.
4 stories per month.

To see which titles are coming soon, please visit

millsandboon.co.uk/nextmonth

MILLS & BOON

MODERN

Power and Passion

Prepare to be swept off your feet by sophisticated, sexy and seductive heroes, in some of the world's most glamourous and romantic locations, where power and passion collide.

01-8208408

0857385818
Work

7589||